# GHOSTS OF HARVARD

# GHOSTS OF
# HARVARD

*A Novel*

## Francesca Serritella

Random House | New York

Published in the United States by Random House,
an imprint and division of Penguin Random House LLC, New York.

RANDOM HOUSE and the HOUSE colophon are registered trademarks of
Penguin Random House LLC.

LIBRARY OF CONGRESS CATALOGING-IN-PUBLICATION DATA
Names: Serritella, Francesca Scottoline, author.
Title: Ghosts of Harvard: a novel / Francesca Serritella.
Description: First edition. | New York: Random House, 2020.
Identifiers: LCCN 2019040833 (print) | LCCN 2019040834 (ebook) |
ISBN 9780525510369 (hardcover; acid-free paper) | ISBN 9780525510376 (ebook)
Subjects: GSAFD: Ghost stories.
Classification: LCC PS3619.E79 G48 2020 (print) | LCC PS3619.E79 (ebook) |
DDC 813/.6—dc23
LC record available at https://lccn.loc.gov/2019040833
LC ebook record available at https://lccn.loc.gov/2019040834

Printed in the United States of America on acid-free paper

randomhousebooks.com

2 4 6 8 9 7 5 3 1

First Edition

Title page art from an original photograph by
haveseen/shutterstock.com
Ivy art by Sodel Vladyslav/shutterstock.com

Book design by Patrice Sheridan

*For my mother,*
*you kept the rickety raft afloat*

Now he has departed from this strange world a little ahead of me. That means nothing. People like us, who believe in physics, know that the distinction between past, present, and future is only a stubbornly persistent illusion.

—Albert Einstein

Anguish is distinguished from fear in that fear is fear of beings in the world whereas anguish is anguish before myself. Vertigo is anguish to the extent that I am afraid not of falling over the precipice, but of throwing myself over.

—Jean-Paul Sartre

# GHOSTS OF HARVARD

# PROLOGUE

IT WAS SILLY to be afraid of falling, considering her intent, but Cady hadn't anticipated how windy it would be on the bridge. She crouched on the balustrade, her hands gripping it so tightly that white crescent moons shone in her fingernails. A gust blew her hair into her face, but she didn't dare lift her hand to move it aside.

She didn't want to fall, she wanted to jump.

After a moment of screwing up her courage, she commanded her legs to straighten and rose slowly to a standing position. She felt a shiver down her back, although the night was warm, or as warm as Cambridge in springtime could be. Across the river, she could see Harvard's campus, the familiar dormitories lit to perfection—but it wasn't perfect, Cady knew that. A glance downward at the black lapping water of the Charles triggered a jolt of fear, but not enough to deter her. She had promised herself she'd go through with it, and she would.

It was easier once she was standing tall. Her jelly legs felt stronger, her balance solid. The night air swept over her body in a caress. She breathed deeply, taking in the scent of the river and this campus in all its bitterness and beauty. She had never imagined she would end up in this place, feeling this way, but here she stood with a lump in her throat, preparing to say goodbye.

Cady closed her eyes and listened to the voices egging her on; they wouldn't let her turn back now. She wished she could slow this moment, but they were counting down—her time was almost up. She raised her chin, pulled her arms away from her sides, and wiggled her fingers in the air, reaching in the dark.

She poised, knees bent, and counted down the final seconds:

"Three, two, one—"

# 1

CADY HADN'T SET foot on Harvard's campus since her older brother's suicide. It was the place where Eric had eaten his last meal, dreamed his last dream, taken his last breath. The sight of the red brick dormitories, a picture postcard of collegiate perfection to so many, made her heart pound. For her, it wasn't a college, it was a haunted house.

And today she was moving in.

Cady couldn't let her doubts show as they drove into Harvard Yard. The sun-dappled quadrangle and its ancient elms were festooned with red balloons and a big crimson banner reading WELCOME HARVARD MMXXIII. She reminded herself that she'd wanted this, insisted on it, sworn that she could handle it, bet everything on it. Yet her knee bounced in the backseat as her father parked right outside her freshman dormitory, Weld Hall. She spied his face in the rearview mirror, his eyes weary, his jowls gray and unshaven. His sister, Cady's aunt Laura, sat in the front passenger seat. Cady's mother remained home in Pennsylvania, too angry at her daughter to come today. Maybe that was for the best; seeing her mother's face would've made Cady lose her nerve.

"Look at this parking spot, I told you I was good for something," Aunt Laura said with a wink. A car accident in her twenties had left her paraplegic and she used a wheelchair, hence the parking privileges, although Cady never thought of her as handicapped. Laura possessed an irrepressibly positive outlook, a trait to be tested today. She had come ostensibly to lend the use of her giant van, but Cady knew it was to fill in for her mother, and she was grateful.

Her father yanked up the emergency brake and took a heavy breath. "Ready?"

Cady got out and helped Laura into her wheelchair as her father went around to the back of the van, their solemn mood at odds with everyone around them. On the front steps of her new dorm, she noticed a boy posing for a photograph with six smiling relatives. A blond girl standing in the bed of a pickup laughed as she pushed a boxed futon toward her father, who waited on the ground, wearing a Harvard T-shirt with his cowboy boots and Stetson. A tall boy in a Lakers jersey wiped his mother's happy tears from her cheeks.

Cady envied them. They didn't have to fake it.

She joined her father at the rear of the van and saw him hauling out her green duffel bag. "Oh, I'll take that one," she said, she hoped not too eagerly.

"I got it, you get the roller suitcase."

"No, Dad, seriously." Cady grabbed hold of the nylon straps and he looked at her, puzzled. Then she deployed the head tilt and tone her mother had perfected. "Your *back*."

He held tight for a moment before he relented and let her have it. "All right, but only because I haven't been doing my exercises."

"When did my little bro get so old?" Laura teased. "You know, some people say back pain can be psychological."

"Then I blame you two," he said.

Cady's dorm room was Weld 23, only the second floor—*only*, she caught herself—she couldn't help but think of the height. The elevator was crowded, so her father decided to wait, but people made room for Aunt Laura to wheel on and Cady to squeeze in after her, hugging the duffel close to her chest. Laura held a laundry hamper filled with linens on her lap.

"Nice that they have an elevator," she said to Cady. It was her official duty to point out every good thing that day.

A middle-aged man overheard. "You know what was in this space before it was an elevator? JFK's freshman dorm room. He went from Weld to the White House." He slapped the back of his reed-thin son. "Might have the next president right here! Right, Max?"

His son's face reddened, and Cady's heart went out to him.

The elevator doors pinged open. Cady and Laura exited, and Laura broke into a grin. "God, can you imagine being here with a young JFK living down the hall? He must have been dreamy. He was probably a horn-dog even then, though."

The first image Cady could conjure of JFK was the last moment of his life, the grainy footage of him waving from that car. She tried to imagine him as a young man her age, full of the nerves and excitement she saw on every face around her. If someone had told him he would be president, would he have blushed like that boy in the elevator, or would he have owned it? Did he sense he was bound for greatness? If someone had told him he would be assassinated, would he still have wanted that future?

"Although," Laura continued, "if you were looking for sexy Kennedy ghosts, you should've gone to Brown. That's where John-John went. He was the best-looking of them all. I had such a crush on him."

*Oh, right,* Cady remembered, *his son,* too. And his brother. And his other brother sort of killed that girl—maybe that was what started it. A lot of ghosts in that cursed family. So far only one ghost in the Archers. Were they cursed, too?

They found the door to her room and Cady reached into the manila envelope to pull out her key, the metal so freshly cut that it felt sharp. She hesitated. It was real now. This place had already marked a turning point in her family's history, and her decision to come here marked another. She knew the pain she was causing her parents. It would either be worth it, or it would be another mistake she couldn't undo.

"You okay, honey?" Laura asked.

"Definitely." *Show no weakness*, she told herself.

Cady opened the door to an empty room. It had a funny layout, the sort that comes from retrofitting a larger space to become multiple rooms; the common room was long and narrow, with an off-center window on one end and the two bedrooms off the side. She crossed to the window and looked out.

"How's the view?" Laura asked, joining her.

"That's Grays over there, that was Eric's freshman dorm. I remember from when we moved him in."

"How does that make you feel?" Laura asked, sounding like a therapist.

"Good, close to him, in a way." Cady was surprised to hear the truth coming out of her mouth. "Is that weird?"

"No, it's nice to remember him." Laura put a hand on her arm. "Just keep in mind, life is for the living."

Cady nodded. She knew it was a common saying, but it sounded so harsh to her ears now. Life was for Eric, too, even if he'd lost sight of that. Maybe they'd lost sight of him.

There was a knock at the door, and Laura went to let Cady's father in. "Is it just you?" he asked, and for a split second, Cady didn't know what he meant. She flashed ahead to a lifetime of not being enough for her parents. *Just you?*

He set the box down with a grunt. "Are you the first to arrive?"

"Yeah. We're first." Cady readjusted the duffel bag in her arms, still holding it close to her chest. "I know we have more to get from the van, but I want to pick my room before anyone else gets here. Do you mind if I unpack a little to claim my space? I promise I'll be right down." It was a lie, one of Cady's two roommates had already requested the single room over the summer, leaving her with the double.

Laura waved her hand. "Of course, call dibs."

"Don't be long. We have to move the car," her father said.

Cady watched them leave and waited a few beats to be sure. Then she darted into the larger bedroom and dumped the green duffel on a bare mattress. She unzipped it and dug under the layer of bras and panties, the final Dad-barrier, to uncover the two items she couldn't let her family see. She'd taken them from the box of personal effects her family had received from Harvard after Eric's death. They'd kept the box in his bedroom at home, but Cady had secretly visited it so often, she had its contents memorized. Most was junk, he'd gotten so messy toward the end, but these two items spoke to her more than the others. As souvenirs or as protective talismans, she needed these relics close to her, especially here.

The first was sentimental: Eric's rumpled gray Harvard hoodie. She lifted it to her face; it still smelled like him, a blend of fresh soap and warm toast. Her parents might've given her this if she'd asked for it, but she couldn't risk their thinking she was emotionally fragile, they'd barely let her come here as it was. Around them, Cady had to hide that crumbly feeling whenever it threatened the corners of her mouth or crept up the front of her throat, and Eric's scent triggered it. But sometimes she needed that feeling, liked it even, to release the pressure. She hugged the sweatshirt to her chest before pushing it to the back of the bottom drawer of one of the dressers.

The second buried item was a clue: a blue spiral-bound notebook labeled lab notes at the top. Lab notes were as close as Eric would've ever come to keeping a journal, so it was the closest she could get to a window into his mind. Cady opened it, flipping through pages soft with wear. She ran her fingers over her brother's familiar handwriting, the ballpoint-embossed lettering speaking to her heart like Braille. The earlier pages were vintage Eric: organized and neat, with logical headings and experimental diagrams, tidy as a textbook. As she flipped farther ahead, however, the notes grew more disorganized and illegible; the math devolved into wobbly columns of numbers and slanted, incomplete equations. These scribblings didn't look like advanced physics, they looked like nonsense. Toward the end, the commentary appeared unrelated to the calculations: misgivings about food in the dining hall, perceived slights from "M"—Cady guessed Matt, his old roommate—and jottings of random people's appearance or behavior, likely those deemed suspicious. His paranoia had taken over by then.

Cady hid the notebook in the same drawer as the sweatshirt. She would look more closely at it later, when she felt stronger.

With those items safely out of sight, she could relax enough to get a look at her new room. She didn't mind having a bunkmate—sharing a room was such a normal misfortune, she found it comforting—and the double was the corner bedroom, large and sunny. She sidled around the haphazard arrangement of metal bunk beds, desks, dressers, and bookshelves. The boxy, light wood modular furniture looked as if it had been built in the nineties; the desks bore decades of pen marks, the dressers were dinged at every corner. She could smell the fresh paint of the white walls, and Cady stuck her fingernail into a soft glob, wondering how many lives in this room had been painted over. Judging by the sloping hardwood floors, the deep windowsills, and the massive trees outside, she guessed about a century's worth. Someone was moving into Eric's old room in Leverett Tower right now, probably finding it as clean and white as this one; they wouldn't know what had happened in it just last year. Cady wasn't here to paint over anything. She was here to chip away.

The bedroom window was open, and Cady pressed her fingertips to the screen, but it didn't give. Eric had removed the screws from his window screen in advance, the police found them and the screwdriver tucked neatly in his desk drawer, that was how they knew it wasn't an accident. Though she supposed that no one really thought it was an accident.

Cady looked out at the busy Yard below. Every new student was acting happy, but no one was at ease. There was all the normal first-day-of-college stuff, living away from home, meeting roommates, and the rest, but Harvard was more than a school. It was validation. It was history. It was expectation. The place crackled with potential energy. She could see the crowd around the John Harvard statue, a reminder that the college was founded in 1636, before the country itself. The legacy of the past and the onus of the future freighted the present moment, like time collapsing inward. It was saying, *This is the launch pad for your extraordinary future, if only you don't blow it.* Behind the smiles and hugs and introductions, the self-doubt: Am I smart enough, talented enough, driven enough to deserve my place here? Will I make good on this golden ticket, or will I crack under the pressure? They were questions for every student here, but only Cady knew the stakes: If I crack, will I survive?

Only the parents seemed unequivocally happy, basking in the proof of their parenting job well done, a sharp contrast to the pall over Cady's family. She thought of her mother with a twinge; Cady missed her today, but didn't blame her for not coming. She knew how her going to Harvard so soon after Eric's death looked from the outside: bizarre, callous, unhealthy, morbid. And the last thing she wanted to do was hurt her parents. They had been through too much, she knew that. But she wished they could see she had her reasons.

Cady thought back to the weeks following Eric's death, when college admissions had been the last thing on her mind. It had been impossible for her to think of her future when he no longer had one. If he was going to stay a twenty-year-old college junior forever, then it seemed that she should stay a seventeen-year-old high school senior for the rest of her life. She and her brother were three years apart, she was never supposed to catch up to him. But when the letter of acceptance arrived, it was as though the decision had been made for her. To go anywhere but Harvard was to willfully *not know,* to stick her head in the sand. She had done plenty of that when Eric was alive, and she regretted it keenly. She had learned that unasked questions were more dangerous than unanswered ones.

Cady had tried keeping the *why* questions locked away, but most of the time, not thinking about Eric was like pushing a beach ball underwater. She had trained herself to run through a series of questions with very specific and unchanging answers—a pilot's checklist against emotional nosedive. Why did Eric change? Because he was schizophrenic. Why did Eric choose to die? It wasn't a choice, it was his mental illness. Was it because she, his only sibling, had let him down? It was nobody's fault.

But did she believe that?

Every single day she woke with the same questions, and every night she struggled to fall asleep in the misery of not knowing. If any answers existed, they would be here, at Harvard.

It would be cowardly not to go, and she had been a coward long enough. She owed it to Eric. It was the least she could do.

She didn't want to be here. She needed to.

Cady looked again at Eric's freshman dorm, catercorner across the green. He had been happy that first year, so excited and hopeful. Cady recalled helping him move in three years ago with fondness. She tried to recall his exact room, her eyes traced the building's facade to find it—*there*, the fourth floor, leftmost room on the center section, his bedroom faced the Yard. Now the window was dark, save for the places where the panes of glass reflected the bright green, yellow, and orange elm leaves, dancing back and forth in the wind. A gust blew, and the colors swept aside to reveal a figure behind the glass.

Cady felt a shiver down her spine.

She had thought she'd seen his red hair, but it was only a reflection from another tree.

Cady stood there looking, wanting it to happen again.

# 2

FIVE MONTHS EARLIER, Cady was sitting between her parents at Eric's funeral. It had been four days since Eric's death, and she was still in shock. He had been at college when it happened, so she hadn't seen him in person since that January, and it was April. He should've been coming home soon for spring break, she'd have seen him again then. But he wasn't, and she wouldn't. It seemed impossible. Only the surroundings made a convincing case: the church she hadn't been inside since she was a girl, now filled with familiar people dressed in uncharacteristic black, the scent of white lilies, the murmuring of sadness. Perhaps this was the purpose of funeral ceremonies, to signal to those minds numbed by grief that this was for real.

Still, her brain rebelled against that reality and bounced everywhere but the present. Cady's parents hadn't called her right away when Eric died, and she held that against them. She had spent the weekend in Myrtle Beach for a choral competition. The drive was so long, the buses didn't get them back until Monday after the school day was over. Cady drove herself home from the parking lot, thinking only of how lucky she was to have missed class. She should have known something was wrong when her father greeted her at the door, but he said he was working from home that day. He should have told her the truth right then. Instead, he let her sit and babble for fifteen minutes about the crazy bus driver and Liz's graduation party. And that was after he let Cady make her usual after-school snack, a package of Top Ramen, so add five minutes for the water to boil and three minutes to cook.

Not once did Cady think to ask where her mother was, she assumed she was out showing a house. She didn't know her mother was in bed upstairs, having been there since the campus police called at four in the morning. Later, the medical examiner said Eric died at 3:17 a.m. It was already 4:36 in the afternoon when the hot soup burned Cady's tongue and her father broke down and told her everything. Thirteen hours and nineteen minutes went by that Cady still thought she had a big brother, but didn't.

She dwelled on this as she sat in the pew. It disturbed her that she hadn't known the instant he passed. He was her only brother, after all. It didn't make logical sense that she would know; she was in a hotel room in South Carolina, he was on the ground outside his dormitory in Cambridge, Massachusetts. But still, she thought, she should have felt the earth shift or the sky crack, at the very least a tiny sting or snap or click, even a hiccup, some signal that he had died, that she had lost someone irreplaceable.

But even knowing that instant would have been too late. She'd have to retrace her steps farther back to find the moment when their paths diverged and she could no longer pull him back. She had lost him sooner than that.

Cady had never known life without Eric. It was one of her family's favorite stories that the surefire way to get Cady to stop crying when she was a baby was to bring in Eric. Growing up, she wanted to be just like him, to the point that when Eric came home with lice in fourth grade, she scratched at her head until her mother agreed to use the smelly shampoo on her, too. There was an old photo from one Halloween in which both Eric and Cady were dressed as the purple Teenage Mutant Ninja Turtle because Cady couldn't bear to be a different color Turtle than Eric. She must have been an awful nuisance, but

Eric was always patient with her, happy to be her hero. He had been happy once.

She remembered when they went to see an exhibit on King Tut and the ancient Egyptians at the museum. The golden sarcophagi, the sculpture of Queen Nefertiti's egg-shaped head, at once elegant and alien, the scale model of the Sphinx, or "Spinks" as she said then— she felt she was meeting history for the first time, and it was love at first sight. Eric's favorite part of the exhibit was the hieroglyphics, which gave birth to one of their favorite games. Eric created an alphabet code with symbols for each letter, and he taught it to Cady so that they could leave each other secret notes. Cady would take a flashlight under her covers and try to memorize their new alphabet, but still she had to carry with her the crumpled cheat sheet he had made her. Eric memorized it right away. She would leave him stupid, short little notes that translated into minor revelations such as "Halloween candy behind coffee can," or "Dad farted at breakfast." But Eric would leave her long ones with real missions, complicated step-by-step directions for childhood adventures, and without fail, when she had completed the final step, Eric would be there waiting for her with a proud smile.

Cady's favorite was the one he titled "Mission: Mantis Mommy Revenge." The week before, Cady had found a praying mantis in the driveway whose abdomen was hugely swollen, and Eric told her it was pregnant. Deciding that the driveway was no place to raise a family, they constructed a praying mantis birthing suite out of a cardboard box, complete with a twig jungle gym, a bowl of water, and a bed of grass and leaves. Eric went around back to catch some grasshoppers for the mantis to eat, while Cady watched it explore its new home. She liked the way the green bug held its hands, as if she was knitting hundreds of tiny socks for her hundred tiny babies. While Cady was alone, their next door neighbor Jeremy and his friend walked over.

"What the hell are you doing?" was his greeting. Jeremy was a sour, pimply thirteen-year-old, with dark curly hair that was tamped down on his sweaty temples. He scared Cady. She looked around without answering to see if Eric was coming back.

"Speak English, dummy?" Jeremy asked. His friend snickered.

Cady leaned protectively over the box. "We found a praying mantis, and she's going to have babies, so we're making her a house."

Jeremy's expression softened. "Shit, really? That's awesome, can I see it?"

The next second, Jeremy was stomping his foot into the box. Cady screamed as the insect skittered from corner to corner before being crushed beneath his dirty sneaker. When Eric ran around to the front yard, the older boys bolted and left Cady crying, the poor praying mantis curling slowly into its death pose, like a clenching fist.

That memory swirled so vividly—a more palatable, childhood trauma to mix with the grief and anguish she felt now. At this moment, like that one, she felt ashamed that this had happened on her watch, ashamed by her helplessness, and most of all, ashamed that she had let her brother down. Surely, Cady thought, she had disappointed him as a sister, or else he would still be here. But that day with the mantis, Eric didn't blame her; when he reached her, he hugged her tight until she stopped crying. He was always too good to her. They buried the praying mantis in the flowerbed with a smooth rock as a headstone.

Eric wasn't having a headstone; he wasn't being buried at all.

A small sound escaped from her mother's mouth before she covered it with a tissue, which brought Cady's attention back to the funeral. She watched as her mother pulled the tissue from her mouth, leaving small particles of white paper on her wet lips, before cramming the tissue back into the crumpled ball. Cady had never seen her mother look so stricken. Her face looked wet with some amalgamation of tears, sweat, saliva, and snot. Her chin-length blond hair looked greasy at the roots and disheveled, a result of her compulsively raking her fingers through it, her eye makeup was smeared around her red-rimmed eyes like bruising, and her cheeks were red, from rubbing or embarrassment. Cady had learned that the family of a suicide victim doesn't get straight sympathy. Every "I'm sorry for your loss" that they received came with a look of curious judgment, the unsaid "How could you let this happen?"

Cady wanted to touch her mother, rub her back, do something to help, but she felt frozen. She was afraid that anything she tried to do to comfort her would be so inadequate, she would only make things worse. Eric had been her mother's favorite, but Cady couldn't hold it against her—Eric was her favorite, too. When Cady didn't get as much attention from her mother, Eric made up for it through his secret eye-rolls and exaggerated obliging smiles that he knew only she would catch. They were the co-conspirators, and their parents were the marks.

While Cady and her mother were still in shock, her father stepped in and took over the business of her brother's death—notifying their relatives, contacting the funeral home, making arrangements for Eric's cremation. Her mother was upset about the cremation, and Cady privately felt the same but didn't want to come between her parents. There was a horror in imagining Eric being burned in some oven and then pulverized, especially because it was so difficult for Cady to imagine him as a dead person.

Cady was upstairs in her bedroom when her father told her mother the decision to cremate had been made; she heard her mother in the kitchen banging pots and slamming cabinet doors and shouting at her father, "How could you? I wanted to see him, I wanted to kiss his face one last time, one last time, to kiss him goodbye. Wasn't that my right as his mother, or did I have to give that up, too? Was that my punishment?" Cady couldn't make out her father's muffled responses, but she could tell he had remained calm, enraging her mother further. Cady normally took her father's side when eavesdropping on her parents' arguments, but even she hated him a little that night.

She imagined her father had set his mouth that day much the way he was now, his bottom lip pulled up and inward, creating little craggy dimples on his chin. His temples had long since gone gray, but now cold glints of silver shone throughout his dark hair. The slack skin on his neck pressed against his shirt collar, and a plum-colored bubble of blood had dried where he must have cut himself shaving. He was only fifty-six years old, but today it seemed everything on him was graying, aging, drying out. Whereas her mother's grief rendered her preternaturally vivified, her father's did the opposite. He had turned to stone.

The regular rhythm of the preacher's monotone speech broke, and Cady looked up in time to see him drop his head and say "Let us pray."

Her mind reverted again to the praying mantis. In the aftermath of its cruel death, Eric produced his longest coded note to Cady, a plot for vengeance he titled "Mission: Mantis Mommy Revenge." The directions, translated, ordered her to first cut open all of their old cat Bootie's toys and empty the catnip into a Ziploc bag, then wait until three in the morning (she had to set her Shark watch alarm), sneak down to the basement to get the ladder, and, without waking anyone up, take it to Jeremy's house and climb on top of his garage. Cady never felt as nervous and important as she did that night. Sure enough, when she had completed everything and reached the top rung of the ladder, there on the garage roof was Eric, sitting Indian-style, waiting for her. Cady remembered that he was pleased to see her, but not surprised—that was the best part about Eric, he was always confident his little sister would come through for him.

She was frozen, crouching on her hands and knees on the roof of the garage; she could see the cedar shingles shine in the moonlight, slick from a recent rainfall. Eric walked on the slanted roof as if it were nothing. He told her not to worry, he had seen Jeremy sneak out on the roof plenty of times, but Cady yelped when his Converse sneaker squeaked and slipped an inch. She watched as he quickly scaled the incline to the roof's apex, then walked along the ridgeline until he reached the wall of the main house. There he bent down and pulled on the last shingle before the wall. It lifted easily, and he revealed a hidden plastic baggie whose contents looked identical to the catnip. When Eric asked her if she knew what it was, she nodded so as not to disappoint him. He laughed and switched the two bags.

Cady could still hear Eric's laughter in her ears, and it joined with the sounds filling the church—Jenny Park chuckled sadly as she stood at the lectern, giving the rest of the mourners permission to follow suit. She had been Eric's high school girlfriend. They had been the academic power couple of Dixon Porter High, valedictorian and salutatorian, nerd royalty—until she dumped him the summer before they went to college, after she didn't get into Harvard but Stanford instead and he wouldn't go to Caltech to stay close to her. Cady had been sad when they broke up, but now she was glad Jenny had known Eric only at his best, before his mind turned on him.

Jenny's silky hair, blue-black like a raven's wing, fell forward as she read from a crumpled sheet of notebook paper. "Eric was the sweetest, smartest guy I'd ever met, but romance was never his best subject," Jenny said—more gentle laughter from the audience. "I told him months before prom that my dress was red, and I kept reminding him that he was going to have to get me flowers, a corsage or a bouquet or something that would match. So the big day rolls around, and there's Eric standing in my doorway with . . . nothing. But he has this big grin on his face, and he leads me to his old VW Golf parked out front, runs around the back of it, and *ta-da!* 'Here are your flowers!' he says. And inside the car were three large clay pots with green, leafy, shrub-type things in each of them. Not a bloom in sight."

Cady remembered this well. Their mother had warned him it was a terrible idea, but he was stubborn.

"And he goes, 'They're hydrangeas! Blue hydrangeas. Or they should be. By mid-June, at least one of them will be the perfect color.' I remember looking at his face all bright-eyed with excitement and then watching it slowly fall as he registered my less-than-ideal reaction. I was furious. What was I going to do with three huge potted plants? I practically threw his perfect red rose boutonnière at him. The entire vehicle smelled like peat moss, and we drove to the prom in silence."

Jenny looked at Cady and smiled. "Regretfully, I didn't realize at the time the effort and heartfelt intention behind Eric's gesture. I found out later, through various unnamed sources, that Eric was hell-bent on getting me a blue corsage because blue is my favorite color. But true blue flowers are very hard to find, so Eric decided to make some. He learned that the color of a hydrangea is determined by the pH balance in the soil, and specifically that a high acid content yields blue blossoms. He bought three hydrangea plants, repotted them in peat moss and conifer needles, and watered them daily with a special solution of aluminum sulfate and iron sulfate. To make sure he got the balance right, he made three attempts, hence the three pots. He had to have been planning it for over a month." Jenny took a long breath before continuing. She wiped her eyes and tucked her hair behind her ears. Her voice was trembling, but she was smiling. "So, I didn't have any flowers on my prom night. But right now, on our back patio, I have three glorious hydrangea plants, and they flower every June. And Eric, I hope you can see that each one blooms the perfect blue. Thank you."

Jenny stepped down from the lectern. As she passed their pew, Cady's mother stood to hug her. When Jenny broke from the embrace, she surprised Cady by bending down and putting her arms around Cady's neck. "I'm so sorry," Jenny said, sniffling. Cady nodded and touched her back but couldn't form the words to answer. All she could think of was how cool Jenny's hair felt against her cheek, like water.

The sound of the organ burst out from the front of the church, and Cady closed her eyes. After the last key was released, the sound lingered before escaping into the air beyond. Cady opened her eyes upward to the vaulted roof of the church.

She remembered looking up at Eric as he stood tall at the garage roof's peak, silhouetted against the moonlight like a wolf on a mountaintop. He motioned for her to climb up to the top with him, then reached out his arm to help her. Eric pointed out their parents' bedroom windows toward the back of the house and his own bedroom window—the one from which he watched Jeremy sneak out to smoke on the roof. He said he saw Bootie sitting in his window, but Cady couldn't, so he held her shoulders to position her in his perspective. Straining to see, she raised her heels from the roof. Suddenly, the light went on in their parents' room. Eric dropped down to hide, tipping Cady off balance. Her feet slipped out from under her.

She slid down the roof face-first, moving too fast to feel the shingles push past her outstretched arms, scrape her cheek, snag her nightshirt, hit her knees. But just before she ran out of roof, a hand closed tight around her ankle and then another yanked on the back of her shirt; Eric was grabbing her wherever he could catch hold. His feet were scrambling to slow their slide until he shoved his heels into the rain gutter. The metal pipe bowed out under the force, but Cady could see that it would hold. He had saved her.

Who would save her now that he was gone? Cady looked at her parents, her inscrutable father, her trembling mother, but neither of them was able to feel her gaze. Eric had always been the center of the family; when he was healthy, they were loving, celebrating, and planning for him, and when he became mentally ill, they were treating, arguing, and worrying over him. She felt they were floating away from one another, clinging to their memories of Eric like pieces of a sunken ship. She wanted to reach out to them, but to let go would be to drown.

Eric always considered Mantis Mommy Revenge their greatest mission, because they got the pleasure of watching Jeremy pretend to get high on catnip for the rest of the summer. He had retold the story to friends many times over the years, but in every instance Cady had to add that Eric saved her life that night, and every time he shrugged it off. She could still hear him give his standard reply: "Would *you* have let *me* fall?"

But in the end, Cady hadn't been there to stop him. She had let him fall. So had they all.

# 3

"I THINK WE'D better hit the road, Cady-Cake," her father said, making her nostalgic for the nickname the instant he used it. They had unloaded all her stuff, reparked the car, and gone out for a nice lunch at a restaurant called Grafton Street across from Lamont Library. Now they were back at the room, and Cady had run out of reasons to keep them there.

"But first, are you sure you don't need anything else?" Aunt Laura added.

Cady was reluctant to see them go, but she also didn't want to hold her father hostage on this campus any longer. "No, thanks, I can take it from here. You guys have a long drive home."

Her father and Laura gathered their things and the empty suit-cases they were taking back, and Cady walked them to the elevator. She bent to give Aunt Laura a hug, thanking her for coming, and Laura gave her an extra squeeze to show she understood. When it was her father's turn, Cady was surprised to see his face full of emotion for the first time that day.

"Now, listen to me," he said, putting his hands on her shoulders. "You're going to be fine here. You earned this, and I'm proud of you, and, deep down, Mom is too."

"Thanks." Cady nodded. She didn't believe him, but she wanted to.

He stroked her hair with one hand, his eyes glistening. "You're gonna make some new memories for our family, right?"

The height of that challenge gave her vertigo. She threw her arms around him, as if she were holding on for dear life.

He hugged her back. "That's my brave girl."

Cady felt anything but.

She walked back, entered the empty common room, and exhaled. It was a relief to be unobserved. But that pleasure was short-lived and replaced with a question: Now what? She had plenty of unpacking to do, she supposed she should get started. Cady arranged, and rearranged, the furniture in the double bedroom, making sure there was parity, each desk facing a window, dressers side by side. She didn't want her roommate to think she was selfish, although she did claim the bottom bunk; she wasn't an idiot. She put away all her clothes, made her bed, and set up the mini-fridge, which consisted of plugging it in.

Cady wasn't sure where to hang the cheap full-length mirror she had brought, or, more specifically, *how*, since the orientation pamphlet said they were prohibited from hammering nails into the walls. She propped the wobbly mirror against the back of the bedroom door and regarded her reflection. She didn't like what she saw. She had gotten up so early to make the drive, she was wearing no makeup, and her skin looked pale and dull, with none of the toasty freckles that would've dotted her nose and cheeks at the end of a happier summer. She wore leggings and a Vampire Weekend T-shirt, she didn't even like them that much anymore, and she wished she had dressed better for a first impression. She still could. Cady changed into better jeans and a blue Henley that she liked, and then her attention returned to the bottom drawer of her dresser.

She knelt and retrieved the Harvard hoodie, pausing before she pulled it over her head. Cady looked in the mirror again. She lifted her hand to her chest and ran her fingers across the crimson felt lettering. She combed her fingers through the end of her ponytail. Growing up, she'd always hated standing out as a redhead, but hers was the same chestnut tint as her brother's, a trait they shared with no other living relative. So now her hair didn't look so much like red, but like Eric. She smiled. People had always said it, but she'd never agreed until now—she looked just like him.

Suddenly, the bedroom door opened, sending the mirror falling forward. Cady lunged to catch it, but not before the corner struck the bedpost and sent a crack splintering across the top.

A middle-aged Indian woman in an azalea-pink tunic stood in the doorway. "Oh, no, I'm so sorry, I didn't realize anyone else was here, please let me help you." She set down the box she was holding and bent to help Cady lift it.

"That's okay, it's my fault."

A girl poked her head in from behind her mother, her long dark hair cascading below her slender neck. Her eyes were framed with heavy lashes, and her finely boned nose was pierced by a sparkly stud. "Mo-om, what did you do?"

"It was an accident," her mother cried. Then, looking at Cady, "I'm very sorry, I will pay for the mirror—"

"Please, don't apologize—"

"Great start to the roommate relationship, Mom," the girl said, playfully, as she entered the room. She was thin and lithe in a way that looked natural, and she was dressed in cool, slouchy jeans and a cropped white tee, displaying a flat, tan tummy. She turned to Cady, her smile bright. "I'm Ranjoo, do you hate me already?"

"Only for those abs." Cady laughed. "No, it's great to meet you, I'm Cady." They hugged, and even her hair smelled good.

"And I am Dr. Vasan, but you may call me Pri." Her mother embraced Cady as well. "And I insist you allow me to replace the mirror."

"Really, it's fine, I think the pieces will stay in."

"We can't use a broken mirror, it's bad luck! And I brought one too, we'll use mine."

"Ranjoo, you are here to study science, not superstition."

"I'm studying art, and now with this bad luck, I'll be unemployed forever. Think of it, Mom, no job *and* no doctorate—what will you tell the aunties?"

"Stop it, you terrible daughter." Her mother grabbed her face and kissed it as Ranjoo scrunched her nose. "You know we are all so proud of you, whatever you decide."

Cady felt a pang of envy. "Is sharing a bedroom okay with you? Our third roommate, Andrea, requested the single, she's a light sleeper."

Ranjoo rolled her eyes. "You got that email from her, too? Last time I checked, being high-maintenance isn't a medical condition. But you're nicer than I am. If I'd been here first, I'd have moved my shit right into that single."

"You still can, I guess."

"No, you were right, it's good to be nice. Plus, I'm not going to stick you with the *crazy* roommate."

Cady's smile faded. "Crazy" was another word that would never mean what it used to.

Weld 23 quickly became a very busy place. Ranjoo's father, the other Dr. Vasan, arrived, and Cady helped them bring Ranjoo's many boxes upstairs. Ranjoo was from California, so most of her things had been shipped ahead of time, which struck Cady as glamorous, if a total pain to unpack. They were knee-deep in cardboard when the front door opened again, and the third roommate, Andrea Kraus-Feldman, and her family arrived.

"Knock knock, anybody home?" Mr. Kraus-Feldman called out in a singsong voice. He had a big smile and brushy mustache underneath a Harvard Class of '88 hat.

Mrs. Kraus-Feldman entered next, gazing around dreamily. "Oh, it's just as I remembered it."

Andrea emerged from behind her. "Cady, I'm so excited to finally meet you!" she cried, throwing her little arms around her. Cady returned the hug and excitement, feeling only a little phony. Andrea gave Ranjoo a cooler greeting, punishment for that unanswered email.

Andrea was petite and waifishly thin, making her appear younger than eighteen. She had big blue eyes behind outdated wire-rimmed glasses and light brown hair pulled back with barrettes. Her fair skin was poreless but stretched tight across her forehead, so you could see a tiny blue vein at her temple. Andrea's silent little sister looked just like her, only less worried. Her family members crammed into her single bedroom to get her unpacked, leaving no job for Andrea, so she suggested the new roommates compare classes in the common room. Cady was happy to learn Ranjoo would be in Psych 100 with her. Neither Cady nor Ranjoo had any classes in common with Andrea's brutal premed course load. Cady glazed over as Andrea agonized over the decision whether to take Chem 17 in fall or spring semester, until she mentioned a Professor Kessler.

"Take the one with Kessler," Cady said. "He's a tough grader, but he makes it interesting. Someone else teaches it in the spring and totally sucks by comparison."

"Really? Good, thank you, that makes me feel so much better to have that decided." Andrea sighed in relief. "Wait, how do you know that?"

"Oh—" *Because Eric took it his freshman year.* "My friend's older brother goes here, and he told me." Cady was afraid the heat of the lie would show on her face, but Andrea seemed not to notice. Cady hadn't explicitly decided against telling people about Eric, but she didn't want to tell her roommates so soon after meeting them. She would wait for the right time.

Ranjoo was discussing the art portfolio submission process for studio classes when Cady tuned back in. Ranjoo showed them pictures on her iPhone of a mural she'd painted on the side of an old warehouse in her hometown. "I didn't get permission or anything, I just did it over three nights one weekend. But people liked it, so they let me do two more panels, see?"

"That's incredible," Cady said, meaning it. "How did I get into this school with you?"

Andrea asked, "And your parents are supportive?"

"Of my majoring in studio art, or my graffiti?"

"Both. I mean, they're *doctors*."

"I know, right? I'm going to have to let them arrange my marriage to make up for it."

Cady laughed with Ranjoo, but Andrea furrowed her brow. "Are you serious?"

"No, I'm kidding! P.S. You're racist for not getting the joke."

"I am not racist." Andrea looked stricken. "I just wouldn't make a stereotype of my family for a laugh."

"Omigod, I'm messing with you. And anyway, they're my family, so joking about them is my prerogative, isn't it?" Ranjoo said.

Andrea raised her eyebrows.

"What's that face?" Ranjoo shot back.

Andrea's smile remained impassive as a doll's. "Both my mother and my father went here, it's where they met. In fact, this was my mother's room freshman year."

"Seriously? That's wild, what are the odds?" Cady interjected in an attempt to defuse the situation.

"I heard they sometimes do that for *legacies*," Ranjoo said. "Makes you feel like your family is part of Harvard's 'living history.' One of their many tricks to secure alumni giving."

"Regardless." Andrea frowned. "I'm proud that I can live up to my family's expectations, even if they set the bar high. And I wouldn't denigrate my own parents to two strangers, but that's just me."

Cady stepped in. "She was just joking."

Andrea took a deep breath. "You're right. I really don't know your situation. I'm sorry if I offended you."

"Whatever, it's fine." Ranjoo bit into the words.

"Friends?"

"Yeah, friends," she answered, smiling tightly.

"Now if you'll excuse me. I have to use the ladies' room." Andrea walked out into the hall.

As soon as the door clicked shut, Ranjoo whirled to face Cady. "Ugh, can you believe her?"

"That was weird," Cady agreed, eager to prove her loyalty. But in the back of her mind, she'd heard what Ranjoo had said about tricks for legacies. Although her parents weren't alumni, she guessed that a sibling at Harvard could count almost as much. She wondered about a dead one.

"I mean, we just met, and she's already judging the shit out of me. Like, we have to live together, can you show a little manners?"

"I know." Cady had assumed the housing was random, but if the college intentionally placed Andrea in Weld, was Cady intentionally kept away from Grays, Eric's freshman dorm?

"And the truth is, I know I joke about my parents, but they're *my* parents. I get it, they get it, I don't need to explain it to some girl I just met."

And she hadn't gotten into Princeton or Yale. The fact was, Cady had applied to Harvard when her brother was a junior there, but she had gotten in three weeks after he jumped out the window of his dorm room. Was her acceptance don't-sue-us insurance? Was she a pity admission?

"You can't judge the dynamic in someone else's family, you know?"

Cady refocused on Ranjoo. "I really like your parents. And I can tell how much you guys love each other."

"Thanks. They're pretty awesome. I'm sorry I missed your mom and dad."

"Yeah, actually, you missed my dad and my aunt, but, whatever." Cady shrugged it off, but something on her face must have betrayed her hurt, because Ranjoo's brows lifted in sympathy and embarrassment.

"Oh, I'm so sorry. Is your mom . . . ?"

"Dead? No, no." *My brother is.* "My mom just wasn't up for the trip." It worked as a vague, passable excuse, as long as you didn't know that the relative who was "up for the trip" was wheelchair-bound.

Ranjoo's father returned from taking the broken-down boxes to the basement to report that the trash area was "quite tidy" and added,

"Ah, and before I forget, Cady, please tell me, where did you buy your sweatshirt?"

She froze—she had forgotten she was still wearing it.

"Oh, no, Cady, don't tell him!" Ranjoo called out from their bedroom. "He's gonna buy them for the whole family. The campus store won't have any left."

Cady yanked the sweatshirt over her head, muffling her weak claim about its being too hot for it.

"My only child gets into Harvard, and you think I want to keep it a secret?" he yelled back.

Ranjoo came out of the room, still needling her father. "You know, I bet Harvard makes them in India, tell the fam to go factory-direct and save on shipping."

Cady darted behind her into the bedroom and tossed the wadded-up sweatshirt onto her bed, then popped back into the common room.

"Such a wise guy," Dr. Vasan said. "Tell me, Cady, how can a good daughter give her father so much grief?"

Cady huffed out her anxiety in a laugh. "You should ask my dad about that."

# 4

IT WAS EVENING when Cady again found herself alone. Ranjoo and Andrea had each gone out to dinner with their parents. Cady had gotten a salad from a chain restaurant in the Square and eaten it hunched over on the futon in the common room, studying the pages of Eric's notebook.

She heard noises outside and crossed the room to peer out the window. Cady watched as boisterous groups of other freshmen barreled around the darkened Yard, their laughter amplified within the quad of aged brick, oak, and ivy. A wave of loneliness washed over her. She had thought that since she and her classmates were all strangers together, a merry spirit of collective neediness would suck her into a burgeoning friend group like a social undertow. She had hoped that she would at least get to hang with her roommates, or that somehow it would be easier than this. Looking out the window, it seemed that for many, it was. She had wanted to feel swept up, but Cady had gone through the day feeling isolated. Secrets had that effect.

The ability to keep a secret was an Archer family trait. Cady remembered the day she heard back from the first batch of colleges. Harvard's acceptance letter hadn't been among the envelopes she pulled from the mailbox after school. That was because her mother had already checked the mail for it, taken it, and hidden it. What her mother hadn't known was that Cady had signed up to be notified by email. The first line of that email—*Congratulations! It is our pleasure to inform you that you have been accepted to the Harvard College Class of 2022*—had been bubbling inside Cady's chest since lunchtime. It was only later that afternoon, after she told her mom she was accepted, that her mother produced the paper version. Her mother said she'd thought it would upset Cady to see it, which was plausible, as Cady had been keeping the secret from her mother of why she actually wanted to go.

But this wasn't what she had thought her first night here would be like. When she first applied to Harvard, she had imagined she and Eric would be moving in at the same time. She mourned that alternate reality, the way it could have been if he were still here. He would already know how everything worked, where you pick up your keys, where you park, whether you got a good dorm. He would introduce her to his friends, and she would be automatically cooler for having upperclassmen who knew her name. He would carry the heavy stuff with his string bean arms that were weirdly strong. He would give her a gross, sweaty hug on purpose.

Back home, she rarely met anyone without having her brother serve as context. She was always "Cady, Eric Archer's little sister." Everyone knew or had heard of Eric Archer; he was the type of kid in high school whom people referred to by his full name. Then, no one had been a stranger. Now, everyone was. And Cady was making it worse. Why couldn't she tell her roommates she had a brother who died? Cady told herself she didn't want to make anyone uncomfortable, but there was the more selfish reason; she didn't want to be tragic. Tragedy taints a person, and no one wants to touch that sadness, just in case it spreads. A genius brother was one thing, a brother dead by suicide was another. She so badly wanted to rewrite that story, to give him, both of them, a better ending. And if that wasn't possible, she didn't want to tell the story at all.

Cady stepped away from the window and returned to Eric's notebook. Maybe Eric could still introduce her to some people after all.

She flipped through its pages once again, looking for any names mentioned. "Prokop" appeared several times on the earlier pages, once where Eric had jotted down "Prof Prokop's" office hours, and Cady vaguely recalled the name as the professor who advised Eric on his Bauer Award submission, a project he never finished. She wondered if his office hours were the same this year.

There was another note that stood out to Cady because it wasn't in Eric's handwriting. It was on one of the earlier pages, when Eric's calculations were still in neatly printed pencil, except on one page there were blue-pen corrections on one of Eric's proofs. And in the margin the pen said, "Cheers!—Nikos."

*Nikos.* An unusual name like that should be easy to find on Facebook, Cady looked him up on her phone and quickly found him. She enlarged his profile picture—chiseled features, dark hair and eyes, looking dapper in a tuxedo. *Damn, Eric,* she thought, *you couldn't have introduced me to him sooner?* She clicked around his profile: He was a senior physics major like Eric, so it made sense they had classes together. Skimming his groups, she saw he was a member of Harvard Intramural Squash Team and University Choir. Cady sang in the chamber choir in high school and had considered going out for one of the choral groups on campus, an idea that had just become more appealing.

Cady heard the suite door open and close from inside her bedroom; one of her roommates must have come home. She got up and poked her head out to see which one it was, secretly hoping it was Ranjoo, just in time to see the door to Andrea's bedroom close behind her.

Cady stepped out and walked to Andrea's bedroom door, hesitating before giving a light knock. "Andrea, hey, it's—"

"I'm *changing!*" Andrea yelled from inside.

"—Cady," she said only to herself. So much for roommate bonding.

She felt awkward just waiting for Andrea to emerge, so she padded down the hall toward the communal women's bathroom, half-intending to wash up for bed and half-hoping to find someone to persuade her not to, but no one else was wandering the halls. She pushed her shoulder against the door's smudgy steel panel. A girl was showering in one of the near stalls, and the smallest sliver of visible flesh between the curtain and the tiled wall made Cady feel like a pervert. She turned her back to the row of showers and put her toothbrush and paste on the edge of a sink, clean except for a squiggle of one anonymous hair. She would have to get used to this communal bathroom thing. Growing up, Eric ceded bathroom territory to her entirely; she had only his ginger beard shavings with which to contend, and they weren't much. Eric was cowed by the sheer force of his sister's feminine mystique; out of respect or fear, he always gave Cady and her strange girl-things like tampons, body scrub, and flat iron a wide berth, although sometimes he did steal her Herbal Essence shampoo. She would catch him smelling of roses or mangoes or whatever the scent du jour was and bust him. "It was the jojoba that gave me away, wasn't it? Damn you, jojoba!"

She looked in the mirror, smiling at the memory, and swept her hair up into a high bun.

The main door to the ladies' room swung open and Andrea entered, dressed in purple plaid pajamas and lavender slippers. "Oh, hi," she said, oddly bashful. "Sorry, I was changing."

"Yeah, no worries." Cady smiled reassuringly. "How was dinner?"

"Fine." Andrea set her matching purple caddy of toiletries on the sink next to her.

The conversation was slower to warm up than the faucet water. Cady bent to wash her face. "Ranjoo is still out."

"I know." Andrea squeezed a line of toothpaste onto her electric toothbrush with an intensity of focus beyond what Aquafresh should require. "We ran into her after dinner in the Square. Her parents had taken her to some fancy restaurant in their hotel. I invited her to get frozen yogurt with us—just to be nice—but she said she was meeting up with some people." Andrea put air quotes around *some people* and said the rest with the toothbrush muffling her speech, her mouth literally frothing. "What people? What's the big secret? I didn't want to join her, I was getting fro-yo!" She paused to spit. "Rude." She replaced the whirring toothbrush in her mouth.

Cady patted her face dry, trying to think of what to say.

Andrea rinsed and spat a last time. "I guess she makes friends easily. I don't know *how*."

Cady felt an unwelcome kinship with Andrea, bonded with the glue of jealousy and self-doubt.

"Can I borrow some toothpaste? I forgot mine."

Andrea handed her the tube. "How did you get that scar on your neck?"

Cady dropped the tube in the sink. "Oh, shoot, sorry." She fumbled to get it, flustered. "I, um, this?" She covered the scar with her hand and lied, "I had a mole removed."

"Skin cancer?"

She pulled her hair down to hide it. "No, but they thought it could be, so . . ." Although the scar was only an inch-long depression into her skin, it traced a shame so deep it cut to her core. "I don't like it, it's ugly."

"You should wear sunscreen daily. Redheads are prone to skin cancer."

"Where did you go for dinner with your parents?" Cady shoved the toothbrush into her mouth so she wouldn't have to talk anymore.

"Bartley's, you know that famous old burger place? My parents had their first date there, so they wanted me to experience it. They said nothing had changed but the menu, which was nice for them, but I don't really like hamburgers. Then my parents went home. They're not the type to waste money on a hotel unless they absolutely have to."

"Same with mine."

"You mean your father and your aunt? Ranjoo told me your mom didn't come."

"Well, right." Cady stole a glance at Andrea in the mirror. *When did those two have a chance to talk about me?* "I meant in general."

"Why didn't your mom come?"

Cady sighed. "She's totally disappointed in me that I'm going to Harvard."

Andrea frowned at her for a moment, puzzled, before her face eased into a smile, and she laughed. "You're joking, I get it this time."

Cady smiled, revealing nothing more. "See you in the room." Walking out, she could see Andrea's uncertain gaze follow her, reflected over and over again in the row of mirrors.

So not one, but two painful memories chased Cady back to her empty bedroom. She changed quickly and climbed under the covers of her bottom bunk, but she couldn't fight off both memories at once. As she tried to sleep, her mind replayed that awful memory of the night she'd discussed those college acceptance letters with her parents at dinner.

SHE REMEMBERED HOW her father sat back in his chair as he said it: "Harvard. You got in—really?"

She remembered the conscious effort it took not to look at her mother's face the whole time.

Then her father took a deep breath and summoned a smile. "Well, that's wonderful."

"Andy." Her mother gave him a look as if he were making a bad joke.

"It is. It's an incredibly prestigious university, not to mention highly selective, and they picked our daughter. That's a very big deal, Cady, congratulations." He raised his water glass in Cady's direction.

"Well, that's true, honey, and I hope you feel proud of yourself, because I am." Her mother nodded to Cady briefly. "She's worked very hard, that's why she got into many other top, top schools, including Ivies, so she has her pick. Of course she's not picking Harvard."

"Have you asked her?" Her father raised his brows at his daughter. "Do you want to go?"

"Actually, I do," Cady answered, softly.

"All right, then I support you. That's an excellent choice."

"Wait, what?" Her mother's mouth dropped open. "Cady, you don't want to go there."

"It was my first choice school."

"*Before*, but not now. How could you want to now?"

Her father turned to her mother. "Don't jump on her. She gets to make her own decision."

"I can't believe we're even having this discussion!" Her mother gave a laugh, but her eyes flared. "Is this about attention? I mean, first the scattering ceremony, and now this?"

Cady's cheeks flushed with heat. "No, that day, I don't know what happened, I didn't mean to—"

"Then why are you doing this?"

Cady looked down to shield herself from her mother's glare. "I just want to—"

Her father interrupted, "Karen, you can't blame Harvard. We have to face the fact that Eric was schizophrenic. It was his mental illness, not the school, that became too much for him. Harvard didn't kill him."

"It didn't save him," her mother snapped. "I brought my son home from Harvard's campus in a body bag. Some cafeteria there is where he ate his last meal. I still get overdue notices from Lamont Library for books he didn't return. I received a letter of condolence on Harvard stationery with that stupid fucking crimson seal that I hope never to see again." Tears brimmed in her eyes. "It is home to the greatest tragedy of my lifetime. It is his tomb!"

"Mom." Cady reached across the table to touch her mother. She felt terrible, and in that moment, she was ready to change her mind, until—

"And *you*." Her mother recoiled from her and stared at her, wild-eyed. "What are you thinking? How could you even think to do this to us? To me?"

"I want—"

"Want what? To drag us through four more years of agony? To keep me up more nights than I already am? Honestly, I don't know why you'd want to go through it yourself. How could you tolerate it? It's like his death means nothing to you."

Cady felt the heat rise to the surface of her skin, reddening her cheeks as though she'd been slapped.

Her father held up a hand. "Enough. That is enough. We are all grieving for Eric, yes, in our own ways, but we are all grieving, and we will be for a long, long time. But I will not allow this family to be defined by this loss forever. I won't. Yes, Eric's death has cast a shadow over our lives. But Karen, you seem hell-bent on drawing some indelible chalk outline around it."

"What do you want me to do? I'm his mother!"

"You're *her* mother, too!"

Her mother's last words before leaving the table: "Not tonight."


CADY AWOKE TO the sound of her own terrified voice, "No, no, no!" Still dreaming, she had put her arms up as if to push someone from on top of her, but instead her hands made contact with the honeycomb wiring of the mattress above her. The room was pitch black, but slowly her senses returned to her: the plasticky scent of her brand-new, extra-long bedsheets; the sound of her heavy and rapid breathing; the cold sweat at the back of her neck; the feeling of restraint coming from the sheets tangled around her legs, as if she'd been tossing and turning for a while. Finally her eyes adjusted to see a girl's hand waving at her over the side of the upper bunk.

"Sorry, sorry, it's just me," said Ranjoo's voice from above. "I tried to be quiet, but I'm still getting the hang of this top bunk thing. It's really creaky."

Cady exhaled a long and shaky breath. "That's okay. I didn't know what was above me. And I think I was having a nightmare."

"Then maybe it was good I woke you? But sorry. Good night."

"Good night," she said to the mattress.

But as Cady's fear dissipated, the loneliness she had felt earlier came back to take its place.

She reached for her phone plugged in on the floor and checked the time: 3:11 a.m. She scrolled idly through her messages, looking for some source of comfort. She had texted her high school best friend, Liz, earlier in the day, but she hadn't responded, probably too busy with her new friends at Penn. Cady went to her Favorites list and let the highlight bar alight on Eric's name. When they were little, if she got scared at night or had a bad dream, she would go into Eric's room and tell him about it. Sometimes she even made up a nightmare to tell him as an excuse to stay up with him. On impulse, Cady keyed in a text message, fingers moving furtively, as if someone might catch her, and clicked Send. She replaced the phone on the floor beside her bed and pressed her face back into the pillow.

A few minutes passed, when a *ping* went off, her cellphone's text message alert. She reached for the phone, and a shiver went down her spine when she saw the screen: 1 New Message. She didn't know what she expected to read, a text message from beyond the grave? But desperate people believe in miracles. Her heartbeat quickened as she unlocked the screen and clicked on her text messages. The screen was blindingly white in the dark. It read:

Delivery Error

Msg: I miss you.

Sent: 3:12 AM

Recipient: **Eric** Not Available

# 5

"AND YOUR NAME is . . ." Dr. Sutcliffe, director of the Holden Choirs, rubbed his knuckles against his brushy white mustache as he looked down his clipboard.

Cady exhaled a shaky breath of nerves. She was standing in a rehearsal room in Paine Music Hall, about to begin the rigorous audition that would decide her placement in one of the seven campus choirs, from the most selective, the Collegium Musicum, to the more welcoming ones with less Latin in their names, like the Harvard-Radcliffe Chorus. University Choir fell somewhere in between, and Cady had hoped to meet Eric's friend Nikos among the members manning the sign-in desk or organizing the auditions. She'd even arrived a half hour early to stake the place out, but to her disappointment, he wasn't there. Now she supposed she'd have to go through with this anyway.

"Cadence Archer."

"Ah. We'll start with the piece you prepared in advance. Soprano, correct?"

Cady nodded, and three of the existing members rose from their seats in the front row. They took their places around her, and Dr. Sutcliffe held his hands in the air, ready to cue them. Cady kept her eyes on her sheet music and waited for the opening measures to begin, trying to keep her breathing slow and steady.

Dr. Sutcliffe cleared his throat and turned over his shoulder to the accompanist. "Nikos? When you're ready."

*Nikos.* Cady met his eyes for only a second before he tilted his face down at the keys, but it was enough to be sure—it was him, and he had been looking at her. His jet-black hair shook as he played the stirring introduction to the piece. But in that brief glance, she noticed he was even more handsome in person.

Cady came in a beat late, flushing her face with embarrassment, but she recovered and sang the rest as well as she could, distracted with thoughts of the boy behind the piano. She pulled it together for the second song, a test of her sight-reading abilities, which were strong, but she was performing for an audience of one.

"Thank you, quartet," Dr. Sutcliffe said when they had finished the second number. "Now for the aural exam. Nikos, I'll take it from here."

Nikos got up from the piano but kept his eyes downcast. Cady was suddenly sure this had been a mistake—he couldn't even look at her, he thought she was a freak, an awkward reminder of a troubled classmate. She wanted to shrink out of the room and—

He glanced up, interrupting her mental spiral with a warm, encouraging smile, and he mouthed the words "Good luck."

Cady blushed again, this time in relief.

Dr. Sutcliffe settled behind the piano. "Shall we begin?"

Cady nodded and the choir director put her through her paces. "Sing the middle note of this chord . . . up a third . . . now down a sixth." And each time, she complied with ease. Finally, Dr. Sutcliffe rose from behind the piano to look at her. "Do you know what note you just sang?"

"An A," Cady answered.

"And how did you arrive at that conclusion?"

"It sounded like one."

"Mm-hm." He rubbed his mustache again. "Sing me an F sharp."

As soon as she had done so, he pressed a finger on a piano key. It matched the tone Cady had just sung. He walked out from behind the piano and folded his arms across his chest. "Absolute pitch occurs in less than one person in ten thousand people. Do you have perfect pitch?"

"I think so." Cady felt squirmy under the directness of his gaze.

"Those with perfect pitch don't think, they know. Do you?"

"Yes."

"I thought so. You were nervous when we started, but you shouldn't be. You have a gift."

"Thank you," Cady said, trying not to look at Nikos.

"So, what do you think of this piano?"

She hesitated. "It's very nice."

"And the tuning?"

This time, no hesitation. "It's about a semitone flat."

Dr. Sutcliffe grinned at Nikos. "Very good."


CADY STEPPED OUT of the rehearsal room invigorated, keyed up on the adrenaline of the audition but even more on finding her first connection to Eric's world at Harvard. She was trying to slow her thoughts and plot how next to "run into" Nikos, when a hand touched her shoulder.

Nikos stood before her. "Pardon me, I just wanted to say, you were brilliant in there. Perfect pitch is like a superpower."

Cady heard his charming British accent; she tried not to get distracted by it. "Thanks, but I was pretty shaky in the beginning."

"Not a'tall. You should've heard the mewling before you. I'm Nikos, by the way."

*I know, I stalked you here.* "I'm Cady." She shook his hand. His brown eyes searched her face, and everything Cady had mentally rehearsed to say to him went out of her head. Her mouth was drier than at the audition.

But Nikos saved her. "I have to confess, I already knew who you were. I recognized your name, and, of course, the hair. Your brother, Eric, was a dear friend of mine. I miss him very much. I'm so sorry for your loss."

Relief washed over her. "Thank you." She liked that Nikos didn't hesitate to use Eric's name like so many others. Cady missed the sound of it.

"I know how lonely this place can be in the beginning, and although it can't compare to how you must feel, I know a bit about how lonely it feels without Eric. I wanted to introduce myself and let you know that I'm around should you need anything, anything at all."

He was saying everything she had hoped he would. She couldn't speak for the lump in her throat.

"He talked about you, his brilliant little sister, Cady."

"He did?" she managed.

"Often." Nikos smiled with one side of his mouth, crinkling the skin beside his eye and under one cheekbone.

"I think I remember hearing your name, too." It wasn't exactly true, but it might as well be. "And if I make the choir, maybe I'll see you around."

"Oh, I'm not a singer. I play the church organ along with U. Choir and occasionally accompany rehearsals on piano, but mostly I practice on my own."

"Ah." Cady hid her disappointment. "Well, then, I'll let you get back to the auditions."

"No need, they have another pianist, I tagged out. But would you like to join me for lunch? I can take you to one of the illustrious river houses. You can't get in alone as a freshman, but—"

Cady gasped. "My freshman seminar!" Cady had completely forgotten she had a class. "Shit, it's the first meeting, and I'm late."

"Oh, no, where is it? D'you know how to get there?"

"Um . . ." Cady rifled through her notebook for her stupid schedule printout. "Sever 207. And no, I have no clue."

"Follow me."

Nikos led her briskly across the green to Sever Hall, a massive red brick building whose entrance was beneath a semicircular archway like a gaping hungry mouth. She bade him a hasty goodbye, heaved her shoulder against the heavy door, and rushed up to the second floor, taking the shallow stairs two by two, even three by three. By the time she reached the door with 207 printed on its frosted glass, it was 2:11 p.m. She opened the door.

"Ah, look, everyone, she's here!" Professor Hines clapped, a show of mock enthusiasm. Wearing gray slacks, a plain white shirt, and a dark blazer, he seemed younger than other professors, save for the baldness that had patterned his hair into a sharp widow's peak. Twelve other students were seated around a long dark wood conference table, looking at her.

"Sorry," Cady said softly, head down. There was only one seat open, and it was right next to the professor. She took it as quickly as possible, waiting for whatever class discussion to resume. But it didn't. The entire room remained silent for an excruciating minute. She saw her classmates' eyes dart at each other in confusion. She mustered the courage to turn and look at Professor Hines, sitting just inches from her.

He was staring at her, resting his cheek in his hand, smiling. But there was nothing kind about the twist of his thin lips, and his hip plastic glasses did little to soften his gimlet eyes.

Not knowing what else to do, she repeated her apology. "I—I'm sorry I was late. It won't happen again."

Professor Hines crossed his arms, still smiling. "Well?" he said, lifting his eyebrows into a wide expanse of forehead.

Cady had no idea what he wanted her to do or say. She looked to her classmates, not a familiar face among them.

"Oh, I'm sorry," he continued. "I assumed, since you're important enough to keep us all waiting, you would have something to say that was worth the wait."

"I don't think I'm important. I just got lost getting here." Cady could barely get the words out.

Professor Hines made an exaggerated pout. "Of course you did. You're new." He paused. "Not like these other freshmen."

She felt a flash of tingly hot embarrassment.

"Speaking of your classmates, you missed the introductions, where we went around the room saying our names, places of origin, et cetera. Now, you'll probably never remember everyone's name and none of these people will be your friends. Of course, everyone will remember *you*, Cadence Archer, because you will go down in class history as the girl who came late on the very first day. That's irony."

The heat in her cheeks had traveled up to behind her eyes, but Cady knew tears would only bait him. She never used to cry easily, not until Eric. "It won't happen again."

"No, usually it doesn't." Professor Hines stood up and faced the class as if he were an actor on a stage. "This sometimes happens with freshmen. You arrive here puffed up and proud. You're used to being the smartest person in the room, the best student, valedictorian of God-Knows-Where High School. Well, kids, you're not in Kansas anymore. This place will humble you whether you like it or not. Or, at the very least"—he put his hand on his heart—"I will."

The class shifted uneasily in their seats.

"Now, where was I? Irony, right. Irony is a topic we'll be exploring at length in this seminar. An excellent example of a poet exploiting irony is in the dramatic monologues of Robert Browning. Perhaps his most famous was 'My Last Duchess' . . . "

For the next forty-five minutes, Cady kept her head bowed to her notebook and didn't dare look up, much less raise her hand. She tried to take notes, but all she could think about was how no paper she could write, no observation she could make, no amount of arriving on time, was going to change this man's first impression of her. Cady had been the most excited about this class; all the freshman seminars required a submission to get into, she had slaved over her essay for it, and this was her only small class, all the rest were lectures. So in the one class where the professor actually knew she existed, he thought she was a snot. *Ugh*, she cringed to herself. How had she let this happen?

When the clock mercifully struck three and Professor Hines dismissed the class, Cady bolted for the door. The freedom of the hallway was in her grasp when a voice called her back. "Miss Archer," said Professor Hines. He beckoned her with his finger. "A quick word. Wouldn't want to make you late for your *next* class."

Cady inhaled, heading back against the exiting students until she reached him. "I want to apologize again for my lateness. It's really not like me, I'm usually very punctual, and I think it may have given you a false impression—"

"I don't care," Professor Hines cut her off. "Really, I don't need your life story. When you show up late in my class, it disrespects me. And when you disrespect me in front of my class, that's embarrassing. So it's simple, every time you embarrass me, I'll embarrass you. And trust me, I'm good at it."

*No shit,* she thought.

"As for impressions, your work in this class will impress me or it won't. That's up to you. Understand?"

Cady nodded.

"That's a good girl. See you next week."

Cady left, fuming as she descended the stairs of Sever. '*Good girl*'— what right did he have to talk to her like that? Who the hell was he? She didn't care if he liked her or not, he could fail her for all she cared, she had two words to say to him and two words only. *Fu*—

"Hey!"

Cady looked up just in time to avoid colliding with the tall boy in front of her, but it took another beat for his greeting to register. "Sorry—what?"

"Are you okay? That was rough in there." He raised his light eyebrows, blond like his close-cropped hair, and looked expectantly at Cady, then added, "My bad, I forgot you missed introductions. I'm Alex from the seminar we just had together?"

"Oh, right, I'm sorry—"

"You can stop apologizing. Professor Hines is gone."

She laughed. "Thanks. And my name is Cady."

"Oh, I remembered *your* name. Hines was kinda right about that part."

Cady groaned.

"No, come on, I'm kidding. I would've remembered anyway." Alex glanced over his shoulder. "And Hines seems like a total asshole."

Cady's whole body relaxed. "He *does*, right?"

"Yeah, he's crazy. You were like five minutes late."

"Erm, more like eleven."

"No, we aren't even expected to be in class until seven past the hour—Harvard's unwritten rules. And I got there just a little before you did, and he didn't say a thing. No idea why he freaked out on you."

"Well, thanks. I'm glad to know his hatred of me is personal more than anything."

Alex laughed; he had a great laugh, Cady thought. They chatted as they descended to the first floor. With his crew cut and denim-blue eyes, Alex looked like he'd grown up on fresh air and a glass of milk a day. She almost didn't believe him when he said he was from Brooklyn.

The ground floor was more crowded, people entering and exiting Sever swarmed around them, and they were jostled apart midsentence among the cattle chute congestion by the front doors. When Cady did emerge, she squinted in the afternoon sunlight, trying to spot Alex among the backpacks and bobbing heads.

"Cadence!"

She turned and saw Nikos waving to her. She smiled and went toward him, happy to see another friendly face.

When she reached him, Nikos put his hands on both her shoulders. "My dear, did you survive?"

She was about to answer, when Alex suddenly reappeared at her side. "See you around," he said with a nod of his head.

"Oh—" Cady turned to him, but Alex was already quickly walking away. "See you," she said anyway.

Nikos grabbed her hand and her attention back. "Let's have a look at you." He pulled her from the herd and twirled her around. "All in one piece? Thank goodness."

"You're surprised?"

"Well, you were late to Professor Hines's class. He's a notorious prick. I was worried about you. But I'm pleased to see you appear unscathed."

"Not exactly." Cady rolled her eyes and told him what had happened. "And then that guy told me that *he* was late, too, and Hines didn't say anything to him. Why'd he get off the hook and I get attacked?"

"What guy?"

"Alex, that guy who, just, a guy in my seminar."

"He was late, too?" Nikos crossed his arms over his red jacket. "Would've been nice of him to stand up for you in the moment, no?"

Cady frowned. She hadn't thought of that.

"You'll soon learn that this is a place full of brown-nosers. Occasionally, you get a warm, fuzzy, we're-all-in-the-trenches-together feeling, but it's a clever trick to lull you into complacency while they steal your notes."

Cady hoped he was kidding. She pulled her quilted jacket more tightly around her. "Did you wait all this time?"

"No, I'm afraid I'm not that devoted, darling, not *yet*. We've only just met this morning."

Cady couldn't help but giggle. Nikos wasn't like any guy she'd met before. He was confident and quick; his brain seemed to work three times as fast as hers. Or maybe it was the accent. "But I did come back 'round after my thesis meeting, so that should count for something."

"It does. I appreciate it." Cady was touched that a friend of Eric's would go out of his way to make sure she didn't feel alone. She had to catch herself from thinking his interest in her could be more than surrogate-brotherly concern. It didn't take much to see that Nikos was a flirt. The only thing Cady couldn't figure out was how he and Eric had been close friends; they were so different. Eric was shy around girls, she had never seen him act flirty, he specialized in nursing a crush from afar.

"And since you were in such a rush, I didn't get to show you the very best part of Sever."

"No, thanks. I'm not going back in there until I have to."

"You won't have to go inside. Trust me."

The Yard had emptied out, and only a few students strolled through the green, the rest were tourists, some in flocks with a leader holding a small flag or umbrella, and others alone with a camera. Cady would have to get used to attending a school that people traveled halfway around the globe just to photograph, and she couldn't blame them. Right now, Memorial Church stood before her, a glorious red brick structure with marble steps, solid round columns, and a snowy white spire that reached toward heaven. It faced the enormous Widener Library, whose facade featured an expanse of marble stairs leading to imposing Roman columns. So far, Cady had been too intimidated to enter either building.

Cady reluctantly followed Nikos back to Sever's main archway, where he positioned her so her shoulder was flush beside it. "Now, what is so very special about this archway is that if you stand very close to it, like this, and whisper directly into the bricks, you can be heard all the way on the other side of the archway there."

"Really?"

"I swear. It's my favorite detail of any building here. Reminds me of the whispering wall in my grandmother's garden in England— magical things are more ordinary over there."

Cady put her hand up against the rough brick. "How do you know all this?"

Nikos's dark eyes flashed as his mouth curled to an impish grin. "I know everything."

"I think you're full of it."

"Let's try it, you'll see. It's just math and acoustical physics, I could explain it, if you like."

"Don't bother, I wouldn't understand it."

"Of course you would, you're Eric Archer's sister."

She smiled.

"But it might bore you to tears, so believe it's magic instead. Now, you stay there," Nikos said, walking backward to the other side. "I'll whisper you a secret message, and then you whisper something to me, and we'll reconvene."

"Okay." Cady waited for him to take his position on the other side. When he did, she put her ear against the archway's edge. At first she flinched; the cold emanating from the bricks cooled her cheek like ice. But the whistling wind already sounded amplified, and her curiosity was piqued. She leaned in a second time and listened to the soft voice funneled into her ear.

*It takes only an error to father a sin.*

Cady felt a chill down the nape of her neck, and not from the cold.

Nikos was grinning at her. He put his own ear up to the wall and motioned her to go ahead.

Cady faced the wall and covered her mouth, knowing it was her turn to play, but it didn't feel like a game anymore. Did he really just say that? Did it mean what she thought it might?

With so many questions swirling in her brain, she couldn't summon a reply.

Nikos pulled back after a minute and strode over to her. "I couldn't hear you at all. Did you hear me?"

Cady eyed her new friend with suspicion. "What did *you* say?"

"No, try and tell me what you heard! That's the fun of it, like playing telephone." Nikos popped on his toes with excitement.

"It didn't work, just tell me."

Nikos checked over his shoulder and leveled his gaze. "I said, 'Professor Hines is a wanker.' Not my best material, but I didn't think I'd bomb this badly."

"Sorry." She gave a weak smile. "I didn't hear it."

"Then I could've gotten away with saying much worse."

She searched his face again. "Is that a joke?"

"Of course it is! A better one if it had actually worked, I don't know what went wrong. What did you say?"

"I said 'Hello,'" Cady lied.

"'*Hello?*' Well that's bloody boring! I was hoping you'd say something flirtatious." Nikos smirked.

But Cady, like the afternoon, had cooled. "I've got to get back to my room."

"Oh, before you go, I want to invite you to a party at the Phoenix, I'm a member—"

"Sure, maybe."

"Right. I'll text you the info."

She nodded and began walking across the Yard to her dorm.

"And we'll have to give the archway another try!" Nikos called after her.

But Cady didn't look back. Instead, she quickened her step and pulled her jacket more tightly around her, the words echoing in her mind:

*It takes only an error to father a sin.*

If Nikos really hadn't said it, who had?

# 6

THE SCIENCE CENTER was the ugliest building on campus, a boxy structure made of concrete and glass tiers in a stairstep formation, like some sort of ziggurat to academia. It encompassed Cabot Science Library, open twenty-four hours, and housed world-renowned physicists, mathematicians, and masters of every scientific field. The Science Center could afford to be ugly, because the people in it were that smart.

*Well, not all of them,* Cady thought as she nearly tripped whirling through the revolving door, *I'm here.* A sense of dread pooled at the pit of her stomach upon entering the main lobby. Perhaps it was her introduction to the place; the first time she was inside had been her mathematics placement exam on her second day—part of Harvard's less-than-welcoming Freshman Week. Or maybe it was just her insecurities about math and science—Eric's specialties, not hers. She preferred history, literature, and other fields open to interpretation.

Thankfully, the only business she had there today was Psych 100, which had quickly become one of her favorite classes. Professor Bernstein was energetic and charismatic, and as a result, the popular course was packed; it was held in one of the building's biggest lecture halls with seating for three hundred, and latecomers still had to sit in the aisles. Cady had missed breakfast that morning, and with a little under a half hour before lecture was set to begin, she figured she'd grab a bite at the Science Center food court, known as the Greenhouse Café, or just Greenhouse. At this hour, they were just starting to prep for lunch, and Cady's stomach growled at the aroma of pizza baking. She walked to the refrigerated section to grab a yogurt and spotted several rows of packaged sushi. Cady remembered Eric talking about his 'science sushi' he ate for lunch every day—her parents had argued with him over spending money on it instead of making use of the residential dining plan. Cady had teased him about the wisdom behind eating raw fish from a food court, to which he'd shrugged: "Builds immunity."

She grabbed a package of the spicy tuna roll and got in line at the checkout counter, a small island of four female cashiers sitting on high stools. When it was Cady's turn, a short, round ball of a woman waved her arm. "Next! Next over here! Have your swipe card ready," she said, the word *cahd* showcasing her thick Boston accent.

Cady rummaged in her tote bag for her ID, or "swipe card." A student's ID acted as an access key and a debit card. "I'm sorry, I know I have it in here."

The woman sighed loudly, her thin red lips flattening into a disapproving line and green-shadowed eyelids sinking over her eyes. "That's why I said 'Have your swipe card *ready*.'"

"Sorry, it'll just take a minute."

"You wanna go ahead a' her?" the cashier asked someone over Cady's head.

Cady glanced back and saw that a tall blond woman was waiting behind her. "It's fine, I'm in no hurry," the woman answered.

"Ah! Here it is." Cady whipped out her card in triumph and handed it over.

"Archer?" The cashier squinted at her ID. "Your last name is Archer?"

"Yes."

"I shoulda known!" the cashier cried, suddenly warm and smiling. "You gotta brother who goes here, don't you!"

"Yes, my brother went here." The cashier hadn't asked it like a question, so Cady figured maybe it didn't need a straight answer.

"The sushi, the total discombobulation, just like him." The cashier chuckled. "But the red hair's the giveaway. You're a dead ringer."

Cady tried not to cringe.

"He's my buddy! He comes here, always gets the same thing, never has his swipe cahd." The cashier leaned in. "I cut him some slack and type him in as faculty, that way he still gets the discount. Last year, he helped me with my Sudoku on my breaks, taught me all sorts of tricks. Before him, I could only do the easy-level books. Now?" She paused for effect. "*Hahd.*"

Cady smiled. "That's cool. Eric has a great head for puzzles."

The cashier gave a hoot. "More than that! He's genius smaht, your brother, even for this school. Always with his notebooks during lunch. You must be wicked smaht, too."

"Not like him." It was the first honest thing Cady had said.

"Don't be like that." The cashier waved her off. "All you girls are like that. You don't got the swagger of the boys. Believe it, hon, you're here, you're smaht." She handed Cady her receipt and ID back. "Your brother hasn't come see me yet this fall. He graduate last year?"

"Yeah, graduated," Cady said, avoiding her eyes. "Now there's just me."

"Well, I'm Eileen. You tell Eric hello from me."

Cady had been seated at a café table for only a few minutes when the blond woman from the line approached her, holding a tray.

"Pardon me, but I couldn't help overhearing in the line, you are Eric Archer's sister?" She spoke with unusual precision.

"Yes, that's right."

"I teach in the Physics Department. Sadly, I know that Eric did not graduate. I'm very sorry for your loss."

Cady's face flushed, busted. "Thank you."

"He was one of my favorite students, and truly brilliant. He had so much potential, to think what he might have accomplished . . ." Emotion flickered in the woman's eyes, but she blinked it away. "I didn't know he had a sister who was a student here. Your name?"

"I'm Cadence."

The woman reached out her hand, which was faintly purple in comparison to the rest of her alabaster skin, as if it might be cool to the touch. "Pleasure to meet you," she said as they shook hands. "May I join you?"

"Of course. But I'm sorry, I didn't catch your name."

"Oh, because I didn't say it. Forgive me, I'm a math person, words are my second language—and English is my *third*." Her smile accentuated her lovely high cheekbones, and rimless eyeglasses did nothing to diminish pretty gray eyes. "I'm Professor Mikaela Prokop."

"Oh—" Cady was taken aback. Of course, she knew the name Professor Prokop, but, for reasons that now felt both stupid and sexist, Cady hadn't considered that Professor Prokop could be a woman, much less relatively young. "You were Eric's adviser last year, right?"

Prokop tucked her cornsilk hair behind her ear. "I advised him on his project for the Bauer Award, and he worked as my research assistant in my lab. I recognized his talent early. It was hard to miss."

That jogged Cady's memory. She generally tuned out when Eric talked about his schoolwork, since he was too paranoid to share any details with them anyway, but she did recall that Eric had taken that research assistant job seriously. He made that and the Bauer project the cornerstone of his arguments with their parents over taking his medication, which he thought dulled his mental acuity, or, when things got worse, against taking time off school for inpatient therapy. But although his commitment to the research may have made him resistant to treatment, it was the only thing that could lift his spirits in those days. Now she understood that the woman sitting across from her had been there for Eric when his illness was at its worst, giving him something to work toward, to live for, right up until a few months before his passing. A wave of gratitude washed over her.

"He was so proud to work with you. It was very kind of you to let him stay as long as you did," Cady said.

Professor Prokop shook her head, her brow creased. "I kept him on as long as I possibly could. I lost many nights' sleep over having to drop him as an advisee. I told him to think of it only as a hiatus. How I wish that was what it had been. I wish I could've helped him better."

"I'm sure you did all you could, and more than most." Cady wished she could've been as encouraging to her brother as the professor. "Your work together meant a lot to him, and to my family. I'll tell my mom I ran into you." Only then she remembered that her mother wasn't speaking to her.

"Are you interested in studying physics as well? It is not too late to switch into one of my classes, not for an Archer."

"Oh, no, I'm like Eric's opposite, a humanities type. The subjects with no wrong answers," Cady joked.

"You're describing the entanglement theory, but for siblings. If one particle spins up, clockwise, the other must spin down, counterclockwise. It is a real theory, no matter how close or distant the two particles are, they affect each other significantly. You define yourself in opposition to your brother, and yet look where you are. Not so different, eh? So challenge your hypotheses." Prokop smiled. "That's just a little quantum therapy for you. Now, unfortunately, I must go prepare for my next class. It was very good to meet you. Please give your family my sympathies. The department misses Eric very much."

Cady said goodbye and watched the professor leave, wishing they could've talked longer. Then she sat back and imagined herself and her brother spinning around each other—not opposite, not the same, but *entangled*.

CADY ENTERED LECTURE Hall C and stretched her neck to scan the upper rows for Ranjoo, like a duckling looking for its mother. This was the only class Cady shared with one of her roommates, and the two of them had quickly developed a routine of sitting together that Cady hoped to upgrade to an actual friendship. She spotted Ranjoo in their usual section, waving to her from the cocoon of an oversized scarf, and joined her.

"Can I catch up on the three chapters I was supposed to read in the three minutes before class begins?" Ranjoo flipped through the pages of her textbook, silver rings on almost every finger. "Or, better yet, did you do the reading?"

Cady smirked. "I did."

"As always, Queen of Homework comes through!"

"Happy to help, even if you make me feel very uncool."

"Girl, no! You're on top of your shit. I want to be like you when I grow up. And until then, I want to mooch off your knowledge. So can you give me the headlines?"

Cady caught her up as best she could before Professor Bernstein appeared. It was a lucky thing Cady was so diligent about her reading, because she had a hard time paying attention to the day's lecture. Bernstein was his typical entertaining self, but instead of taking notes on her laptop, Cady's mind wandered back to her conversation with Professor Prokop. Their brief meeting had left her with an unexpected feeling of shame. Prokop had been, without question, a main character in her brother's daily life on campus, and yet Cady hadn't even known her gender. At some point, Eric surely mentioned Prokop was a she, but Cady had forgotten, or worse, she hadn't been listening. It highlighted a fact that Cady preferred to repress: At the end of his life, she and Eric had become strangers. That she was now left to piece together clues from his notes was embarrassing enough, but to make such an obvious mistake . . . it rubbed salt in the wound. They weren't always like that. Eric's leaving for college put literal distance between them, but his freshman year they would email and text often, even talk on the phone occasionally. He was still a part of her life. She had sensed during that first year that he was depressed, he had indicated as much in pessimistic emails, but she hadn't known what to do about it. When it got worse his sophomore year, his grades faltered, and he shut down. At first, Cady had tried to lay off him, tried to be the one person in the family who wouldn't ask him questions. But as he'd gotten sicker, they'd argued more when he was home. Cady challenged him on his paranoid theories, even though the therapist had told her it wouldn't make a difference. She thought if she could just bear down on him, she could unearth the logic that had anchored his intellect for his entire life. But soon she'd grown tired of fighting with him, and she stopped saying anything at all. She told herself she was giving him space, but she had let Eric float away.

She decided she would get lecture notes from Ranjoo, a favor she could easily repay. Instead, Cady navigated to the Physics Department faculty pages to learn more about Professor Prokop. She looked up her office hours, and she emailed her saying how nice it was to run into her and asking if she could come in and talk a little more about Eric. It took three drafts before Cady felt brave enough to put Prokop's address in the To: field, and she didn't click Send until the end of class. But apprehensions aside, it was the first time since she had moved onto Harvard's campus that Cady felt she had accomplished something.

CADY AND RANJOO joined the throng of exiting and entering students forced to squeeze through the revolving doors of the Science Center, like competing schools of fish, until finally it was her turn to be spat outdoors into the bright sunlight. Outside, people rushed by all around her. Ranjoo peeled left toward Annenberg, the freshman dining hall, per their post-Psych routine.

"Should we text Andrea to get lunch with us?" Cady asked. Ranjoo widened her eyes in a way Cady knew meant *Please don't.* "I know she's not your favorite."

"No, it's fine, go ahead." Ranjoo sighed. "I suppose I have to get used to her."

Cady preferred Ranjoo and didn't want to irritate her, but something about Andrea tugged at her heartstrings. She was fishing for her phone in her bag, when suddenly she felt its vibration in her coat pocket. She was getting an incoming call from Home. "Oh, hold on a sec," she said before answering it, "Hey, Dad, I'm about to go to lunch—"

"Honey, it's Mom."

"Oh. Oh, hi." Cady stopped in her tracks. It was the first time her mother had called her since she had moved in. Every night she went to bed hoping her mother would call, but she hadn't. Just how much she missed her mother came crashing over her at this moment, and she was terrified of screwing it up.

"How are you? Is it a bad time?"

"No, I—" She met Ranjoo's questioning gaze and waved her on ahead. "It's fine, I'm fine. How's home?"

"Empty."

Cady felt touched. "I miss—"

"Are you making friends?" her mother spoke over her.

"I like my roommates. One is really cool, Ranjoo, we just had a class together. And I met a good friend of Eric's, a British guy named Nikos."

"Nikos? I don't remember him, but I forget everything lately. How did you find him?"

She saw no need to tell her mom about her audition stakeout. "He found me, actually. He recognized my name and introduced himself."

"That's so nice."

Cady heard her mother sniffle, and her heart sank. She decided not to tell her about meeting Professor Prokop, either. "It's okay, Mom. It's nice to meet people who knew him. It's supportive. It's nicer being here than you thought." It wasn't true yet, but she needed it to be.

"That's good." Her mother seemed to collect herself. "And how's your mental state?"

"What do you mean?" Cady tensed up, sensing where this conversation was headed. "Mom, it's normal to have some anxiety about being at college for the first time."

"I know, the transition to college for the first time is a huge one, for anyone, under any circumstances. And these aren't normal circumstances. You're fragile right now."

"We all are, we're grieving. It's *normal* not to feel completely normal."

"Cady, you had a major episode—"

"That was once!" Cady shot back. "It was an accident, I mean—it was an emotional day. And I've apologized."

"I'm not blaming you, in fact I wish we had done more for you this summer. I'm afraid you haven't dealt with—"

"I deal with it every day! It's awful, it's hard, but at least *I'm* trying. I'm going to school, I'm living my life, I'm moving on. What more can I do?"

"But at Harvard? I still think it's too much for you."

That touched a nerve. Deep down, Cady didn't believe her mother ever thought she could get into a school like this, even when her brother was alive. She saw her son as the genius, her daughter the hard worker. Her mother's doubt irked Cady all the more because she often shared it. "I can handle it. Today I nailed my choir audition, I made a friend, and my seminar professor told me he would never forget my name. So actually, I'm doing great."

"Good. I'm truly glad to hear it, that's why I called."

Cady tried not to give herself away with tears.

"Just promise me one thing," her mother added. "Don't stay there to prove something to me. If you're unhappy, or if, God forbid, you have another episode, come home. I'm on your side."

"Doesn't feel like it."

"Well, I'll work on that. But will you promise me?"

"Okay, yes, I promise. I have to go, I love you, 'bye." Cady hung up and wondered if she would be lying to her mother for the next four years.

# 7

CADY HATED WHEN her mother referred to her *episode*, meaning how she'd acted at Eric's scattering ceremony. It felt like her mother was rubbing her face in it, although perhaps it merely recalled Cady's own shame about that day.

Her parents had chosen Lake Wallenpaupack as the place to scatter Eric's ashes because they'd rented a cabin on the lake every summer when Cady and Eric were growing up. Everyone else in her family had agreed that it was what Eric would have wanted. Cady had no idea what Eric would have wanted. She still couldn't imagine he had wanted to die.

Cady held Eric on her lap for the three-hour drive to Lake Wallenpaupack. Eric was in a wooden urn, a small chest of polished walnut burl, which she gripped tightly but at a slight distance from her body, more on her knees. She felt nervous and carsick. She tried to look out the window, but she kept glancing down at the chest.

Their car was leading a caravan of close family: Directly behind them in the Saab was Grampa, her mother's father, and his second wife, Vivi; Aunt Laura and Uncle Pete brought up the rear in their van. In their SUV, Cady's father was driving, with her mother in the passenger seat, while Cady was in the back next to her grandmother, Gloria, or Gram, her father's mother, who was eighty-seven and hard of hearing. Age had made her body small and frail, so the seatbelt hit high on her collarbone; she hadn't wanted to wear it, but Cady's dad had insisted. Now she sat very still and quiet, except that she repeatedly reached a shaky hand to pull the seatbelt down and away from her stringy neck, only to have it migrate back. Cady felt a pang thinking about how much longer Gram was likely to live. There she sat, her only sign of stimulus and response the nagging irritant of a nylon belt. Otherwise her body was shrinking, thinning, bending, disappearing before their eyes. Her life force was a fading ember, and yet Eric was now ash.

"How's everybody doing?" her mother asked from the front seat.

Cady answered reflexively, "Okay."

Gram hadn't heard the question, but she turned when Cady spoke, smiled, and put her hand on her granddaughter's wrist. Her knuckles were knotted by arthritis and the skin on her hands was thin and papery, but the gesture was warm and comforting, and Cady needed it— she wasn't okay.

The Pennsylvania countryside seemed static, as though their car was the only moving object on the landscape. Cows grazed in place, their bloated barrels hung low from jutting hipbones, as they flicked their tails at flies. Calves slept in the grass beside their mothers, lying flat. Split-rail fence posts ticked by regularly, as if keeping track of something. At one point, she spotted two turkey vultures sitting on a fence rail, one facing backward and the other forward, its featherless red head set low on its hunched black body. In the moment they passed by, Cady felt caught in the vulture's beady-eyed gaze, as if it knew there was death inside. She recoiled. Cady knew it was ridiculous, but it felt like a bad omen. In retrospect, it was.

"This was right," her mother said suddenly.

"I told you, I remember the shortcut," her father said.

"No, I mean what we're doing for Eric today. Our decision to, to do what we did with him, for him. And the lake means so much to all of us, it's . . . it's right."

Cady wasn't sure whether this was an implied forgiveness of her father's hasty decision making, or if her mother had brainwashed herself into thinking the choice to cremate had been made jointly.

"I agree," her father said.

"Wha-at was that?" Gram asked.

"I was just saying"—her mother raised her voice—"that I feel good—I feel at peace with our decision."

Gram turned to Cady and blinked slowly. "I can't hear her, what is she talking about?"

"Gloria, our *decision*," Cady's mother raised her voice, "about Eric, what do with his, to scatter—" Her voice broke. "Dammit, I wish she would get that effing hearing aid."

"Karen, get ahold of yourself," her father snapped.

"I'm *trying*!" her mother shouted back.

"She's an elderly woman and—*shit*."

The car suddenly swerved to the right, and Cady heard the squealing of the brakes, a small thump, and then the gravel along the road's edge grinding and snapping into the undercarriage, until the car came to an abrupt halt. Then total silence as they all caught their breath.

Both her parents turned to the backseat and started speaking at the same time.

"Mom, are you okay?" her father asked Gram.

"Cady, you have the urn, right, it didn't drop, did it?" Her mother's eyes were wide. "Oh, thank God."

During the swerve, without thinking, Cady had hugged the urn tightly against her stomach.

Gram looked more feisty than frightened. "I'm fine, but this darn seatbelt—"

"Well, you know what, Mom? I'm really glad you were wearing it just then." Her father undid his seatbelt and got out of the car, slamming the door behind him. Cady thought he was coming around to check on Gram, but instead he stalked back past the car.

Her mother gave a snort. "Now where is he going?"

Cady craned her neck to see. Grampa's Saab pulled over, and behind him, Laura and Pete's van slowed to a stop, but her father wasn't interacting with either. He stood in the center of the road between their tire tracks, looking down at something.

Cady carefully set the urn on the backseat, got out of the car, and jogged over. She slowed down when she saw how upset her father looked, his face bright red, his eyes glistening. "Dad, what is it? Did you hit something?"

Her father didn't answer, the muscles beneath his cheekbone flickered as he clenched and unclenched his jaw, he didn't even look up. A tear dripped off his nose and fell on the ground beside the body of a gray squirrel.

Cady's heart sank, but she hid her dismay. "Aw, you didn't mean to, you tried to avoid it." It wasn't as gruesome as she had anticipated, and she was relieved. The small animal lay on its side, completely intact; the plush fur on its fluffy tail shivered in the breeze and its onyx eyes were open, but there was no question it was dead. *Died on impact,* the familiar words echoed in her head.

Her father gave a gurgling sniff. "I can't believe I killed it."

Cady put a tentative hand on his arm, touched but surprised by his tears. Her father hadn't cried since Eric died, at least not in front of anyone, not even at the funeral. The emotion he bottled up typically emerged in anger, so Cady considered this progress.

"Everything all right out there?" Grampa yelled from his car window.

Cady waved him off and turned back to her father. "Dad, it's okay. I'm sure it didn't feel a thing."

When Cady returned to the backseat, Gram was still strapped in by her cruel seatbelt, looking troubled. "No one tells me what's going on!"

"A squirrel ran out in front of the car. Dad swerved to avoid it, and we all just wanted to check to see what happened."

"Did he hit it?" Her eyebrows jumped behind her glasses.

"No." Cady put her hand over Gram's. "It got away."

She relaxed and smiled. "Oh, good."

Cady looked out the window and wondered if Eric had felt a thing.


PEBBLES GRUMBLED UNDER the tires as they pulled into the small parking area on the northern banks of Lake Wallenpaupack. Cady's family had discussed the logistics of a scattering ceremony with the park rangers, and the only stipulation was that the scattering "must be done out of sight of any public access, such as roads, trails, parking areas, et cetera," in other words, "Don't freak anybody out." The only thing that mattered to the Archers was for it to be in the water. So they had chosen a spot off a long dock, seldom used since the main recreation center had relocated to the opposite side of the lake years ago. The bank on this side was wooded and heavily overgrown, only a thin strip of rocky beach remained visible with a clearing around the dock. From where they parked, Cady could barely see it through the brush.

Her mother had taken the urn from Cady and gone first. Grampa helped Vivi try to negotiate the rough natural footing in her heeled rubber booties. Cady's father followed, guiding Gram with one arm and holding Laura's folded wheelchair in the other, while Pete carried Laura in his arms as if she were a new bride. Cady was left with no one to help or hold.

Once they were through to the clearing, the lake spread out like a clean sheet settling on a bed, waves fluttering across the surface. Cady remembered the bright days of summer, when the blue skies, a few lone clouds, and the far tree line reflected on the lake's mirror surface with dreamlike movement, but today was different. The sun had disappeared behind a shroud of thick clouds in watercolor grays, veiling the horizon completely. Dark wooded hills in the distance rose out of the haze like disembodied spirits. The long, narrow dock seemed like a gangplank into the River Styx.

Cady was reminded of an old campfire story she'd been told some summer long ago. Lake Wallenpaupack used to be a town called Wilsonville, until an electric company bought all the land and intentionally flooded it. Now the waters were murky and dark, but supposedly when they first flooded it, you could see the whole town underneath, and to this day, during very dry summers, you could still glimpse the church steeple poking through the surface, although Cady never had. The part that scared little Cady the most, the part she remembered now, was about the old Wilsonville cemetery. Before they flooded it, they dug up all the graves and moved the remains to higher ground, but there were many more bodies than expected, and many were children. Legend had it that if you swam above the graves, the ghosts would grab your feet and pull you down. It was a good ghost story, because no one knew where the cemetery was, so it could be anywhere and everywhere, and there was always something touching your toe in a lake. Usually, it was Eric, trying to scare her. It always worked.

Her family had gathered at the near end of the dock, the only spot broad enough to hold them all. Cady edged outside the huddle, the wet, cool breeze chilling her. Aunt Laura spoke first: "Okay." She took a deep breath. "Andrew and Karen asked me to lead this ceremony on this sad, sad day. The three of us talked for a long time about today's purpose and hope, and our wish for today is that it may provide each of us with some individual closure, and hopefully a degree of peace with this tragedy. We're going to take turns with the scattering. There's no right or wrong way to go about this. If you would like to say something or share a particular memory, of course, you are welcome and encouraged to do so. But if you would just like a quiet moment with Eric and your thoughts and prayers, please feel free to simply . . . let go. There is no right or wrong way to say goodbye. Just do what's in your heart. Who would like to begin?"

"I will," answered her father, surprising Cady. He took the urn from his wife's hands and looked down, inhaling through his nostrils like a bull. "This didn't have to happen. I'm not sure I'll ever understand why it did. I know we loved him so much, and we would have supported him through anything. I know we could've gotten through his struggles if we'd had more time. He should be here still."

He rubbed his eyes; when he opened them again, they were filled with tears, honest and vulnerable, the anger that had held him together released. When he spoke again, his voice broke, breaking Cady's heart with it. "But he was sick. That sickness was not my son. I will remember my son as the brilliant boy he was, a lover of learning, of nature, this lake, these hills, a joy to his family, my buddy. And I will always mourn that bright future that is now lost to him, and to us, forever."

Gram put her hand on his arm. He hugged her close to his side. Her mother hugged him, too, and pulled Cady into the embrace. He kissed Cady on the forehead, then broke free of them and walked to the end of the dock alone. With his back to them, he lifted a handful out of the urn and let his only son pass through his fingers into the water.

He walked back, and since Cady's mother was crying, Aunt Laura went next. "I remember the day Eric was born." Tears welled in her eyes. "He was so beautiful. Perfect and pink. Eric filled my heart with the happiness a child can bring." She looked at Cady. "You both did. I never missed having children of my own, thanks to you two. And I felt so proud and blessed to have him in our family. I still do."

Pete coughed some tears away and roughly wiped his eyes before adding, "Little dude, it was a privilege to watch you grow up. I love you, and I feel lucky to have known you."

"We are lucky. We'll miss you, Eric."

Laura tapped Pete's arm, and he wheeled her to the dock's end. Cady saw them hug each other and say something she couldn't hear. They were always there for each other. *You only need one person*, Cady thought. Eric was her one. Had she been there for him?

"Mom?" her father said, voice cracking. "Do you want to say anything?"

Every line on Gram's face was shaped by sorrow. Her pale blue eyes looked on, searching, as she gripped her son's arm and shook her head. "This is not right. He was a good boy!" Her mouth hung partly open, her tongue panting in distress—in that moment, Cady saw the DNA of the same directionless anger her father had of late. But just as quickly, Gram's energy was spent, and her expression regained a more familiar cast of resignation, soft and sad. She began again, "I am old. Why I am the hand and not the ash, I do not know. If I could trade places, I would. But the Lord works in ways we cannot understand, and He loves us all. I hope this child may find peace with Him now."

"Ready?" her father asked, after a moment.

Gram nodded, and he carried the urn while helping his mother walk down the dock. She was unsteady, more than usual, so they didn't go as far down as the others, only about fifteen feet, to the side of the dock where the wind was in their favor. Cady could see Gram put her shaky hand into the urn and hear her say "Then shall the dust return to the earth, and the spirit shall return unto God who gave it. Sweet child, I will see you soon." Gram released the ash from her knotted fingers.

Cady blinked and saw all of their eyes aimed at her with expectant expressions. It was her turn. "I don't know what to do," she muttered, her lips sticking to her teeth.

Her family nodded in sympathy, although Cady hadn't meant it metaphorically. She felt panicky, and her gaze flitted from person to person for guidance.

"You don't have to say anything, sweetie," said Aunt Laura. "Just take your time, let yourself say goodbye."

She reluctantly took the box that held her brother and turned to walk down the dock, her horror increasing with every step. When her feet reached the end of the wooden planks, she knelt at the edge of the dock and placed the urn beside her. Cut into the swirling wood was a small keyhole with a smaller golden key already in it, tasseled with crimson silk cords. Her hand trembled as she turned the key.

Inside was gray sand. With her heart pounding, her eyes scanned the contents for any piece that might be recognizable, a tooth, a finger bone. Any small token of Eric's humanity would be both grotesque and comforting, but she found none. Just a pile of crumbs, some big as a chip of gravel and some small as a grain of sand, but all gray, dead.

The first time she touched the pulverized bones, her hand jerked back involuntarily—her index and middle fingers were tipped in the ashy powder, as if they were as lifeless as the substance that covered them. She tried again, and this time her hand sank in deep like quicksand, as if the bones possessed a pull.

Her vision blurred under the thick veil of memory. Images of her brother at different ages and states flashed in succession, images she had seen a thousand times and ones only imagined: as a teenager, in profile, driving her somewhere; as a boy with his back to her, facing the lake, the breeze blowing the fine hair on his oversized head; and one imagined memory, the sight of him lying on the ground, dead, eyes open, eyes closed, she didn't know which so she saw them both ways, as if he were blinking at her. And now this was all of him, burned down and in a box, small enough to fit under her fingernails.

*Say goodbye.* It was so surreal. She had lost her sense of reality when reality became so frightfully unreal. Her brother, her point of reference for the world, was dead. Reality had become something for which she took other people's word. But other people's words plagued her. Everyone had been saying the same things since it happened, repeated so often as to become unintelligible—*such a shame, all that potential, could have been, how did he do it?, he was so bright, jumped, I heard, and at Harvard, everything going for him, did you know? whole life ahead, what he could have accomplished, died on impact, at the beginning of his, it's horrible, could've done something, bright future, what a waste, a shame, the potential, lost*—this unceasing murmur played over and over in her mind, a stream of numbing platitudes punctuated by the occasional innocent, careless comment that could rip out her heart. Numbness and anguish. She felt both right now.

She lifted a fistful of his remains and let the excess spill back into the urn, the light fragments of bone tickling the inside of her wrist as they tumbled down, then she reached over the water and stopped. Ashes covered her entire hand, but instead of rendering her hand lifeless, it was as if she were giving life to his ashes, reanimating him. Cady's heart beat so fast it hurt. It didn't feel like a goodbye, it only felt like getting rid of him, and she wasn't ready to do that. She didn't want to let him go. She wanted to put him back together again.

She squeezed her fist tighter and a small quantity escaped and fell into the water. She looked over the edge of the dock and watched the heavier particles sink while the ashes swirled and bloomed over a rippling image of her own reflection. She brought the handful of ashes close to her mouth, maybe with the idea to kiss him goodbye or something else, Cady couldn't recall, because when she gave in to the next impulse, her mind was blank. All she remembered was how Eric's ashes felt gritty as she rubbed them on her face, the dust stung her eyes, stuck to her wet cheeks and lips so she could taste it, and how she pressed harder and harder until the bone ash dug into her cheeks, but she couldn't feel them enough, not enough to last forever.

Cady brought her hands down from her face—they were white but empty, and shaking terribly. Horrified at what she'd done, a small cry escaped her lips, releasing more ashes in a puff of her breath. She turned toward the voices now shouting her name. First she saw her father's mouth agape, Gram slumping against him, Aunt Laura leaning forward in her chair while Pete threw an arm across her chest, to comfort her or hold her back. But her mother looked the worst—her eyes were wild and her lips pulled back in a horrified grimace, and she had both arms outstretched in front of her. Soon they were all moving toward Cady, they looked terrified and terrifying.

Panic seized her. Cady didn't think. She turned and leaped to follow him into the water.

# 8

HAVING MISSED LUNCH with Ranjoo, Cady felt her stomach growl as she took her seat in her next class, "The Medieval Imagination," a small lecture course in the History Department. The reading was incredibly dense—biblical apocrypha, the writings of Augustine, and other esoteric texts—but Cady had made it a priority to keep up with her assignments, largely because of how much she liked Professor Watkins. He was warm and wacky, a fifty-something-year-old Englishman with longish hair and a single earring, a hippie medievalist. He couldn't be more different from Professor Hines. When a student arrived late today, full of apologies, he waved her off.

"Not at all, my dear. It would be hypocritical of me to blame you for tardiness, as I myself was running a bit behind today, as these more diligent students will tell you. So I say, O Tosco, ch'al collegio de l'ipocriti tristi se' venuto. Translation: 'My Tuscan, you've reached the college of the hypocrites.' However, I endeavor not to be among them. Does anyone know what that's from?"

Remarkably, a hand went up in the front. Cady craned her neck to see who could possibly know the answer. Professor Watkins called on the girl, whose hair was dyed pink at the ends, and she answered: "Dante's Inferno."

"That's right! Now, for bonus points, do you know what canto?"

The girl paused. "Canto Five?"

"Twenty-three. But very well done. Soon we will all get to know Dante as well as—"

"Jessica," the girl filled in.

"—as Jessica here, later in the course. But today, we'll discuss the Passion of Saint Perpetua, one of the most important, albeit little known, of the early Christian visionary texts. This text is significant because it was written, at least in part—the pre-gruesome-martyrdom-part—by Perpetua herself. We have very few female voices on record around 200 c.e., and I think you will find hers to be one of the most compelling . . ."

Cady gave a weary exhale. She'd known she would have to work harder to keep up with her classmates here, but for someone to nail the source of one random quote—in Italian, no less—was next level. She sank lower in her chair.

*"Don't be too impressed,"* whispered a voice at her ear.

Cady looked over her shoulder to the desk behind her, where a guy was slumped back in his desk like a low-rider; he didn't appear to be the one who had said anything to her. She glanced around, a girl beside her was diligently taking notes on a pad, a boy to her left was furtively texting on the phone in his lap. Where had it come from?

*You already know.*

Anxiety bubbled within her—was she the only one hearing this?

*You know how she cited* Inferno, *you just said the clue she used. It's simple.*

She wanted to jump out of her seat, out of her skin, but she didn't want to flag for anyone else what was happening to her. What *was* happening to her? Was she speaking to herself? But it was a man's voice. And it wasn't stopping.

*The quote was in Italian. How many books on your syllabus are in Italian? Check.*

Cady slid her syllabus out from under her notebook. The only listed text with an Italian title was *Inferno*. This voice was definitely speaking to her.

And it was right.

*I told you. She correctly surmised that the professor would reference something from class. I'll bet she hasn't read a word of* La Divina Commedia. *Anyone remotely familiar with Dante would know that a sin on the level of hypocrisy would occur much later than Canto 5. And anyway, Canto 5 is* Paolo e Francesca, *everyone knows that.*

Cady didn't know that.

*Really?*

Cady heard the voice snigger.

*You'll find that most people here are more adept at appearing intelligent than actually being so. They're mostly dolts.*

Cady raked her fingers through her hair, pausing to press them tightly over her ears, willing the voice to stop.

*Don't get upset. I didn't mean you. Did it sound like I did? Forgive me.*

Why is this happening? Cady thought. Make it stop.

*Sorry, I'll go.*

"Today, we would call them hallucinations," Professor Watkins said, and for a moment Cady thought he was answering her directly. He continued, "But at the time there was real credence given to a 'spiritual vision' under certain circumstances. As Perpetua was left in prison to await her impending execution, knowing she was soon to become a Christian martyr or a lion's plaything, she was poised to receive such a vision."

Auditory hallucinations. Cady remembered that her mother used the term after meeting with one of Eric's doctors at McLean, Harvard's affiliated psychiatric hospital, when they first got the diagnosis of schizophrenia. Was that what had just happened to her?

"However, Augustine wrote at length about the process of 'discernment,' meaning the practice of discerning whether a vision is of divine or demonic nature." Professor Watkins wrote "discernment" on the chalkboard with a sharp, hollow *clack clack clack*. "A spiritual vision was subject to the imagination and thus could be fooled, vulnerable to demons. Or, the mind could be the access point for divine clarity, wisdom, even prophecy. Thus the ability to discern the difference was of the utmost importance. We'll talk more about this and the Neoplatonists next week. In preparation for Monday, please read Augustine's exegesis in *The Literal Meaning of Genesis*, as well as his personal account in *Confessions VII*. Thank you."

Cady needed to calm down—she needed to be *discerning*. There was no need to jump to any conclusions; there could be a reasonable explanation for whatever she just heard. She was bored, she was daydreaming. She hadn't eaten, or slept well, she was stressed by that call from her mom. Cady wrote down the reading assignment like a normal, sane student, but gathering her things, her hands shook.

There remained a question in her mind more frightening than the voice itself: *Is this how it started with Eric?*

# 9

CADY COULDN'T MAKE it all the way home. She found a quiet corner in Lamont, the undergraduate library, booted up her laptop, and opened her Gmail account. Cady needed to learn everything about Eric's life at Harvard during his last year. All she had gathered from home was that he had been consumed by the Bauer project, and when he'd suddenly refused to submit it, it was the first sign that he was worse off than her family thought, much worse. But Cady didn't even know the topic of his Bauer project, much less why he ditched it. Was that really the first sign of his illness taking over, or was it only the first loud enough to be heard back home? There were so many blanks to be filled in, her ignorance suddenly struck her as staggering, maybe even dangerous. Her whole life, the question had been *Will I ever be as good as Eric?* Not *Could I ever be as sick?*

Somehow it had never occurred to her that she could suffer from Eric's illness. Eric was always different, special, marked. It made sense that the eccentricities of genius would be disposed to warp into mental illness. Cady thought of herself as the average, or at least more average than Eric, and she expected shelter in the bell curve. Now she felt stupid never to have considered it; they were blood relatives, they have, or had, shared genes. As her Psych book said, only genotype is inherited, the phenotypic behavior is triggered by environment. Well, now she had put herself in the exact same environment as Eric. What if her mother was right, and she couldn't handle it any better than he could? She had all of Eric's emails of the last year or so archived in a folder named E. She had made the folder right after he died, when she couldn't bring herself to delete the emails nor could she bear to see them sitting in her inbox. She hadn't opened the folder until now. Their last email correspondence was February twenty-fifth, almost a month before his death, and it wasn't much.

**Cadence Archer** to Eric Archer Feb 25, 2019
You coming home for Dad's birthday? Mom wants to make reservations.

**Eric Archer** to me Feb 25, 2019
no. can't.

Cady remembered how annoyed she had been at his short reply—annoyed but not surprised. He had become very distant by that point. She hadn't even bothered to follow up with him. She recalled feeling relieved that he wasn't coming to their father's birthday dinner, relief for which she now felt guilty, but she had known it would be more relaxed if Eric wasn't there. He had become so difficult, his moods so unpredictable. Eric's attitude and behavior wore on her father, who would get short with him, and then her mother would get snippy in Eric's defense, and before long, every family get-together was a tightly wound ball of tension, if not an all-out fight. None of them had truly understood how much Eric was suffering, herself included. If she had written him back, encouraged, cajoled, begged him to come to that stupid dinner, then maybe they would have seen how bad he had gotten. Maybe something could have been done.

Her eyes ran down the list, skipping most. All of the ones from January on were short and clipped. He rarely came out of his shell by then, and he was even less forthcoming in email. One particularly cheery Re: line from an email Cady sent him in early December 2018 triggered something in Cady's memory; it read: "When do we get to celebrate?!!" But despite her exclamation points, the memory was as dark and heavy as a storm cloud waiting to break. Reading her initial email first, she recognized the false enthusiasm in her words.

> What's up with your Bauer project?? Are you almost done? We all have our fingers crossed, not that you need it. They're going to love your submission, and next year you're totally gonna win. I'm already happy for you, that's how confident I am. Love, C

She thought back a minute. This was the project Professor Prokop had been advising him on. The Bauer Award was one of the most prestigious academic prizes offered at Harvard, a one-way ticket to any graduate school science program and a clincher for job interviews. The adjudication process was so in-depth, students submitted their work their junior spring and didn't hear back until senior fall. Winning it had been Eric's dream since he first set foot in Harvard's Physics Department, but that had been back when he was a freshman, when it had seemed like only a matter of time for him to grow old enough to receive it. By junior year, nothing was certain. Still, as his mental problems worsened, his science grades stayed up. Her family had hoped that if he could stay on track, the satisfaction of winning the Bauer could pull him out of the depression that threatened to swallow him whole. They had all tried to act extra-supportive during that time. Cady recalled thinking the worst that could happen was that they would build it up and then he might not win—how naive she had been.

His response was devastating then and now:

> I'm not going to submit. working on something way more important. can't waste time on the Bauer. I'll tell you about it some other way, this email account is not secure.

The paranoia. This was when he had stopped trying to hide it. He had become suspicious of those around him, even close friends and family. He was on high alert, fearful of surveillance of any kind. He changed his cellphone number three times that year. Within the family, their father, inexplicably, caught the brunt of Eric's mistrust. Whenever their father would leave a room, Eric would fall silent for a few minutes because he believed that his father was eavesdropping just behind the door. Whenever he was made to meet with a concerned or disciplinary Harvard administrator, which was increasingly often, he believed his father had put them up to it. He occasionally thought his mother was conferring with his therapist, seeking to learn his secrets, but Cady wasn't entirely sure this was untrue.

In a heartbreaking variation on the theme, the way his paranoia manifested with Cady was in concern for her. Growing up, he had never been the type of brutish big brother to intimidate guys or beat up school bullies; more often Cady was the one defending Eric's quirky behavior. But when he got sick, his protective instincts went into hyperdrive. Even when he was away at school and she was home, there would be some nights when Cady would find ten text messages and five missed calls from him checking up on her. When she would ask him why he was so worried, he would never explain.

Her eyes returned to the rows of subject headings until one burned like acid. It was dated January 4, 2019, from the email account of Dr. Mark Rowan, Eric's psychiatrist; the subject was

Holiday break episode, moving forward.

She reflexively rubbed her hand on her neck; her pulse thumped against it. It had taken her three days to summon the courage to open that email when she first received it, and she didn't want to open it again. She never wanted to open it again.

So she didn't.

Cady scrolled way down to October 12, 2016, his freshman year, when Eric was still Eric. And when she was still Cady.

**Eric Archer** to me:

A little bird (Mom, don't be mad) told me that Justin broke up with you. The most simple observations are usually the most accurate, and in this case it is obvious that the man is a fool. I know that love is rarely simple, so this fact is probably not much comfort. But he sucks.

**Cadence Archer** to Eric:

Thanks for that. I love you.

**Eric Archer** to me:

Love you too, kid. Hang in.

The tension in Cady's chest unwound. This was the brother she grew up with. This was the brother she so terribly missed. This was the brother she wanted to remember.

Sometimes this was the only brother she remembered. Her mind did not go willingly back to that difficult period. It was as if her brain had dismantled the timeline and hidden the bad memories, switched them around like a magician hiding a ball beneath a trio of cups. When it came to the progression of his illness, emotion clouded the waters of her memory, and it surprised her how little she could now recall. She couldn't remember when exactly he got his diagnosis of schizophrenia, or discussion of how his symptoms began, certainly never explicit talk of hearing voices. She did remember what her father had said after the diagnosis: "Things will get better, because now that we know what it is, we can fix it and get back to normal." They hadn't known then that normal was a long way away.

But searching through their emails, she hoped to find something, somewhere, that would offer a peek into Eric's interior world. She found only one email that dealt directly with his illness. On April 20, 2018, she had written:

**Cadence Archer** to Eric:

I know you're freaked out about the diagnosis, but I think this is a

good thing. Now that they know what's going on they can give you
better treatment. Soon you will be feeling like your old self. This is
just a bump in the road . . .

**Eric Archer** to me:
I'm aware of things that I didn't used to be. I just have to accept that
these changes are a part of me now. I need to adapt to them, learn
to live with them. It's just hard. I miss my old brain. It's different now,
I'm different.

**Cady** to Eric:
You're not different. You're still my brother. I know you. I love you. I
don't think you're crazy.

**Eric** to me:
I do.

Was Cady becoming "different," too?

She closed the email and exited the E archives, returning to her
inbox. At the top, she noticed that a bold new email had arrived from
Prokop@fas.harvard.edu. She opened it:

Pleasure meeting you as well. My office hours this week are busy,
but perhaps next Thursday. Alternately, I will be speaking at the
Cosmology Colloquium this Friday at 2pm in the Science Center,
Lecture Hall B. You are welcome to attend if the topic interests you,
it promises to be an interesting panel discussion, and I should have
a little time to chat afterward. We will make a physics student out
of you yet!

"Well, hello there."

This was a voice, and an accent, she recognized. "Nikos, hi." She
quickly closed her laptop.

Nikos was wearing a crisp white shirt tucked into dark jeans and a houndstooth blazer, she noticed he even had little braided cuff links. On most people their age, the outfit might have looked stuffy or pretentious, but Nikos carried himself with such confidence, he pulled it off. "How have you been?"

"I've been good." Cady chided herself for saying 'good' instead of 'well'; his accent made her self-conscious of her English.

"What are you working on?"

"Nothing. Well, actually, I have something you might be able to help me with." She pulled the blue notebook out of her bag. "I found some of Eric's old notes, but I can't understand them. It looks like part class notes, part math I'm too dumb to get, part personal calendar, part I don't know what. Can you tell me what this might mean?"

"Surely. Let's have a look." Cady handed it to him, and Nikos began slowly flipping through the pages. "The front half is definitely physics notes, I recognize this class, I was in it with him fall semester. Then it looks like experiment results, probably from a lab. But toward the end . . ." He shook his head and slid it back to her. "These letters aren't like variables in an equation or anything, it's nonsense. It must've been from when he was sick. I'm sorry."

Cady nodded. "Thanks, that's what I thought."

"Thank *you*. Eric was always such a freak about those notes, everything with him was top secret. I took them once as a goof, and I thought he was going to kill me. I always wanted to sneak a peek."

She smiled, although it made her feel regretful for showing him just now. She asked her next question with the notebook tucked to her chest. "He wrote down 'M' a lot, with times, like social plans. Do you know who that could be?"

"Probably Matt Cho, his roommate."

Of course, Cady thought, how could she forget Matt Cho? Well, probably because she hadn't seen him in years, when they first moved Eric into his dorm freshman year. Although they had been friends and roommates all three years, Matt hadn't come to the funeral. Cady had invited him via email, her parents had offered to pay for his flight and everything, but he hadn't even replied. On the day of the service, they had all been too distraught to notice his absence, but his not responding to her email had stung. Maybe that's why Cady had blocked him out.

"I'm sorry this hasn't been more enlightening. Is there anything else I can help you with?"

A different thought crossed her mind. "You know what I need for a class? A copy of Dante's *Inferno*."

"My blessed Beatrice, that should be easy to find." Nikos tapped at the computer keyboard and quickly summoned the call number. "Ah. Widener. Let's go."

CADY FELT A bit anxious about including someone else in an inquiry into her own sanity, but she reasoned the voice wasn't the *only* reason to look up *Inferno*; she would need the book for her Medieval Studies class eventually. Plus, Nikos's company put her at ease.

They scaled the grand gray marble steps of Widener. Though it was still only autumn, it was already cold, and the wind made it colder. A few people were scattered on the steps; a couple cuddled together sipping matching coffees, an Asian teenager posed and smiled while her parents snapped a picture, an attractive guy sat absorbed in a thick novel, hoping someone would notice his absorption. At the top of the stairs, they passed between the enormous columns and Nikos held the heavy door for her.

They were about to pass through the small antechamber to the main lobby, when Cady stopped. On each wall, there was a large white marble plaque. The left one read:

HARRY·ELKINS·WIDENER

A GRADUATE OF

THIS UNIVERSITY

BORN JANUARY 3·1885

DIED AT SEA APRIL 15·1912
UPON THE FOUNDERING
OF THE STEAMSHIP
TITANIC

And the right:

THIS LIBRARY
ERECTED
IN LOVING MEMORY OF
HARRY·ELKINS·WIDENER
BY HIS MOTHER
ELEANOR·ELKINS·WIDENER
DEDICATED
JUNE 24·1915

"Sorry, I assumed you knew the backstory," Nikos said at her shoulder.

"I did." Cady had been briefly obsessed with the history of the *Titanic* after she saw the movie, so she knew all about Widener the man, but she didn't know the story behind the library. "I guess I imagined he gave the money to Harvard while he was alive or in his will or something. I didn't realize his mother did it for him."

"Quite a costly memorial. I wonder if Mummy had something to feel guilty about. I crossed an ocean to get away from my mother, too, but lucky for me, I made it to the other side."

Cady bitterly remembered her own mother saying *It is his tomb.*

They passed through the security turnstile to a short but grand staircase in cool white marble, its brass handrails reflected in the smooth, gleaming walls on either side. The landing above looked like something out of a Roman palace. There was a central doorway framed by tall columns, intricately detailed, and two great arched frescoes on either side, all in the same heavenly white marble and bathed in cool natural light from a domed skylight. Through the doorway, a great golden chandelier glowed warmly even in partial view. Cady stepped toward the staircase, awestruck.

"Wrong way," Nikos said.

"But," Cady began, unable to hide her disappointment.

"I know it's beautiful, but the stacks are this way. Come along. Call me Virgil." He gave a little bow and a flourish of his hand, directing her away, and she reluctantly obeyed. Nikos added, "Sadly, nothing, where we now arrive, is shining."

They took a sharp left, bypassing the staircase, and suddenly Cady found herself in a darker, more ordinary room with computer screens against the wall and a central, curved information desk. He led her past the beeping, stamping, shuffling sounds of people checking out books, through to an even smaller room with an elevator on one side and a metal door like those on a gymnasium on the other, and against the third wall was a small desk with photocopies of maps, scrap paper, and tiny pencils. Nikos glanced at a cluttered library map, which appeared utterly incomprehensible to Cady, before he pressed through the metal door.

The door led to a concrete staircase lit with harsh fluorescent wall sconces. She followed Nikos down an odd interval of a flight and a half when he pressed through another door. As the door clicked shut behind them, Cady realized they were finally in "the stacks." Rows upon rows of putty-colored metal bookshelves stretched out before them with only a narrow walkway alongside. There seemed to be no one around, the air was stale, and the lights were off.

"Why is it so dark?" Cady whispered.

"Watch this," Nikos whispered back. He took a giant step forward, thrust out his hands, and cried, "Let there be *light!*"

In the next second, the fluorescent ceiling lights above him clicked on with a loud *ka-chunk*, and one hissed and flickered. Nikos looked back over his shoulder, grinning. Cady laughed nervously.

"They're on motion detectors," he said. "No need to light this crypt at all hours. Come on, this way."

As they passed each row of books the lights around them clicked on, *chunk, chunk, chunk,* buzzing and crackling with age and electricity. It reminded Cady of Dr. Frankenstein pulling the succession of the levers on his machine, vivifying the corpse with lightning bolts.

"It's kind of creepy down here." Cady followed him. "Where is everybody?"

"You can do an awful lot of wandering in the stacks before you see another soul. But that's mostly because Harvard students would rather do anything in a library other than actual research. Speaking of—" Nikos stopped and turned around to face her. "You've heard about the stacks tradition?" One dark eyebrow lifted.

Cady shook her head.

"There are three things every Harvard student is supposed to do before they graduate. One, take a piss on the foot of the John Harvard statue, the same foot all the tourists rub for good luck, poor bastards."

"Ew."

"Yes, it's not really for girls, that one. Second is Primal Scream. That's where the night before the finals period begins, in the dead of winter, you get naked and run round the Yard screaming like a lunatic. It would be all right, except that's another one in which the girls are a bit reluctant to participate, so it's sort of a mishmash of bobbing male bodies with their knobs spinning about like pinwheels. It really doesn't show a man to his best advantage. I learned that the hard way." Nikos gave a sheepish pout that made her giggle. "And the third, well, the third is the very best one. The third is you have to have sex in the stacks of Widener."

Cady managed only "Hm."

Nikos maintained eye contact. "Are you trying to guess whether I've done it?"

Cady could feel her cheeks flushing. "No."

"I have not. I am saving myself for someone special, so get that hungry look out of your eye."

She laughed. "You're terrible."

"Flattery will get you nowhere. We have a job to do here, and I am very focused on your studies." Nikos started back down the aisle. They stopped when they reached the row labeled with the correct combination of letters and numbers and decimals, and he crouched to scan the titles. "Here we are. *Inferno*," he said, rolling the *r* dramatically. "By Dante Alighieri. This Kirkpatrick is a good translation. Have you ever studied it before?"

"No, I'm embarrassed to say I've never read a word of it."

"Ah, you'll like it. We studied it at Eton, and I remember particularly loving that flatterers have to lie in a river of shit. I don't remember what circle or canto that was, but . . ."

Cady wasn't listening. He'd triggered an idea. "Nikos," she said abruptly.

"Cadence," he answered, mimicking her serious tone. "Yes, what is it?"

"Sorry, but can you check, what's Canto Five?"

Nikos looked down at the book, checking the table of contents and flipping to the appropriate page. Suddenly impatient, Cady fought the urge to snatch the book from his hands. "Canto Five is . . ." He clicked his tongue as his eyes scanned the page. "Paolo e Francesca."

A chill tiptoed down her spine, vertebra by vertebra. Cady replayed her voice saying it.

*I've never read a word of it.*

# 10

IT WAS A relief to close the door of Weld 23 and hear it latch behind her. Her dorm room hadn't felt like home until being outside it got so scary. Cady took a deep breath, inhaling the familiar scent of microwave popcorn, Andrea's study fuel of choice. She grabbed a can of La Croix from the mini-fridge, cracking the tab with a trembling hand. It was her own fault, she told herself, she had let her worries spiral out of control. First the call from her mother had triggered traumatic memories, then she made it worse by revisiting those emails from Eric, and Cady had overwhelmed herself. Maybe imagining the voice in Medieval Studies class was a bizarre coping mechanism, a self-made puzzle for distraction. Her mind felt so cluttered, she couldn't think without tripping over some new fear or old memory. She needed to reset. Cady went to her bedroom and undressed, slipped into her robe, grabbed her towel and toiletries caddy, and headed down the hall for a nice long shower.

The women's bathroom had a row of four toilet stalls facing four shower stalls, each with a flimsy, peach-colored shower curtain not quite wide enough for Cady's preferred degree of privacy. She had arbitrarily chosen the second-to-last shower stall as her favorite, if only to create comfort via routine. She relaxed a little to find she had the place to herself today, checking for feet beneath the stall doors to be sure. Cady disliked being nude in front of girls she didn't know, and the bright fluorescent lights in the Weld bathroom didn't make it any easier. It felt like getting naked in a lab.

Cady hung her towel on the hook, pushed up the sleeve of her robe, and reached in to turn the water on. The showerhead sputtered with a metallic whine that she could feel in her teeth, but soon it got going smoothly and quietly and the water grew hot. She pulled her ponytail holder from her hair, slipped off her robe, and hopped behind the shower curtain.

The hot water pounded her head and shoulders, melting the tension that had knotted there. She leaned her chin back, exposing her neck, and let the water soak her hair, face, and ears. She was working shampoo into her scalp and squeezing her eyes shut, when she was shocked by the loud crash of a cymbal.

Startled, Cady swore to herself. It took another moment for her brain to register that the blast of sound was actually music.

The tinny peal of a trumpet and the writhing whine of muted brass horns sounded all the sharper for pinging off the tiled walls, but she recognized the old-time tune "Happy Days Are Here Again."

Was this some kind of prank? Who was blasting Depression-era jazz in the women's bathroom?

"Who's out there?" Cady shouted over the music. "Ranjoo, Andrea? Is that you?"

No answer.

"Yo, whoever, can you *lower* it?" Her voice echoed off the tile.

The music bounced along at the same uncomfortable volume. Cady grumbled and gave a rough rinse to the suds on her brow, turned off the water, and poked her head out.

No one was there. "Hello?" The only answer was the lilting clarinets' cheerful melody and the plucky bass line, unnervingly out of place in the empty restroom. Fear crept from the top of her head down her spine like a drop of cold water.

Cady checked every stall for some sort of bluetooth speaker, an iPhone, any possible source for the sound, but came up with nothing.

Soaking wet and wrapped only in a towel, she swung the door open to the hallway, where she could still hear the music. A guy was walking toward her, texting on his phone.

"Hey, do you know who's playing that music?" she asked him.

He looked up in surprise, then confusion; Cady guessed he hadn't expected a nearly naked girl in his way.

"Sorry, what?" He pulled wireless earbuds out of his ears.

"Oh, you had headphones." Cady huffed in relief. "That music, do you hear it now? 'Happy Days Are Here Again,' like an oldies station or something? It's driving me crazy, where is it coming from?"

He frowned at her, uncomprehending. "What music?"

"Are you kidding? It scared the shit out of me in the shower, I can still hear it out here. Someone is *blasting* it."

He paused for a moment, tilting his head, then shrugged. "Sorry, I don't hear anything." He replaced his earbuds and gave Cady and the growing puddle at her feet a wide berth.

By now the vocals had come in, a quartet of men's voices singing the familiar lyrics in four-part harmony. Cady looked around her in every direction, down the hall, up the entryway stairwell, but no one seemed to be bothered in the slightest.

No one seemed to be hearing anything unusual at all.

Cady slammed the women's bathroom door behind her and locked it from the inside. The jaunty music only grew in volume, heedless of her panic. Her heart thundered in her chest, she couldn't catch her breath, her thoughts spiraled, but one fact had become clear: No one else could hear the music. The music was in her head.

The realization curdled in the pit of her stomach and rose up. She hurtled into the nearest shower stall before she doubled over and dry-heaved, with every muscle in her body straining for some relief. None came.

She turned on the water, letting it soak her and her towel as she crumpled to the tile floor. It washed her tears and muffled her sobs. But the water could do nothing to drown out the music, taunting her.

*So let us sing a song of happy cheer again,*

She knew she could be predisposed to mental illness, she knew this terrible potential was in her blood. And yet she had come here and risked it, dared it to show itself. Now it had.

Her new question was—

*Happy happy happy days are here again!*

—Would she survive?

# 11

WHEN RANJOO FOUND Cady in their shared bedroom later that evening, she didn't know that Cady had been sitting on the bed in her towel, paralyzed with anxiety, for nearly two hours. Ranjoo thought she was just being lazy and insisted she get ready for the party at the Phoenix. She even went so far as to pick out Cady's outfit for her—dark wash jeans, black ankle boots, and, after most of Cady's wardrobe was dismissed as too "basic," Ranjoo's own slinky off-the-shoulder top that Cady, admittedly, coveted.

"Now I have to go meet Dev, who's going to get us in, so you should meet me there. And please put some eye makeup on. You know I love the Puritan beauty thing you do, but tonight we're going to a party, not a barn raising."

Cady saluted her. She had never been more grateful to be told what to do.

Alone, Cady looked in the mirror, searching her reflection for evidence of the cracks she was feeling. But she looked good, she looked normal, she told herself, she was normal. Songs get stuck in people's heads all the time, no big deal. But at that volume? And that old vintage tune, when had she last heard it? Not recently, maybe not ever. Like she'd never read *Inferno,* or heard that voice, or— Stop. Don't dwell on it. That will only make it worse.

Cady got extra close to the mirror and drew a shaky charcoal line over her lashes. She remembered when she'd first tried eyeliner in ninth grade, and Eric saw her at breakfast and immediately quoted Charlie Sheen's line from *Ferris Bueller*, "You wear too much eye makeup. My sister wears too much. People think she's a whore." Eric had thought it was hilarious, but Cady rarely wore it again as a result. Now that seemed so overly sensitive; she had always been too easily influenced by Eric. She wasn't like him, she wasn't like him at all—she said it to herself like a pep talk. Cady applied two coats of mascara, only flinching and smearing it onto her cheek once.

Cady pulled her hair aside to slide the right earring in, revealing the still too short chunk of hair behind her ear and the faint mauve scar on the side of her neck. The sound of her own voice played in her mind, terrified: *Eric, what are you doing? Stop, it's me, Eric, it's me.* She covered the scar with her hand and shut her eyes to that memory, though her pulse beat against her fingers, as if that night were pounding on the door.

She threw the hoops back onto the desk. She didn't need jewelry anyway.

"Cady, I'm ready when you are," Andrea called from the common room. Somewhere during Ranjoo's fashion intervention with Cady, Andrea had caught wind of their evening plans, and Ranjoo had reluctantly extended an invitation.

Cady opened her bedroom door to find Andrea looking like a girl who had broken into her mother's makeup case. She had put on face powder a shade too light, giving her fair skin a ghostly pallor; her eyelids were covered in sparkly lilac shadow, and she was wearing oddly dark lipstick. The ends of her pin-straight hair had been curled under. She wore black slacks and ballet flats, and a purple scoop-necked shirt with a purple ribbon choker and amethyst earrings.

"You look cute!" Cady said at slightly too high a pitch.

Andrea scrunched her eyes into a wince. "What's wrong?"

"Nothing! But maybe save the necklace for another night? The shirt's neckline is so pretty by itself."

"But it matches the shirt. And my earrings, do you see?"

"Oh, nice." Cady pressed her lips together to keep her mouth shut. Andrea smiled. "I'll get my coat."


AS THEY WALKED down Mount Auburn Street, Cady had to rock forward on her toes to avoid getting her heels stuck in the brick sidewalk, and Andrea took the opportunity to explain how damaging high heels are to orthopedic health. "You really don't want to have bunion surgery before you're forty. Anyway, do you know which building's the Phoenix?" Andrea asked.

"No, but we'll find it." The Phoenix was a final club, one of the twelve all-male party houses on campus. Some were nicer than others, but most were gorgeous homes staffed and maintained by alumni where members could hang out during the day and host parties at night. The majority of the final clubs were located along Mount Auburn, but none of the clubhouses were marked. Cady had tried texting and calling Ranjoo, but she wasn't answering. They passed two barred windows, and although the curtains were drawn, she could hear the faint thumping of music. The only sign was for a used-record store called In Your Ear, but beside it was a grand door, blood red in color and crowned with ornate molding—the market for vinyl couldn't be *that* good, she thought. Cady climbed the front steps, her eyes drawn to the small brass knocker set high on the lacquered door. Her hunch was correct, the knocker was in the form of a golden phoenix. "This has to be it."

Andrea remained on the sidewalk, reluctant. "What do we do to get in?"

"I guess knock." Cady said it with nonchalance, but she shared Andrea's apprehension. Still, after the day she had had, Cady knew one thing and one thing only: She needed a drink. She knocked on the door and waited. Nothing. She tried again, harder this time. Cady had heard that girls could get into a final club more easily if they opened their jacket at the door, but she wasn't playing that game. It was demeaning, and worse, it was cold.

A few moments passed before the door was opened halfway by a young man blocking the entrance with his body. He was wearing Wayfarer sunglasses and a white button-down stained with some sort of liquid. "You on the list?"

"Um, I'm not sure . . ."

He cut her off. "Who do you know inside?"

"Ranjoo, our roommate—"

"Girls don't count. You have to be invited by a *member*. Final club rules."

"Okay, sorry, never mind," Andrea interjected, eager to admit defeat.

Cady couldn't remember the boy's name Ranjoo had mentioned, but she had a backup. "Nikos Nikolaides invited me. Tell him Cady Archer is here."

The Wayfarer pulled out his phone and shut the door in their faces.

Cady deflated but stayed put. Andrea bounced on her toes. "C'mon, let's just go."

Just then, the door swung wide open, and now a tall boy with curly blond hair was smiling down at them. "I'm sorry, ladies, I hear Rob's being an asshole again. Come right in. There's always room for a redhead." Cady hated comments like that, but she supposed she was getting her way. *This is normal, feel normal, be normal,* she commanded herself. They went inside.

They followed the two boys up red-carpeted stairs to a dimly lit landing that formed the head of two side staircases and the foot of a grander center staircase up to the second floor, where the real party was taking place. Cady could barely see what the room looked like for all the bodies crammed inside, mostly girls, but it looked big. Resigned to their admittance with the same apathy with which he had met them, the Wayfarer offered to take their coats and disappeared. An enormous gold-framed mirror over the mantelpiece reflected the crowd of heads bobbing like apples in the stairway. Cady met her own wide-eyed gaze like a stranger's. She was wearing too much eye makeup.

"So." The blond guy from the door placed his hand on her bare shoulder and leaned close to speak over the music. "What can I get you to drink?"

"Vodka cranberry?" It was what Liz had brought to prom in a Gatorade bottle, and it was the only hard drink Cady had ever had.

"Sure thing." He looked to Andrea, who shot Cady a desperate glance.

"She wants the same."

"Two vodka cranberries. Be right back."

Cady watched him sidle through the crowd. Guys slapped him five and a couple of girls kissed him on the cheek, but he moved quickly through. *To get me a drink*, Cady thought, with an inward smile. Maybe she should forgive him for the creepy redhead comment.

Andrea tapped her on the shoulder. "Let's find Ranjoo."

On the second floor, the room throbbed with a hip-hop bass beat and a mass of grinding bodies, the windows had fogged up with the heat of them. A grand antique wooden table with clawed feet shook as four girls danced close together on top of it. Cady led Andrea through the crowd of dancers to the quieter half of the room, where a few couples were snuggled on an enormous leather couch in front of a fireplace and three people were crammed into a single armchair. They passed a group of girls squealing high-pitched greetings to one another, and Andrea nearly got smacked by a tipsy blonde as she swung her skinny arms around a man's neck in either affection or inebriation.

Cady heard someone call her name. She looked around just in time to receive Ranjoo's wobbly embrace.

"Hey, girl! You made it!" Ranjoo spilled a little of her drink on Cady's shoulder as she hugged her. Cady could guess by her volume and her wobble that she was several drinks deep and had likely pregamed. Ranjoo swung her unfocused gaze toward their roommate. "And Andrea, coo-ool," she added. "You never come out with us."

"You never invite me," Andrea said sharply.

But Ranjoo had turned to say hello to a guy passing by, and Cady felt relieved that she had missed Andrea's edge. Until Ranjoo turned back and her smile was hard and her eyes had regained their acuity. "Nice choker."

Andrea crossed her arms but had no retort.

"You guys need drinks! Hold on." Ranjoo walked away before Cady had a chance to stop her.

Beside her, Andrea was quickly unfastening her necklace. The sight broke Cady's heart.

"Oh, don't listen to her, Andrea, it looks fine."

She shook her head, lips pressed tightly together, and dropped the choker into her purse. "She's such a bitch. I don't know why you want her to like you so bad."

Cady grimaced; nothing got by Andrea. "I'm sure she didn't mean it like that. She's just drunk."

Andrea heaved a big sigh. "I'm going to go home."

"What? No, stay! We just got here." Cady actually wanted her company.

"You should stay. I have to study, I hate the taste of alcohol, and let's face it, this is *not* my scene. I'll see you back at the room." Andrea hugged her goodbye and wedged through the crowd toward the stairs.

An elbow tapped her back and she turned to see the blond guy had returned with a red Solo cup in each hand and a third in his teeth. She took one from him so he could talk. "Two vodka cranberries. Where's your friend?"

"She had to go."

He grinned. "Darn."

Cady smiled back but felt a little guilty for it. She took a sip of her drink, wincing as the vodka hit her palate—the drink was strong.

"Is it okay?"

"Perfect." Cady squinted through the burn. "You didn't tell me your name."

"My bad. I'm Teddy."

"Cadence, but everyone calls me Cady."

"You a freshman?"

She nodded. "This is my first time at a final club."

"All right! Well, you've chosen wisely. The Phoenix is the best one. We throw the biggest parties, but not like those cokeheads at the Spee—unless you're into that, then I can find someone for you." He must have seen Cady's eyes bug out. "I'm kidding. I'm genuinely not into that shit. My only weakness is skirts."

"*Skirts?*" Cady laughed at him.

"Women," he explained. "Sorry, I'm on a noir kick. Raymond Chandler is my favorite."

"Seriously? Mine too!" Eric had turned her on to the genre; he had every Hammett and Chandler novel on his bookshelf at home, and his indoctrination of Cady had begun, appropriately, with Chandler's *The Little Sister* when she was eleven years old. "But I don't think you're hardboiled enough to pull off the lingo."

Teddy laughed and slung an arm around her. "We've got a funny one!"

Cady leaned into him and took another sip of her drink. The burn was getting softer already.

Teddy didn't leave her side for the next hour. He suggested they move to the smaller room where the bar was so they could actually hear each other. Their conversation was mostly small talk, sharing their personal stats—hometown, residence, concentration—and Cady was a little bored but flattered by the attention. She was happy for the distraction; a little underage drinking and talking to a boy at a party, it was nice to feel like a carefree college student for a change.

Then something Teddy said cut through her buzz: "My older brother's at Wharton now. He was Harvard '17—"

"Your brother went to Harvard, too?" The words escaped her mouth before she could check herself.

"Yeah, is that weird or something?"

"No." Cady paused, it wasn't a commonality, not anymore. "Your family is very impressive."

"They say most Harvard students are firsts or onlys. So I like to think I beat the odds as the overachieving baby of the family. Do you have any siblings?"

She shook her head.

"See? You're an only child! The theory is true."

Cady fought a lump in her throat. She wasn't sure what drink she was on, Teddy really kept them coming, but she felt like she was losing her poker face. She needed a break from the family talk. "I love this song. Do you want to dance?"

"For sure."

When Cady stood up, a brief wave of dizziness washed over her, but Teddy led her by the hand, and she focused on his broad back and the blue check on his white shirt. The dance floor was crowded already, and Teddy took her to the center of it. He was a fun dancer, if not the most rhythmically skilled; despite the hip-hop beat, he spun her around like a ballroom dancer and made her laugh. She was still feeling a little imbalanced, but his strong hand on the small of her back kept her steady.

The music was loud, and Cady's head was already pounding when a girl squealed too close to her ear. But Teddy kept her moving, and he held her hips as his silly dance moves gave way to a more intense grind that Cady wasn't into. She would break from his grasp every few moments to give him a hint. But the last time she tried to put a little space between them, Teddy yanked her back and slid his hands over her stomach and up her rib cage, grazing her breasts.

*Watch it.*

She jerked away, at the warning or his touch, she wasn't sure, but she had definitely heard a woman's voice clearly. She looked around her to see who might've spoken, if she'd bumped anyone, but everyone seemed to be focused on the music or their dance partners. But on another level, she knew already—the voice belonged to no one. It was a voice in her head, a new one, and it sounded like a threat.

Teddy spun her back around to face him. "You okay?" he asked, with his hands on her shoulders.

*Listen to me.*

Cady forced herself to smile and nod at Teddy, but a sobering chill went through her. These voices, auditory hallucinations, weren't something she could dull with alcohol or hide from in a crowd. They were something inside her, and they had multiplied: a man, music, now a woman. She was terrified, but she couldn't give in to it. She made herself focus on Teddy; he was real, he would keep her grounded and safe from her own mind.

His kiss took her by surprise. It was wet and strong, his teeth pressed on her lips, his tongue thrust inside her unsuspecting mouth, before he eased his grip on her and ended the kiss softer than it began, with a few sweeter kisses on her lower lip, as if it had been romantic from the start. Cady recoiled, but his heavy-lidded eyes were fixed on her mouth. "You're good at that," he said.

Cady felt a flash of guilt that the feeling wasn't mutual and spun her back to him to avoid the prospect of more sloppy kisses.

*He ain't gonna stop when you ask him to. Boys like him think everything is theirs for the taking.*

Don't listen, she commanded herself. It was just an awkward moment, a harmless miscalculation on his part. Be nice. Be normal.

*Get out of here.*

Still, Cady cringed as Teddy's fingers stroked her hair aside, and when she felt his mouth on the back of her neck. His other hand slipped up her waist, this time under her shirt.

*Before it's too late.*

Cady pulled out of his arms.

"What's up?" Teddy asked with a guileless expression.

"I'm tired." She wanted to get home in case the voices got worse, even though the prospect of dealing with it alone scared her, she didn't want to have an episode in a public place.

"Sure, let's go."

He's not so bad, Cady reassured herself, as they shuffled through the crowd. People get sloppy on the dance floor, they had been hanging out all night, she could see how he got the wrong idea. She hoped his feelings wouldn't be hurt when she bailed.

"You want another drink?"

"No, thanks, I think I ought to head home."

"One for the road?"

"Seriously, I don't think I could take another. You'd have to carry me home."

Teddy slipped his arms around her waist and slid his hands down her backside. "You don't feel too heavy." He leaned in close, his eyes dreamy and his breath smelling of liquor.

Cady didn't want to embarrass him, but the voice had made her uneasy. *Before it's too late.* When his lips were an inch from hers, she whispered, "Where's my coat?"

She had intended to say it in a flirty, lighthearted way, but she must have missed the mark; his affect turned suddenly icy. "Rob put it upstairs, I'll show you."

Teddy led her by the hand past the bar to a skinny door that hid a narrow servant's staircase. As if the vodka cranberries weren't enough, the stairs were completely dark; she took a tentative step.

*No. Don't go in there. Turn back.* The voice was even louder here.

But Teddy tugged her hand, and Cady obeyed. She couldn't trust a strange voice in her head. Still, it was awfully dark. She dragged her one free hand along the wall to feel for a railing, but there was none. Her toe missed a step and she fell on her shin.

She heard Teddy's voice in the dark say, "I got you."

*Don't trust him. Don't go with him.*

She had a bad feeling, but she wasn't clear whom it was coming from, the voice or Teddy. She wanted to be nice, cool, normal, anything but paranoid. Cady felt Teddy's hand pulling under her arm—but he was helping her, she told herself, it was okay, chill out.

When they emerged upstairs, it looked more like the mansion

that it was, with oriental rugs, lovely old lamps, and plush furniture. He took her down a hall and opened a door to an elegant, if minimally furnished, bedroom.

"I'm sorry, but, I don't see my coat?" She didn't know why she was apologizing, maybe because it was awkward. But then, if it was only awkward, why did she feel so scared? There was no voice to blame now. And her own sounded smaller than ever. "I just want my coat, Teddy."

"Are you cold? C'mere." He pulled her farther into the bedroom, wrapped his arms around her, and kissed her, hard.

She turned her head to pull her mouth away, but he didn't let go. "I have to go, I'm really tired—"

"Me too, lie down for a minute." He sat down on the bed, pulling her onto it with him.

Cady forced a laugh and scrambled back to her feet. "I'm sorry, but I should go." She turned to reach for the door, but he was still holding her hand, and when she shifted her weight away, his grip tightened. She looked back at him pleadingly, but his bloodshot eyes were impassive. In that moment, her last shred of embarrassment surrendered to the chill of undeniable fear. "I want to go. Now."

Teddy smiled. "Oh-kay, bring it in," he said, as if he was going to hug her goodbye, as if he didn't still have a death grip on her wrist. He nuzzled her neck. "You smell good, I bet you taste good, too," he murmured. She squirmed in his grasp. "C'mon, baby, we've been having a good time all night." He pressed her hand to his crotch so she could feel his erection. "See what you did?"

Cady pulled her hand to her side, but the skin of her wrist was twisting and pinching in his grip. With his other hand firm on her shoulder, Teddy pressed her against the door, closing it behind them, his strength overpowering her. Cady knew she was in trouble, but in a fog of shock, fear, and vodka, she stood frozen. He pushed his mouth on hers again, biting her lower lip. Even the pain didn't pull her consciousness back into her body, not until she heard it again:

*You scared? Good. Use it. Fear makes you strong.*

It was as if the woman's voice had taken the place of her own. Cady couldn't speak. She could barely breathe, he was kissing her so hard. But the voice was coaching her back into her body, slowly, and she began to dig her fingernails into Teddy's forearm. He didn't react.

*Fight, girl. Fight for yourself, fight to get free.* The voice was growing louder.

Teddy tried to force her hand back to his groin, but she made a fist and hip-checked it into him. He flinched.

MOVE! The voice was so loud it startled her. Cady wrenched free and lunged aside, a split second before the bedroom door flew open, slamming into Teddy and knocking him halfway to the ground.

"What the hell?" Teddy clutched his shoulder.

She was stunned to see Nikos standing in the doorway, looking at her with eyes as wide as hers must have been.

"Cady! Are you all right? Ted, what's going on?"

"Relax, we're hanging out, having a good time. Weren't we, Cady?"

She felt overwhelmed by shame; she couldn't look Nikos in the eye, but she knew she wouldn't get another chance to escape. Her voice was small but firm: "I want to go home."

"We're going." Nikos put a comforting hand on her shoulder. As they passed Teddy at the door, Nikos muttered, "Bastard."

"Sorry, dude. Didn't know you were hitting it, too."

Nikos spun around and punched him square in the jaw.

Teddy stumbled backward, clutching his chin. He spat on the ground and swore, but he didn't dare look back at Cady. "What the *fuck*, man?"

Nikos swept her out of the room, leaving Teddy to shout after them. He led her down a hall and down a different staircase. Cady was completely disoriented. The whole night felt like a bad dream.

When they reached the first floor, he pulled her into a small sitting room that was relatively quiet. "Here, sit for a second. You're shaking. Tell me what happened."

Her voice sounded barely above a whisper. "He said we were getting my coat. I feel so stupid."

"Innocence is not the same as stupidity."

Cady shook her head. "I was warned, this voice told me, I didn't listen—"

"The voice . . . inside you?" Nikos's eyes searched her face with worry. His earnest concern sobered her.

"Yes," she made herself say.

"I'm not surprised. Unfortunately, your gut was dead on with Teddy. He's the Phoenix's resident asshole, I swear we're not all like that, but don't blame yourself. You couldn't have known."

Cady nodded. Maybe it *was* her own intuition speaking to her. "I mean, you're right. I just—" But why didn't it sound anything like her? "I can't think straight right now. I feel crazy."

"Don't worry, you're safe now, you don't have to say anything more." He put an arm around her and rubbed her back. "I'm just glad I was there."

"How? How did you know where I was?"

"Rob told me you had asked for me, and when he said Teddy was with you, I knew you were in trouble. We all know his routine." Nikos must have felt her tense at the word "routine." "God, that sounds bad. He should be kicked out."

"Of school?"

"I meant the Phoenix, but fuck, yes, probably both."

Cady hung her head. "I'm so embarrassed."

"Why? You did nothing wrong."

But that wasn't true. That hadn't been true since last Christmas. Since losing Eric, she had learned things about herself that she hated. She was a person who misjudged people, who took things for granted, who lied. And tonight only proved it. She'd misjudged Teddy. She'd drunk too much. She hadn't stopped him earlier or more forcefully— although the memory of his grip twisting her skin argued that more force wouldn't have made a difference. She felt guilty for burdening Nikos, and for lying to him. She felt ashamed of hearing things that weren't there, or for not knowing what was real and what wasn't, or for believing something was real that didn't make any sense.

But she couldn't say any of that. "What I mean to say is, thank you. I owe you."

"I owed it to your brother."

That stopped her heart.

"Let's get you home."

# 12

NEARLY FIFTY VOICES soared and swirled, blending and washing over one another in harmony. The song Collegium was working on, Rheinberger's "Abendlied," soothed Cady's troubled spirit like a lullaby, driving out the nightmarish voices of the night before—Teddy's lies, his lewdness, and that strange voice and its warning she didn't heed. She had replayed every word and every action as she tried unsuccessfully to sleep, retracing her mistakes. But now the four-four time kept her anchored in the present, her sole focus on the sheet music and the confluence of sound as the group lit upon each chord.

Collegium was composed of mostly undergrads with a handful of graduate students, but it was by far the most serious and professional choral group Cady had ever heard. She still couldn't believe she'd been accepted; she was one of only five freshmen brought on that year, and many in the group were pursuing music as their main course of study. So she could tolerate today's unusually early morning rehearsal at Paine Hall. Dr. Sutcliffe, their choral director, had had to cancel one of their thrice-weekly rehearsals for a conference this weekend, so he called a makeup session this Friday morning from seven to nine. Cady sensed that Dr. Sutcliffe never canceled a rehearsal. An hour in, and they had only sung through half a page of music, which was typical for Dr. Sutcliffe's perfectionism.

"Can you hear that?" Dr. Sutcliffe called out over their singing. "Can you hear the overtone? No, no, keep going!"

But his interruption had broken the spell of their collective concentration, and as a smattering of the voices dropped out, the harmonies crumbled into dubious melodies and elementary thirds.

"Gah!" Dr. Sutcliffe smacked his palm to his head. "I didn't mean for you to stop singing!" He rubbed his knuckles against his brushy white mustache, his signature tic. "I interrupted not to nitpick, which you know is my favorite pastime, but to get you to hear the *overtones*. That will require you to listen while you sing. Tune in to the person next to you, that's why I have you seated in quartets. The other voices are your *guides*." He looked down at the score and rubbed his mustache again. "Do you know what I mean by 'overtones'?"

There was an uncertain murmuring in the crowd.

"Every note produces a fundamental tone, the tone we recognize and name, and a quieter, secondary tone known as an overtone or harmonic. When you all hit the notes of your chord in tune, the resonance from each of your notes gives birth to a second, ghostly chord made of the overtones. Releasing the overtones from within our bodies to float above us will elevate the musical experience from the corporeal to the *divine*."

A few students giggled.

"I feel your skepticism. Maybe we need a demo. Peter, Jamal, Elizabeth, and Annie, would you mind performing from measure twenty-six to the end of the page?"

This was one of the practices that most frightened Cady, when Dr. Sutcliffe would cold-call a singer from each voice part and ask them to sing. Her heart beat faster every time in dreaded anticipation of the day he called hers. But this time, he had chosen four of the most confident and accomplished singers; all four were seniors, Peter was an aspiring operatic tenor and Annie sometimes assistant-directed Collegium. They each rose from their seats and carried their sheet music to the front to face the group.

Peter started them off, but as soon as the other three joined, all four voices melted into one. They rose and fell and shrank and swelled together, rounding the hard-edged German words into soft aural elements. When they reached the final chord, Dr. Sutcliffe directed them to hold it out. Cady closed her eyes. She might have been imagining it, but she thought she could detect a fifth tone above their notes, like the sound of a finger on a crystal goblet, fragile and ethereal—the overtone.

When they finished, the rest of the choir applauded and chattered to one another. Dr. Sutcliffe quieted them down. "Did you hear it that time?"

The group murmured a jumbled response. Cady penciled in a note to herself above the triplet rhythm she kept missing.

"Some of you? More than half? It's okay, we'll keep practicing and keep learning. All I ask is that you remember to listen to the other voices."

She looked up from her sheet music.

"Now let's try it from the top."

When Dr. Sutcliffe dismissed them an hour later, Cady was loath to leave. During rehearsal, she had felt lighter than she had all weekend. Cady was putting on her coat when Nneka, a pretty Nigerian second soprano, approached with a smile.

"Hey, Katie, right?" asked Nneka, mistaking Cady's name as nearly everyone did.

"It's Cady, actually, but I answer to both."

"Oh, Cay-dee, I got you. Please, if anybody can spare a second to get your name right, it's me, 'Nneka' with two n's," she put in air quotes. "Nobody nails that on the first try."

Cady laughed.

"If you don't have class, some of us are going to this brunch spot across from Wadsworth House that we love, wanna join?"

"Sure, I'd love to." Cady had liked Nneka since she first met her. It would be good to make some friends outside the tension of her roommate triangle.

"Great! I'm going to go grab some more people on their way out, but find us, and we'll walk to the Square together."

Nneka led Cady and a small group of five Collegium members to the restaurant and claimed the long high-top table toward the front. They decided to order at the counter in shifts so they could hold the table; Cady didn't know what she wanted, so she let others go first. She sat facing away from the big glass window so the sun would warm her back. Cady felt a tingle at the back of her neck, either a draft from the door, or the sensation of being watched. She looked up from the menu and met the pained gaze of Rachel, a senior soprano sitting across from her, staring. Rachel leaned forward to speak softly. "I just wanted to say, I lived down the hall from your brother last year. I'm really sorry about what happened. He was my laundry room buddy, we used to play chess while we waited. He was a sweet guy."

"Oh, thank you. That's nice to hear," Cady replied, but Rachel still looked concerned, so she added, "That he actually did his laundry, I mean." She had grown adept at releasing people from their uncomfortable sympathy for her.

Rachel laughed politely. "Eric certainly had his quirks. But I'm a psych concentrator, I hope to be a clinical psychiatrist, so I'm familiar with what he was dealing with. I knew the signs." Rachel eased back and picked up a menu, satisfied with the interaction.

What had seemed like perfunctory condolences had just become more interesting. "Like what?"

"I'm sorry?" Rachel's blue eyes looked icy and innocent in the sunlight.

"The signs, you said, what signs specifically did you notice?" Cady no longer cared about Rachel's comfort level, she needed this information.

"You know, I shouldn't have overstated it. I didn't, like, diagnose him or anything."

"No, I know, but I'm curious what his illness was like last year. Did he say anything to you during your chess games or whatever? Did he ever mention hearing voices?"

Rachel's neck grew pink and blotchy. "I'm sorry, I feel like this is coming out really badly. I don't even know what I'm doing explaining this to you. He was *your* brother, you knew him better than I did—"

That was the problem, Cady thought, she hadn't known him better, because she was a shitty sister whose only insight into her brother came from the possibility that she might currently share his mental illness.

"I only meant, I could see he needed a friend. I'm glad he was mine."

Because I let him down, Cady thought.

"You guys are up!" Nneka said as she and the other three returned to the table. "Only bad news is, I got the last chocolate croissant. You can fight me for it." Nneka glanced at their faces. "Y'all okay?"

Rachel said something to cover for them, and Cady excused herself to go to the ladies' room, if only to put some people between her and Rachel in the line. As she walked toward the back of the restaurant, her temples throbbed.

The memory haunted her always and yet never showed itself in full, only in shards. Frantically grabbing at Eric's arms. *Are you afraid?* Hearing him say *I'm sorry* and knowing the words should be hers. Recollections that rose in her throat and threatened to choke her with self-loathing. She reflexively covered the scar on her neck with her hand and tried to push them out of her mind.

*Psst.*

Cady snapped her head over her shoulder but saw no one.

*Pardon me, miss, but I been watching you.*

It was the woman's voice from the Phoenix. Cady stepped into the empty hallway to the restrooms, safe from view of the other patrons.

*I saw you talking to that Negro girl, and the light-skinned one last night. They slaves of yours?*

She blanched at the notion. Slaves?—she thought—No! Of course not, they're my friends. And Ranjoo? She's my roommate, and she's Indian.

*Knew a Pequot Indian when I was small. Master treated him like he treat everyone with skin darker than his own, like filth. But he was a medicine man, learned and respected in his tribe. He taught me how to read plants and herbs, cure any ailment. Holyoke's youngest be dead from smallpox if not for his lessons. So, black, Indian, you call them friend?*

The voice was talking so fast, Cady felt three steps behind in her understanding— It was *you* last night. You were trying to help me.

*I did, and I just ask this small thing in return. Please, help me, I beg of you.*

Who are you?

*I'm Bilhah, the Holyokes' girl. I need a friend, miss, a friend who knows her letters. I need you to read this to me, please.*

Read what?

*This, this paper here. Should take only a moment—*

I can't see—

*Please, I have to get back to Wadsworth House. I can't read it, but I need to know if they put my baby for sale, how much time I have. I'll smell fire again before I let them take him.*

Sell your baby, why—?

*'Cause the president of Harvard don't need a mute houseboy, least of all one with blue eyes that insult him! Now, please, I need your help to save my son!*

Cady was so disoriented at the fever pitch of this information coming out of nowhere, and yet the uncanny sensation when certain familiar details were mentioned, like Wadsworth House, the administrative building across the street. She shook her head— But what does this have to do with *me*?

"Hey." The nonchalant greeting clashed with the panicked confusion inside Cady, and she turned to see it had come from Ainsley, a blond alto, who had suddenly appeared in the hallway to the restroom. Cady couldn't muster a hello back, so torn between reality and whatever the voice was. Ainsley, luckily, didn't seem to notice. "Ugh, a line? Always, right?" She rolled her eyes and began tapping at her phone.

Cady coughed to stall replying when Bilhah's voice returned, only its tone had completely changed at Ainsley's arrival. Gone were the desperation and urgency, she sounded entirely deferential and poised. *Thank you kindly. I'll be right back with your tea, chamomile and rose hips, miss, fix that cold right quick.*

"You know, um. I'm sorry," Cady stammered, recovering slowly. "I'm so stupid, I actually didn't test the door yet."

"Oh." Ainsley frowned up at her. "Well, are you gonna go?"

"Yes, I am, now. Sorry." She tried the door; it opened easily. Cady gave a pathetic laugh and slipped inside.

Locking the door behind her, she braced herself against the sink and gulped for air. This was bad, bad, bad, she told herself. These voices weren't going away, they were coming more often, and now they wanted something from her. She was losing it. Cady looked up at her reflection in the mirror, trying to see the sane, healthy girl she used to be.

# 13

CADY HAD BEEN circling the Ginsberg Reading Room for a sufficiently deserted chair for the last five minutes. She had retrieved the
book she came for and tucked it deep inside her shoulder bag, now she
just needed a private place to read it. The contemporary study space
outfitted in the keep-calm colors of beige and sage was packed with
diligent students, but none were paying any attention to her. Their
eyes were glued to their laptop screens, ears stuffed with headphones,
no one would care what Cady was reading. For another, the subject
matter could easily pass as an academic interest instead of a personal
one. Any psych student might pull a book on abnormal psychological
phenomena; they weren't all crazy.

Like her.

Cady settled for sitting at a table with only one person at it. The
table was set up with two desk lamps at the center, so she had to face
her companion, a boy with dark hair and hip glasses, but at least they
were separated by his laptop screen and stacks of economics books.
She pulled out the book *Origins of Schizophrenia*, with its troubling
subtitle, *The Makings of Madness*. Until recently, she'd felt she knew
all she needed to about schizophrenia. She understood the basics of
the illness and its horrors; her family had lived through them. But
it took Eric more than a year to get that diagnosis. First they said it

was depression, then bipolar disorder, for a while her mother thought the antidepressant medications were *causing* his psychosis, but finally everyone agreed on schizophrenia—except Eric—but what did he know? He was only the patient.

Cady realized now that she only knew the words other people had said, labels for her brother that were disputed and refined but never confirmed. She knew nothing of his experience with the illness; she had been afraid to ask. She could no longer afford the luxury of denial. Cady had quickly abandoned her search online, too easy to get paranoid and hypochondriacal, she figured. She'd surmised that a book, with its comforting physical weight and peer-reviewed levelheadedness, would offer her a greater chance of reassurance, or at least a higher bar for panic. Her heart pounded as she looked at the book's cover.

Cady skipped to the second chapter, titled "Diagnosing Schizophrenia." She feverishly read the first paragraph:

Schizophrenia shares many symptoms with other mental illnesses, sometimes muddling an accurate diagnosis. However, there are highly characteristic symptoms, such as the belief that someone else's thoughts are being inserted into one's mind or hearing (nonexistent) voices discuss one's behavior.

Cady's eyes raced down the next few lines, which listed the criteria for schizophrenia from the *Diagnostic and Statistical Manual of Mental Disorders:*

A.  The presence of characteristic psychotic symptoms in the active phase: any of 1, 2, or 3 for at least a week:
    1.  Two of the following:
        a.  Delusions
        b.  Hallucinations throughout the day for several days or several times a week for several weeks, each hal-

lucinatory experience lasting more than a few brief
moments.

   c.   Incoherence or marked loosening of associations

   d.   Catatonic behavior

   e.   Flat or grossly inappropriate affect (emotional
tone)

2.   Bizarre delusions (i.e., involving a phenomenon that
in the person's culture would be regarded as totally
implausible—e.g., thought broadcasting, being con-
trolled by a dead person)

3.   Prominent hallucinations of a voice with content having
no relation to concomitant depression or elation, or a
voice keeping a running commentary on the person's
behavior or thoughts . . .

Cady stopped reading. She had already made mental check marks
next to too many of A's subsets—1. she was having auditory hallucinations, although they hadn't lasted a week, yet; 2. it hadn't crossed her
mind they were dead, exactly, but it was true they didn't speak to her
like contemporaries, and there was that old music. . . . and they weren't
controlling her, yet, but this morning, the woman's voice wanted her
to read something . . . did asking for help count as control?; 3. the
voices were unrelated to her mood and arrived without warning, and
they did comment on Cady's behavior and thoughts. Her own thoughts
intruded—*But what if they were right? Canto Five in* Inferno, *Teddy and
the danger—you can't be making it up if they're right.* But what explanation did that leave her with?

*Slow down*, Cady told herself, *don't jump to conclusions.* Crazy people don't know they're crazy, right? She thought the fact that she was
questioning had to count for something, until she read:

Unlike patients suffering from other forms of dementia, schizophrenics can remain fairly high-functioning, with a seemingly

clear and conscious grip on reality, and with intellect intact. Studies show that schizophrenia has a statistically greater occurrence
in those persons of genius IQ.

*But Eric was the genius*, Cady reasoned, *not me*. Eric was an unusual, precocious child; Cady had never stood out the way he did. Her
parents had his IQ tested at a young age and he scored extraordinarily
high; when Cady had asked why she was never tested, her mother had
said there was no need for competition, which Cady always took to
mean they had wanted to spare her feelings when she inevitably fell
short.

But had they been wrong? Cady had excelled in all her classes easily, especially in the humanities, and only she had perfect pitch. She
didn't share Eric's relish for math and science, but she had never struggled in either. Eric's SATs were perfect, Cady's were nearly the same,
though she'd attributed her score to studying, not genius. If Eric's outlier IQ had marked him for this illness, was she far off?

Cady skipped to chapter 5, "Family Studies," and started skimming pages. She read that siblings, along with parents and children,
counted as "first-degree" relatives of the schizophrenic patient. Already that sounded bad. A large bar graph was captioned "Figure 7
presents the grand average risks of developing schizophrenia; there is
a high correlation between risk and genetic relatedness." Her eyes
scanned the mini-skyline of bars at all different heights: the bar labeled "siblings" was one of the highest, showing a 9 percent increased
risk of developing schizophrenia in their lifetime. The only groups
with higher risk were twins and the children of two schizophrenic
parents.

Searching through the interpretation of the graph data, she found
a passage that was even more troubling:

While parent-child pairs share *exactly* 50 percent of their genetic
material, it is important to note that sibling pairs share an *average*

of 50 percent. So it is possible for some sibling pairs to have considerably more or less, with obvious impact on their similarity in all polygenic traits, including the liability for developing schizophrenia.

Cady reflexively touched her hair. She and Eric were the only ones in their entire family who had red hair. Uncle Pete always kidded their dad that he should give "that redheaded mailman" a talking-to. But it was that recessive gene from way back, hidden for generations, until it resurfaced for both of them. Cady's memory flashed through pictures of her and her brother when they were little, particularly a photo that still sat on their mantel in the dining room despite her hating it. Cady was around six, so Eric was eight when it was taken, the same year her mother had given her an unforgivably boyish bowl haircut. She and Eric looked nearly identical.

She jumped in her seat when her phone started vibrating, rattling against the hard desk. The boy across from her peered over his glasses in annoyance. The words Home Calling gave her a bolt of anxiety, as if her parents could see through the phone. With one clean swipe, she cleared her things from the desk and darted out to the hall to pick up the call. She pushed through the heavy swinging doors into the hallway and clicked Accept on the last ring.

"Cady-cake. How are you? Bad time?" her father's voice said. He had a way of sounding in a hurry even as he asked you if you were.

"I'm in the library, but I can talk for a minute."

"Good, I wanted to run over your flight details for tomorrow."

"Flight?"

"For me to pick you up at the airport. Grampa and Vivi's thing is this weekend, remember?"

Cady's mouth opened in a silent gasp—she had completely forgotten she was flying home *tomorrow* to see her grandfather and his new wife renew their two-year-old wedding vows. She felt like an idiot for letting it slip her mind, but with everything going on . . .

"Cady? You there?"

"Sorry, I'm here. I'll have to email you the itinerary, I don't have it in front of me right now. I know it was a morning flight."

"I imagine so. Luckily the ceremony isn't until six, so we'll have plenty of time to go home and get changed and everything. I can't wait to see my girl."

"Um, yeah, same." All Cady could think about was how she could possibly face her parents with these voices echoing in her head. Over the phone was one thing, but would she be able to hide her fears in person?

"Listen, you sound stressed," her father said—maybe Cady wasn't so good at hiding it over the phone either, she thought. He continued, "I know it's only a short trip, but it'll be nice to get a little time at home to recharge. I know I always cherished those weekends home from college when I could get a couple home-cooked meals in me."

The tension in Cady's chest began to ease. Maybe he was right, maybe she just needed a break. The small crack of hope was enough for her to muster more convincing enthusiasm. "It'll be fun, I'm looking forward to it. But I should probably get back to work."

"On a Friday? Relax. I don't want you working too hard."

That didn't sound like her father, the man who made her and Eric recite the preamble to the United States Constitution for the firm's partners on Take Your Child to Work Day; they were aged seven and nine. "Dad, you love working too hard, I get it from you."

"Yes, but I wasn't always like this. Not when I was your age. I had fun back then. I was the irresponsible one, Aunt Laura was the worrywart."

"I don't believe you."

"It's true. I was fun until Laura had her accident. Then we switched places. There was only one positive outlook between us, and she needed it more than I did. So I've turned my worrying on you now. I'm afraid I've thrown you to the wolves."

"How do you mean?" Cady asked.

"College is supposed to be a happy time, and I'm worried I encouraged you to choose an unhappy place. Maybe we should've kept you closer. On the other hand, I didn't want you to get stuck with your mom and me. But I could have helped you escape somewhere . . . easier."

"I wanted to go here."

"Are you sure? Because I let your mother push me around sometimes. She can be bullheaded, in her way, you know? And I couldn't stand to see her do it to you. But I want you to feel you had a real choice."

"I did. I chose this."

"All right, then. That makes me feel better. I'm second-guessing everything lately."

They were alike this way.

"Mom called me," Cady said.

"Oh? How was that?"

"She cried."

"Ah, yes." Her father breathed heavily. "No one suffers like she suffers. Her idea of checking in is letting you check on her."

Cady felt a pang; she hadn't meant to elicit such cold words. Her parents had never had a perfect relationship, but as Eric had gone downhill, so had their marriage. Now her father often had an edge when he spoke of her mother. "It wasn't a big deal. I was the one who brought up Eric," she lied.

"You're allowed to! It's not your fault she's sad, all right? You didn't do this to us."

Cady felt doubly guilty now; she hated when her father blamed Eric. She hesitated before asking the next question. "Are you and Mom okay?"

His sigh sounded like a hurricane over the phone. "We're fine, don't worry about us. Just, the—"

"I know."

"Right."

Her conversations with her father included more and more of this shorthand.

"I want you to know I'm proud of you," he added.

"I haven't done anything yet."

"How can you say that? You were accepted into one of the most selective schools in the country, you've triumphed over personal tragedy, and possibly most remarkable, you stood up to your mother. You're the brave one in the family, remember that."

And she was terrified. She wished he would stop saying that.

"Anyway, I'll let you go. Don't forget to forward me your flight info. And I love you."

"Love you too."

Cady clicked End and slid her back down the wall, suddenly too tired to stand. Cady hated lying to her father, but she had to get a better sense of what she was dealing with before opening up. He was the only one in her corner and she liked the way he saw her, she couldn't bear the thought of disillusioning him. She hoped this trip home wouldn't prove to be a mistake.

Sitting on the top step, she realized she still had her index finger saving her place in the book. She flopped it open on her lap and picked up reading:

"Genetic material alone cannot result in schizophrenia. Likewise, no environmental factor, on its own, has been proven to cause schizophrenia."

*Not even Harvard?*

"Instead, it is a combination of the two. Genes form a hereditary vulnerability or predisposition, known as *diathesis*, to the development of schizophrenia, and these latent genetic traits, when combined with environmental stress or trauma, can manifest in full-blown mental illness. This is known as the *diathesis-stressor* theory." It went on:

Environmental risk factors fall into general groups including (a) brain injuries, (b) emotionally traumatic experiences, acute or persistent, (c) demoralizing or threatening physical environments, termed "toxic environments. . . ."

*Emotionally traumatic experiences, acute or persistent*—Cady had both. Eric's illness had weighed on the family for the last two years, and his death was the greatest trauma imaginable. As for environment—as Cady had assured her father, she had chosen an academically grueling, freezing-cold university that happened to be the same "toxic environment" that had led to her brother's suicide on campus.

*But other than that,* Cady thought bitterly, reading ahead:

In principle, those at high genetic risk of falling victim to schizo-phrenia could avoid tipping the balance into psychosis by avoid-ing the kinds of environmental factors that act as triggers or *stressors*. In reality, these factors are not always preventable or foreseeable.

But hers were. She knew she was hurting after Eric's death, and yet she chose to place herself in the very same "toxic environment" that had been the stage for his suicide.

*What have I done?*

# 14

CADY HAD ALREADY surveyed Linden Street to make sure no one she knew was in sight before she approached the historic clapboard home that housed the offices for campus counselors, tutors, and mental health services. The place was euphemistically titled the Bureau of Study Counsel, as if the only thing a Harvard student could admit to needing counseling for was studying.

The weathered gray and white clapboard might seem charming to someone in a cheerier frame of mind, but to Cady it resembled the sort of spooky old house that kids subject to Ding-Dong-Ditch. The wooden boards of the porch steps were cracked and peeling and creaked beneath Cady's feet, so she stepped lightly, not wanting to call one decibel of attention to her entrance. The Bureau looked closed, as the windows had both exterior and interior shutters, but it had to be open. It was a building designed for discretion. And not everything on the exterior was aging; there was a wooden bench on the front porch, brand new, or at least barely used. Nobody wants to sit and relax on the porch of the school shrink.

She hadn't heard anything else unusual since the café with Nneka, but she suffered from a sort of reverse separation anxiety, so fearful that every minute of quiet would be her last. The suspense of when her mind would next be invaded was nearly worse than the voices themselves. She felt on the verge of a nervous breakdown.

Cady pushed the doorbell and a moment later the door buzzed open. The waiting room looked like a regular living room except none of the mismatched pieces of furniture faced one another. A girl wearing a hijab sat behind the reception desk with an open textbook. "Sorry, hey, what can I do for you?"

"I don't have an appointment, but I thought maybe I'd try and just walk in and meet with someone. Is that possible?"

"There's always someone to talk to. Are you already a friend of the Bureau's?"

"A friend?"

"Are you in the system—have you met with a counselor before or participated in a wellness workshop?"

"Oh, no. I'm new."

"Then you'll need to fill out these forms. Greg is free to talk when you're finished."

Cady accepted the clipboard and sat on a sagging forest-green loveseat to fill the papers out. Her hand shook as she wrote her name. She would prefer no record of her being there. She suddenly remembered how Eric felt a loss of control when he got psychiatrists involved, especially the ones at school. "It's official. There's no going back now," he'd said after his diagnosis. At the time, Cady had thought he was being melodramatic and stubborn, but now she understood. She wanted to talk to an expert about what she was hearing, but not at the expense of her autonomy or privacy. Her parents could not know she was here, especially not her mother.

"You can go right up," said the girl at the counter when Cady brought over the forms. "Upstairs, first door on your left."

The stairs creaked under Cady's feet. The second-floor hallway was dark save for a shaft of light coming from a barely open door. Cady knocked. "Hello?" She got no answer, so she pushed it open.

"Yo! Hey there, come in." The man seemed surprised, hastily pulling out headphones that were plugged into the MacBook in front of him. He looked to be in his early thirties, wearing a gray hoodie over a plaid shirt. With his wool beanie hat, thick glasses, and big, bushy beard, Cady thought he looked like Hipster Freud. He rose from the desk and reached out a lanky arm to shake her hand. "I'm Greg."

Cady returned the handshake and awkwardly introduced herself. "Sorry, I don't have an appointment."

"No worries, that's why I'm here. Please, sit down." Greg motioned to a navy blue loveseat against the wall. The office was small but cozy, with a muted oriental rug, plush upholstered furniture, and lacy grandma curtains on the window. He sat down in a tartan armchair across from her. "So, what's up? Give me the lowdown on you, your year, house, concentration, whatever."

"I'm a freshman, I live in Weld. I haven't chosen a concentration yet."

"Good, take the time to explore. Do you like it here so far?"

"It's hard."

"Why is it hard?"

"It's Harvard, it's supposed to be hard, right?"

Greg smiled. "True. But try to be specific. What's making it hard for you?"

Cady took a deep breath before answering. "My brother. That's why I came here tonight, actually. My brother was a junior here, last year, when he died."

"Oh, I'm sorry. How did he pass?"

"It was suicide." It was still hard for Cady to attach the word to him. "He suffered with schizophrenia, and then . . ." She trailed off.

"I'm very sorry."

"It's okay." A reflexive answer she always hated herself for saying.

"It must be very difficult to be here with that history."

Cady nodded. Greg seemed nice, but she was losing her nerve. "There are things about his illness that I wish I understood better, that I feel like I need to understand better to move on, and that's why I thought you could help me. I don't know who else to talk to."

"Whatever you want to talk about. I'm not an expert in schizophrenia, but I'll try to answer as best I can."

"My brother told me that he heard voices. Do you know anything about that?" It was a weak version of the old "asking for a friend . . ." trick but Cady couldn't own it, not yet.

"Auditory hallucinations. They're common among schizophrenics."

"What are the voices generally like?"

"I think that sort of symptom varies pretty greatly from patient to patient."

"One thing Eric said that stayed with me was that the voices told him things he didn't otherwise know."

"Eric was your brother?"

"Yes, did you know him?"

"No, I'm just trying to follow your story."

"Oh. Anyway, I mean the voices would tell him about a book he'd never read, or the history of a building on campus that was before his time, and it was accurate information, pretty much."

Greg nodded but appeared otherwise blank.

Cady couldn't understand his lack of surprise. "I mean, that's weird, right? I remember him being kind of scared by it."

Greg parted his lips with a smack. "I'm sure it was scary for him. And it must be very difficult for you to walk through the same halls your brother walked, see the same sights. I see how that could be upsetting."

"But how is it possible to hallucinate something you didn't know? Eric thought it proved the voices were real, you know, not just in his head. I mean, how could a figment of his own imagination tell him something he didn't already know?"

"Well, there are a lot of explanations for that apparent . . . phenomenon, I guess you could call it. One possibility is that the facts the 'voice' gave are inaccurate. Schizophrenics are often good at sounding highly informed and educated, or privy to special knowledge, and because they believe what they're saying is true, they deliver it with confidence. Throw in a couple of big words and it can sound official, but in reality, it's fiction."

"But what if all the facts checked out, one hundred percent correct? I mean, theoretically, is that possible?"

"It can happen. Sometimes we've read or heard something at one point or another, and we forget that we did. Then, when we see those same facts packaged or presented in a different way, they appear new." Greg scratched his chin through his beard. "Like unintentional plagiarism. Some of the world's greatest scholars have accidentally plagiarized another scholar's work, because they forgot the origin of that information. This famously happened to the historian Doris Kearns Goodwin, a former Harvard professor, I might add. The point is, the mind can play tricks on you. The brain is a fallible organ."

Cady chewed on the inside of her cheek. The Dante reference could have been floating around sometime in her past, *Inferno* gets enough play in pop culture, it might've been a *Jeopardy!* question or something.

He went on, "You know, suicide is a tragedy unlike any other. It leaves a lot of complicated emotions in its wake. Anger, sorrow, guilt. There's a reason we call the family and friends of the victim 'suicide survivors.'"

Cady nodded, already trying to think of a way to leave as quickly and gracefully as possible.

"Have you participated in any grief counseling, with a psychologist, or perhaps a pastor or rabbi? Feelings of depression would be normal in this aftermath."

"No, it's not that. I'm okay on my own for now." *For now*—it echoed in her head.

"Something made you come here today."

Cady looked at her lap—now the only voices warring in her head were her own. She tried to summon the courage to tell the truth: *I'm afraid it will happen to me.*

She settled for a half-truth. "Sometimes I just feel so distracted. I came here with a clear idea of things I wanted to do and learn, but now that I'm here, I can't clear my head." She wanted to understand her brother, and now her own mental troubles were threatening that goal, one she had risked her family's well-being to pursue.

"So this isn't just about your brother. You want help focusing."

"Yes."

"Ah, I see." Greg sat back in his seat, his affect suddenly guarded. "We would need to be in more regular sessions before I could recommend a prescription, and until then, I would strongly discourage you from trying any of your friends' medication to help you focus. Adderall and its ilk are not candy."

"What?" Cady recoiled. "No, I'm not—I don't want *medication*."

"Good. You know what you should try?" Greg pressed his palms together and smiled. "Yoga."

# 15

CADY STEPPED OUTSIDE feeling like an idiot. No counselor was going to open Eric's file and hand it over, nor could anyone help her if she wasn't honest about her own experiences. But she couldn't be honest, not yet. Because once you're diagnosed with a mental illness, you don't get a say—she had seen that with Eric. For the first time, Cady felt she was gaining some insight into what was happening to her brother before he died, and she needed her freedom now more than ever.

So she flinched when she heard someone call her name as she was trying to discreetly descend the steps of the Study Bureau. Andrea waved as she scampered uphill on the brick sidewalk, her giant backpack thudding against her slight frame.

"Hey, I texted you. Do you have a class right now? Have you eaten lunch?" Andrea asked, slightly out of breath from her hustle.

"I'm supposed to be in Psych lecture, but—" Cady checked the time on her phone. "I've already missed half of it, I might as well make it official. I can get the notes from Ranjoo. She owes me."

"Oh, thank God. I hate eating alone."

Andrea said she wanted a change from Annenberg, so they walked around the corner to a restaurant called Clover. Clover was a funny mix of old and new; its walls were historic white tile with an upper border of tiled pennants belonging to private schools and other Ivy League colleges that, according to a sign, dated back to 1913, juxtaposed with a giant natural wood slab communal table in the center and digital menus on the wall. Cady and Andrea joined the long line of people waiting to give their order to a server holding an iPad.

"How was the rest of the Phoenix party?" Andrea asked. "You got back late. I heard the door, it woke me up."

"Sorry about that." Cady considered telling Andrea what happened but decided against it; she already felt overexposed leaving the bureau. "It sucked. You made the right call."

"What were you doing at the Study Bureau? Were you seeing a therapist?"

She hesitated to answer. "I was just checking it out. I don't think I'll go back, it wasn't that helpful."

"Okay. But you don't need to be embarrassed. I went to a psychiatrist back home. I used to have anxiety. But I beat it."

"With yoga?"

"No. Zoloft."

Cady snorted. Andrea could be annoying, but Cady admired how unfiltered she was. Maybe she didn't have to be so guarded all the time. "To be honest, I went to talk about my brother. He died last spring."

"Oh my God, I had no idea."

"I know, I didn't tell you. It's hard for me to talk about. It was suicide."

"Oh my God, that makes it worse!"

Again the blunt honesty made Cady laugh.

"I meant, worse for your family." Andrea made a pained expression. "Sorry, I don't know the right thing to say."

That made Cady only laugh harder. "Nobody does! And you're not wrong. It's definitely the worst."

"Did you see it coming?"

*That* stopped her giggles. "He'd been struggling with mental illness for the last couple years, schizophrenia, but I never thought . . ."

Her voice trailed off. "Now, looking back, I do see the signs. I think back all the time about where was the moment it turned for him, the moment before the point of no return, when we could have done something to save him. But we missed it." It was painful to say it out loud, but there was some relief in telling the truth for a change, even if she was still leaving out that he went to Harvard. "All we talk about at this school is potential, like what you do here is going to set you up for the rest of your life. But not all potential is good. Mental illness can be hereditary, and so I get scared sometimes, like, what if I have that in me?"

"No way. You seem so together."

"He did, too."

Andrea shook her head. "You can't think like that. It's like manifesting in reverse. If you worry about something too much, you can make it come true."

Then Cady was in real trouble.

"Why didn't you feel like you could mention this before?"

"I wanted you to get to know the normal me, not the tragic-story me, but the thing is, I don't feel normal since Eric died, so I end up just feeling fake. But I don't want people to tiptoe around me, you know?"

"Don't worry. I'm bad at that kind of thing anyway."

It was finally their turn to order. The server swiped their credit cards on her iPad and assured them they'd bring the food over. Cady and Andrea took window seats at the counter that faced Mass Ave.

"I wouldn't normally spend money like this, but it's my birthday, so it's okay."

"It's your birthday today? Happy birthday!"

"Thanks."

"Are you doing anything to celebrate, like a party or something?"

Andrea shrugged. "I don't really have enough friends here for a party."

"Aw, well, it's only because it comes up so early in the school year, nobody knows anybody yet. We should do something fun, you and me. Let's go out for dinner tonight."

"We're already out for lunch. And anyway, I can't. My Orgo study group is meeting over dinner."

"Oh my God, skip it. Your birthday celebration can't be a study group."

"I don't want to skip it," Andrea said, defensively. "I need to review." Then, a little softer, "and I like this one guy in my group, Marko. It's the only time I talk to him."

"Ooh, *Marko*," Cady said with a shimmy. "I take it back. Tell your study group it's your birthday and invite them, mainly Marko, back to our room for cake!"

"I can't invite him to a party with no other friends. I'd rather not celebrate at all than look pathetic."

Cady thought for a minute. "I have a better idea. When your study group is wrapping up, text me. Find some reason to get Marko to come back to our room, can you do that?"

"I'm supposed to bring copies of my chapter four notes for everyone. I could forget his." Andrea giggled.

"Perfect. So you text me when you're heading home, and I'll be in the room, waiting with the lights out and everything ready, and when you guys walk in, I'll shout 'Surprise!' I'll get Ranjoo in on it too, if I can." Cady was still determined to make the two of them get along better somehow. "You can play it cool like, 'Gosh, I wasn't even going to celebrate until later this weekend.'"

Andrea rolled her eyes with a smirk. "This is a full-on scheme."

"Yes, a birthday mission! We'll call it Operation: Marko Polo."

Andrea cracked up at that, and Cady laughed, too. She was thinking of the fun missions Eric used to set up for her, and for the first time on this campus, Cady felt warmed by his memory and excited to be sharing a moment with a new friend. "C'mon, we'll get a cake at Mike's Pastry after this, my treat."

A smile tucked into Andrea's rosy cheeks. "I've never had a surprise party before."

*　*　*

THE TWO ROOMMATES headed back to campus with their Mike's
Pastry booty: a luscious fudge layer cake in a big box, and, since they'd
agreed delayed gratification is overrated, they had each gotten a cannoli for the road—classic chocolate-chip for Cady and caramel pecan
for Andrea. They gossiped in between crunches as they walked
through the fallen leaves and bit into the crisp cannoli shells. Andrea
stopped walking just inside the great wrought-iron gates of the Yard
and began to giggle. "Cady, you are literally covered in powdered
sugar."

"I am? Oh my God, I really *am*! How are you not?" Cady said
through a mouthful. "Help me!"

Andrea began brushing her chest—"Are you trying to touch my
boobs?" Cady teased, making them both laugh harder—but it only
seemed to press the white sugar into her black wool coat. Andrea tried
to find more napkins through her tears of laughter, as Cady discovered
a new patch of snowy sugar on her person. "But seriously, how did I get
it on my shoulder?" Yet as Cady craned her neck, a small stone plaque
on the exterior of the yellow clapboard administrative building beside
them caught her eye.

As Cady read the words engraved upon it, the humor drained from
her like blood.

## WADSWORTH HOUSE

### TITUS & VENUS
LIVED AND WORKED HERE AS ENSLAVED PERSONS
IN THE HOUSEHOLD OF
PRESIDENT BENJAMIN WADSWORTH (1725–1737)

### JUBA & BILHAH
LIVED AND WORKED HERE AS ENSLAVED PERSONS IN THE
HOUSEHOLD OF
PRESIDENT EDWARD HOLYOKE (1737–1769)

Her memory replayed the words from that morning: *I'm Bilhah, the Holyokes' girl.*

"Okay, where else?" Andrea held a wad of napkins in her hand. Then she noticed what her roommate was staring at. "Oh, yeah, Harvard had slaves. Did you know that?"

Cady couldn't speak. *The president of Harvard don't need a mute houseboy.*

Andrea chattered on. "It's okay, nobody knew it for a long time. I read an article about it in the alumni magazine; my parents subscribe. The fact had been effectively buried, left out of every historical narrative, either by bad record keeping or willful ignorance. Doesn't really fit with the 'progressive bastion of higher education' label, right? Although in a way, it's progressive that they're acknowledging it now. Harvard deserves credit, even if I think Brown copped to it first."

But Cady heard only the terror, and the desperation. *I need your help to save my son!*

Andrea looked from the plaque back to Cady's ashen face. "Are you okay?"

This wasn't a well-known passage in a classic book, information she had learned but forgotten. This wasn't her imagination or a hallucination. This was etched in stone.

This was proof.

This was real.

# 16

CADY DIDN'T HAVE to pretend to feel normal with Andrea much longer, as she had had Prokop's physics colloquium to attend, so she sent Andrea home with the cake and walked the rest of the way herself. Was it better or worse that the voice she'd heard was coming from outside rather than inside her? If they weren't her own delusion, what did that make them, *ghosts*? Could she really believe that? She needed to stay skeptical, stay grounded. Thankfully, there was no place better to do that than the Science Center.

Cady arrived at the designated lecture hall and felt a pang of guilt to find it so close to where her Psych lecture was held. As soon as Cady pushed through the double doors, the smell of chalk filled her nose, and she quickly realized this was going to be nothing like the relaxed TED Talk style of Professor Bernstein's Psych lectures. The seats faced a full wall of blackboards, three across, and Cady could see that one on the far left was pushed upward to reveal another underneath. She took a seat near the back right corner and shuddered to imagine the type of math problem that would require six blackboards to solve.

*If you'd been here last year for Niels Bohr's lecture, you'd have some idea.*

Cady's breath caught.

*My dear, you look stricken.* Je vous demande donc grâce—*I only meant that his theories of atomic structure could fill the room. He just won the Nobel Prize in '22, they don't give those out for arithmetic. But he was mesmerizing, well worth the calcium carbonate.*

Cady recognized him from her medieval class, the Dante one.

*Yes, I'm a fan of Mr. Alighieri, though I'd prefer you call me Robert. I love literature, but at my essential self, I'm a man of science. Bohr only reminded me what a dreadful error I'd made declaring chemistry instead of physics. Men under twenty shouldn't be permitted to make life decisions.*

She debated whether or not she should leave. "Robert" prattled on.

*I was glued to my seat. No easy feat in these god-awful wooden chairs. The angle's all wrong, I think I'm too tall for them.*

The seat Cady sat in was molded and upholstered plastic. What world was this voice coming from?

*My two great loves are physics and New Mexico. It's a pity they can't be combined.*

She still wanted to believe this was a figment of her imagination, but his references were so specific, and not to her. How could she be imagining this when she'd never been to New Mexico?

*Never? Then you must plan a trip, it's the most remarkable country you'll ever see. So beautiful, wild, pure. That place changed my life, truly.*

Professor Prokop entered, along with the visiting speakers, Professor Daley from MIT and Professor Zhou from Columbia, and a moderator (all men, Cady noticed), plus a small phalanx of teaching fellows. More of the seats had filled in while Cady had been distracted, and now, to her surprise, the audience began to applaud. This lecture was a bigger deal than she had realized, and she was having either a paranormal experience or a psychotic episode in the middle of it.

Cady tried to calm herself by thinking of the soothing song they rehearsed earlier that day at Collegium. It was just like in choir—she didn't have to understand the lecture or even participate—all she had to do was blend.

And listen to the voices around her.

She shook that last thought from her head.

Cady redirected her gaze to the front of the room. The moderator

was introducing each professor, listing their numerous degrees and accolades. Prokop's list of accomplishments went on for a solid minute.

The voice, thankfully, seemed to have fallen silent, and the lecture got under way. Cady looked around the room. Although fewer
than half of the seats were filled, none of these students seemed like
the casual lecture attendee who half-listens and surfs the Internet.
Few had laptops at all, and most sat forward, listening intently, occasionally posing questions beyond Cady's comprehension. Those in at-
tendance were a rarefied group, even by Harvard's standards, and they
were all held in rapt attention by Professor Prokop.

But it remained difficult for Cady to focus on the content of the
lecture. She was trapped in anxious anticipation of the possible return
of the voice that called itself Robert, anticipation and something
else—curiosity.

Her mind wandered, and as if sensing an opening . . .

*I met Katherine in New Mexico.*

In spite of her saner judgment, Cady listened.

*We stayed at her dude ranch in Los Piños. This was the summer before
Harvard, I was only nineteen. She was twenty-eight. Married. Utterly un-
attainable. Which I suppose added to her allure. But it was more than that.*

*She ran that ranch all by herself. She had hidalgo blood. The ranch
hands respected her, so did the horses. Even the mustangs seemed to recognize her as one of their own. She was commanding.*

*Commanding*—the word resonated in Cady's mind as she watched
Professor Prokop. Prokop was wholly transformed from the soft-
spoken, self-effacing woman Cady had met in the Science Center
café; this woman was confident and, yes, commanding. She strutted
across the lecture hall floor dressed simply in black slacks and a white
oxford shirt. She wrote on the blackboard with flourish, her marks
slanted and large, striking the chalk with such force that the garments
on her slim frame trembled.

*She took an unlikely shine to me. She'd take me out riding through the
Jemez Mountains for days at a time, with only whiskey and peanut butter
sandwiches for sustenance. Despite her beauty, there was nothing precious*

*about her. She'd think nothing of kneeling in the mud to pick up a horse's hoof and hammer a nail into a loose shoe.*

Prokop was barely letting her colleague Professor Daley talk, and when she got excited, she had the funny habit of raking her fingers through her hair until it began slipping from her ponytail in pieces.

*Katherine had grown up in the Pecos. She could read the land like a Hopi tracker. She was in her element.*

Just then, the young male teaching fellow assisting her made some sort of math joke, and Prokop burst forth with a boisterous laugh that Cady wouldn't have guessed she had in her. Here she was masterful and charismatic. This was *her* element.

*I was probably in love with her.*

Listening to the voice, Cady saw Prokop in a new light.

*Or I came to crave her approval, which might be the same thing.*

She tried to look at her through Eric's eyes. How did *he* see this professor?

*I would have followed her to the ends of the earth. Luckily, she took me only as far as Los Alamos.*

She didn't hear from "Robert" again after that, but Cady remained preoccupied by his story and how it might be analogous to that of Eric and Prokop. She wondered if this was the connection she was intended to draw. Was this the voice's purpose, to give her insight into her brother? Eric had always been proud of his academic abilities, and he had a strong work ethic, so it hadn't seemed unusual when he was adamant about staying on campus to continue working on his Bauer project, despite his family's begging him to come home. But now, as she watched Professor Prokop—masterful, charming, "in her element"—she could see how he might have had other motivation to stay on campus. Surely Eric, too, had "craved her approval." Had he thought he was in love?

Absorbed in her thoughts, Cady didn't realize the lecture had ended until the people around her started to shift and get out of their seats. She gathered her things slowly; she had come to talk to Prokop but found herself newly intimidated. Cady loitered in the middle of the seats, waiting for the stragglers to have their moment with the professors and planning her opener. She hoped Prokop would notice her, but she was speaking animatedly to her TF as he erased her calculations from the board, leaving behind a ghostly outline of the letters and symbols. It was the TF who finally spotted Cady waiting. He leaned over and said something in Prokop's ear; Cady noticed he touched her arm when he did so.

Prokop's head snapped in Cady's direction with the precision of an owl.

Cady took tentative steps forward. "Hi, I'm—"

"Cadence, good to see you. I'm glad you could make it." Prokop smiled. "Did you enjoy the lecture?"

"Yes, or what I understood of it."

"Take my class next semester, we'll fix that." Prokop diverted her gaze to some papers on the desk in front of her.

Cady felt suddenly dry-mouthed. Prokop had a way of charging the atmosphere. "You mentioned you might have time to talk?"

"I did, didn't I?" She paused to squint, then returned her gaze to the papers. "I'm sorry, my schedule has become compacted today, perhaps next week would be better. I have office hours on Thursdays at four."

"I know, but I'd rather not wait, and I won't take much of your time, if you have a minute now . . ." Cady waited for Prokop to finish writing something down, fearing she had already lost her attention. "Do you have a minute?"

Prokop finally looked up. "You are persistent like your brother." Then she turned to the TF and said something in what sounded like Russian; he answered her in kind. She took her time putting her things into her laptop bag, saying goodbye to Professor Zhou when he passed, thanking the other TFs. Cady had the sense Prokop was daring her to leave, and she wanted to, but she fought the creeping sensation of awkwardness and stood, waiting. Finally Prokop ceased moving, smoothed her hands over her clothes, unaware of the faint chalk marks she was leaving on her black slacks, and met Cady's gaze. "Come. You can walk me to the T."

Cady would take what she could get. What she got was scampering at Prokop's heels through the halls of the Science Center. Prokop had to be five foot nine at least, and she took long, purposeful strides.

"Please, go ahead," Prokop said.

"I want to know what Eric was working on before he got too sick."

"Well," Prokop began, "his initial research for the Bauer involved taking data from the Large Hadron Collider experiments, searching for Kaluza-Klein modes, and interpreting their properties in order to draw conclusions about the geometry of the hidden, extra dimension whence they came." Without breaking her stride, she threw a glance at Cady. "I imagine you don't know what that means."

"Not really, but I can follow along."

Prokop sighed. "It's very complicated. It is not a conversation for a walk to the train."

"That's all you would give me."

"You couldn't wait until next week." Prokop pushed through the revolving glass doors, slipping between the rotating panels before Cady could catch her. "Even if we had time, I'm afraid you wouldn't understand."

"My big brother killed himself, it can't be any harder to understand than that."

Prokop stopped and her pale eyes scanned Cady's face, her expression softening. "I'm sorry, I've upset you, and this is exactly what I don't want to do. I can speak to you about any abstraction in quantum physics, but I'm not as fluent with the spectra of emotion. The last thing I want to do is add to your pain."

"No, I'm fine." Cady quieted her tone. "Please, I just need the headlines of what you two were working on. Don't worry about upsetting me, leave the emotion out of it."

"All right. I can do that."

They walked through the Yard, which was quieter on the weekends, and this Friday afternoon, it was warmer than it had been. People had laid out blankets on the grass, some chatted and ate, others read, a trio tossed a Frisbee, all enjoying an afternoon in the dappled sunlight beneath the fiery-colored trees. Cady longed to know the school and the life those students knew, the one of new friends and carefree afternoons. She felt no more a part of that scene than one would while watching a movie.

Meanwhile, Professor Prokop was doing her best to describe another foreign world to her. "Let me try to give you a quick frame of reference. There are certain questions posed by our universe that are not explained by the standard model of particle physics. The classic example is, why is gravity so weak?"

"Is it weak?"

"Of course it is. A small magnet will allow a paper clip to defy gravity. It is disproportionately weaker than the other three elementary forces, which are . . ." Professor Prokop shot Cady a teacherly glance.

"You're asking me? I have no idea."

Prokop lifted an eyebrow. "You are lucky you're not in one of my classes. The other three are electromagnetism, strong nuclear forces, and weak nuclear forces. When we consider the disparate weakness of gravity, it raises big questions, such as, is our world what it appears? The short answer is no." An errant soccer ball bounced across their path, which Prokop deftly stopped with her foot, even in her low-heeled pump. "We experience the world as having three dimensions, back-forward, left-right, and up-down. See?" She demonstrated each direction with the ball, even lifting it on the bridge of her foot. "We are not physiologically capable of perceiving anything more. But there is no theory that dictates there are only three dimensions. It is only logical to think that there are others." A final swift kick sent the ball sailing back to the students on the green with surprising accuracy. A few clapped, but Prokop barely acknowledged them and resumed walking.

Cady was dazzled, struggling to follow the logic. "There are more than three dimensions?"

"Yes, without question. Einstein introduced time as the fourth dimension, and his theory of relativity proved that time and space are inextricable, woven together in a fabric he dubbed space-time. String theory postulates nine or ten dimensions. There could be more hidden dimensions, we don't know yet."

"When you say 'hidden dimension,' what does that even mean? Like a parallel universe?" Cady felt silly even saying it.

"Parallel universes—in the community, we call them supersymmetry theories, and they had their moment, but they've fallen out of favor," Prokop answered matter-of-factly. "Warped geometry, to borrow my colleague's term, is the current hypothesis."

"Warped how?"

"Hidden dimensions could be any size and shape. One could be 'compactified'—squeezed into a circle whose diameter in centimeters is ten to the negative thirty-third power, or one thousandth of a millionth of a trillionth of a centimeter. Or an extra dimension could be infinite and expansive. The shape could be curved, rolled up like a spool of thread, or doubled back on itself like a snake."

"Doubled back?" Cady thought of the voices in her head, seemingly coming from the past. "What would cause distortion like that?"

"Any matter or energy can distort space-time. Are you familiar with the terms 'dark matter' and 'dark energy'?"

Cady shuddered and shook her head; they sounded sinister.

"Dark energy is energy in the universe that we cannot see but that we know is there. Only about four percent of the universe as we know it is observable light matter. The other ninety-six percent is dark matter and dark energy."

Invisible forces. "So we can see almost none of what's really there?"

"Correct."

"If we aren't capable of perceiving this matter or other dimensions, how can we tell they exist?"

"They leave behind tracks in our three-dimensional world. We can discover indirect evidence of these hidden dimensions and build from there, the way a shadow gives us information of size and shape of an object or an echo can tell us direction and distance of a sound. I tell my students to think of it like a crime scene, we can dust for fingerprints of the hidden dimensions left behind in our world. This is what your brother's project looked into: the study of those particles that travel in the hidden dimension yet leave traces in our recognized three-dimensional world."

"He was trying to find proof of the extra dimensions?"

"Yes, but proof means something very different for a physicist than it might for a mathematician or a detective. Many of the phenomena we are considering are difficult or impossible to measure. It is hard to find *the* answer, so we search for the best answer. The universe will always have its secrets." They had passed out of the Yard and stopped at the streetlight, waiting to cross Mass Ave. Now that they were out of the shade of the elm trees, Cady could see that Professor Prokop's expression had relaxed since they started their walk. "Eric was wonderful," Prokop continued. "Such passion. He wasn't afraid to tackle the big ideas. Other students want to approach only the problems they know they will be able to find the answer to. Their work is a means to an end, or rather, to an A. Your brother was different. He threw himself at the impossible questions with the true spirit of discovery. No challenge I gave him was too great. He had such promise."

"So what went wrong?"

The light turned green and Prokop set off across the street with haste, the tightness at the corners of her mouth reappearing. "He forgot the cardinal rule that you must let the evidence and data speak to you, you must let the math pose the questions. You can't go hunting for other dimensions. They are elusive and intangible by definition. If you pursue your own agenda, you poison the process."

Cady scurried after her. "You think he was looking for something specific?"

"I didn't know what he was looking for. He lost sight of our original objectives for the project and veered off track. Before long, work that could've been brilliant became ridiculous. I tried to talk to him, but he wouldn't listen. My constructive criticism was viewed with great suspicion, what I later understood to be his paranoia. It wasn't his fault, of course, I suppose his illness took over. It interfered with everything. That's why I had to relieve him of his duties in my lab."

They had reached the Harvard T station, a glass-covered outpost with stairs and an escalator to the underground. Cady leaped onto the escalator ahead of Prokop, just to slow her down. As they descended into the dark subway station, Cady asked more questions. "What if he was trying to explain phenomena he was experiencing?"

"Experiencing how? Psychologically?"

"Or, I don't know, subatomically? What if he was tapping in to an extra dimension?"

"I don't understand what you're asking."

"His mental illness." Cady stumbled as she stepped backward off the escalator. "He was having delusions, paranoia, maybe hallucinations, voices. He had been diagnosed with schizophrenia. But maybe he was looking for another answer."

"It's possible that he thought that, but he would have been wrong, that's a delusion in itself." Prokop tried to step around her, but Cady stayed at her shoulder.

"But it's like you said, 'fingerprints' of other times, space-time folded over itself. What if the things he heard were echoes of voices, from this same place but from the past, like strings reverberating from a different era?"

Prokop shook her head, exasperated. "No, no. You're extrapolating and twisting my words. There is real quantum mechanics behind this that you simply don't understand. It isn't science fiction. I told you, we are not capable of registering any extra dimension."

"But what if one person could?" Or two.

"It's not possible. Please, I have to go." Prokop slipped by her, swiped her CharlieCard to pay the fare, and pushed through the turnstile.

"Just one minute." Cady hopped over the turnstile to keep up. A low rumbling began in the station like faraway thunder.

"The train, it comes."

"How can you know for sure someone couldn't sense another dimension?" Cady was shouting over the shudder of the train.

The banshee wail of the train screeching into the platform silenced any further argument as Prokop shook her head in dismay. When it quieted to a stop, she put a hand on Cady's shoulder and said, "Your brother had a brilliant mind taken over by illness. Don't follow him down that path, it leads nowhere. That's why I had to let him go. I advise you to do the same."

Prokop disappeared inside the subway car, leaving Cady behind as bodies pushed past her in both directions. When the train pulled away and the platform finally emptied, Cady was still standing there, unmoved by the professor's warning. It couldn't be pure delusion. How could she have conjured Bilhah's name? Imagined New Mexico? Read books she'd never opened? She was tapping in to something, some dimension on this campus where time had warped.

And there was no time to waste.

# 17

IF CADY HAD been thinking clearly, she might have regretted losing her composure with Professor Prokop, but she wasn't thinking clearly. It felt like an electrical storm firing in her brain, with each burning question briefly illuminated before a new one took its place. Did Eric hear voices like the ones she was hearing now? Was he trying to explain the voices in his research on multiple dimensions? Or was she alone in that?

But she couldn't ask Eric about the voices he had heard, if he'd heard any at all. His voice was lost to her now, and as Professor Prokop said, the universe will always have its secrets. But something about the science Prokop described resonated with Cady's experience. The two voices she heard did sound as if they were from different eras in Harvard's past—in their references, their music, their dated descriptions of her campus surroundings. It was like space-time folded over, the past layered on the present, echoes from another era.

Prokop didn't believe it was possible. She said Eric's research had become "ridiculous." But maybe that was only because Eric never shared his best evidence with her, knowing how crazy he would sound. He wouldn't risk losing the esteem of his crushworthy professor. Cady knew she was speculating wildly, but she also knew how fiercely Eric guarded his reputation around teachers he admired. She knew how much the respect of his teachers mattered to Eric, and how much their pity crushed him. She had seen it firsthand last year.

Eric had surprised her by picking her up at school. It was the fall of her senior year, his junior year at Harvard, and he was home on Thanksgiving break. She remembered the way he looked leaning against the side of the blue Volkswagen, wearing rumpled plaid PJ pants and a cat-hair-covered fleece pullover.

"You didn't have to dress up for me," Cady said. She was making a joke of it, but Eric cared less and less about his personal appearance since he'd gotten sick, and she wasn't thrilled for people to see him like this. But she supposed she should be happy that his disregard for other people's opinions remained intact.

"I'm on vacation," Eric said, walking toward her and away from the car.

"Where are you going? I'm supposed to get in the car, not you get out of it, that's how this driving me home thing works."

"I want to go in and say hi to some teachers."

"Seriously? Come on, let's just go."

"I haven't been back since graduation. You can come with me or wait in the car."

Cady made a show of being annoyed, but of course she was going with him. She plucked cat hair off his fleece the entire way to the lobby.

As soon as they walked through the big glass double doors, Cady realized why Eric wanted to visit—he was given a hero's welcome, not by the students, who were blasé about everything, but from the adults in the building. The office ladies popped out to give him a hug when they saw him through the glass, and every passing teacher stopped to say hello and make flattering small talk; they didn't, or pretended not to, notice his schlubby appearance. Eric wasn't the only Dixon Porter graduate to get into an Ivy League college, but there was something about him, his prodigious intellect mixed with boyish sweetness, that never failed to charm. People wanted good things for him.

In the past, watching Eric eat up the attention might have irritated the little sister in Cady, but he looked happier than he had in a while, certainly since his diagnosis last spring. These were the people who knew only a healthy and happy Eric, and around them he became so. Cady liked seeing him like this; it relaxed her.

Eric said he wanted to see Mr. Moore, his old physics teacher and track coach, a particular favorite. Cady currently had him for AP Physics. She had just that day received a B on her last test, practically failing for her, which both she and Mr. Moore knew. She didn't want to see him today. As they walked into his classroom, she thought, *Eric, you owe me for this*.

"Hey, man! What a surprise, get over here." Mr. Moore sprang up from his desk, arms outstretched, and gave Eric a bear hug. He kept himself in good shape for a man his age, but he always looked a little crazy in his trademark Hawaiian shirts and curly salt-and-pepper hair. "How the heck are ya? What's new in Beantown?"

They talked a bit, Mr. Moore brought up an educators' conference he was organizing later in the spring and asked Eric to be a student speaker. Eric said he would like that and would have to get back to him. At the time, Cady remembered naively thinking—*good, by next spring, he'll be better.*

"Cady tells me you're working on some big project, how's it going?"

"It's going."

"What's the topic?"

Eric's attention wandered to a small desk toy with five steel balls suspended between two racks. "What are these things called again?"

"Newton's Cradle, because of the—"

"Conservation of energy, equal and opposite reactions." Eric smirked. "I listened in class."

"Sure did, best student I ever had," Mr. Moore said, clapping a hand on Eric's back. "So the project, it's like a contest, right? The Bayer Award?"

"The Bauer." Eric pulled back one of the metal balls and let it drop. The silver ball collided with the resting ones with a loud *clack*, causing the one on the other side to follow suit, instigating a tennis match of percussion.

Mr. Moore did his best to talk over the noise. "That's it. I've actually heard of it before. It's awesome that you're going for it, man. We're all rooting for you."

"Thanks." Eric wouldn't make eye contact.

"So what's it about?"

Instead of answering, Eric caught two balls on one end and released them so that the lineup clattered back and forth like galloping hooves.

Mr. Moore smiled and eyed Eric and Cady both, as though they were playing a joke on him. "What is it, top secret?"

"Eric," Cady said under her breath, shooting him one of their mother's *Stop fidgeting* glares. But he didn't look up to catch it. He continued to tweak the silver balls to change the rhythm.

Mr. Moore lifted his eyebrows in mild annoyance. "Well, whatever it is, we're all behind you. Dixon Porter High is very excited to see what you become."

Just then, one of the balls snapped on Eric's finger and he yanked his hand back, pulling the entire contraption off the desk and sending it crashing to the ground. Cady and Eric both quickly knelt to get it, nearly knocking their heads like the Newton's Cradle balls, but Eric beat her to it. He picked up the toy with shaking hands. The strings were tangled and the corner was chipped.

"You okay, Eric?" Mr. Moore asked.

"I broke it."

Mr. Moore took it from his hands. "Oh, don't worry about it. But are you all right?" His eyes searched Eric's face, which was now beet red.

"I'm sorry," Eric said, backing away.

"It's just a ding on the base, it's not a big deal."

"Sorry," Eric repeated.

"Buddy, I teach sixty teenagers every day, you think you're the first to break something?"

But Eric wasn't listening. Without a word to either of them, Eric hurried out the door.

"Wait, Eric, don't go," Moore called after him, before turning to Cady in confusion. "Is he serious?"

Cady apologized quickly and darted out into the hall. She called Eric's name, but he didn't turn around. He was storming down the hall toward the exit. She had to jog to catch up to him. "What's your deal?"

"I didn't want to talk to him anymore."

"So then you say, 'Goodbye, Mr. Moore, nice talking to you.' You don't just leave. That was rude."

"We have to get home."

"I have to see him in class tomorrow, so it'd be nice if we didn't burn bridges for no reason."

Eric didn't seem to be paying attention. Cady felt like a dog scampering at his heels as they crossed the driveway to the parking lot. She didn't speak again until they got into the car.

"Eric, all I was saying is that I think you overreacted. You're making this big thing out of it in your head, but it really was just a ding. He wasn't mad at you, okay? He didn't even care."

"I care."

"About a stupid science toy?" Cady looked down to plug her seat belt into the buckle. When she glanced back, she gasped.

Eric held on to the steering wheel with his arms locked, bracing himself against the surge of emotion now contorting his face. His chin and lips trembled and his eyes were squeezed shut, but when the tears came, every joint seemed to loosen as he slumped in the seat. Saliva bubbled at his lip as he sobbed through the words: "I don't want him to know. I don't want him to know about me, about the way I am now."

Cady had never seen him break down like that. He kept so much in.

She roughly wiped a tear from her cheek and refocused on the present. Yes, it was possible that Cady had no idea what she was talking about when it came to Eric's symptoms or quantum physics. Much like it was possible that Eric was simply crowbarring scientific theory onto textbook symptoms of schizophrenia. But what if he had been right? What if they had found a way to tap in to another dimension?

*They.*

Now that she was hearing voices, too, Cady needed to understand exactly what was going on with Eric that last year of his life. Her own life might depend on it.

There was another person who had been close to Eric, who had been there for him during his years at Harvard, even if he did skip the funeral. He was likely the only person on campus who had witnessed Eric's day-to-day symptoms firsthand. And Cady couldn't put off finding him any longer.

# 18

AS SOON AS Matt Cho answered the door, Cady doubted her decision to come. Matt had been Eric's best friend and roommate all three years, and as Cady had known him, he'd had a pleasant chubbiness to him, a mischievous smile, and an infectious laugh. Matt's charm had been irresistible, and Cady had once thought Eric was lucky to have him as a sort of social Seeing Eye dog. Now he stood before her looking completely different. He'd lost a significant amount of weight; his polo shirt draped over his small shoulders and was tucked into his belted jeans. His eyes looked tired behind smudgy glasses. When he saw her, a flash of warmth and surprise passed over his face but evaporated just as quickly.

"Hey, Cady, wow. Good to see you."

Cady said hello back and made the hasty decision to hug him, maybe because he looked as if he needed it. "How are you doing?"

Matt shrugged. "I heard you were on campus. I'm sorry I haven't been by to say hello or anything. I've been meaning to, but . . ." He trailed off.

"Oh, gosh, don't worry about it." Cady shook her head. "I know senior year must be insanely busy."

"I'm not technically a senior, because, you know, I took last spring off." He pressed his lips together in a flat line and looked down.

Cady hadn't known that he'd taken a semester off after Eric died.

"But anyway, yeah, this place is kind of always busy. So." He made an effort to brighten his expression. "What's up?"

She was reluctant to make Matt relive last year's events but desperate for answers. Desperation won. "Can we talk?" Cady suggested Starbucks, but Matt nixed it. "I've cut out coffee, I haven't been sleeping well." Instead, he took her to Tealuxe, a small, cozy teahouse in Harvard Square. She could see how this place could soothe one's nerves—the place was small but uncrowded, painted midnight blue and perfumed with the spicy-sweet scent of chai, and with only a few tables up front and a few more at the back, it felt quiet and private. Behind the counter was a giant apothecary cabinet with rows and rows of every possible tea variety; Cady let Matt choose.

"It seems I'm always fighting a cold, so let's go with Echinacea."

The man behind the counter had curly hair like a wilted plant. "I'm sorry, but we're out of that. My co-worker dropped the whole bag today and spilled it." He sniffed, and Cady noticed his septum piercing.

"What else is good for colds?"

"Chamomile and rose hips," Cady blurted out.

"That's right, actually, rose hip has a lot of vitamin C, most people don't know that. Are you an herbalist?"

Cady shook her head. She had learned it from Bilhah that morning but instantly regretted sharing it.

"We put rose hips in our Throat Tender blend. Is that good?"

Matt agreed, and Cady insisted on paying. She was about to drop the spare change into the tip jar, when she noticed that it was an actual funerary urn. GLAD WE URNED YOUR TIP! read the sign. Cady pointed to it. "Morbid sense of humor."

"Death is everywhere at this school. Plaques in memorial to this person or that, the colonial cemetery right across from Johnston Gate. Once you start to notice it you can't stop," Matt said, matter-of-factly. "You're probably the only person I can say that to and not sound crazy, but it's true. It's everyone else who's in denial."

They sat at one of the small café tables in the back; its copper tabletop showed hundreds of tiny dings, dents, and scratches. Cady marveled that teacups left such scars, while the wounds that she and Matt had left no marks at all.

Cady poured him a cup of steaming amber tea. "Have you been okay this past year?"

"Have *you?*" He tilted his head. "The answer is, not really, but you're the last person I'd complain to."

"Well, you can. That's part of why I wanted to talk to you. You're the only one who gets it. Like you said, this place is different for us. I feel crazy to everyone else."

He nodded. "I hear that. I mostly try to distract myself, sometimes it even works. I'm not very good at 'self-care,'" he said with disdainful air quotes, "but I started going to Mem Church services. I don't know if church is your thing, but it's been good for me. I work a lot in the church student center downstairs; it's new, so it's like the one place I didn't used to hang out with Eric, which gives me a break from re-membering. I can actually think clearly there."

Cady missed "thinking clearly." Right now, all she could think of was how to broach the subject of Eric's illness when Matt had just finished telling her he was trying to forget about it. She could hardly look at him, and she wondered if her pain was as obvious as his. In any case, she was losing her nerve. It was Matt who broke the silence again:

"I'm sorry I didn't go to the funeral. It was a piece of shit thing to do, I feel terrible about it still." He took a sip of his tea and Cady could see his hand was shaking. "I couldn't face your family."

"Matt," Cady said softly, wishing she knew him well enough to reach out and touch him. She remembered learning that Matt had been out the night Eric had jumped; he had stayed in the library all night studying for an exam the next morning. When she searched for someone to blame, his name had certainly come to mind, but her anger then had been scattershot, and most of her recriminations boomeranged back on herself anyway. Looking at Matt now, she felt only compassion. Matt had been a friend to her brother when Eric was at his worst; Matt had been there when she and her parents weren't. She had been disappointed in him when he skipped the funeral, but now she recognized it was an oversight that her family hadn't checked in with him.

"I hope you know we don't blame you for anything." Then Cady heard herself say all the canned comfort phrases that she hated: "Eric had an illness. It's not your fault, it's nobody's fault. It was Eric's decision."

"I should have been there." Matt's face and neck became red. "I knew things were bad, but things had been bad for so long, I guess I got used to it. I thought he would just coast like that. But I think all the time how things might've been different if I hadn't stayed late at Cabot studying for a stupid test."

"No, don't do that. You couldn't watch him every minute, that wasn't your responsibility. And you could never have expected he would do what he did, none of us did."

"Even if I couldn't have stopped him, I think, what if I'd been there to call the ambulance, what if they'd gotten to him faster, what if something could've been done?"

"There was nothing. He died on impact." *Died on impact*—she sounded like her mother. In the weeks after Eric's death, her mother had become obsessed with the exact sequence of events following Eric's fatal fall, hunting down every first responder and Harvard official involved. Her mother had talked herself, and Cady, and her father, through Eric's final moments often. The grieving mind seems to fixate on certain details, and the knowledge that her son didn't suffer in his last moment seemed to mitigate the knowledge that he suffered so badly in all the moments leading up to it. Cady, on the other hand, found little comfort in these details. They only armed her nightmares and imbued her imagination with the knife-sharp clarity of a memory. In her mind's eye, she could conjure the image of his death as if she had seen it firsthand. *Died on impact*—the words were quick, but brutal and violent. Sometimes she wished he had taken pills, so that she could at least envision his face peaceful.

But maybe Matt was more like her mother. She continued, "Someone did call 911, we don't know who, but someone did, and the ambulance came right away, but there was nothing anyone could do."

"Really?"

Cady nodded.

Matt sniffed and blinked away the wetness in his puffy eyes. "I guess it was stupid to think that would make me feel better." He took a slow sip of his tea before looking at Cady again. "Anyway, you don't have to make me feel better. You want to talk about Eric, right?"

"Is that okay?"

Matt nodded.

Cady took a deep breath and tried to remember the questions she had rehearsed. "Eric experienced the worst of his schizophrenia symptoms here at school, and the times he did come home, I tried to give him a break from talking about it. But I feel like I don't even know the version of my brother that killed himself, and it just feels . . . wrong. I want to know the truth about what was going on with him his last year here—what he was working on, what his illness was like. I was hoping you could help me fill in the blanks."

"Eric didn't really open up to me about his symptoms. Maybe he complained about his meds from time to time, but he certainly didn't go into details with me."

"But you lived with him, you must have seen the changes in him."

"Yeah."

Cady could tell he was uncomfortable with the conversation, but she needed to know more. "So what was the first change that you noticed?"

"He got more withdrawn. We stopped goofing around like we used to. Some days, he'd be real quiet and sort of zone out. Other times he'd be anxious and jumpy and talking a mile a minute. I knew something was wrong."

"Do you know if he heard voices?"

Matt shrugged. "Like I said, he didn't like to talk about it. When he told me he'd been diagnosed with schizophrenia, I knew a symptom like that was possible—I watch TV—but he didn't get into it. He talked to me less and less, especially that last winter, when I guess he got paranoid."

"How so?"

"He became super-secretive about everything. He'd lock his bedroom door, he wouldn't tell me what he was working on, he'd leave the room, and if I asked him where he was going, he wouldn't tell me. I was his best friend, and he didn't trust me. I knew it was his sickness, but you know, it hurt."

Matt blew his nose into a napkin. "I probably took it too personally, but I stopped trying with him. I was over it. I was over Eric." As soon as he'd said his name, the tears welled again. "I feel terrible about it now."

"No, I understand," Cady said with sympathy. "I backed off, too. It was a lot, and you were the one here dealing with him."

Matt took off his glasses to wipe his eyes. "I don't want you to think I was sitting around the room being a dick to him. I loved the guy, he wore me out, but I loved him like a brother."

"I know—"

"He pulled away from me, not the other way around. He was never in the room, he practically lived at the Science Center, working with his adviser at all hours. And when he wasn't in the lab, he was busy with errands for her. I felt like he was avoiding me. We never got meals together anymore—God, I sound like his jealous wife."

*All hours.* Cady thought of Prokop in that lecture earlier, charismatic, masterful, and, as Cady saw it now, attractive. She remembered Robert's voice saying *I was probably in love with her.*

"He was close with that adviser. Obsessed. I swear, he didn't shut up about her after he took some class with her freshman spring. I think he took every class she taught after that. There was no other professor he wanted to advise him for the Bauer. He dropped every activity to devote more time to whatever she needed him for. He thought she was a genius."

Again, her memory returned to that voice: *I came to crave her approval.* Her hunch that Eric's admiration for Prokop was more than just academic grew stronger, but she was reluctant to embrace any idea suggested by a strange voice in her head. "When she fired him from that research assistant job, it must have crushed him."

"He wasn't fired, he quit. At least that's what he told me." Matt took a sip of tea.

Cady frowned. Maybe Eric had lied to him to save face.

Matt continued, "I didn't even know there was trouble until his adviser showed up and banged on the door."

"On the door of your dorm room?"

"Yeah, it was nuts. She was demanding that he talk to her, begging at one point. He hadn't been answering any of her calls or emails— I could hear her saying that from the other side of the door. But he wouldn't open it, and he told me under no circumstances should I let her in, like she was *dangerous*. He said we could get in trouble with the FBI." Matt made an incredulous face. "When he got delusional like that, I didn't push it. All of a sudden, Mika went from being his favorite person to enemy number one."

"Wait, who's Mika? I thought we were talking about his adviser, Professor Prokop."

"Oh, right, same person, but Eric called her Mika, so that's all I ever heard."

*M. M is for Mika, not Matt,* Cady thought. His notes were about her. Eric had been the favorite of many teachers in high school, but he never called any by their first name, much less a nickname. A nickname was intimate, validating Robert's hunch again. "Do you think he was in love with her?"

"I don't know about love. It didn't hurt that she was a tall blonde. She doesn't do it for me, she's got that Ice Princess thing going on a little too much, but I got it. She's youngish, pretty, and has a PhD—by geek standards, she's smoking hot."

"But seriously. Is it possible that the feeling was mutual, that they were . . . involved?"

Matt frowned at first, but then his brow softened. "It certainly didn't occur to me then, but looking back, he was so sick, he had already bailed on the Bauer—it's hard to think of another reason that she'd keep him working as her assistant when he was in that state."

"He bailed on the Bauer before he quit?" Prokop had made it sound as if she had reluctantly fired Eric after his Bauer project went south; she hadn't mentioned his helping her with anything else, and she certainly hadn't mentioned trying to get him back.

"Yeah, he dropped that pretty early that fall. He was just working on her research stuff, he said he couldn't tell me what it was. But look, I don't know what happened between them. I'll only say she must have cared about him a lot, because when she was at our door that night, she seemed genuinely distraught. When he wouldn't talk to her, I thought she was going to cry." Matt paused. "Cry, or break the door down."

# 19

CADY LEFT TEALUXE with her thoughts churning. The M in Eric's notebook wasn't Matt, it was Mika, his pet name for his adviser. She reviewed every mention of "M," rereading with new eyes notes like *Dinner at M's, call M, birthday drink for M, M 8pm, M 10:30pm, M 7am*. They clearly spent a lot of time together, often outside normal school hours. But then something happened between them, something bad. Prokop said she fired Eric, Eric said he'd quit; until an hour ago, Cady would have believed a professor over her mentally ill brother without question, but after hearing Matt's account of Prokop's visit to their dorm room, banging on the door, begging to talk to Eric, Prokop's version no longer made sense. Prokop had wanted him to continue working with her—desperately, it seemed.

But why would Prokop lie?

It wasn't like firing Eric made her look better in regard to his death. Eric's suicide wasn't explicitly anyone's fault but his own, but Prokop's assertion that she fired Eric, a fragile student who took his own life soon after, arguably made her look worse than if Eric had quit of his own accord. The lie was more awkward than the truth.

Or was it?

Cady hated that her maybe-imaginary friend first planted the idea, but she now fully accepted the notion that Eric had loved Prokop—the long hours "working" with her at the lab, after-hours errands, Eric's obsession with "Mika"—it made sense. Prokop's oversized reaction when he broke things off indicated that she had strong feelings for him, too.

Did Prokop lie about firing Eric to cover the fact that they were having an affair?

She was almost home when a text pinged on her phone. It was Ranjoo saying she was having friends over to "pregame" before going out, which meant doing shots, taking photos, and blasting music. It was the last thing Cady felt like doing. She stopped walking in front of her dorm, newly reluctant to enter. She craved privacy, some peace and quiet, a place where she could think. But where could she go? The campus transformed on Friday nights. The pall of pending exams, paper deadlines, and unread reading assignments was temporarily lifted, or at least drowned in cheap alcohol, and she knew that everyone inside the warm, bright building would be boisterous and loud. She looked across the Yard and saw Memorial Church, lit with warm spotlights on its robin's-egg-blue door and red brick and white spire, giving it the idyllic appearance of a building in a model train set, and remembered what Matt had said about how it had helped him. It was late, but she wondered if the student center was still open. She figured it couldn't hurt to check. She bypassed Weld and crossed the green.

Up close, the church looked dark and closed, but Cady mounted the church steps to read a board with the service schedule. Maybe she would go to a service that weekend, although treating possible hallucinations with religion felt uncomfortably close to seeking an exorcist. But from the corner of her eye, she noticed the farthest right door to the church was ajar. It felt like a sign. After a quick glance over her shoulders to make sure no one would see her, she slipped inside.

Even in darkness, the church's beauty took her breath away. Cady didn't expect the interior to be so lofty and open, larger than it seemed from the outside. Moonlight streamed from high windows on one side, lighting the far edge of the wooden pews but leaving the aisle and other side in shadow. Smooth white pillars lined either side of the pews and lifted the arched ceiling to a great height. Although it was dark, everything—the pews, the walls, the pillars, the embellished ceiling—was painted the same clean white, which now glowed a lunar gray. Cady stepped lightly down the aisle carpet, the only true color in the room—it must be vermilion in the daytime, but now it was a deep blood red. Her eyes followed the color to an altar table draped in matching crimson velvet, with the Harvard seal stitched in gold. On the left side stood the pulpit, a grand hexagonal structure of dark wood, carved like ebony. Atop the lectern on the right was a golden statue of an eagle poised to take flight, wings outstretched, head lowered, sightless eyes fixed in Cady's direction.

She took a seat in the pews and let the silence of the space wash over her, focusing on her breath as she inhaled and exhaled deeply. The exhaustion of the day caught up with her. She had so many questions, and the one person who could answer them was the one out of reach. She wished she could talk to him, then found herself doing just that:

*Eric, why did you leave? Did Professor Prokop break your heart? Did the pressure here become too much? Did you think you'd never get better? I looked up to you, challenged myself to achieve at your level, to get into the school you went to, I wanted to be you—but do we share an illness? Did you hear things like what I'm hearing, is this how it starts? Or are these voices something completely different? Am I channeling another dimension, some version of the past made present? But why? What's the message? Even if you didn't experience anything like this, you'd know what to do, you'd know how to interpret them better than I do. You were the one who taught me the meaning and the purpose of things, until the moment that you made the most senseless decision your last. It's not fair. What kind of sick joke is it that I start hearing the voices of dead people, but I can't hear yours?*

*Eric, are you still mad at me?*

Cady strained to listen, tensing every muscle in her body.

Someone was humming.

As she recognized the tune, the hair on the back of her neck stood up. It was the song from the shower, "Happy Days Are Here Again."

"Who's there?"

*Oh, sorry, I didn't mean to creep up on you.*

It wasn't Eric, it was a stranger, a new voice, a man's. Cady felt instantly vulnerable and afraid.

*You don't need to be frightened, I'm a student here.*

Cady jumped to her feet, ready to run—but from what? Could she escape this voice even if she wanted to? She stopped herself. She felt unsafe but had to know what was going on.

*Please, don't leave. I'm just laying out programs for tomorrow's service, I'm an usher. Normally I'd do it in the morning, but I have crew practice tomorrow. Reverend Phillips leaves the door unlocked for me.*

Cady's memory leaped back to the open door . . . was it possible?

*All right, now you.*

Me what?

*What are you doing in a church in the middle of the night?*

I'm either talking to ghosts or I'm losing my mind.

*Really?* His laugh was warm. *You make it look good.*

Cady softened a bit in spite of herself. —Who are you?

*You want the whole story? I'm James Whitaker Goodwin, Jr., but everyone calls me Whit. Only son of Emmeline Goodwin and the late James Whitaker Goodwin, Sr., of Savannah, Georgia. I'm a junior, varsity rower, physics concentrator, record collector, and all-around music enthusiast. Pleasure to make your acquaintance, Miss . . . ?*

Cady.

*Nice to meet you, Cady. Now, what really brought you here?*

My brother, Eric.

*Has he passed on?*

Yes. Have you?

*Talked to those who've passed? Why, sure. My father died in the Great War when I was a tyke, if I didn't talk to ghosts, I wouldn't have gotten to tell him anything.*

Did he ever talk back?

*I wish. I s'pose he does, in his way. Through his record collection, he left me his old Victrola. Through his military service, I grew up hearing those stories. I don't feel him much here, though. If my father were a ghost, he wouldn't haunt Harvard. He wouldn't be caught dead sitting around a classroom, so why would he after death? High school and then straight into the Navy. He wasn't the type to pore over a book. I don't know if I'm the type either—or maybe I just hate that I am.*

*Your brother, how does he answer?*

He doesn't.

*Maybe just not in the ways you're expecting. If I may ask, how did he pass?*

He killed himself on this campus.

Another sound came from somewhere behind her. She spun to look toward the back of the church, but nothing was there. She forced herself to say its name aloud. "Whit?" Her own voice speaking the unusual name for the first time sounded eerily foreign in this space. Did she really believe this was a harmless "fingerprint" from another dimension? Cady stood still and listened, light-headed, every muscle in her body tense. She closed her eyes, the next name coming out as more of a whispered prayer: "Eric?"

"Cady!" a new voice echoed in the church, loud and more present, making Cady jump. "Look up!"

She lifted her gaze to the balcony at the back of the church, where a dark figure was leaning over the railing, his face only half-lit by the moonlight. "Nikos?"

"Yes, hold on, I'll come right down," he replied. He scurried across the balcony and disappeared, while Cady all but collapsed in a pew, trying to catch her breath. He reemerged from a side door on the ground floor of the church. "Whatever are you doing here?" he said on the way, but when he reached her, Cady simply threw her arms around him and hugged him tight.

"Oh my God, I was so scared!"

"*I* scared *you?*" Nikos delicately unwound her arms from his neck.

"Do you know how utterly creepy you looked, standing in the middle of the aisle like some sort of bride of the damned? I thought I'd seen a ghost!"

Cady heaved an exhalation. "Then we're even."

"What are you doing here, conducting some sort of séance? I'm not standing atop a pentagram, am I?"

Cady gave a laugh, mostly to stall—she didn't have a good answer for his question. "I was passing by and I heard something, I thought, I don't know, I was curious." The truth blinkered in her mind as she rambled: *I was talking to a ghost.* "The door was open," she added, a little too defensively.

"Was it? I was sure I locked it behind me."

"You have keys to the church?"

"Blasphemy, isn't it? But yes, unlike you, I have permission to be here. It's my practice hour."

"Practice for what?"

"The organ."

"You're kidding."

"Come up if you don't believe me." Nikos held out his hand.

Cady hesitated for only a moment before letting him lead her to the back corner of the church; she liked the feeling of his hand around hers—warm, alive, real—she had to will herself not to squeeze his fingers. When they reached a stone spiral staircase, Cady glanced once over her shoulder at the vacant pews, half-expecting to see someone watching them go.

The balcony was up out of reach of the moonlight streaming in from the windows, and Cady's eyes struggled to adjust at first. She was distracted by the height, looking down into the nave of the church, still scanning for a figure to go with the voice she'd heard. So when she finally looked to the right and saw the organ, it took her breath away. It looked like some sort of heavenly gate; the great arc of its height reached all the way to the ceiling and almost the full breadth of the balcony, and its golden pipes glowed without any light reflecting from them. Nikos let go of her hand and walked up the choral risers to the bench at the dark wooden heart of the instrument. He sat and flicked on a lamp above the music stand, illuminating the keyboards but silhouetting his torso, the stray light creeping up the pipes whose open mouths cast inverted shadows, like a kid with a flashlight beneath his chin. When Nikos turned to look back at her, the light shone all around his head but obscured his face in shadow. For a strange moment, Cady thought she saw someone else's features, but then, that accent: "Are you joining me?"

Cady sat close to Nikos on the bench. Four keyboards lay before them, stacked one on top of the other, like rows of shark teeth. "I can't believe you actually play this."

"I'm playing at service this Sunday, which is why I have to brush up. Normally my practice hour is Thursday nights, eleven to midnight, but I swapped with Yumee. There are a few of us organists."

"Why so late at night?"

"They have to find time when the church is closed so we don't bother anybody. And you know, it's hard to sort out the schedules of overbooked Harvard students, we're far too busy and far too important."

Cady reached out and brushed her fingers against the thirty-some knobs that lined the keyboards.

"Those are the stops. Like the expression 'pulling out all the stops'? It literally means to engage all the pipes at once, full blast. It'll blow your hair back."

"I knew you played the piano, but this? You have to be a serious musician to play this. I thought you were all physics all the time, like Eric."

"Music and physics have always gone hand in hand. Eric didn't share your supernatural ear?"

*Supernatural.* Cady knew he meant her perfect pitch, but she blushed with embarrassment anyway. "You clearly never sang karaoke with Eric."

"Never had the chance." They were both quiet for a moment, silenced by the finality of it. "This is a Fisk organ, Charles Fisk was a Harvard grad and accomplished physicist, he worked on the Manhattan Project during World War II before devoting himself to organ construction."

"From the nuclear bomb to church organs—atonement?"

"I don't know if there's atonement to be had for that," he said with a grimace.

"Is it like the piano?"

"Not quite. A piano is a forgiving instrument; it's easy to control the volume, all the notes linger and glide over one another, and the sustain pedal can mask any mistakes. An organ is the opposite. When your finger hits a key, even if it only grazes it, wind is released into the pipe at full blast. And as soon as you lift your finger, the wind stops. The pipes speak at a fixed volume—"

"The pipes 'speak'?"

"That's the term, funny, isn't it? Anyway, they 'speak' at fixed volumes, depending on the size. So no sins are forgiven."

Cady's eyes scanned the enormous instrument with its four keyboards and countless stops on either side. "Sounds impossible."

"I like the challenge." The side of Nikos's face crinkled with a smile. "The piano is like a high school girl; pliable, sensitive, easy to please." Nikos ran his hands over the keys in a light caress. "But an organ is the sort of woman who's out of your league, maybe a little older, aloof. On the surface, she's an ice queen, but if you touch her in the right ways"—he paused and walked his fingertips across the keys—"she'll make you feel like a god."

Cady elbowed him with a laugh. "So, do you have to sit here in the dark, or is that just your mood lighting of choice?"

"They ask us not to turn on the houselights at this hour. I won't lie, it's a bit spooky. See here?" Nikos reached up to adjust a mirror poised above the music ledge. "You're supposed to look in this to watch the choir conductor. But these rehearsal nights, when I'm all alone and the wind is howling, I find myself compulsively checking the mirror. Like I expect a ghost, or perhaps a wayward freshman girl, to be lurking behind me."

Nikos laughed but Cady didn't. Her thoughts returned to the voice. "Do you believe in ghosts?"

"Please, I'm a man of science."

*I don't know.*

Whit—had her thoughts summoned him? Hearing the voice with Nikos beside her made her panicky again. She wanted to turn it off.

*I want to believe, don't you? That the ones we've lost aren't really gone.*

"Do you?" Nikos asked.

She shrugged. "Maybe."

"Is that why you came here?" Nikos's voice was gentle, but the question cut her to the quick.

Cady couldn't bring herself to answer, her heart rate quickening. He thinks I'm sick, she thought to herself.

*No, I don't.*

"Play something for me."

"Okay, what do you want to hear?" Nikos asked.

"Anything," Cady answered.

*Do you think it's sick I want to enlist when my father died in the Great War?*

"How about . . . Bach's Toccata and Fugue in D minor?"

*Way I look at it, when someone's taken from you too soon, there's a finite number of things you can share with that person, so you want to share them all.*

Cady hadn't responded, so Nikos added, "You'll know it when you hear it."

The first notes poured from the organ at such a high, reedy pitch, it tickled the eardrum. Then the lower chords erupted, vibrating through the organ bench and up her spine. Nikos's hands moved quickly and expertly across the manuals, and she recognized the piece immediately, a Halloween classic.

*Music, Navy, these are my chances to having something in common with my father beyond blood, so how can I resist that pull?*

The music's quickening tempo and menace only magnified her anxiety, but Nikos's playing was a distraction from Whit, and she didn't want him to stop.

*With no more future, the past is all you have.*

The cascading notes crashed over Cady, and she was desperate to submerge her consciousness and drown out Whit's voice, but it wasn't enough. Like the rattle of a bathtub chain beneath a thunderous faucet, the voice was only louder underwater.

*So you make their past your present, it's almost like they're with you.*

"Can you play it louder?"

Nikos obliged, pulling out two more stops.

Cady nodded.

Nikos hesitated. "We're not supposed to pull out all the stops at night—"

*You want to know about keeping the past alive, you ask a Southern boy.*

"Please—" she cried.

*Ghosts don't haunt the living.*

"Louder!"

*We haunt them.*

The organ roared. Cady flinched at its earsplitting volume as if she'd been struck. The subterranean rumblings of the bass chords twisted in her gut and drummed in her chest, the wind from the pipes blew on her cheeks, the tempo like adrenaline coursed through her veins. Any emotion, any thought in her brain was wiped out, her skull scraped clean. But the obliteration was a relief; the visceral discomfort soothed her. She had the easy, frightening sensation of surrender.

And she didn't hear the voice anymore.

CADY RETURNED TO her dorm room punch-drunk, desperate to lie down and quell the ringing in her ears. The suite was dark and quiet, everyone seemingly had gone to bed. Emotionally and physically exhausted, Cady collapsed onto her bottom bunk.

*Squish.*

She sat up and twisted around to see a piece of chocolate cake smashed onto a paper plate, and now, her bedspread. She reached to her back, and her fingers found the sticky icing clinging to her sweater. A Post-it Note lay on her pillow, written in precise purple handwriting:

*I saved you a piece.*
*—Andrea*

# 20

CADY HAD FELT sick to her stomach with guilt all morning, a situation not helped by her father's aggressive driving, as they were running late to Grampa and Vivi's vow renewal. She'd slept badly the night before, berating herself for blowing Andrea's birthday. Just as Cady had instructed her, Andrea had indeed texted her that she and Marko were coming to the room, but Cady had been so preoccupied with Matt's new information about Eric, Mika, and the voices that she had completely missed it. She could only imagine how humiliated Andrea had been when she walked into a dark dorm room with no surprise waiting for her, and in front of her crush no less. Worse still, Cady had had to leave that morning to catch her flight to Philadelphia before Andrea woke up, so she hadn't been able to apologize in person. Not that she knew what she would say—how could she sincerely apologize without making herself sound crazy? "I'm sorry, I got distracted by the voices in my head." "I'm sorry, I might have schizophrenia, but I'm pretty sure it's ghosts." She'd spent most of the flight trying to compose a text, and after a dozen drafts in her Notes app, Cady managed to send only:

Andrea, I am so, so sorry.

She checked her phone again in the backseat. Andrea still hadn't replied.

Self-loathing sloshed in Cady's gut as her father changed lanes.

Cady opened the other note she had written in her iPhone on the plane, a secret inventory of all the facts she had gleaned about each of the voices, who they were, and whence they came:

Whit—full name James Whitaker Goodwin, Jr., from Georgia, calls WWI "The Great War," so pre-1940.
Father died in the war, Whit too little to remember him. So Whit born sometime between 1910 and 1914.
Currently a junior, so he's about twenty years old. Current year for him between 1930 and 1934.

Robert—expert in literature, science, mentioned recent Nobel prize 1922, prob mid 1920s

Bilhah—slave during Pres Holyoke's time (1737–1769), her current year is ?? Can't read, son is mute, afraid they will sell him!? Needs my help.

Cady looked out the car window and mulled over her theory. Professor Prokop might not approve, but Cady had incorporated what she'd said about hidden dimensions—in which time and space could be warped and folded over, leaving traces in our world—into her interpretation of the voices, but in layman's terms, they were ghosts. People from different times poking through the same space. They spoke to her as if their time was the present, and they seemed to experience her in their world in whatever way made sense for their period. They didn't know they were dead, because in their own dimensions, they weren't yet. Could she help them? Could they help her? Bilhah already had, that night with Teddy. Cady wondered how they died, or would die. Was she supposed to help them avoid that fate? Was it some sort of test?

Cady hadn't really believed in ghosts before, not the type that rattled chains or made the room temperature drop. The closest she'd come to a paranormal experience was years ago, when Cady and her mother were driving by their old house and her mother decided to knock on the door. The new owners invited them in, and although the walls were new colors and Cady and Eric's shared bedroom was now an office, she could feel her younger self there. She could hear Eric's little-boy voice echoing around the stairwell. Her family's past selves were captured between those walls, preserved in memory, like an insect in amber. These ghosts felt like that, and she was starting to believe in them.

"Chilton Gables, that's the name of the place, right?" her father asked. "I think we're here."

After driving around the labyrinthine retirement village, they finally found the correct tan clapboard home, which looked nearly identical to all the others save for a few details, like garage placement or shutter color, as if all the homes were genetic relatives. However, Grampa and Vivi's stood out thanks to Vivi's collection of stone statuettes on the lawn: a boy and girl sitting on a bench, a pig pushing a wheelbarrow, a bunny rabbit with white balloons tied troublingly around its neck, and the Virgin Mary.

"Looks like I'll have to park down the street," her father said. Cady saw the driveway was already stuffed with cars and more along the curb.

"That, or we can just turn around and go home," her mother said.

He shrugged. "They're *your* family."

"It's Vivi's family, I don't know these people," her mother muttered. Vivi had three children, a little younger than Cady's parents, and a bunch of grandkids, but her mother was right, Cady hardly knew them beyond a refrigerator Christmas card. *Blending* hadn't been a priority on either family's side. "It's ridiculous. A vow renewal? They've only been married two years."

"I think it's kind of nice, since they didn't have a real wedding," Cady piped up from the back, overcompensating for her mood.

Grampa and Vivi had eloped; they'd gotten married on a Carnival cruise ship somewhere in the Atlantic. They didn't even tell anyone they were engaged, or maybe people don't get engaged at their age. So it took the family by surprise, most of all Cady's mother. It had been only eighteen months since Cady's grandmother had passed away from a brief but brutal battle with pancreatic cancer.

They parked a few doors down and plastered smiles on their faces before Cady pressed the doorbell. The door swung open and Vivi greeted them, beaming.

"Hello, hello!" Vivi cried. She was swathed in a champagne chiffon dress and jacket set that matched her peachy-hued hair, and her makeup level was set to "showgirl." The three of them shuffled slowly through the front door as Vivi hugged each of them, her many bangles jangling as she threw out her soft arms and pulled Cady into a heavily perfumed embrace. Vivi kissed her cheek and Cady could feel the creamy pink lipstick leave its mark.

"Care-bear!" Grampa came ambling into the entrance hall in a tan suit, arms outstretched. He looked healthy and happy, younger than his eighty-one years.

"Hi, Dad," her mother said, hugging him.

He spotted Cady over her shoulder. "And my munchkin!" Grampa's bear hug leapfrogged from his daughter to granddaughter. "Come in, come in, wait'll you see the spread we got in here!"

The party was more elaborate than Cady expected: a white carpet rolled out through the entrance hall and into the living area, which was missing its usual furniture and filled with three rows of white fold-up chairs and a pink-rose-covered altar. Gauzy white curtains hid the kitchen from view, but well-dressed catering staff emerged with trays of drinks and hors d'oeuvres, and the place was packed with older faces Cady had never met before. She and her father oohed and aahed while Grampa grinned so broadly, Cady feared for his dentures.

"Wow, Dad, you weren't kidding," Cady's mother said, her eyes wide.

"You know what they say, you can't take it with you!" He laughed.

"I gotta spruce up before the ceremony. Then afterwards, they're gonna set up some tables *tout suite*, and we'll have a nice buffet dinner. Now enjoy yourselves and eat some shrimp—they're jumbo!"

Her mother lifted a glass of champagne off a passing silver tray.

Cady and her parents made small talk with a few of the guests, but mostly they stood around, an awkward triad. The octogenarians around them were in livelier spirits than they were, and it was a relief when Vivi came back with some of her immediate family. Her father got busy talking sports with Vivi's sons-in-law, leaving Cady and her mother to fall prey to Vivi.

"You remember my grandson, Jackson." Vivi threw her arm around the beanstalk of a boy, easily six feet tall but thin enough that he shook when his grandmother patted him on the back. "He just made the varsity basketball team at school."

"That's awesome," Cady said, only half-recognizing him.

"Thanks." Jackson shrugged, his blue eyes peeked through his floppy bangs for a whole second before looking back at the floor. Then he murmured something to Vivi that Cady couldn't hear.

"Okay, sweetie, in the kitchen," Vivi answered him—her voice had only one volume setting. She looked lovingly after him as he ambled away before turning back to Cady. "Isn't he handsome?"

"And so tall!" Cady's mother said. "When did that happen?"

Vivi's glow faded. "You haven't seen him since his confirmation. That was over two years ago, he's sprouted. He just turned sixteen."

Cady remembered Jackson's confirmation reception with a wave of embarrassment, the whole thing having taken place at the home of Jackson's mother, Linda:

"Did someone let the dog out?" Linda had asked, fear thinning her voice. Shadow, their black lab mix, had a bad habit of chasing cars; the family must have mentioned keeping him in ten times when everyone had first arrived. When the room quieted in reply to her question, there was no question; there was barking coming from outside. And, Cady noticed, Eric was missing.

The front door was found hanging open, the winter air chilling the cozy party. Jackson ran out the door and onto the lawn, his dress suit billowing on his teenage stick-figure frame. Cady remembered Jackson calling the dog's name, his panic and hormones cracking his voice, then the sound of screeching tires and the dog's yowl.

Thankfully, Shadow had yelped out of fear, the car had missed by the slimmest margin, and they eventually got the dog safely back in the house, but the ordeal made Jackson cry. The poor kid was so humiliated that he'd cried on the day he was supposed to become a man that he hid in his bedroom for the rest of the reception, only to be dragged out when it was time for cake.

It seemed that only Cady's family remained concerned for Eric. He had walked out without his coat and without a word to anyone. Grampa and Cady's father and mother went to look for him; Cady's role was to stay behind and make nice, but the drama was *the* story of the party. For the rest of the reception, there was a murmuring speculation about why a young man would just walk out like that. Cady overheard someone suggesting Eric was a drug addict. Meanwhile, Vivi was annoyed at having attention diverted from her grandson. It took Cady's family more than an hour before they found Eric casually eating at a roadside Burger King over a mile away.

So Cady could understand why Jackson wasn't eager to catch up with her. She looked at her mother to see if she recalled the incident, but her mother was occupied with a member of the catering staff, swapping out her old champagne for a new one. "Which way is the bathroom again?" Cady asked.

Vivi pointed her in the right direction, and Cady excused herself.

She walked to the bathroom, preoccupied. She shared some of her mother's dislike of Vivi. Vivi was hard to accept, not because she wasn't nice, but because she was so different from Cady's late grandmother. Her grandmother had dressed simply and aged gracefully, and she was wonderfully mysterious. She had had the mind of a scientist. She'd made her small greenhouse into a laboratory, and Cady wouldn't be surprised if she had taught Eric how to grow those blue hydrangeas for Jenny. When they were younger, Grandma would orchestrate little secrets to entertain Eric and Cady. She pressed flowers into their children's books and said that fairies left them. On Easter she'd set up an egg hunt that was rather difficult but for her clues—Easter bunny "tracks" left in baking flour, dropped carrots unearthed from her own garden. To Cady and Eric, Grandma was the good witch, moody but full of surprises. Cady got the sense from her own mother that Grandma was different growing up, that her darker moods didn't always pass so easily, but it's simpler to be a grandmother than a mother.

On the other hand, everything about Vivi was obvious, from her makeup to her feelings. Jackson's confirmation fiasco might not have been such a big deal if Vivi had just let Cady and her parents deal with it quietly. Vivi was a drama queen; she wailed when Shadow returned as much as if he *had* gotten hit, she clucked that they should call the police to locate Eric instead of just helping, and she complained openly that Grampa had missed Jackson cutting the cake, as if a thirteen-year-old boy could care in the slightest.

A forgotten snippet of that confirmation day came back to Cady: when Grampa and her mother had finally gotten Eric back to Linda's house and set him up on the couch with an electric blanket, tea, and a hot foot soak to warm up. Vivi had come over with a plate as a peace offering. "We saved you some dessert. Now, Eric, do you have anything to say to Jackson?" Vivi had asked, prompting him to apologize as one would to a small child.

Eric had looked at her with neither affection nor malice and said, "If I believed that cake to be edible, I wouldn't have left in the first place."

This was the only Eric that Vivi knew—the odd, arrogant, selfish boy who caused trouble. Unpredictable. Unstable. An attention hog. A danger to himself and others. Thinking about Vivi's perspective reminded Cady of a truth of the last two years: They were difficult. Eric was difficult. Vivi's was a fair assessment made under unfair circumstances.

On the way back from the bathroom, Cady noticed Vivi had converted the guest bedroom into a scrapbook palace, with bookshelves full of her bedazzled photo albums. Such a quaint hobby, sweet but a little cheesy, like everything else about Vivi. Curious, Cady detoured inside.

All of Vivi's scrapbooks and photo albums had titles on the spine; Cady pulled an old one titled HAPPY HOLIDAYS '72! She looked at the pictures, roughly able to identify which of the little kids were which of Vivi's now-adult children despite their seventies haircuts and clothes. She guessed the man with sideburns whom she didn't recognize was Vivi's late husband, Cady recalled his name was Michael, but he looked happy and kind. In one Polaroid, he played on the floor with the kids on Christmas morning, in another he held up some sort of casserole with great pride. Cady wondered if he was as good a husband and father as these chosen photos made him seem. Cady had thought she remembered her family history with such clarity, but then she had "forgotten" Eric's misbehavior in front of Vivi. Do we all pick only the best snapshots to remember in our mental scrapbooks and throw away the bad? Perhaps all photo albums should bear the subtitle "The Past—The Way You Want to Remember It."

Cady replaced the album on the shelf and turned to leave when something else caught her eye: a scrapbook in progress atop a desk strewn with colored paper, ribbon, tape, and scissors. It looked like a gift for Grampa. The pictures on the open page were of them golfing together, with little captions written in the loopy script of a Catholic schoolgirl, but Cady couldn't help but be charmed. Maybe she had been too cynical. She had wondered if the only reason Grampa remarried so quickly was a fear of dying alone, but this woman clearly loved Cady's grandfather, and judging by Grampa's goofy grin in most of these shots, the feeling was mutual.

"Do you think he'll like it?" Vivi stood smiling at Cady from the doorway.

"He's going to love it."

"I can't wait to surprise him." A girlish smile appeared on her well-lined face, and Cady could imagine what a pretty young woman she must have been. "Did you see these?" Vivi crossed the room and, with some effort, bent down to the bottom shelf to grab a shoebox. "I rescued a bunch of photos from Matty's old house. Lots of oldies but goodies in there."

Cady took the box from her and opened it; inside was a mishmash of old pictures, including some worn black-and-white ones of him and Grandma in the fifties with her mom as a baby. Others were more recent, of her and Eric as little kids. Cady held up a photo of Grandma and Eric together—Eric looked barely three—and felt her heart break. She missed both of them so much.

"You're welcome to take the box home. I thought maybe you and your mom could go through them together."

Cady fought the lump in her throat to say "Thank you."

"Which album were you looking at?"

"Huh?" Cady had to pull herself from the shoebox photos. "Oh, an old one."

"Which?"

She squirmed a bit. "Happy Holidays '72? But you might not want to—"

Vivi pulled it from the shelf before Cady could finish. She opened it and started flipping through the pages, her eyes softening around the edges.

"I'm sorry if it's sad or uncomfortable for you to look at them today."

"Why, because Mikey's in them? Nah." Then she looked up and said something that floored Cady: "Mikey approves of me marrying your Grampa—he told me."

A few months ago, Cady might have brushed the comment off as another wacky belief of her step-grandmother's, but given the voices she had been hearing, it didn't sound so silly. "How? Does he speak to you?"

"He has his ways. When your grandfather asked me to marry him, the next day I saw a rainbow, and I knew that that was Mikey saying 'Go ahead, Viv, be happy.'"

It wasn't anything like what Cady had been experiencing with the other voices, but it was clearer than anything she was getting from Eric. Cady would kill for a rainbow. "But how do you reach him?"

"I don't reach him, he comes to me. Oh, sweetie—are you crying?"

Cady couldn't hold it in. "Eric never comes to me. I'm listening, but . . ." She shook her head. "It's never him."

Vivi came over and hugged Cady to her perfumed bosom, gently shushing her like a baby. "The spirit world gives us what we need, when we need it. You can't chase it. Try to be open to whatever form the messages take."

Her words resonated, and Cady thanked her, meaning it.

"There you go, don't cry, you'll ruin your mascara. Now, let's go back in, we're going to start the ceremony soon."



THE CEREMONY WAS surprisingly affecting. Grampa and Vivi recited handwritten vows with a sense of humor, promising "to keep the TV loud enough for me to hear it without my hearing aids, but to turn it off at dinner," to keep each other young, with love, travel, healthy eating, and "watching one new show our grandkids like." Everyone was laughing. Cady looked over at her mother: almost everyone.

Afterward, they had a buffet set up in the kitchen.

"This food looks good," said Cady's father, but her mother only shrugged. "What, you don't think so?"

"I keep remembering my mother clipping coupons when I was little. Dad was so stingy. Do you remember when she wanted to build the greenhouse? How he dragged his feet on that? Now he marries this woman and he's spending money like water."

"Maybe he has regrets. Maybe he wants to live differently now."

"Nice of him to get it right for *Vivi*." Her mother said her name like it tasted bad. "Forgive me if I'm not thrilled his new wife is burning through his cash on a fixed income. You want them to move in with us?"

"God help him, no one should have to live with us," her father sniped.

"Mom, Dad, can we not?" Cady said, shaming them both into silence.

They sat down at the largest table, reserved for family, but they were the only representatives of Grampa's side. Vivi had three children, Michelle, Linda, and the wild thing, Mikey Jr. Her daughters were both attractive women, put-together, French-manicured tips on their nails, five good-looking kids between them. The only difference was Michelle wore her chocolate-brown hair straight and Linda left hers in crispy curls. Mikey Jr. lived up to the stereotype of the baby in the family and the only boy; Vivi and his sisters doted on him as if he were a teenager, though Cady was pretty sure he was pushing forty.

As the meal was winding down, Cady's grandfather stood up and clinked on his glass. "I want to thank all of you for coming. My Vivi has such a big family, it's wonderful to see everyone and to feel so welcomed. I look out at my three beautiful girls, my bride, Vivi, my Kare-Bear, that's Karen to all of you, and my baby granddaughter Cady, who I guess I have to concede isn't such a baby anymore. I don't know how I became so blessed. Thank you, Vivi, for bringing love into my life again."

The room gave a collective "aww" as Grampa leaned to kiss Vivi, his starched collar pulling tight against the loose skin of his neck.

Vivi's elder daughter, Michelle, stood and made a short speech about how grateful she was for her mother to find love after her dad passed, and how Michelle thought her late father would have liked Cady's grandfather if they had met.

When Michelle sat back down, Vivi was busy grabbing her cheek and kissing it, so Cady's grandfather put a hand on her shoulder and stood up again. "Wow, Michelle honey, thank you for your kind words, no thanks for making an old man cry in public." Grampa and everyone laughed. "I don't want to put my family on the spot, but, Karen, do you want to say anything?"

Cady glanced over at her mother; she looked exhausted, her eyes a little red. Cady didn't know how many champagnes deep she was, but she was guessing a speech was a bad idea. Before her mother could answer, Cady said, "I'd like to say something."

"Oh?" Grampa looked surprised. "Well, that's wonderful! Everyone, my granddaughter, Cadence."

Her mother shot her a grateful glance, just the confidence boost Cady needed. She smoothed cake crumbs off her skirt and stood up. "Hi, everyone. I just wanted to say that it was really a pleasure getting to be a part of today and celebrate my grandfather and Vivi's marriage. Our family has been through some hard times recently, and to get to celebrate something so positive and happy has been a gift to all of us." She sneaked a sip of water. "We're still getting to know you, Vivi, and your family, but just today when I got a chance to see your scrapbook room, I was struck by how perfect you are for Grampa and for our family. He is so lucky to have found a woman who understands the importance of honoring the past, but who also gives him the courage and hopefulness to move forward and start anew. I feel like that special combination is what all of us want, even those who are no longer with us."

Vivi dabbed away tears, Grampa nodded solemnly.

"Um, so, cheers!" Cady said, raising her glass, and the entire table clinked glasses and laughed. Cady sat down.

"Nicely done," her father said quietly, filling her with pride. Even her mother smiled. Grampa reached over the table to take her hand in his warm leathery one. He seemed too choked up to speak.

Vivi came around behind Cady's chair and put her plump arms around her shoulders. "Cady, that was so lovely, thank you so much, you sweet angel. Karen, you never told me you had a poet in the family all this time." She tapped the table with her pink fingernails. "I had no idea you had such a gift for public speaking, Cady. It's nice to see you finally have a chance to shine."

Cady was about to thank Vivi when her mother snorted. "She's shined, she's always shined," she said, sounding a little slurry.

"Well, I've always known Cady to be the quiet one," Vivi said, taking an open seat beside Cady so that the two women were on either side of her. "But maybe this is just the first time I've gotten to see her in the spotlight, without any distraction."

"What do you mean by that?" This time there was no softness to her mother's pronunciation; her words cut like acid.

Vivi sighed. "I was trying to pay your daughter a compliment. Don't turn it into something else."

"But so we're clear, the 'distraction' was my son?"

Cady sucked her body into the back of her chair as flat as she could.

Vivi looked at Grampa across the table and said, "I can't say anything right with her."

"She didn't mean anything by it," said Grampa to her mother.

Cady's mother ignored him and spoke directly to Vivi. "You can't say anything right, because you're being insensitive to my son's memory."

"It's not insensitive to acknowledge that it was a struggle."

"For *you?*" her mother said incredulously.

"For everyone. You can't pretend it didn't affect us. We could never have had a wedding celebration like this." Vivi lifted her penciled brow. "Why do you think we eloped?"

Her mother turned to Grampa. "Dad, is that true?"

"Well . . ." Grampa's mouth hung open, his eyes darted between the two women in his life, his lips quivering in indecision.

But his silence was answer enough. Cady was shocked, too. She had always thought their marriage aboard the cruise ship was an act of romantic spontaneity, not a planned escape from Eric.

Her mother, shaking her head, fixed on Vivi. "It's not enough to trample on my mother's grave, you have to shit on my son's, too?"

"That's it," snapped Michelle, as she stood up from her seat. "You've got a lotta nerve talking to my mother that way. It's supposed to be *her* day."

Linda threw up her hands in disgust. "Just like at Jackson's confirmation. This is what they always do, make it all about them."

"Oh, fuck you, Linda," Cady's mother said.

With that, hell broke loose. Mikey Jr. jumped up and started yelling in defense of Linda, Michelle shouted at Mikey to sit back down, Linda remained laser-focused on Cady's mother, and Vivi was trying to say something over them that no one heard.

"Okay, time-out." Cady's father wedged himself between his wife and the rest of the table, then turned his head to say, "Cady, get our stuff. It's time to go."

They sidled quickly around the other tables of confused and curious guests as quickly as possible. Grampa, rushing as fast as his wobbly legs could carry him, caught up with them in the entry hall.

"Karen, wait, you've got it all wrong. We were only waiting for Eric to get better, I always thought he'd get better."

Cady's father tried to placate them, but her mother wasn't slowing down and Grampa continued to try to get through to his daughter, scurrying after her, saying, "Vivi didn't mean it to come out like that. Don't leave like this, I love you, you're my baby girl."

Cady's mother spun around and held up a shaky finger to her father, but Cady could see there was more pain than anger in her eyes. "You have no loyalty, Dad. Not to Mom, not to me, and apparently not to your grandson." She stormed out the front door with Cady's father, apologizing, following close behind.

Only Cady looked back at Grampa, who stood helplessly and watched, his birdlike chest heaving. His eyes fell to meet hers, and his entire face crumpled. Then he pulled her into a desperate hug.

"I'm so sorry," he murmured into her hair, choked up.

She braced as he leaned his shaky weight into her. "It's okay, everything will be okay."

When he pulled back, she saw his face was pale, his watery blue eyes were limned in red, and dried spit was caked at the corners of his mouth. As vibrant as he had looked when they arrived, he now looked enfeebled and distraught. "Take care of her for me, will you?"

Cady nodded and kissed him quickly on the cheek before hurrying out after her parents. The car was running, her father sat stone-faced in the driver's seat, and her mother was slumped in the backseat with her hand covering her eyes. Cady climbed into the passenger seat without a word.

"You all right?" her father asked.

Cady was shaken, unable to get her grandfather's face out of her mind. She felt anxious and ashamed about the fight, they had ruined the reception, and she knew everyone would be talking about them. At the same time, she could tell her mom was in such pain—the pain of a grieving mother and of a little girl. And Cady had no idea how to take care of any of it.

# 21

CADY FLEW BACK to Boston the next day. She had hoped going home could be a reset button to send her back to school refreshed and strengthened, but her nerves felt only more frayed. Andrea hadn't replied to her apology texts or spoken to her since she'd returned, charging the air in their suite with tension. But Cady had only ever had one coping mechanism for stress anyway—work. Lamont Library's café had a comforting level of hubbub. The café was at the front of the building; the entire front wall was made of glass, filling the room with light, and Cady had snagged one of the coveted squishy brown armchairs facing the window. She had her MacBook open and warming her lap, her Medieval Studies binder out, and her latte beside her, but she was struggling to get started. She was on tenterhooks, waiting for something. She was waiting for the ghosts to come back.

She hadn't heard a single voice or anything else unusual since the moment she left Harvard's campus. Their absence had been a relief, but it was a slippery kind of hope that *that* trip home could have cured her of any mental health crisis. But then she no longer believed the voices were her mental illness talking. More and more, she had come to believe the voices were extrinsic, supernatural, or extradimensional. She didn't know how or why, but she was intersecting with them here. They were ghosts of Harvard. But where did that leave her? Trying to do homework in a haunted house.

A chat message pinged on her email window:

How's it going?

The webmail provider identified the sender as abrousard@fas .harvard.edu.

**me:** Who is this?
**abrousard:** Sry, it's Alex. From Hines's class. Also, from across the room.

Cady lifted her head and scanned the room. Most students were bent over their work, and one guy was slumped sound asleep in an armchair while still holding a precarious coffee cup. Then her eyes lit upon Alex's disheveled blond hair, his neck stretched up like an ostrich's. He waved when she made eye contact. She smiled in return. He looked back down at his laptop.

In seconds, another chat message:

How's the paper coming?

She typed back only an ellipsis.

**abrousard:** Same here.
**me:** I don't believe you.
**abrousard:** ha! Come over and see. There's an open armchair next to me.

Cady considered it, but she knew she'd only procrastinate more.

**me:** I would but I gotta focus :(
**abrousard:** ok. bye.

In the next second, his name grayed and the chat window read:

abrousard@fas.harvard.edu is offline.

Cady felt a jab of regret, but she pushed it away and opened her medieval history sourcebook to that week's reading. She flipped through the pages, mostly photocopies of ancient texts, early biblical writing, and simplistic diagrams of the cosmos. She turned to the section titled "Early Visions: Biblical and Apocryphal, 200 B.C.E.–400 C.E." She had to remind herself that c.e. stood for "Common Era" and signified the same time period as a.d., Anno Domini, medieval Latin for "In the Year of Our Lord." Generally, she had a great mind for dates, but she had always been thrown by the fact that the b.c. "Before Christ" years counted backward; she drew a small bracket beside the time period and wrote **200 BC to 400 AD = 600 yrs** so that she wouldn't forget.

In her high school history classes, it had been nearly impossible for her to comprehend that the advent of Christ permanently modified the way an entire culture conceptualized time. They'd been taught that it was a gesture of devotion and a way to ratify Christ's importance. But Cady couldn't imagine how people in the years around Christ's earthly existence mentally reversed time's arrow and counted backward. It had seemed so confusing and inconvenient, she'd doubted that laypeople changed it in practice. Now, since her brother had died, it made sense. It's how the brain wants to work. When something profound occurs in our lives, that becomes the start, and everything before is only a countdown. This was Year One of Life Without Eric. The year before was Year One Until Life Without Eric. The only difference was that she was counting backward from his death, not his birth.

Cady tried to put Eric out of her head—not easy, as her alternative was pages of dense text—when the appearance of an illustration caught her eye. The first drawing was labeled "Figure 2: Late medieval idea of the location of the ventricles in the human head—with decoration (by Guillaume Leroy II, pub. 1523)." It was a diagram of a head in profile; the cranium was displayed in cross-section with Latin labels, but the face was illustrated with bulging eyes, open mouth, and protruding tongue. A wreath of lush grapevines bordered the diagram. It may have been scientific for its time, but to Cady it looked like something out of a book of spells. The caption read:

> Bartholomaeus Anglicus's thirteenth-century encyclopedia gave this derivation of the term *ventricle*: "The brain has three hollow places that physicians call *ventriculos*, 'small wombs.'"

*Small wombs*. Cady waffled, was that what had been happening? Was her brain giving birth to the beings whose voices she heard, the immaculate conception of insanity? That was a pretty decent explanation of schizophrenia in thirteenth-century terms. But they didn't feel like her creation; they felt like strangers, unknown but fully formed, from another time, but real. They felt like ghosts.

So she perked up when she saw the Middle Ages definition of *spirit* as "a liquid found in the ventricles of the brain," spirit as a synonym for soul, spirit as a medium between body and soul, and spirit as a "physical quantity like breath."

*Like breath*—or like voices? It reminded her of what Vivi had said: *The spirit world gives us what we need, when we need it,* and she should *try to be open to whatever form the messages take.* What if these voices were messages from the other side, a spirit dimension? These spirits were reaching out to her for a reason, she just had to figure out what it was. Lingering there was the temptation: If she made herself open to these spirits, would Eric reach out to her, too?

Work. She had work to do, reading and a response paper. She rubbed her eyes to rid herself of the distraction and returned to the email with the assignment prompt. The TF had included a general note on the readings:

> The biblical and postbiblical visions in this week's reading testify to the importance of dreams and other kinds of revelatory experi-

ence in the Jewish culture from which Christianity sprang. *Apoca-lypse*, from Greek *apocalypsis*, or "revelation," was used as a genre description for a certain sort of visionary writing, often involving a mix of disaster and promise of transformation. Write a reader response paper to the text of your choice.

Cady never knew "apocalypse" meant "revelation." If only real-life catastrophes came with some revelation. She profoundly hoped for one, but in her experience they left only rubble behind.

She flipped to the first assigned text, *The Vision of Paul*, which was very long and organized in the biblical style of simple sentences on numbered lines. Next. The following option, *Revelation*, was the same. The third text she turned to seemed a little more interesting. It was called *The Passion of Saint Perpetua*, about the martyrdom of Vibia Perpetua, a twenty-two-year-old woman in Carthage, and the head-note said it was believed to be the work of Perpetua herself. Cady was intrigued. There were so few female authors on her syllabus, and certainly none so close to her in age.

Perpetua's account was written in first person and felt as candid as a diary entry. She wrote of being tormented with visions of her dead brother, Dinocrates, who was suffering in the afterlife. In her visions, Dinocrates seemed to be in neither heaven nor hell, but somewhere between life and death. Cady thought of Whit the other night, saying his father died in World War I, meaning that Whit also had to be dead. But he'd spoken to her as if he were her contemporary, a fellow student, alive and well. Where was he? Where was Eric?

*Stay focused*, Cady scolded herself. Back to Perpetua:

Yet I was confident I should ease his travail. . . . And I prayed for him day and night with groans and tears, that he might be given me.

On the day when we abode in the stocks, this was shown me.

I saw that place which I had before seen, and Dinocrates clean of body, finely clothed, in comfort.

And I awoke. Then I understood that he was translated from his pains.

Could she have eased Eric's pain? Surely she had suffered, watching him transform from her funny, sweet, awkward, genius brother to an angry, deranged stranger. Even before he died, she had suffered the loss of her closest confidant, her most trusted adviser. Throughout her entire life, on Cady's internal compass, Eric had been north. When he became lost within his illness, she, too, lost her way.

But Cady never had confidence like Perpetua. She hadn't had faith that she could steer the ship herself. She had anxiously watched while her parents and a revolving door of doctors and experts failed to help Eric. And when she'd had the chance to intervene, she'd missed it.

She returned to the Perpetua reading; she had only the grim ending left. The prisoners who were not sufficiently mauled by the leopard or bear were sentenced to death by the sword. Perpetua's executioner was a "novice" and lacked the nerve to go through with it, and in the end, Perpetua took the sword and "set it upon her own neck." The last line read, "Perchance so great a woman could not have been slain . . . had she not herself so willed it."

So Perpetua killed herself. Which, if you do it for religious reasons, makes you a martyr, a hero, a saint. If you do it as a mentally ill undergraduate, then people assume you're pathetic, weak, or selfish. She hated that some people thought those things about her brother, but people wanted to know the reason, and without one, they'd come to their own conclusions.

She gazed out through the glass wall before her. Everything looked clear and sharp, the sort of day you could tell was cold just by looking. Far across the green, Memorial Church's snow-white spire pierced the perfect blue sky, yet the clouds racing across the sky betrayed the bitter wind outside. Fallen leaves skittered and bounced across the ground, like fledglings wanting to take flight but losing their nerve. Only a small maple refused to part with its red leaves, fiery and defiant. If she had lost her nerve when Eric was alive, could she find it now that he was dead? Could she undo that wrong from here? If the ghosts were reaching her from the past, could she reach back?

*Vision confirms faith,* Cady wrote in the margin. Perpetua wasn't born brave; she found that courage after her hallucinations. Last year Cady had been too passive, cowardly even; the changes in Eric had scared her. But that was before. The voices she was hearing scared her, too, but what if the experience could "translate" to Eric? What if letting these ghosts infiltrate her mind was a key to reaching his, or at least to understanding him? Cady sensed that the voices were leading her somewhere, either to madness or to clarity, but she didn't know which. If she had any dream, any sign, if she had any faith at all, maybe she could be brave, too.

*Thwap!*

Something slammed into the window. Cady jumped in her seat, knocking over her water bottle. As she fumbled to protect her laptop from the spill, the students around her reacted to see what had just happened, talking at once: "Holy shit!" "Was that a bird?" "Aw, poor thing."

Cady rose and approached the window, where a couple of students had gathered. "I don't even see it," said one. "Maybe it flew away," said the other. "Did you see how hard it hit? It left freakin' *feathers.*"

Sure enough, there was a smudge on the glass with a few tiny wisps of down clinging by some grisly glue. Cady pressed her forehead against the window to try to see down to the ground but couldn't. She took a step back. *Was that bird her sign?*

She headed for the door, leaving her laptop open and her damp notes on the chair. She passed through the double doors of the library and a cold gust of wind hit her, blowing her hair across her eyes and mouth. She held it aside and hurried around to the front of the library's main window. A thick hedge lined the foot of the library, and when she thought she was in the right area, she knelt down on the ground to look beneath the bushes.

A pigeon lay on its side with one wing outstretched, revealing a shock of white feathers where the rest were gray, its scaly toes curled close to its body. But as she inched closer, she was relieved to see its feathered breast rise and fall with regular breath. If only Cady's own breath were so steady. She had asked for a sign, and the universe had literally flung one out of the air: a pigeon, like a carrier pigeon, with a message. The echo of Vivi's words: *Be open to whatever form the messages take*. Messages delivered by birds, or by spirits. Maybe she needed to stop doubting and start paying attention.

The pigeon's lava-red eye rotated in her direction, and Cady was about to touch it, when crunching footsteps approached.

"Cady?" Alex peered down at her in a puffy coat that made his tall, lanky frame look even thinner. "I saw you rush out, is everything all right?"

"Did you see that bird fly into the window? I think it's hurt." Cady brushed the mulch off her knees.

He tilted his head and smiled. "You came out to check on the bird?"

"Yeah, is that crazy? Don't answer that."

"No, it's nice. And it's more interesting than doing work. So where's our suicide bomber?" Alex crouched down beside her. "Aw, poor guy. This happened once at my aunt's house, a bird whammed into the patio window and fell right into a trashcan. He was fine, but we had to shake him out. They get stunned or something and they think they can't fly away, but they can. We've got to get him out of the bushes."

Cady reached for the pigeon.

"Whoa, what are you doing?" Alex asked.

"Getting it out of the bushes, like you said."

"With your bare hands? Are you insane? Pigeons are disgusting, you'll get bird flu or something."

"He's injured. I can't just leave him." She needed to help *something*.

"Then hold up." Alex yanked a striped scarf from his neck. "Wrap your hands in this."

"And contaminate your scarf?"

"It's fine, but this is the full extent of my helping. And I'm warning you, if that pigeon flaps in my face, I'm going to scream."

Cady crept deeper into the shrubbery and gently clamped the scarf around the pigeon's wings, though it didn't struggle at all. Its only movement was in its pink toes, which closed around her exposed thumb, tight like a baby's hand. Its skin was surprisingly warm. "Where should I take him?"

"Um, um—how 'bout over here." Alex jumped back and pointed her to the stone steps around the side of Lamont. "Beside the stairs, this area gets less foot traffic."

Cady ducked under the metal handrail and stepped into the thick, tangled ivy blanketing the hill. She gently placed the pigeon down on a spot where the drape of the vines propped the bird in a semi-upright position. The pigeon allowed her to do this, only blinking one lavender eyelid when an ivy leaf touched its head.

She backed away, keeping her eyes on the bird, but it didn't move. Cady felt a pang of guilt that maybe she ought to have let the animal rest in peace. She looked over her shoulder at Alex, who was frowning.

Suddenly she heard a coo and flutter of wings, and Cady turned to see the bird take flight up into the sunlight.

Alex clapped his hands. "Ha! What'd I tell you?"

"I can't believe it!" Cady threw her arms around Alex with relief.

They both realized they were embracing a moment later and loosened their hold, although Alex didn't quite let go. Instead, he said, "Do you know what you need to do now?"

Did she? He had inadvertently asked the very question she'd been asking herself. Cady searched his sky-blue eyes for the answer.

"Wash your hands."

BACK INSIDE, CADY began to head back for the café, but Alex said he had to start his shift and motioned toward Lamont's front desk.

"You work at the reference desk?" Cady's wheels began turning.

He nodded. "It's a nice campus job. Pretty easy, gives me plenty of time to get my own work done, but it can be boring. Unless someone wants to keep me company." He raised his eyebrows at her.

"Yeah, I'll hang for a bit."

"You will? Awesome!"

"Great. I'll just get my things . . ." He looked so happy, Cady felt a little blush in her heart. But not quite enough to distract her from her newfound focus. "And maybe you can help me with something I've been researching."

"Absolutely, I'd love to."

It was only a few minutes before they reconvened behind the reference desk, but it was enough time for Cady to come up with a vague American History assignment on slavery at Harvard, more specifically, the slave at Wadsworth House named Bilhah. Excitingly, Alex was familiar with the topic and seemed eager to help her.

He frowned and typed quickly while Cady peered over his shoulder. "Okay, searching Hollis—that's the library database—I'm getting a ton of hits on Harvard history in general around President Holyoke's time, ooh, here's George Washington in Cambridge, *Harvard: Cradle of the American Revolution*," he said in a mock-serious voice. "We can pull some that look good. As for specifically Holyoke's slaves . . ."

"Bilhah and Juba," Cady supplied.

"Hm?" Alex looked up from the computer.

"Those are their names, Bilhah and Juba."

"Juu-bah," he played with the word in his mouth. "So cool. Well, this whole slaves-at-Harvard thing must be pretty new, like, not new in actuality, but new to academic writing, because these are some lean search results." He pushed back from the computer. "The best shot for small details like that would be the Harvard Archives, but they're closed on Sunday, and they can be kind of strict about letting students near the primary docs. But they like me down there. I'll follow up on it for you this week and let you know if I find anything."

Cady thanked him. She was grateful for Alex's help, sincerely, but she couldn't match his casual attitude as they hunted down the books in the stacks. They weren't "cool," and they weren't "details." Bilhah was a person, she had a name.

And she was trying to tell Cady something.

# 22

IN HER BEDROOM, Cady spread out on her desk the library books Alex had given her, filling her bedroom with the pleasantly musty, resinous smell of aged paper. They had titles like *Three Centuries of Harvard; VERITAS: Harvard College and the American Experience;* even a booklet from the National Park Service, *George Washington's Headquarters and Home, Cambridge, Massachusetts,* which Alex the library ninja had found included a chapter called "Wadsworth House Pre-Revolution." The only book that seemed remotely focused on race was a newer one titled *Ebony and Ivy.* Cady figured she would try to learn whatever she could about Bilhah and the time in which she lived. Maybe that would help Cady understand what she wanted from her, and what might come next.

She flipped through the index of the first book, *Three Centuries of Harvard,* but there was no "Slavery" under *S,* no "African" under *A,* no "Race" under *R,* and definitely no mention of the names of any of the slaves at Wadsworth House. However, there were plenty of mentions of President Holyoke and an entire chapter titled "Good Old Colony Times." Well, she would gather what she could by learning about the slave woman's general historical context. All she knew was that she worked for President Holyoke sometime between 1737 and 1769. The rest she would have to read between the lines.

President Edward Holyoke's tenure was described as one of "prosperity and progress." It said he oversaw a period of modernization of the library texts, scientific instruction, and moral and ethical philosophy. He believed in "aggressive liberalism" and the book's author noted, "It is probably more than a coincidence that so many of the New Englanders who took a leading part in the American Revolution had their education under him." Cady saw Holyoke described over and over again as a 'gentleman.' "A polite Gentleman, of a noble commanding presence." "A gentleman of innate dignity and sense of justice."

And yet, Cady thought, he was a slaveholder. This book didn't mention that. She noticed how easy it was to edit someone's past so that all the pieces of a person fit neatly together. Simple narratives were easier to tell, to teach, to understand, to remember. The lie endures for generations, while the truth dies with its victims. But what were the consequences?

Then Cady saw something that reminded her of Bilhah's talk of "smelling fire again": the "worst disaster in the history of the College," a devastating fire in Old Harvard Hall, the original library, in which all five thousand volumes were consumed. Cady opened a notebook and jotted down the date of the fire, January 24, 1764. Perhaps that was Bilhah's approximate present. It described how all the townspeople came out in a snowstorm and tried in vain to save the library and "its treasures." Cady felt almost moved until she got to the inventory of said treasures: listed without comment, after items such as portraits of benefactors, various taxidermy, and a model ship, was a "piece of tanned negro's hide, 'Skull of A Famous Indian Warrior, and in fact the entire 'Repositerry of Curiosities,' were seen no more."

The word *hide* turned her stomach. These were human remains, not curiosities.

"*Boom!*" Ranjoo jumped into their bedroom brandishing a Sharpie. "I did it!"

"Holy shit, you scared me," Cady said, recovering her breath. "Did what?"

"Catch." She tossed Cady a small plastic toy lizard. "For my draw-ing class, I had to draw that sucker *one hundred times* from different angles—in permanent marker, no less. Check it." She buzzed her thumb through her sketchbook pages revealing a flip-book of impec-cably drawn lizards.

"Whoa, you did amazing. But that assignment is insane."

"I know, this school finds a way to make studio art type-A. So, my hand is too cramped to do anything but shovel food in my mouth. Want to break for dinner with me? Or is this nightmare due tomor-row?" Ranjoo peered over at the books spread out on Cady's desk.

"Oh, yeah, a paper." Cady stood so she blocked her view. "But it's not due for a couple weeks. Let's go."


THEY WERE GETTING ready to leave, when an absentminded peek at her phone gave Cady pause. It was a Facebook notification that she had been tagged in a photo posted by their old neighbor, Patti Regan, one of the many women her mom's age and older who had friended her in recent years. The picture was of a pool party at the Regans' back when their kids, Eric, and Cady were young, maybe fourteen and eleven. The kids had all swum up to the pool's edge for the photo; the twins were in the center, looking indistinguishable with their wet hair, Liam Regan mugging mid-cannonball into the water, and Cady sitting tall atop Eric's shoulders. They were the reigning neighbor-hood champs at playing chicken, Liam and his sisters could never beat them even if they rotated the twins. Patti's caption read, "#tbt ~ Sum-mer Daze ~ Missing When These Kiddos Were Little! <3." They had moved away so long ago, she wondered if Patti knew Eric had died; Cady doubted she would have posted it if she did.

But it wasn't the photo or the wacky mom-caption that unnerved Cady, it was the tags. When she touched the image, "Eric Archer" popped up as an active tag. How was that possible? He hardly used social media when he was alive, he certainly wasn't accepting new tags now. She clicked on his name and was redirected to his profile page—only she was blocked from viewing it. The top of the profile asked: "Do you know Eric? To see what he shares with friends, send him a friend request."

"Ready?" Ranjoo was waiting at the door, already bundled in her oversized leather jacket and scarf.

"You know, I just remembered something, an email I have to get back to. I can do it faster on my laptop. Give me five minutes, and I'll meet you there."

Ranjoo's voice was muffled by the scarf. "A'right, see you at Annenberg."

Cady watched her go, then returned to frowning at her phone. Of course, she was friends with Eric on Facebook. She messaged technical support last summer to turn his profile into a "memorialized" account so that it couldn't be hacked; she was its new admin. She quickly typed her brother's name into the search field, and the top results showed two Eric Archers with identical profile images. The first one led her to the "Remembering Eric Archer" page she recognized and had full access to, Eric's old page. The second one, the one Patti had accidentally tagged, had to be an imposter.

She supposed it was possible Eric had made the duplicate account himself—in his paranoia, he often suspected hacking of various accounts and devices—but he had largely abandoned social media in the last year of his life. If he had begun to distrust Facebook, she didn't think he would make a second account, certainly not with his real name and image. Cady took a closer look at the second account, at least to the areas she could see as a non-friend. The fact that the profile and banner images were identical pointed to deception, whoever made this was intentionally trying to impersonate Eric. She knew this thing was fairly common. Once in high school, a handful of Cady's Facebook friends started messaging that they had received friend requests from a "new account" of hers and asking if it was legitimate. It wasn't, and Cady was able to flag the fake account as abuse, and Facebook removed it. It was little more than a nuisance, and Cady hadn't given it much thought. She didn't even get the angle on why a person would bother to make these dupe accounts, she just knew it happened often, as she had seen other friends post "This is my only account! Don't accept new requests from me!"

But this fake Eric profile struck her as unusual for a stranger taking a random shot at scamming someone. It didn't look hastily made; it looked like a real, cultivated Facebook profile made with Eric's stolen information and photos, just not the way Eric would have made it. For example, this fake Eric had "liked" the Philadelphia Eagles, Fandango, The National, Kendrick Lamar, and Harvard University. It wasn't that Eric *didn't* like those things, he did—but he would never, under any circumstances, have "liked" a corporate or promotional page on Facebook.

Similarly, the photos on the imposter page weren't fake or doctored, they all belonged to Eric at some point, but they were . . . curated, a selectively edited personal history. Not to mention they were set to "public"—very un-Eric. The account's deceit lay not in what it displayed, but by what it omitted. It was Eric's life, minus the darkness. For instance, real-Eric had grown so paranoid in his last year, he had stripped his social media of most photos and information. His final Facebook profile picture was one Cady hated. In it, he was sitting at his desk, unremarkable from the chin down, but starting at his nose, the image was distorted, twisting his entire face into a whirlpool of color: the pink of his lips smeared across his brow, the blue of his eyes spilled out like running water, the rest a blur of flesh tone and red hair. Posting it just months before his death, Eric had captioned it SELF-PORTRAIT.

But in the perfect world of the imposter page, the profile image was a beautiful landscape shot of Eric in his happy place—outdoors, on a hike, looking off atop a summit. She had seen it online in the past, it had been taken when Eric participated in one of Harvard's Pre-Frosh activities the summer before his first year, for which he'd chosen a week-long backcountry excursion. Cady remembered he'd come back from that trip more grown up, confident, in the perfect frame of mind to enter college. Cady's summer had been so chaotic, with her mother barely speaking to her, that she hadn't had the wherewithal to sign up for any of the Pre-Frosh offerings. The next featured image on the fake account was one she recalled from his freshman year of Eric asleep with his mouth open during what was clearly a lecture class and captioned, Photo credit: Matt Cho. Then a close-up of their family cat, Pickle, maniacally chewing the tassel on one of their window curtains, over which Eric had photo-shopped the words STRNG FEERY TASTE SCIENCY. But God, how long ago were LOLcats a thing? That was pre-Instagram, ancient history.

Cady clicked to the final photo and the furrow in her brow eased. It showed Eric in a Santa hat, sitting in front of the fireplace and holding their old Westie, Bowie, who was half-wearing a green elf hat. The photo must have been at least four years old, because Bowie died before Eric left for college. In the picture, Bowie was squirming in his arms, tongue out like he was smiling, and Eric was laughing, rendering the photo slightly blurry from the dog's movement or Eric's or both. Or maybe it was Cady's giggling that had shaken it. She'd been behind the camera.

She felt the tidal pull of nostalgia. And she understood how white-washed histories got committed to print and how a fiction could get committed to memory. They were so much more comforting, because they made more sense than the truth ever could. Cady wanted so badly to believe that Eric had made this second profile. It was like visiting a parallel universe where Eric never got sick, and she would give anything to stay there. It was Eric, as he was supposed to be. Eric, healthy. Eric, confident. Eric, plugged-in. Eric, happy. Eric, alive. It felt more real than the alternative.

But it wasn't.

She looked one more time at the Christmas photo. Nothing in that picture existed anymore. Not the dog, not the boy, not the laughter. Nostalgia had an undertow, and it threatened to drown her.

But for one detail that bobbed to the surface. Eric had never posted that picture on Facebook. Cady had.

So whoever had created this profile had been on her page, too.

# 23

THE SOUND OF Cady's cellphone ring burst into the quiet room. She reached for the phone on top of her dresser, half-dreading, half-hoping that it was her mother calling.

"Cadence." Nikos's familiar accent filled her ear. "I'm passing by Weld and I thought of you. Have you had dinner?"

"No, but I'm meeting my . . ." Cady checked her watch, surprised to see it was already seven. Ranjoo had left more than a half hour ago, she was probably finished by now. "Never mind. No, I haven't eaten."

"Good, me either. Come down, let me squire you to Lowell House. The dining halls close in a quarter hour, but our head kitchen lady fancies me, so she'll still feed us if we're a bit late."

The low moon was a gold button on a navy sport coat sky. On the walk to Lowell, Nikos talked enough for both of them, telling Cady about taking the math and physics GREs last Saturday and his top choice graduate programs. She was only half-listening, preoccupied with thoughts of Eric's imposter profile. It wasn't until they turned up a wide driveway off Mount Auburn Street that Cady's attention was pulled into the present. "Whoa."

The beautiful and imposing bell tower of Lowell House dominated the building's Georgian facade. The spotlit tower shone bright white, and the interior bells glowed in warm amber, like a jack-o'-lantern.

Cady followed Nikos through the main archway and into a courtyard where stone walls dripped with lush ivy and a flagstone footpath cut across the manicured lawn to the dining hall. A small tree in the courtyard was wound with twinkly white Christmas lights.

"Is this your first time at Lowell? It's the prettiest house, at least on the outside. Inside there's an occasional roach situation, but I shouldn't tell you that before dinner."

But the dining hall itself was even lovelier on the inside. A cream-white arched ceiling and butter-yellow walls made the space airy and inviting, and one long wall was filled with floor-to-ceiling windows. Nikos jogged across the checkerboard-tiled floor to the kitchen on the left, leaving Cady to admire the two large crystal chandeliers that bathed the room in warm light.

Nikos returned. "So, they've already taken away the hot entrees, but Marcia is working the grill, and I know I can get a couple more plates out of her. She's only just been divorced." He flashed a grin.

"You're terrible."

"I'm a man who can put food on the table. So what'll it be? Want a cheeseburger? That's what I'm getting."

"Sure, but make it a veggie for me."

Nikos rolled his eyes. "As you wish," he said, and hurried off toward the kitchen.

Cady dropped her coat and bag at an empty table and followed him. She scanned the buffet counters of mostly empty wells where the hot food had been and snagged a few tomatoes and sorry-looking lettuce leaves from what was left of the salad bar. She couldn't find a hamburger bun, but the dining halls kept a bread and bagel bar out all night for people working late, so Cady popped two slices of bread into the toaster. While she waited, her mind was swimming with thoughts of the imposter profile and its implications—had Eric seen it while he was alive? She heard a woman laugh and looked across the kitchen to see Nikos making the middle-aged grill cook giggle.

A few minutes later, Nikos met her at the table juggling three plates of food. "Here's your Resistance Burger," he said, deftly setting down her plate without disturbing the other he held in the same hand.

Cady gave a laugh. "It's not a political statement, it's just a kinder, healthier choice."

"Don't talk to me about health with whatever you've got there. What do you call that, a poor man's *pain au chocolat?*"

"What? It's just toast—" Cady stopped, suddenly at a loss for words. She was looking down at her plate, bewildered to find a piece of toast with peanut butter and a squiggle of chocolate syrup. She was seeing it for the first time.

"It looks disgusting," Nikos said. "But if it's delicious, I want a bite."

She hadn't made this, had she? Had she taken someone else's plate by mistake? But there'd been almost no one in the kitchen with her.

"Is something wrong?"

Cady met his gaze. His bushy black eyebrows were tilted like a roof over his soft brown eyes, his lips were pursed with concern. She felt a wellspring of emotion in her chest; he was the only person on this campus who would look at her like that. But she couldn't tell him that, so instead she told him all about Eric's second Facebook profile in a gush of words.

"That's very weird, I'm sorry you had to find that all alone." Nikos gently covered her clenched fist with his palm to comfort her. "But I suppose it doesn't matter now."

"Of course it matters! Someone was stealing his information and using it to impersonate him. That's huge! Can you imagine how that would have affected him?"

"Did Eric know about the fake profile?"

"He could have. I scrolled way down and checked, the first posts were started in the fall of last year, *before* he died. Toward the end, Eric was so paranoid. He was always thinking he was getting hacked. His doctor told us those sorts of groundless fears were typical. But what if it wasn't just paranoia? What if he was *right?* Someone was messing with him. Messing with me, even, I told you they took one of my pictures, too. This goes deep!"

"Okay, but before we get carried away with conspiracy theories, let's slow down. Those Facebook dupe accounts are a common scam. It's happened to me before. And it doesn't take a rocket scientist to infer that one Cadence Archer on Eric's friend list might be a relation. You said that Christmas photo was your banner photo, right? And the banner photo is always set to public, so it doesn't even mean you were hacked."

"No way a random scammer made this profile. It was made with care."

Nikos picked up her phone to see the profile again. "It's very thorough."

"But who would do this? Who would want to torment him? Like the poor kid didn't have enough on his plate. He never bothered anybody. Even in the end, he only hurt himself. Why target Eric?"

Nikos looked down at his hands. "This is hard to say, but in the last year of his life, Eric wasn't exactly the most popular person. His illness changed him, made him difficult to be around. I'm not sure he had many friends."

"Did he have enemies?"

"None that I can think of." Nikos shrugged. "I'm not ready to discount the possibility that the timing was coincidental, and it was simply a random Internet attack. I'm sure Eric didn't even know, and if he did, he wouldn't care."

Cady shook her head. "If Eric knew, it would've triggered a lot of bad memories for him. He was sensitive about that stuff. He got bullied as a kid, bad, especially in middle school. By high school, it was clear he wasn't just smart but brilliant, and he gained the confidence to own his nerdiness, so people let up. He worked so hard to get happy with himself. Which is why, you know—" Cady felt a familiar tightness in her chest and throat "—why what happened was so unfair."

Nikos reached out and put his hand over hers for the second time.

But Cady pulled her hand back and blinked away the wetness in her eyes. She hadn't wanted to lose control at that moment, she wanted Nikos to take her seriously. And she didn't want him to touch her out of sympathy.

"You know, I was bullied." Nikos sat back in his chair. "Don't give me that look! I was a short, hairy know-it-all with a funny name. Of course I was bullied."

"Nikos Nikolaides." Cady pronounced it slowly, letting her tongue click against her hard palate. "It's a lot."

"The repetition aside, Nikos is a name more befitting a Greek god, and then I show up, barely eleven stone, a hundred seventy-three centimeters, and I'll tell you that's about five foot ten, but that's rubbish, and this is *after* my growth spurt. For most of my young life, my name was a joke at my own expense, like when someone names their Chihuahua 'Killer.'" That made Cady laugh, and Nikos feigned being wounded, although one dimple betrayed an impish smile. "It's a terrible fate, really, you should pity me."

"I don't feel sorry for you." Nikos was heartbreakingly handsome, and worse, he knew it; Cady couldn't let him fish for compliments and win. "You're not completely disappointing in person, and my name is annoying, too. People always think it's Katie. Sometimes I think only my closest friends and family know my real name."

"You should go by Cadence."

She took a sip of her soda. "Maybe someday."

"No, I'm serious. Cady is cute, but it's for a little girl. And look at you." His gaze was steady and assured. "You're all grown up, Cadence."

They held eye contact for a beat longer, until the frisson made them both look away, pleasurably embarrassed. Nikos spoke first.

"For now, I think you need to put this Facebook stuff out of your mind, focus on your own agenda. It's Sunday night, you must have work."

Cady groaned. Tomorrow was Monday—the mere thought brought her down to earth. "I have a paper due Tuesday. I haven't even chosen a topic. I am so screwed."

"Tell you what, I've a pile of problem sets to grade for the math class I teach, they're up in my room. I'll get my things together, you finish your strange little supper, and I'll meet you back here. We can work together in the dining hall till they force us to relocate. Sound good?"

Cady agreed, and he left her alone. The dining hall had almost emptied out by now, the few who remained were just hanging out. Her stomach growled. She lifted the top bun of her veggie burger, which, she had to admit, didn't look so appealing now that it was cold. She replaced the bun, and her eyes traveled to the peanut butter and chocolate thing that lay untouched. She picked it up, and, with a last glance of skepticism, took a bite.

*Pardon me, but you're eating my black and tan.*

# 24

CADY QUICKLY REPLACED the peanut-butter-and-chocolate toast in its exact former position on the plate, like a thief restoring the objects of a victim's home.

*Well, goodness, it's yours now. I don't want it after your mouth touched it. It's contaminated.*

She recognized that tone—a mixture of childishness and superiority—Robert.

*The black and tan is my own culinary invention. I make one every day. I would've made one for you if you'd only asked nicely.*

You made me make this?—the realization sent a chill down Cady's spine. While her mind was elsewhere, his consciousness had reigned over hers.

*So? What do you think?*

Robert's casual question broke through the spiraling anxiety. She took a bite. It wasn't bad.

"Are you done?" A woman dressed in the gray and black Dining Services uniform appeared at Cady's left shoulder.

*"Are you finished."* Robert corrected.

Thankfully, the woman didn't hear his reply, nor did she wait for Cady's, "If not, keep the plates, but we're trying to get the trays up and cleaned."

"I'm finished, but I'll take it, I don't mind." Cady pushed her chair back from the table and asked where to bring it, and the woman pointed her in the right direction.

*You could have let her take it,* Robert said, as she walked across the room.

That's not her job.

*Where are the waiters?*

It's a dining hall, not a restaurant.

*Don't be silly, all of the dining halls have formal waitstaff.* Robert sounded genuinely confused.

Cady slid the tray into a vertical conveyor marked by a goofy, handmade sign that read "The Tray-o-later" and imagined a more elegant past.

She was walking back to the table when Robert added, *I overheard you talking about your brother, Eric.*

She instantly perked up—Did you know him? Did you ever speak to him?

*I haven't had the pleasure of meeting him. Is he my year?*

Cady sank back into her chair. —No. He's dead.

*Oh, dear. I'm sorry. How's your mother?*

What makes you ask that?

*I had a baby brother who died. He was only an infant, I myself was barely ambulatory, so I wouldn't presume to know your pain. But my brother's death changed my mother, and thus changed me. She kept me in a protective cocoon, utterly sheltered. So when I left my cosseted existence for boys' camp at fourteen, she might as well have thrown me to the wolves.*

She wanted to listen to him, but she had to be smarter about covering for these episodes in public spaces. Cady pulled a book from her bag and laid it open on the table. At least it would look as if she was doing something sane. She wondered how much time she had before Nikos got back.

*Although many things came easily to me as a child, relating to boys my age was never my forte. I couldn't help it, I related better to adults. I was always a teacher's pet.*

The same was certainly true of Eric, Cady thought.

*"Cutie" was the mildest name they called me. I was regularly roughed up. I never retaliated. Firstly, violence is against my personal ethos, and secondly, I calculated that most physical confrontations, I'd lose—I wasn't so tall as I am today. So I ignored them and hoped they'd get bored and leave me alone.*

Cady kept her eyes lowered to the pages of her open book, but she was listening intently.

*I was precocious, but naive. I learned the facts of life from some fascinating reading material a counselor had—lad mags. Accustomed to my curiosity being rewarded, I wrote about it in a letter home. My mother called the camp director, who in turn instigated a campus-wide crackdown on pornography, and I was branded a traitor.*

*I was asleep in my bunk when some boys shook me awake and dragged me outside my cabin. One pulled my shirt up over my head so I couldn't see a thing, and they marched me, stumbling, through the woods at midnight. We finally stopped and they shoved me down. As soon as my hands and knees touched the frozen floor, I knew where we were. The icehouse.*

She felt the chill in her teeth as Robert continued.

*I was stripped naked. The ringleader was holding a pail of something, I feared it was water, but that was wishful thinking. It was green paint. Two boys held my arms back so I couldn't cover myself. Then a sucker punch to the gut to make me double over, and they threw paint on my . . .*

His voice trailed off, but he didn't need to say it—the hot flush of embarrassment Cady felt on her cheeks told her exactly how he was humiliated.

*They said it was to find the other boys 'like me.' And then they left me there, naked, locked in from the outside. I spent all night in that icehouse.*

That's horrible.

*I suppose my bunkmate told them. He was probably my only friend, and he was the only one who knew about my letter.*

He betrayed you.

*Or he simply let it slip. There are such things as unintended consequences. But it did change me. And it taught me a valuable lesson:*

*It takes only an error to father a sin.*

Cady got goose bumps. She had heard those words before . . . at the whispering wall outside Sever. So that had been Robert speaking to her, not Nikos.

A stack of papers slapped down on the table in front of Cady, making her jump.

"Two sections, totaling thirty-three students, each with a four-page problem set, equals one hundred thirty-two pages for me to grade by tomorrow morning at eleven o'clock. Can I do it?" Nikos collapsed into the chair across from her, lolling his head back and his arms out to each side in a gesture of utter helplessness.

Cady tried to push Robert's story out of her mind. "Sounds tough."

"It's not for me. This is Math Xa, it's kid stuff."

"I thought all the teaching assistants were grad students."

"They are, usually. But occasionally professors employ advanced undergrads, especially for subjects like maths."

"But aren't you a physics major?"

"Physics 'concentrator' in Harvard-speak. Like 'teaching fellow,' hence TF. If we aren't needlessly different, how would people know we're so elite?" He uncapped a red pen with glee.

"Before you get started." Robert had given Cady an idea. "I was thinking more about Eric. What about his academic rivals? He must have had them, if he was going out for the Bauer Award."

"He didn't end up submitting."

"Yeah, but no one could've predicted that. And Prokop, this hot-shot professor, picks him as her advisee." Robert's story echoed in her mind. "Eric was a teacher's pet, people don't like that, they get jealous. So maybe that's a lead on who did this. Who does Prokop advise now?"

"Me." Nikos chuckled.

"Oh." Cady blushed. "I didn't realize."

"My Bauer project required experimental research this summer, Prokop was the best suited to the material, so I switched. But I know I'd have Eric's blessing. He and I always made each other better."

"No, I know, of course. But someone who wasn't his friend, someone who might have resented him, can you think of anyone like that?"

Nikos puffed out his cheeks and blew out a sigh. "No one in particular comes to mind. The Physics department isn't as crass about its competitiveness as say, the Maths department, those animals actually tear up each other's notes, but there is a hierarchy in Physics. I wouldn't say Eric was top dog, but he was a *darling* of the department."

"Was he Prokop's darling?"

"She chose him to advise out of many, she's in demand, like you said, so she certainly believed in him."

Cady took a shaky sip of her water, unsure of how much to share. "I went to one of her lectures to talk to her about Eric. She said she felt really bad when she had to dismiss Eric as her assistant. But then I talked to Matt, his roommate, and *he* told me that Eric called her 'Mika,' that they spent a ton of time together, and, get this—that she didn't fire him, he quit." Cady waited for a shocked reaction, but Nikos's affect remained flat, so she pushed on. "And when he quit, Prokop showed up at their room *begging* him to talk to her." Still nothing. "C'mon, how often do professors make house calls?"

Nikos shrugged. "She was likely disappointed he was quitting his project for the Bauer, as was I. And as for the 'Mika' thing, a lot of people refer to professors by their first names in conversation, it's a form of posturing to seem like you're on their level. You don't say 'Professor Lemke is advising me,' instead you say, 'Peter and I are working on . . .' It doesn't necessarily mean much."

"But how do you explain her lying about firing him?"

"Isn't it more likely that Eric was lying about quitting?" Nikos said gently. "She was advising him on the Bauer, after he refused to submit, it didn't make sense for her to keep him on as a research assistant."

It was the same conclusion Cady had first come to, and it sounded even more sensible coming from Nikos, but she couldn't deny that in her gut, she believed Matt. "But what if there was another reason Prokop would want to keep Eric around?"

"Like what?"

Cady leaned over the table. "Matt thought Eric had a crush on Prokop. Is it possible that, maybe, she reciprocated those feelings?"

Nikos leaned in to meet her. "Like an affair?"

Cady raised her eyebrows.

A great guffaw burst from Nikos as his body rocked back in the chair. "Unless Prokop has a fetish for awkward gingers, I don't think your brother was getting a piece of the faculty's Hitchcock blonde. Nabbing a professor, especially one like that, calls for some serious finesse, a pro. Eric was brilliant, but he was not a pro." Nikos laughed again, this time drawing the attention of a few people sitting nearby.

Cady sat back, peeved. "I think it's in the realm of the possible. And something like that might've made someone jealous of Eric. But I don't know, you were his friend, you probably have a better sense."

"Honestly, I can't see it. Bedding Prokop would've been the greatest coup since Napoleon. If Eric had pulled that off, he would've told me. The bragging rights would be irresistible."

Cady frowned. Eric had never been one to brag. "Okay, so maybe not an affair. But something went south between them. Something personal." She sat back in thought. "Matt made it sound like Eric cared more about Prokop's research than anything he was working on for his Bauer submission. If she's your adviser now, that research assistant job must be yours, too, right? What's she working on?"

"No, actually, I'm her advisee but not her assistant. She can help me with my research, but I'm not allowed to work on hers, because I'm a 'foreign national.' Is America great again yet? I've been meaning to ask."

"Are you being serious?"

"Yes, her current research is restricted. It's funded by the U.S. government, and the federal grant stipulates that no 'foreign nationals' can participate. Last time I checked, Britain was an ally, but it'd be politically incorrect to say what they mean, which is, 'No Arabs, No Chinese,' so they discriminate against all of us equally."

"They're afraid of what—spies?"

"I'm a bit short to play James Bond, but I have the accent, and I can wear the shit out of a tuxedo."

"So her work is top secret."

"Well no, it's not *that* exciting. This is still a university. So, generally speaking, I know that she's refining the method of using wave particles to scan freight for uranium or nuclear material. She's been researching related topics in particle physics for the last decade, she's preeminent in the field, it's no secret. But the specific technology that she's developing is proprietary, so the details are classified. That way some other country or company can't swoop in and piggyback on all the research, that's the expensive part."

Cady's thoughts swarmed like bees around this new information. Eric had been working on restricted government research with Prokop—it sounded like the beginning of one of Eric's paranoid theories. Cady could imagine how such a scenario might've exacerbated Eric's paranoia, made him even more difficult to work with, maybe that necessitated Prokop firing him. Or what if he broke one of the rules, compromised the research somehow? Maybe that's why Prokop cared enough to come to his room, maybe she lied about firing him to cover her own liability. But one question remained: why would Prokop want a paranoid schizophrenic working on sensitive material in the first place?

. "But I would like to amend one of my previous statements," Nikos broke through her thoughts. "I *can* think of one person who might have had knives out for him, I forgot her because she's a joint-concentrator in Physics and Comp Sci. Her name is Lee Jennings. I believe she did submit for the Bauer competition, although I doubt she stands a chance."

"Comp Sci—*computer science?*"

"That's right. For someone like her, I'm sure hacking Facebook is child's play."

"Oh my God, it has to be her. Should we go to the Ad Board?" One minute ago she hadn't had any idea who Lee Jennings was, now she wanted this person who hurt her brother punished.

"And say what? You suspect she created a false Facebook account?"

"She was harassing a mentally ill student at his most fragile time. Hacking his social media could have exacerbated his paranoia and his depression. We still don't know what exactly pushed him over the edge. It takes only an error to father a sin."

"Is that a Chinese proverb or something?" He chuckled. "Look, I hear you. If it was her, and we don't know for sure, but if it was, she should be ashamed of herself. But Cadence, she's a petty loser, a nobody. She'll get hers when I destroy her in the Bauer competition."

"How do you spell her name?" Cady had her phone out, already looking her up on Facebook. "Never mind, got it. Ugh, her profile picture is private." Cady navigated around what little wasn't blocked by the privacy settings. But she was tagged in one group affiliation. "She's in ROTC for the Navy?"

"Perhaps, yes, I've seen her around campus in fatigues. I thought she was just butch."

ROTC for all of the branches remained a very small group on Harvard's campus, Cady knew only two people in her Freshman class who were members, and they were both men. In her mind, it only added to Lee's strange, threatening mystique. She navigated to the NROTC group page and looked through their pictures. Lee was easy to spot as one of the few women. Seeing her in uniform triggered Cady's memory. "Oh my God, I think I know this girl. She's in my French class."

"Perfect, next time you see her, you can shout *J'accuse!*"

"Don't joke."

"I'm sorry, I'm only trying to make you laugh."

Cady opened another Safari window on her iPhone and looked up Lee's room in Harvard's student directory. "She lives in Kirkland N-42. Where's that?"

"It's part of the Kirkland annex, but Cadence, why are you looking up her room? You're not seriously thinking of going over there."

"Why not?"

"Because it's mad! You don't know if she had anything to do with it."

"So, I'll ask her." Cady bristled at his judgmental tone.

"You said yourself you have French class with the girl, so sleep on it, let yourself cool off a bit. And really think if this quest for revenge is worth your time. You can't go backward. Eric wouldn't have wanted you to spend your freshman year fighting small battles for him."

"You don't know what he would've wanted."

Nikos looked stung.

Cady instantly regretted snapping at him, embarrassed by her behavior. She knew that for all his joking, Eric's death had taken a toll on Nikos as well. "I'm sorry."

"I didn't mean to tell you how to feel—"

"You didn't, I just have to go. I have this paper due Tuesday for Hines, who hates me, I haven't started it, and I realize I left the poetry book I need in my room. I should've checked before you went and brought all your stuff down. Sorry."

"Oh, no worries at all." Nikos did a poor job of masking his disappointment.

She gathered her things, and he rose to hug her goodbye.

As they embraced, he said, "Just remember to look out for yourself, all right?"

She nodded into his shoulder.

But she was already planning her next move.

# 25

CADY KNOCKED ON the door of Kirkland N-42 and waited, working her tongue to unstick her lips from her dry mouth.

The girl who answered the door wore thick glasses and light brown hair pulled tightly back. Her skin was pale, save for her nose, which was red and glistening. "Yeah?" she asked, before blowing her nose loudly into a wad of tissue.

"I'm looking for Lee, is she here?"

"No." The girl coughed and hocked something into the tissue.

"Oh." Cady cleared her own throat, out of sympathy-disgust. She had come up with a contingency plan on the walk over. "Well, my name is Julie, and Lee and I have French 27 together, and she's in my project group. Can I drop off some papers for her in her room? She has to write the conclusion for our skit tomorrow."

"Okay. Come in." The girl turned around and Cady saw that her braid went all the way down her back. "Hers is the second door on left." Cady thanked her, and she reentered the cocoon of a comforter and tissues scattered all over their futon.

Cady closed Lee's bedroom door behind her with a soft click. She had no clear objectives beyond getting a sense of the girl, but whatever she was looking for ought to be easy to find—Lee's bedroom was Spartan and immaculate, as though she was in the military already.

The old wood floors were bare and clean, and the bed was made with tight hospital corners. Cady scanned her desk for anything that might give her a sense of the person who lived there, a day planner, even a Post-it, but the surface was completely clear except for a large monitor and a jack for a laptop—Cady inferred with disappointment that Lee's laptop must be with her. The only evidence of personality was on the walls, which were covered in photographs. But not personal photos of family or friends; instead there were careful rows of black-and-white photographs of birds in flight. Geese flying in formation over the Charles. Pigeons fighting over a piece of bread. A cardinal, drained of its sanguine color, about to alight on a branch.

Lee is a lonely person, Cady thought, or an envious one. Although it would have been hard to envy Eric on that front, as he isolated himself pretty well. But he had Matt, and Nikos, despite going for the Bauer at the same time. Maybe with Lee, the budding soldier, everything was a rank, a battle, zero-sum. Maybe that was her motive for targeting Eric online, to throw him off balance for the competition. Lee hadn't known he was already so close to the edge.

Cady's eyes fell to the bookshelf, where a Nikon 460 lay with a telephoto lens beside it. She picked up the camera and started clicking through the images on the digital screen: birds, birds, and more birds. Then, a picture of the back of a blond woman's head, taken from far away, seemingly without the subject's knowledge. Cady clicked through a succession of images of the woman, which, going in reverse, showed the woman getting out of a car. She kept clicking, hoping she'd get one shot that showed the woman's face, with each click the woman's head rotated closer and closer, *beep beep beep*.

Cady gasped.

"What are you doing?" The roommate was standing in Lee's doorway. "You said you were just dropping something off. Don't touch that."

Cady clicked the camera off and set it down. "Sorry. I was just looking at it."

"You need to leave right now."

Lee's roommate walked her out of the suite and slammed the front door shut behind her. Cady stood momentarily stunned on the fourth-floor landing before the vertiginous entryway staircase. She was full of adrenaline, but not from getting caught.

Why was Lee Jennings taking photos of Professor Mikaela Prokop?

# 26

WITH RANJOO GENTLY snoring above her, Cady lay in her bed, squinting against the brightness of her phone screen a few inches from her face. She was reviewing every aspect of Lee Jenning's social media presence. Unfortunately, her initial assessment of Lee's Facebook in Lowell House was correct, there wasn't much to see. She'd thought she'd hit pay dirt when Cady found Lee's Instagram set to public, but it appeared only to show off her photography hobby; Cady didn't think Lee was very good, but she wasn't in a charitable mood. Very few of Lee's photos were of people and nearly zero of herself. The closest thing Lee had to a selfie was one in which she was reflected in a broken mirror propped against a stop sign. In the reflection, Lee's face was mostly blocked by the same fancy-looking camera that Cady had found in her room, all of her that was visible was one dark eye above a haughty cheekbone, and half of a full mouth. She was not smiling.

The screen's glare at last became too much, and Cady squeezed her eyes shut, rubbing the greasy skin of her forehead where a headache bloomed. What grudge did Lee have against Eric? Cady asked herself. Why go after my brother?

*Not him*, Bilhah's voice cut into her thoughts, *someone else.*

Cady's eyes flew open. She saw nothing but the fuzzy darkness in her bedroom, but she knew better than to think she was alone.

*If somebody disguising hisself as your brother, it's not him they after. You don't wear a mask to fool the mask. You wear one to fool someone else. So the better question is, who they trying to fool?*

Yes. Cady had been too preoccupied with protecting Eric. Who was the imposter profile meant to fool?

*I'll tell you a story. Some months ago, a stranger came to Cambridge village, Mister Bristol, looking for someone to help his sick little boy. I told you I know Indian medicine, so I thought I might help, and the Holyokes let me go. Mister Bristol took me in his buggy, and he whipped his horse so fast, I thought the wheels would spin off. But by the time we reached the house, it was too late. Child been dead for hours, skin white as flour, but the mother wouldn't let go of him, wouldn't let anyone near who might try and take him from her, she wouldn't even look at me. I wept for her the whole way home. That Bristol boy, they only son, reminded me greatly of mine own. Eli is the same age, same soft curls—it was like I seen my baby's ghost.* Her voice trailed off. *I couldn't wait to get home to feel him safe and warm in my arms again.*

*That's when I knew: If Missus Bristol saw my boy, she wouldn't think twice, she'd take him in.*

What do you mean?

*Eli will never be safe with me. But the Bristols would think they prayers was answered if Eli was found on the doorstep of they parish church. A precious white child, an orphan boy who needs a home, just like the one they lost.*

Cady didn't understand—But . . . your son isn't an orphan, or white.

*He might as well be. I'm mulatto, and he take after his father—light eyes, Christian hair.*

What little Cady knew of this woman came together in a bleak picture—a slave with a biracial child, a woman who knew to warn Cady from the dangers of drunk, entitled, privileged men—Cady didn't need to press farther. She knew his conception was just one of many horrors Bilhah had likely endured, but she could also hear that the pain in her voice came from the deep love she felt for her son.

*The Bristols will want to believe it. If I get Eli the proper clothes, genu-ine leather shoes, they'll believe he's one of them, no question. And once they do, so will others. People see what they want to see.*

But how can you part with him?

*Tell me how can I keep him? White mothers get to hold on to they chil-dren even in death. Black babies been taken from black arms since birth. I either wait for my son to be sold a slave, or give him a chance to be reborn a white man. I love him more than anything in this world, but if I try and hold on to him, they'll take him anyway, he'll forever be a thing to be owned, and used, and broken. If I can set him free of me now, before he grows, before he remembers, he can live free forever.*

*I won't be the chains around my child's feet.*

Her words flattened Cady in her bed, her heaving chest her only movement.

*People have many reasons to disguise themselves. You're trying to un-derstand why this person used your brother as the lie, then you need to ask, who was they after? Who was they lying to?*

Cady blinked away a tear and picked up her phone in a trembling hand. But how could she concern herself with this after what she'd just heard? Her mind felt too clouded by the voice to think clearly.

*Look for who would believe that lie,* she insisted. *Go on.*

Eric's fake profile reappeared on the screen. She navigated to his Friends list, which was blocked from view except for one profile listed in "Mutual Friends:"

Andrew Archer

Her father.

"Oh my God," Cady whispered aloud.

*I been too long. My candle's almost done.*

Wait, please, just wait—Cady couldn't even process the bomb-shell she'd just seen, but she didn't want to let the voice go without answering some of her questions—Why do you come to me, why do you want to help me?

*Because you listen. Because nobody here seems to know you or ever seen you except for me, which makes you the perfect person to help me save my son. I'll explain more next time. I hope you will agree to help me when I come again.*

Yes, yes, I will. I wanted to help you before, I went to Wadsworth House—

*—No! You mustn't tell them I spoke to you, don't tell anyone.*

No, no, I didn't, I won't. —Cady felt especially insane reassuring someone she wouldn't tattle on her more than two hundred years into the future, but here she was. She wondered how she could explain herself without alarming her. —Your secret is very, very safe with me.

*It has to be. That awful fire—*

The library fire?

*Oh, the sorrowful bellowing over those burned books last year. But no, those aren't the flames that chase me in my nightmares.*

Then what is?

*My first autumn here, two slaves named Mark and Phillis, killed their master by poisoning him. (They only caught them because they stole the arsenic. Pity they didn't know how to do it with mushrooms). They was dragged through Cambridge Commons and executed right outside these gates of Harvard. Everyone gathered to watch. Mark was hanged to death. But poor Phillis, she was old enough to be a grandmother, she was burned alive at the stake. Her smoke blew right through the Yard. Ten autumns since, and when the leaves turn, I can still smell her burning.*

*If you tell anyone, it will be me next.*

# 27

WAKING UP THE next morning was a mercy, as Cady had never had such vivid nightmares as she did after Bilhah's visit, and she vowed that whatever she could do from this dimension to help her, she would. As for her own agenda, Cady had been given a new hypothesis to test: that Lee was catfishing her father with an idealized version of Eric. It seemed utterly bizarre that these two people should be connected, and yet it appeared to be true. Cady hadn't even known her father had a Facebook account, was this one a fake, too? Was someone impersonating her entire family? But she checked, and neither she nor her mother had a dupe account. There were too many unknowns to speculate; she needed to go to the source and call her dad.

Ranjoo was getting ready and blasting Lizzo, her current morning jam, in their bedroom, and Andrea was in the common room, snowed in under a flurry of white index cards for Organic Chemistry and still giving Cady the silent treatment, so she went out to sit in the hallway just outside their door to make the call. She tried to keep her voice down for some modicum of privacy.

After a brief small chat, she got right to the point. "Dad, do you have a Facebook profile?"

"I'm not on it, per se, you know me, I still miss my BlackBerry, but yes, I made a rudimentary profile."

"I saw it. I was so surprised, I thought it was a fake. Did you friend Eric?"

"Yes."

It was off topic, but Cady couldn't help herself. "You didn't friend me."

He chuckled. "You actually talk to me! You remember how Eric was with me that last year. Facebook was the only way I could keep up with him, see how he was doing. He was the only reason I made an account in the first place."

Cady did remember. Eric was the most combative with their father. "Dad, that account—"

"That stupid account was a huge comfort to me. I know, it's absurd, I 'friended' my child. Virtual crumbs of a connection to my only son. But it was something, I was completely shut out of his life, and then with that Facebook, it was like the door opened a crack."

Cady bit her lip.

"And he seemed happy on it. All we got at home was the Sturm und Drang of his illness and the business of trying to get his life back on track, but on his profile you could tell there was some good stuff left too, you know? I still visit it sometimes, just to see the pictures. That he accepted his dopey dad's friend request was your brother's final gift to me."

And Cady wouldn't be the one to take that away from him, she decided. He deserved this bit of softness, even if it wasn't real. She had gotten what she needed—confirmation that her father's profile was legitimate. The rest of her questions she would have to answer for herself.

"But I will happily add you as a friend. I need pictures of you, too, now that you're not under my roof anymore. Was that what you wanted to talk about, Cady-Cake?"

"Parents' Weekend," Cady pulled out of her subconscious. "I forwarded you that email a while back, but I think it's soon, like next weekend. You guys should book your hotel if you haven't already."

"Oh, dear, I meant to discuss this with you in person when you were home, but then everything became"—another gale-force breath—"*chaotic*. Anyway, I feel terrible about this, but I realized Parents' Weekend coincides with my firm's partners' retreat. It's when the Management Committee votes on new partners, and it's absolutely mandatory. I looked into coming for part of the weekend, but the retreat is all the way out in Bolton Landing, so a hike to sit in Adirondack chairs with men too old and fat to hike, and I think it's not gonna work out."

"Oh." Cady tried to hide her disappointment. "That's okay."

"I know, you just saw me, so you're probably relieved. But I'm so sorry to miss it. I hate thinking of you with nobody there."

"So, Mom isn't coming either?"

"She hasn't made a decision, but . . . I wouldn't get your hopes up."

Cady fell silent. A moment ago, Parents' Weekend was nothing more than a convenient excuse to call home, but now she felt the full weight of what she would be missing. She had been worried about how she was going to manage her mother without her dad as a buffer, but instead of relief, she felt anger. "She's never going to be okay with me being here."

"Not never, but not yet. That place holds such bad memories for her."

"Does it for you?"

"We're going to make some new ones, aren't we?"

Cady nodded, since it was easier than talking with the lump in her throat. Her father kept counting on the fact that Cady would make up for Eric. That was worse than her mother thinking she couldn't.

"There's something else I should mention," her father continued. "From now on, the best way to reach me is by calling my cell or here at my usual office number, not at home."

"Why?"

"I've taken on almost double the workload lately, and I'm spending more time in the city, so I've decided to rent an apartment."

"Wait. You're *moving out*?" Cady asked, stricken.

"Not permanently, just for a while, to get some space."

"Whose idea was this?"

"Mine."

"What does Mom think?"

"Neither of us is happy about it, but it's a decision we discussed. I'd prefer to keep the details between us."

"Are you leaving her?" Cady's voice caught on the word *her*; it sounded like a line from a movie, not a question about her own parents.

"It's not that simple. Your mom and I made a promise to each other that will bind us together in ways more profound than a shared living space."

She felt panicky. "Mom can't be alone." They couldn't *both* leave her, she thought.

"We all have to learn someday." Her father's voice was suddenly gruff.

"But how can you?" Cady's feelings of protectiveness of her father and resentment of her mother completely inverted. "After everything we went through, she's the only one who understands. You're going to go meet some woman who doesn't even know Eric, who never even knew he existed?"

"Whoa, whoa, whoa, slow down. I'm not moving out to meet women. We're not getting divorced. But I'm trying to move forward, and I can't do that living with your mother right now."

"Why? Because she reminds you of him? Because she's still sad?"

"No, that's not it."

"It's like you want to erase him. And Mom reminds you of him, so now you have to erase her, too. What about me? I'm still sad, I still miss him. And I look like him! Am I next?" Cady was yelling now. "I can't win with you guys! Mom will never be happy because I'm *not* him, and you won't because I'm *too much* like him."

"Cadence, listen to me." Her father spoke low and steady. "I love you more than you can possibly imagine. You are my child, you are the most precious thing to me, and I would do anything, *anything*, to protect you. But I have gotten myself into a situation with your mother that is dark and toxic. I'm not the man I thought I was. I need some time and space to think, so that I can look in the mirror and recognize myself again."

"Now's not the time to split apart. Hard times are supposed to bring families together," Cady said, her voice breaking.

"We haven't been together for a long time."

Cady affected calm sufficiently for her father to let her off the phone, but she ended the call feeling more disturbed than ever. She rose and put her hand on the suite room door, then paused, suddenly embarrassed her roommates might have overheard her when the conversation got heated. They probably hadn't heard anything, she thought hopefully.

Cady opened the door to their suite. The futon had been completely cleared of Andrea's study materials, and her bedroom door was shut. So was the door to her and Ranjoo's room, and the music was off. So, they had heard everything and fled the awkwardness, which Cady wouldn't have minded if she hadn't had to get her stuff from her room. She exhaled a massive sigh, but it did little to expel the building tension in her chest.

# 28

CADY HAD NEVER been so alert and focused in that morning's French Lit class before, only her attention wasn't on Madame Dubois—it was on the young woman in a khaki naval uniform.

Lee Jennings was sitting one row ahead and two seats to the left, and Cady had been staring at her through the whole lecture. Lee was short and compact; she couldn't have been taller than five foot two. Cady could tell she bit her nails, possibly the only mark of vulnerability on her. The rest of her aspect was serious, her mouth seemingly naturally downturned, her direct gaze magnified behind rimless glasses. She looked Asian, or maybe half, her brown hair was wavy at the temples, even as it was pulled back in a bun with regulation severity. Cady wondered if Lee would recognize her as Eric's sister the way Nikos had, and she brushed her own hair off her shoulders and onto her back, as if that could hide its color. But Lee was looking straight ahead at the blackboard, where Madame Dubois was writing about the themes of Stendhal's *Le Rouge et le Noir* in loopy script.

The class was conducted entirely in French, and it required concentration to follow the lecture. Madame Dubois turned to pose a question to the class, which Cady translated in her head: "There are some who say the protagonist, Julien, is a narcissist, or even a sociopath. Do you agree?"

Gideon, a French Canadian whom Cady resented for his native advantage, raised his hand first, as usual. "Yes, he uses people, especially women, as tools. He's manipulative and without remorse. He has no empathy."

Cady took halfhearted notes as he spoke, but she perked up when Lee raised her hand to answer next. "I disagree," Lee said, in French. "He's not a sociopath, but he is not sentimental, like the other characters. He is small, and he is poor. His only mode of advancement is his wit. Julien's not cruel, he's cunning."

Cady huffed—*you* would *think that*, she thought—and Lee glanced in her direction. Cady quickly dropped her gaze to her notes.

Cady spent the rest of class rehearsing what she would say to Lee if she confronted her—*when* she confronted her. She was frustrated with herself that the girl intimidated her. But according to Nikos, Lee was both brilliant and ruthless, and Cady could sense her edge in that single glance. Still, she had to know more about this girl. If Nikos was wrong, she was harmless. And if he was right, Cady reminded herself, Lee had already hurt her in the worst way possible, by hurting Eric. In that case, Lee should be afraid of *her*.

As soon as class was dismissed, Lee flipped her empty notebook closed and was out the door. Cady grabbed her things in one motion and rushed after her. Boylston's main hall was congested, and although initially Cady had a bead on Lee's tight bun weaving through the crowd, she soon lost sight of her. She thought she saw the brown head near the glass doors at the entrance, so she ducked and shoved her way through. Cady emerged and hurried down the steps to Boylston's cobblestoned courtyard and stopped. Her eyes scanned the Yard, which was bustling with students crossing the green on the long diagonal footpaths, weighed down by overstuffed backpacks and bags, like ants—but Lee had vanished. Cady cursed under her breath.

She turned around and nearly slammed right into the uniformed chest of Midshipman Jennings.

"Why were you at my room last night?" Lee said, arms akimbo.

Cady hadn't expected to be on the defensive. "What?"

"My roommate said a redhead from my French class stopped by, 'Julie.' I know it was you. What were you snooping around for in my room? Did you take anything?'"

"No." Cady heard her own voice sound like a scolded child.

"I'll find out if you did." Lee had a way of tilting her chin up so that, despite being a few inches shorter than Cady, she seemed to be looking down at her. "Don't mess with my stuff again." She turned to go.

Lee got two paces away before Cady's anger revived her courage. "Why are you taking pictures of Professor Prokop?" she called out, loud enough to make a few passing students' heads turn.

Lee stepped in close again, crowding her. "None of your business," she said, her voice low.

Cady squared her shoulders. "It is my business, because I think you're spying on her because she's advising your competition for the Bauer Award, currently Nikos, my friend, but first my brother, Eric. And I don't actually care if you want to play dirty for an academic award. But I do care if you were following or in any way harassing my mentally ill brother right before he committed suicide, and I think the Ad Board might be interested in that, too." That came out better than she'd rehearsed.

"Look, I'm sorry your brother died, but I hardly knew him. And if Nikos Nikolaides is your friend, you should find a new friend."

"I think it was you who made that fake Facebook profile for Eric."

Lee gave a laugh. "You're crazy. I don't know what you're talking about."

But Cady registered a flicker of fear in Lee's eyes. "The one you used to catfish my dad."

When Lee glanced back at Cady this time, her eyes had softened. "We need to talk."


LEE TOOK HER to Café Gato Rojo, a campus spot near the language building. The small coffee shop was filled with students and TFs speaking in all different tongues, the United Nations with chia lattes. They didn't order anything, and Lee sat at a corner table with her back to the wall facing the entrance. For the first time, she seemed as nervous as Cady.

"Let's clear this up. I wasn't cyberbullying Eric. Your dad paid me to hack Eric's profile."

Cady's jaw dropped. "He *paid you?*"

"I work at the Computer Help Desk on campus, our website has a bulletin for small IT jobs, it's supposed to be for students and alums, but I saw an Andrew Archer posted a message saying he was the father of a student and to email for more info. I admit, I recognized the last name, I was curious, so I answered it. What he really wanted me to do was to get him access to Eric's social media accounts."

"Wait, back up." Cady squeezed her eyes shut. "Why would my dad hire someone to hack his own son?"

"All he said was that Eric was going through a hard time and shutting him and your mom out, and that the school wouldn't communicate with him." Lee shrugged. "He's a dad. He sounded like he just wanted to know more about his son's life. And like a dad, he thought Facebook was the best way to do it, but Eric had him crazy blocked, he couldn't see a thing."

"So you hacked his—"

"No, I didn't. I don't know how to hack anything. People like your dad watch movies, and they think every Asian kid can hack into the 'mainframe' in thirty seconds from the back of a van. And even if I could, he wasn't paying me enough for that shit." Lee must have caught Cady's scowl. "*And,* I wouldn't do that to Eric. So I figured, if I just make a second profile for Eric and friend your dad, then it's win-win. Eric gets his privacy, and your dad is reassured everything is okay."

"But . . . everything wasn't okay." Cady suddenly saw the what-could-have-beens in new light. "Eric was worse than ever. He was posting dark stuff, he was in crisis. If my dad had seen the real thing, he might have intervened or done something—"

"You didn't."

That knocked the wind out of her.

"Look," Lee continued, oblivious to her sucker punch. "All social media is bullshit anyway. I tried to do as close to the right thing by your brother."

Cady shook her head. "You didn't care what happened to him. You wanted to take him down."

"Not him," Lee said, her lips tight. "*Her*."

"Who? Prokop?"

Prokop's name ignited something within Lee, her nostrils flared and her jaw clenched. "There's one female professor in the whole Physics department, one, and I was the only female applicant for the Bauer. I'm joint concentrating in Physics and Comp Sci, and after college, I'm going to be an officer in the Navy—I get what it is to be a woman in a man's world, okay? But I thought for once, I found someone who could take me on my merit and not make me double-time it to be considered. I looked up to Professor Prokop, I identified with her. I have the highest GPA in the Physics concentration, higher than Eric and Nikos had, and I submitted a great application."

"You were angry that she picked a guy?"

"No, I'm angry that she picked her *boyfriend*."

Even as it confirmed Cady's own suspicion, it was strange to hear it validated.

"Her favoritism of him was so blatant that even after Eric missed the deadline to submit his Bauer project, Prokop *still* wouldn't choose another advisee. I had a hunch they were hooking up on the side, so I was interested in building a sexual harassment case against Prokop. That's when I started following them with my camera."

"So you *were* stalking Eric!"

"No. Only when he was with her."

"Did you photograph them . . . *together* together?" Cady was disgusted at her gross invasion of his personal life.

"No, no, I never got anything I could use," Lee answered, missing the point.

"And you had the gall to say you gave one shit about his privacy? You have no boundaries."

"Boundaries are a privilege. Rich people have boundaries, I have limits, obstacles I have to work around. Accusing a star professor of sexual harassment is serious, the faculty here doesn't just roll over when they're threatened, there are repercussions—especially for someone like me. You and your brother waltz into a school like this, your daddy can pay people just to keep an eye on you. My mom's an immigrant, my father didn't go to college, without my ROTC scholarship and financial aid, I wouldn't be able to pay for any of this. If I was going to call out what I saw, I had to come prepared, I needed *proof*. Any extent to which that involved your brother was completely harmless."

"Harmless?" Cady felt the heat rising in her face. "He was a paranoid schizophrenic, you think impersonating him online and stalking him with a camera and trying to blackmail his professor was harmless?"

"I was careful, Eric had no idea—"

"You don't know that."

"I had to get evidence—"

"It was none of your business!"

"Take that up with your dad!"

Cady had heard enough. She pulled her bag over her shoulder and pushed up from the table.

"Wait." Lee grabbed Cady by the elbow. "I am sorry, okay? I'm sorry about what happened, really, you have no idea. But it wasn't right what Prokop was doing, not to me, not even to Eric. He was vulnerable. People like her are predators."

Anger steadied Cady's voice. "And what are *you*?"


CADY FOUGHT BACK tears as she hurried out of the Gato Rojo. She almost couldn't believe her father's involvement, but Lee had too many details for her story to be false. Did he decide to hack Eric's computer behind her mother's back, or was Cady the last to know? She replayed the arguments her mother and father used to have about how to handle Eric's illness; they always seemed on opposite sides, with her mom being the hyperinvolved empath, swayed by Eric's complaints, open to alternative treatment, and her father as the medical hardliner, advocating tough love to get Eric to stay on his medication. Maybe he had second-guessed that tough love after all.

And the affair. Lee hadn't found proof, but her suspicion confirmed Cady's own. Still, she didn't think it was so terrible. So what if Eric had been fooling around with his teacher? It didn't mean that he wasn't brilliant, it didn't mean he didn't deserve the accolades he got. Cady was glad Eric had had someone who loved him on this campus, or at least who cared, someone who stuck by him, at least for a while.

Unless the drama of a secret affair had added to his mental pain. Had the breakup been what pushed him over the edge? If only her family had known, they could have supported him better. How had she known so little about what was going on with Eric? Well, nobody told her anything. If her own father hadn't been open and honest with her, whom could she trust? No one had been looking out for him properly, least of all—

"Cady!"

She was relieved to see Ranjoo waving hello and walking toward her, until her eyes fell on the guy beside her.

Ranjoo hugged her and said, "Do you know Teddy?"

The blood rose high in her cheeks. She couldn't look him in the eye, much less reply.

Teddy didn't have that problem. "Sure we do. Cady's my drinking buddy." And he hugged her, too.

Like muscle memory, Cady's body froze, her heart raced. As Teddy casually threw his arms around her rigid shoulders, her mind dissociated from the present and jumped right back to that night—*See what you did?*—her paralysis shaming her all over again. By the time Ranjoo's voice brought her back to the safety of the sun-dappled Yard, Teddy had already let go.

"Right, at the Phoenix! I saw you guys, I forgot. I was wasted that night."

"Me too." Teddy laughed. "We all were."

"I wasn't that drunk." She dared a glance at Teddy to see if he'd heard her, but he was looking at his phone. "How do you guys know each other?"

"*Arcadia.*" Ranjoo must have noticed Cady's blank stare. "You know, the play I'm painting the sets for? You've been really spacey lately, but I definitely told you about it."

"No, yeah, *Arcadia*, I remember." Cady didn't remember.

"Teddy's my work wife. He's one of the few actors who actually pitches in with the crew. When they're not rehearsing his scenes, he helps me paint backgrounds."

"She tolerates my having no artistic talent."

"You did a great job with that solid gray, boo."

"What can I say? I know my way around a roller."

Their easy banter gutted Cady. She hadn't told Ranjoo what had happened at the Phoenix yet, because she was humiliated, and the facts still felt tangled up with the voices. Now it seemed too late. Would Ranjoo believe her over Teddy? He was her "work wife," and Cady was just her roommate who didn't listen.

Ranjoo frowned at her with concern. "Are you okay? You seem stressed."

She had to get out of there. "I'm fine, I have stuff, I have to go to the room—"

"That will *not* destress you. Andrea is melting down over some test. And did you know she's mad we missed her birthday or something? I couldn't even follow it. She's so exhausting."

Cady rubbed her face, because her nails weren't long enough to claw it off.

"Come to lunch with us, we're going to Darwin's, Ted says it's the best sandwich spot in the Square."

"No, I just can't, sorry." Cady waved them off and began walking swiftly away. She had her back to them before they could reply.

"Uh, okay, 'bye!" Ranjoo laughed at her abruptness.

"See you around," Teddy called out.

Cady rushed away from them both, from everything that brought her shame and anxiety and fear on this campus, and escaped through the great wrought-iron gate to Mass Ave. She took out her phone and texted Nikos to see if she could get lunch with him at Lowell. Maybe she would just go there, she so badly needed a friend right now. Beyond the Yard's sheltering canopy of ancient oaks, the noon sun shone brightly in her face, making her squint. A large group of visiting high schoolers wearing matching red T-shirts flooded through the gate as she was exiting. Their tour bus was parked near the crosswalk, unloading rowdy students like a clown car, all of them talking and joking and ignoring whatever instructions their chaperones shouted over them. She struggled to pick her way through the sea of bodies and the enveloping cacophony—the shrieks of laughter, the yelling adults, the grinding idle bus engine—all made her grow more frustrated and claustrophobic by the minute. When some girls moved and a space opened up by the curb, Cady rushed through it.

*Beeeeeep!* The car horn blared, and Cady turned to face a Yellow Cab bearing down on her.

# 29

Just as Cady flinched in anticipation of the impact, two hands gripped her firmly around the shoulders and pulled her backward with such strength that she was lifted up off her feet. The cab barreled past her, close enough for her to feel the hot exhaust as it screeched to a halt.

People and noise rushed in around her where Cady had fallen back on the street, but all she could do was try to catch her breath. The smell of burned rubber filled her nostrils. She saw her messenger bag on the crosswalk in front of her, its leather strap flattened and embossed with tire tracks.

"I got you," said a soft voice belonging to a young man over her shoulder. She noticed then that she was nearly in his lap; clearly he had broken her fall.

"Oh, I'm so sorry." Cady scrambled to get off him, though she winced in pain when she set down her hand.

"No worries. You a'right?" He helped her to her feet, and Cady thanked him. But standing eye to eye with the boy, she was surprised that he was no taller than she, with a nascent fuzzy mustache; he couldn't have been older than fifteen. Cady retrieved Eric's blue note-book herself, but as the boy bent to gather the others scattered on the street, she noticed the base of his bumpy spine on his slight frame and marveled—*his* were the hands that had so forcefully lifted her?

"Holy shit! That girl almost got run over!" a nearby teenage girl squealed, waving a cellphone with a glittery pink cover. "And I got it on video!"

"For real? Tiana, show me." Newly distracted, the boy darted to join the group gathering around the girl with the phone.

Cady wanted to see, too, but the cabbie, newly sprung from his taxi, cut her off. He'd run around the hood to see if he'd hit her, and as soon as he realized she was fine, his panic turned to anger. "Jeezus, were you lookin'? I had the light! Whaddya tryin' to do, kill yourself?"

Her mustached protector reappeared, stepping between them and puffing his bird chest. "Hey, fuck off, man!"

The light changed again, and other cars began to honk. The cabbie threw up his hands and stormed back to his car.

"Hey, hey, hey!" A pot-bellied school chaperone finally pushed his way through the throng and pointed at the boy. "Javi, I don't wanna hear that language again, you hear?" Then he hitched up his pants and shouted over their heads, "Come on, everybody, outta the street."

As they jostled with the crowd back to the sidewalk, Cady turned to the boy. "Javi, is it? Thank you so much. Did your friend really get it on video? Can I see it?"

A sly smile carved his cheeks. "Sure, *guapa*, give me your number. I'll get it and send it to you." He handed her his cellphone and grinned, showing off his braces.

Cady quickly tapped her number into his phone, just as the chaperone began to corral the students back toward Harvard Yard. Javi gave her one last moony smile before he disappeared among his classmates.

Cady still felt shaken from the near miss and embarrassed for making a spectacle. She quickly, and carefully, crossed Mass Ave and strode toward the Smith Student Center, taking a seat at one of the outdoor tables to collect herself. She turned over her right hand and grimaced; the heel of her palm had been badly skinned, and she was definitely going to have a huge bruise on her buttocks. Although she supposed she should be thankful—if not for Javi, she could've been hurt a lot worse, or even killed. She sucked air as she picked out the pieces of gravel pressed deep into the heel of her palm. Droplets of fresh blood appeared in the tiny craters left behind.

A pinging sound of a text message on her phone distracted her from the pain. It was a message from an unknown 617 number, consisting of mostly emoji: a taxicab, a gust of wind, and prayer hands, with a video attachment. A second text followed: "Follow me snap and ig @hollajavi04" and the sunglass smiley emoji.

Cady clicked to play the video. It started by showing Harvard's giant gate, with the girl narrating their arrival over a lot of ambient noise, then it panned down and back toward the street to a boy on the curb. "Devon, give me that Ivy League glamor, hunty!" Her guy friend snapped into a pose, fanning his painted fingernails around his fluttering doe eyes. While he vogued in the foreground, Cady spotted herself in the background hustling toward the street. The Yellow Cab barreled down the frame, and even at that angle, it was clear that the two vectors were doomed to intersect, until the very last moment, when Cady was yanked backward. She replayed those last seconds, watching as Javi reached for her, his skinny right arm outstretched, and only his right arm—when she was sure she had felt two hands, on either side of her. Cady touched her left biceps—did she feel a tenderness there, or was she imagining it? Cady played the part again, pausing to zoom in on the moment, viewing the segment frame by frame, and while it was clear Javi touched her, the force of it, enough to reverse her momentum like a crash-test dummy, didn't make sense to her.

*Good grief, that was close.*

Cady recognized the voice right away, it was the one from Memorial Church—Whit.

*I saw you walking ahead of me, and I was trying to screw up the courage to say hullo, when I saw that roadster coming right for you.*

Whit was there. Seeing her and, not a taxi, but a "roadster." She remembered what Prokop had described, hidden dimensions, the fabric of space-time folded over. What if the past had folded overtop the present at that precise location where she needed help?

*I'd like to take credit, but it was reflexive, I was in the right place at the right time.*

Or the right place in the wrong time.

*Anyone would've done it.*

Anyone could try, Cady thought. A fourteen-year-old boy weighing 120 pounds soaking wet probably couldn't. But a collegiate rower like Whit was?

You saved me, thank you.

*Shucks, like I said, I was lucky to be there.*

Cady stared at the chair opposite her, searching for any sign of movement, any glimmer, any sign of a presence. She leaned all the way across the table and waved her hand over the seat of it, feeling only air.

*Hey, hey!* He chuckled, a low laugh like ice clinking in a glass of whisky. *You could buy me dinner first.*

She yanked her hand back. "Sorry," Cady said aloud. A couple of tourists at a nearby table stopped talking to look at her.

*You left in a hurry that night at the church. I hope I didn't talk too much.*

No, I . . . I just had to get home.

*They give you Cliffie's a strict curfew, keep the "Betty Co-Ed's" in line.*

A what?

*You know, like the song? "Betty Co-Ed has lips of red for Harvard . . ."* he sang. *Nothing?*

*It's a stupid novelty tune. My music taste is better than that, I swear. My cousin works at Brunswick records in New York City, he sends me records all the time, sometimes before you can buy them. Anyway, any girl who goes to college has my utmost respect. You've probably got big plans for after graduation.*

Cady sighed, graduation seemed light-years away, she was trying to get through this week, or this day.

I haven't thought that far ahead.

*You haven't thought past your brother.* He'd said it gently, and yet the words still knocked her back in her seat.

*I'm sorry, there I go again, getting too comfortable. You were so open in the church the other night, made me feel like I know you better than I do.*

No . . . I know exactly what you mean, I just didn't know it until you said it.

*I haven't thought past my father. He died a few days shy of his thirtieth birthday. When I picture my future, I can imagine my Naval career, start-ing a family, but I can't picture myself as a geezer, or really any older than he got to be. It's like he's the horizon line in my head, I'm always moving toward it, but I can't imagine getting to the other side. You ever feel like that?*

Yes—Everything Whit said resonated with her. She had the un-canny sense of being truly seen by someone invisible. It thrilled and frightened her.

Cady caught a tourist couple stealing glances at her again, but she didn't care. She didn't want to lose contact with Whit. She wanted to know more about him, to find more of his connections to her or Eric, but maybe just to know him.

—What do you want to do in the Navy?

*Have you ever seen a dirigible? They're airships, enormous blimps with a steel skeleton. The Germans called them Zeppelins.*

Zeppelins . . . like in the *Hindenburg* explosion?

*I don't know that one. Is that one the Krauts used in the war?*

Cady racked her brain for the year of the *Hindenburg* crash, but Whit was excited and kept talking.

*Wouldn't surprise me—the Zeppelins were filled with hydrogen, highly combustible. But the Navy has a new Lighter-than-Air division that has improved on the technology using helium, which improves stability. Ours are so stable that the latest prototypes double as an aircraft carrier. I'd love to work in that division, I'm studying applied physics and mechanical engi-neering to give me an edge.*

If you join the Navy, don't go to the base in Pearl Harbor, okay?

*What, you don't think piloting a seven-hundred-foot airship while drinking Mai-Tais is a bright idea?*

No, it's—Cady wanted to warn him without freaking him out or disturbing world history with some sort of butterfly effect—that base is vulnerable to attack.

*Exactly. All the more reason we need dirigible aircraft carriers for recon and defense. There are miles and miles of currently unguarded Pacific Ocean between us and the Far East. Something's brewing in the Orient, and it ain't green tea, I read the papers. These dirigibles could avert disaster. It's beautifully simple technology. Airplanes are heavy, they need lift, drag, and fuel to propel into the sky. But dirigibles are literally lighter than air— they float! The papers are calling them the Leviathan of the Skies. They're a modern marvel, and we need that right now, a reminder that we can build our way out of this depression. Something people can literally look up to in the clouds and say, "My country made that." The Navy has figured out how to harness the wind.*

It was a big idea, the kind of thing Eric would've liked, Cady thought.

*What's that you're working on? You seemed so eager to rescue that notebook from the street.*

It was my brother's. It's all I have of his from his last year. It starts out as lab notes, but toward the end, I can't understand it. I feel like I need to know what he was trying to work out, it's my only insight into what was going on in his head. I thought these notes could give me a clue, but his best friend looked at it and says it's just nonsense, that Eric had lost it by then.

*So? Why do you think his friend is the authority?*

Because he studies physics like Eric, he would know how to interpret this better than I would.

*Better than his sister? I find that hard to believe.*

Cady felt her cheeks flush with shame.—He was here with him his last year. I wasn't.

*Distance doesn't matter with family. Trust your gut. There's no better decoder ring than shared history.*

What kind of ring?

*Little Orphan Annie? C'mon, I thought everybody knew that radio show. They ask kids to send away for the decoder ring—it's just a simple Caesar cipher, the alphabet shifted over five or so letters—and then the radio show puts out a coded message that only the kids with the ring can decipher at home.*

A coded message, Cady repeated in her mind, the notebook gibberish is in code. She flashed to coded directions Eric used to leave her when they were kids, the hieroglyphs, the word puzzles, the missions . . .

*This might be a tougher puzzle than a kids' radio show. But he was your brother. Nobody knows how to interpret him better than you.*

. . . the codes that only she could break.

Cady dug in her bag for the notebook and threw it open on the table. She was paging to the back, when she recoiled: a streak of red smeared across the page and dampened the edge of its pages. It was blood, and it was coming from her.

"Boo-boo!"

Cady looked up to see that a little girl was pointing right at Cady; when their eyes met, her small face crumpled. "Mommy!"

The girl's mother swooped in and lifted her daughter just as the child began to wail. Cady glimpsed the mother's expression as she turned her daughter's face away.

Fear.

A stream of fresh blood had sprung from a divot in the heel of her palm, a puncture wound from road debris that was deeper than she had realized. The blood filled the creases of her hand, tracing her lifeline like a palm reader. It must have been like that for some time, because the blood had dripped down her arm and darkened the wrist of her jacket and even smeared on the aluminum tabletop. It seemed impossible that Cady hadn't noticed; she was as dumbfounded as the people now staring at her.

But she'd been listening to Whit.

It seemed that suddenly every passerby was looking at her. All wore similar faces of curiosity, concern, and revulsion. A middle-aged man in tortoiseshell glasses approached her. "Miss, do you need help?"

"I'm fine." Cady sprang up, hooking her arm under her purse straps and swiftly wiping the tabletop clean with her sleeve.

"Do you know where UHS is, University Health Services? I can show you," the woman with him added.

"No thanks, really." She hoped they weren't faculty.

Cady kept her head down as she entered the student center and beelined to the restroom. A girl rose from a nearby seat and beat her to the bathroom door but, upon catching sight of Cady, blanched and stepped aside to let her go first.

When she got to see herself in the bathroom mirror, Cady understood why. A bloody smudge marred her cheek and lip from where she'd touched her face, and her injured palm continued to sponge-paint in red everything she touched. She pawed at the toilet paper with her left hand and ran the right one under the hot water. The cut hurt more as she cleaned it, but luckily it didn't seem too deep.

Wounds on the palm bled a lot, Cady knew from past experience.

She gingerly dried her hands. As she pressed a paper towel to her palm, a plum spot bloomed in the middle, but instead of focusing on the pain or the deepening color, Cady conjured the faces of the people staring at her, paralyzed between the tug of pity and the recoil of disgust. She imagined them talking about her right now, speculating, judging, and later, when they got home, Cady would be their story of the day.

Just like Eric.

# 30

CADY HAD BLOCKED out how hard it had been to go out with Eric in public. Now she recalled an afternoon at the King of Prussia mall, when her brother was home for spring break, and they had gone out to get their mom a birthday present. It was a Saturday, and the mall was packed. Eric had always hated crowds, even before he got sick, so Cady hadn't intended to take him with her, but she wasn't given a choice. Eric and their father had been fighting again, so their mother had insisted Cady get Eric out of the house. Cady made it a one-stop shop at Williams Sonoma, where she grabbed the first pretty serving platter she saw and raced to the checkout line. But even so, it hadn't been fast enough for Eric.

"This line isn't moving at all," he said, visibly agitated.

"It is, just slowly."

"All these people are making me claustrophobic." Eric kept licking his lips, though the white buildup at the corners of his mouth remained; his medication made his mouth dry. "We should go."

"If it's making you really uncomfortable, you can wait outside. There's an Auntie Anne's pretzel kiosk outside the store, you like the cinnamon sugar ones, right? Here." Cady handed him a twenty-dollar bill. "Get whatever you want and I'll meet you there. Make sure you wait for me."

"I hate when you act like Mom." He took the money and walked away.

She didn't like it any more than he did. She waited in line, which *was* moving awfully slowly, glancing over her shoulder to keep an eye on Eric. Finally she paid for the gift and rushed outside, but Eric wasn't in front of the Auntie Anne's. Her heart pounded as she hurried out onto the main atrium of the mall. Faced with three congested corridors going in separate directions, her eyes scanned for her twenty-year-old brother as panicky as if he'd been a lost child.

She spotted him. He was standing by a large fern, rocking back and forth on his toes, talking to himself, with his eyes fixed on a security camera—these days he never missed a security camera. But Cady saw something he didn't see that broke her heart: two teenagers were filming Eric's strange behavior on an iPhone and laughing at him.

Cady called his name, hoping he would turn in the opposite direction. He didn't respond, so she tried again, hustling to him. "Eric, we're done, let's go."

He ignored her and motioned to the camera with his head. "This is a decoy, the real one is somewhere else. They want you to believe the technology hasn't improved since the eighties."

"We can go home now." Cady took him by the arm, trying to steer him away, but not before he caught sight of the boys over his shoulder.

"Hey, you!" Eric shouted to them, his volume attracting the attention of passing shoppers. "Are you filming me? Are you following me, who told you to film me? Who sent you?"

That only made them laugh harder.

Cady kept her hand on his arm, feeling his muscles tense as the teens approached them. She kept her voice calm. "Ignore them, let's get—"

The one wearing a Phillies cap jutted out his chin. "This retard belong to you?"

Cady recoiled at the nasty word as if she'd been hit.

"*What* did you call me?" Eric snapped.

"All right, then, how 'bout batshit crazy," said the other, still holding up his phone. "This is going on YouTube."

"Give me that." Eric shoved his hand out. "How did you know I would be here? Were you waiting for me?"

"He makes it sound romantic. Yeah, I've been waiting for you my whole life."

"Eric, stop." Cady tugged at his sleeve.

"Give me the phone," Eric commanded.

The punk met Eric's glare and shrugged. "Make me."

Eric's arm burst out of Cady's grasp and caught the boy by the wrist, sending the phone clattering to the floor. They started scuffling, the boy pushing and trying to swing while Eric maintained his death grip. The friend had just lunged at Eric when a mall cop came jogging over, middle-aged but beefy. "Hey, hey, hey, everybody calm down and back off." The mall cop pushed his body between the boys and finally Eric let go. "What's the problem here?"

"This motherfucker tried to steal my phone! Probably broke it!"

Cady spoke up. "These guys were filming my brother, he asked them to stop, and they wouldn't."

"Miss, a lot of people take pictures on their cellphones, that's not against the law."

"My brother is disabled. They were making fun of him."

The cop's expression changed. He looked at Eric, then turned to the boys. "You got your phone?"

They muttered acknowledgment.

"Then nobody stole it. Get outta here, stop making trouble." The cop shooed the boys away, then turned back to Cady and gave Eric an embarrassed smile. "Sorry about that. You have a nice day, young man."

Cady thanked him and steered Eric in the opposite direction. Walking away, she noticed all the shoppers who had stopped to watch the altercation and continued to stare at them. She wondered if Eric noticed, too, but he was silent beside her, rubbing his arm, eyes downcast. "Are you okay?" she asked.

He still wasn't looking at her, but she could see his lips were drawn with hurt. "Why did you say I was disabled?"

She didn't know why she'd lied, it seemed easier than explaining, but the shame made her defensive. "I was trying to keep you from getting arrested."

"Did you see how that cop looked at me? I'd rather be in jail than have people look at me like that."

"He was trying to be nice, he took our side."

"You don't get it."

Someone banged on the other side of the bathroom door, startling Cady.

"Just a minute," she called out. She finished drying her hands and gave her face one last check in the mirror. She was about to unlock the door, when she glimpsed her bloodied paper towel at the top of the trash heap. Cady flashed on the blond girl whom she'd frightened, the concerned man in the tortoiseshell glasses and the pitying woman with him, the startled classmate who'd let her use the bathroom first, and all the other unknown faces that had shot her an identical look.

She had wanted to come to Harvard to know how Eric felt.

She "got it" now.

# 31

CADY WAS SUPPOSED to be writing her poetry paper for Professor Hines, due tomorrow at two o'clock and not a minute later, and she had so far written only one page of a required five to seven. But it was impossible to focus on Keats and his Grecian urn after what Whit had shaken loose in her brain—that Eric's scribblings weren't gibberish, but *code*. She had Eric's blue notebook open on top of her *Norton Anthology of Poetry*, and several Internet browser windows open on top of her Word document, searching for something, anything, that might help her break it.

Eric had made a list of three numbered sections with three separate dates and times, but the notes below them were incomprehensible.

1.  10/15/18 8:36pm
    WFIKP KNF KYIVV JVMVE FEV JZO QVIF EZEV—
    JVMVEKP FEV FEV FEV JZO VZXYK WFLI QVIF✓

2.  10/31/18 11:10pm
    WFIKP KNF KYIVV JZO EZEV JVMVE JZO WFLI—
    JVMVEKP FEV FEV KNF WZMV WFLI EZEV JVMVE✓

3. 11/20/18 9:07am
   WFIKP KNF KYIVV JVMVE KYIVV KYIVV WFLI
   WZMV—JVMVEKP FEV FEV FEV VZXYK VZXYK
   VZXYK EZEV✓
   WFIKP KNF KYIVV JVMVE WZMV QVIF KYIVV
   VZXYK—JVMVEKP FEV FEV FEV EZEV WZMV KYIVV
   FEV

She thought back to the way he used to do it when they were kids. She hadn't known the term for it that Whit had used, but it had been as he described, the alphabet shifted a certain number of letters forward. But she remembered Eric using all different numbers, and he usually told her what it was, didn't he? No, a few times he made her guess, but it was easy to guess. Why was it so easy for her to guess back then? She closed her eyes and envisioned herself as a little girl, bouncing on the balls of her feet in front of her older brother, excited to play his game.

Aha!—she guessed easily because she usually guessed her age first, Eric knew that, and so he always made the number key her age. She was eight years old when they did their Mantis Mommy Revenge mission, and she remembered now, writing out the entire alphabet and counting to eight over and over again.

Eric had turned twenty years old last spring, but that was too long to count out by hand. She needed some assistance. She googled the terms Whit had used, "Caesar cipher" and "decoder," and found "to decode something, subtract the encryption N from 26." She found an encoder/decoder translation tool on another site, filled in the fields on the decoder tool with the copied lines under number one, and entered 20 as the "shift" number.

More gibberish.

She looked again at the dates above the gibberish. At the time Eric had been writing these down, she was seventeen. She tried 17 as the shift number.

She gasped. The decoder yielded recognizable words: FORTY
TWO THREE SEVEN ONE SIX ZERO NINE—SEVENTY ONE
ONE ONE SIX EIGHT FOUR ZERO.

Her heart swelled. It was as though he expected her to be the one
to crack the code. Encouraged, she quickly copied and pasted in the
other four lines, jotting down the translations below Eric's notes:

1.    10/15/18 8:36pm
      WFIKP KNF KYIVV JVMVE FEV JZO QVIF EZEV—
      JVMVEKP FEV FEV FEV JZO VZXYK WFLI QVIF✓
      forty two three seven one six zero nine—seventy one one
      one six eight four zero

2.    10/31/18 11:10pm
      WFIKP KNF KYIVV JZO EZEV JVMVE JZO WFLI—
      JVMVEKP FEV FEV KNF WZMV WFLI EZEV JVMVE✓
      forty two three six nine seven six four—seventy one one
      two five four nine seven

3.    11/20/18 9:07am
      WFIKP KNF KYIVV JVMVE KYIVV KYIVV WFLI
      WZMV—JVMVEKP FEV FEV FEV VZXYK VZXYK
      VZXYK EZEV✓
      forty two three seven three three four five—seventy one one
      one eight eight eight nine
      WFIKP KNF KYIVV JVMVE WZMV QVIF KYIVV
      VZXYK—JVMVEKP FEV FEV FEV EZEV WZMV KYIVV
      FEV
      forty two three seven five zero three eight—seventy one one
      one nine five three one

Electrified as she was to have broken the code, her next thought
was—now what? She had broken one code to yield another. She wrote
out the numbers in numeral form:

1. 42 371609—71 116840
2. 42 369764—71 125497
3. 42 373345—71 118889
   42 375038—71 119531

What were these numbers? Passwords to something? Phone, credit card, or bank routing numbers? The formatting didn't seem to fit, but maybe she had that wrong. What on earth had Eric been up to?

Her cellphone rang, annoying her with the distraction, until she saw who it was. "Mom, hi."

They remained tentative with each other, making small talk as they warmed to the conversation. Cady felt doubly anxious wondering whether she should ask her mother about her father's moving out or wait for her to tell her. Cady wanted to be there for her mother, to tell her she was on her side. But she hadn't felt on her mom's side in a long time. Finally she mustered, "So, Dad called me."

"He did," her mother said. Cady didn't know if it was a question or an acknowledgment.

"About using his cell to reach him instead of the home phone?"

"Mm-hm."

"Are you okay?"

"Of course. I'm fine. We'll figure it out."

They both let the line go quiet. Cady and her mother had never been the best at communicating, but they had become pretty adept at navigating the unsaid.

"I want to talk about you. How are you? You sound down."

"I have a lot going on."

"Are you happy there?"

The direct question surprised Cady; she had become accustomed to roundabout, surface-skimming conversation with her mom, so this was an unexpected opening. She wanted to tell her no, she wasn't happy, she was exhausted and overwhelmed and scared. She wanted to tell her about the voices, and how at first she was afraid she was getting sick like Eric. She wanted to explain why she thought the ghosts were real—whatever that meant—how they were helping her figure out Eric and feel less alone, how she might even like talking to them—and how that frightened her most of all. She wanted to tell her about Lee and Professor Prokop and Teddy and everything. She wanted to cry to her mommy and receive that comfort that she remembered as a kid, but she couldn't. She couldn't say anything. Not after defying her mother's wishes by going to this school, certainly not now, knowing everything going on in her parents' marriage. At this moment more than ever, her mother needed her to be okay. "Yeah, it's fine."

"Good. I'm glad."

Cady bit her lip to keep from crying.

"Do you need me to bring you anything from home on Parents' Weekend?" her mother asked.

"You're coming?"

"You don't want me to."

"No, I do, I really do." She was shocked but elated. It felt like a lifeline—if her mother was coming, she could make it through the week.

"I know Dad can't, and I want to see you. I want to make sure you're okay. That's my job as a parent. It's not your job to take care of me, you're my kid." Suddenly her mother's resolve faltered, and her voice broke. "I messed up before, when you got in, and last weekend at Grampa's. I've been wrong a lot before, but I want to make it right."

"Mom, are you crying?" It was the admission she'd wanted to hear from her mother, and yet now that it came with muffled tears over a phone line, it brought no satisfaction.

"I love you, you know that, right?" her mother managed to squeak out.

"I know. I love you, too. Don't cry, really, I'm fine. I'm excited to see you."

They said their goodbyes and Cady hung up the phone. All of her hope and happiness at seeing her mother instantly dissipated, with regret and dread taking their place. She had just asked her grieving and fragile mother to return to the site of her son's suicide alone. Cady felt sick at the prospect of seeing the living proof of the pain that she was causing her mother. Just because she had some morbid impulse to retrace Eric's final steps didn't give her the right to force her parents to relive it with her.

She looked back down at the notebook in her lap and the numbers she had deciphered.

Unless these steps were leading her to an answer.

Cady heard a knock on their suite door. She waited for someone else to answer it—she was pretty sure Andrea was home, Cady had ceded the common room to her as part of her penitence—but the knock sounded again. Cady pushed herself up from the desk and went to answer it. She opened the door to a young man with a swish of brown bangs over his brow, wearing a powder-blue polo shirt and khakis and holding several plastic bags. He was good-looking, and a little out of breath.

"I have a delivery for"—he glanced down at a scrap of paper—"Cadence Archer? Chinese food from the Kong, still hot."

"I didn't order Chinese."

"My name is Zach, I'm a sophomore, I'm punching the Phoenix, so I pretty much have to do whatever they say. Tonight, Nikos said to bring this to you." Zach thrust forward three bags.

"This is all for me?"

"He told me to get every vegetarian entrée they have."

"Oh my God." Cady covered her grin with her hand.

"Will you tell him it's hot? That was one of the requirements. I ran here."

Cady told him yes and thanked him. She placed the bags on the coffee table and opened the first one, releasing the delicious aromas of curry, black bean sauce, and lo mein noodles. Her mouth watered. But before she dug in, she had an idea.

She knocked on Andrea's bedroom door.

"Yeah?" her small voice called from inside.

"Hey, I just wanted to see if you're hungry."

Andrea opened the door a crack. "You got food?"

"Chinese. And I have plenty for both of us, three times over. Please, have some."

She padded out in her purple robe to inspect it. "Are you sure?" Andrea asked, already pulling out the cartons and chopsticks.

They both made their plates, and Andrea took a seat on the futon.

"Well, I have that paper to write. Good luck with your studying." Cady headed back to her room with her food.

"You can work out here with me," Andrea said.

Cady looked over her shoulder.

"There's more room, and it's nice to have company on an all-nighter."

Cady exhaled in relief and smiled. "Okay. I'll get my laptop."

After Cady and Andrea had enjoyed their first normal conversation since the birthday debacle, and split the scallion pancakes because they were inedible cold, Cady texted Nikos:

> I can't believe you sent me all this food?!
> You are crazy and too sweet, thank you!!!

His response chimed in a second later.

> Not at all! Was sorry I missed your text earlier, wanted to make it up to you. Stupid punches are good for something.
>
> He was nice!
>
> You liked him? Then he's out. I must be your favourite.

Cady wrote a response, hesitating before she clicked Send.

> You are ;)
>
> Phew. Good luck on your paper xx

Cady sat back and held the phone to her chest, unable to suppress a smile. Forgiven, or close to it, by Andrea, indulged by Nikos—it was the lightest she had felt all week, and just the boost she needed to get through her paper.

She had just begun writing the second paragraph, when she received another text:

Ps. Was it hot??

# 32

THE NEXT DAY, Cady slumped in a chair in Sever 207, dead tired, waiting for Professor Hines's seminar to begin. Her eyes stung from lack of sleep, and her stomach churned from an excess of MSG and caffeine. She and her classmates were seated around the conference table, and Alex sat directly across from her. Alex looked chipper and handsome in a neatly buttoned shirt, while Cady kept both hands on the tabletop, as if to hold herself upright. Yet, by some miracle, a completed paper lay stacked in front of her, although its overall quality was anyone's guess. She had stayed up all night working on it, practically sleepwalked through writing it, and had woken up with her face planted on her desk. Hitting Print had been all the proofreading she'd had time for this morning.

Professor Hines entered the room, his suit jacket billowing around his slim frame. Without any greeting, he stood at the head of the conference table and clapped his hands once. "Papers. I want to see papers. Fork 'em over."

The class passed them forward to him in a flutter of white. Cady was glad to be rid of hers. Professor Hines muttered thank-yous as he gathered up the papers. He cracked the stack against the table to align it and gave a yelp. For a moment he was entirely absorbed in looking at his index finger, then he brought it to his mouth and sucked. When he became aware of the class staring at him, he still had his finger in his mouth. "It hurts!" he whined.

Some classmates laughed. Cady hated him.

"Whoever's paper delivered this injury gets knocked down a grade."

Again, cloying, brown-nosing chuckles from the crowd. Now Cady hated them.

"So, who wants to start our discussion of today's reading?"

The room fell silent.

"Well." Hines crossed his arms. "I recognize we had a paper due today, but you also had a reading assignment, a single poem, very manageable. Here at Harvard, we have to walk *and* chew gum. So come on, get out your Nortons."

Cady had not read any poem for today, she didn't even know which had been assigned. As the other students pulled out their heavy *Norton Anthology of Poetry* books, she followed suit, stealing a glance at the page number of the boy beside her, rushing so her clumsy fingers nearly tore the ultrathin pages.

"Page thirteen forty-four, for those lost." Professor Hines continued, "Here we meet another Harvard alum, T. S. Eliot, class of 1910. He wrote 'The Love Song of J. Alfred Prufrock' at the tender age of twenty-two, just one year after graduating. No pressure to any aspiring poets in the room. You still have four years to catch up." Hines was the only one who laughed this time. "Today we're discussing Eliot's most famous poem, 'The Waste Land.' Some of you may have read it in high school, although I doubt many of you were equipped to understand it then. Some of you may not be equipped to understand it now, it's a challenging work of art, but we're going to muddle through it together." He cleared his throat and used his favorite nickname for Cady: "Girl Who Was Late. Why don't you get us started and discuss the opening?"

Her mouth went dry. She had found the page, at least, but the first line alone was indecipherable.

*Actually it's Latin,* said Robert's voice. *Oh, how I adore Eliot. And don't worry, I can read it.*

Robert began to slowly read it aloud to her, Cady simply repeating his words and becoming his mouthpiece: "For I myself have seen with my own eyes, the Sibyl hanging in a bottle at Cumae, and when those boys would say to her: 'Sibyl, what do you want?' she replied, 'I want to die.'"

"Yes, thank you for reading us the translation contained in the footnote, but I was looking for actual insight. Moving on . . ."

*Footnote? Why didn't I see that there? But that's mere translation. It doesn't tell the story.*

"It doesn't tell the story," Cady parroted.

"Pardon me?" Professor Hines turned back around.

Desperate, she wasted no time on caution and repeated verbatim Robert's words as they came, letting them slip from her mouth as quickly and easily as if they were her own. "The Sibyl of Cumae was a prophet of Apollo. She asked him to grant her immortal life but forgot to ask for everlasting youth, and so her wish became a curse."

Professor Hines eyed her from behind his rimless glasses, and although his dislike of her was apparent, she could also tell she had said something correct. "I see you did a bit of extra legwork looking up the reference. Commendable."

But Robert wasn't done yet, so neither was Cady. She was sick of Hines underestimating her, even if this time she deserved it. She added, "Yeah, it was interesting, because the allusion to this idea of immortality as everlasting death is repeated in the last stanza of this first section, beginning with line sixty, when Eliot writes 'Unreal City, Under the brown fog of a winter dawn,' et cetera."

"Ah, but you're mistaken." Hines brightened. "Line sixty refers to Baudelaire's *Fleurs du Mal*, the flowers of evil, written in the 1850s. It's a completely different text."

"A different text with the same idea. *Fleurs du Mal* is the collection, the specific poem is '*Les Sept Vieillards*,' or '*The Seven Old Men*,'" Cady translated from Robert with confidence. "Eliot quotes only the first line, but the rest of the poem describes Paris as a city 'stuffed with dreams, where ghosts by day accost the passer-by.' Then there's a frightening procession of seven wretched old men, and Baudelaire says, 'for all their imminent decrepitude, these seven monsters had eternal life!' Like the Sybil who asked for immortality but not eternal youth, it's another example where eternal life appears as the walking dead."

Professor Hines's mouth remained set in a patronizing smile, but his eyes relayed panic.

*Tell him to look it up, if he doesn't believe me.*

"Yes, well, that's a good observation." Hines smacked his lips as if his mouth was dry.

Thank you, Cady thought to Robert.

*Pas de problème.*

Professor Hines continued, "Moving on, the poem begins, 'April is the cruelest month.' What do you make of this as an opening? Yes, Lindsay."

Lindsay was a tall, pretty girl with a high ponytail and a Harvard volleyball sweatshirt. "I'm a psychology concentrator, and I was just reading that statistically, the most suicides per month occur during April."

March 26, Cady remembered, that was when Eric did it.

Hines said, "Interesting, I would've guessed closer to final exam period." Everyone but Cady laughed. He then asked, "Is there a hypothesis as to why?"

"Some think the seasonal change alters serotonin or hormones. I don't think they know for sure," Lindsay answered.

"I imagine Eliot would have been an interesting psychological case, don't you?"

"Definitely." Lindsay held the floor. "His thoughts are so scattered, the way he jumps around from past to present, referencing different poets, and the narrator constantly channels all these different characters, different languages, different voices. Seems a little schizo to me."

"What seems spontaneous, or *schizo*, as you call it, Lindsay, is actually brilliantly devised, revised, and contributing to all sorts of shades of meaning. A genius masquerading as a madman, as opposed to the other way around." Hines turned toward the class, but his eyes homed in on Cady. "Anyone have some ideas on a close reading on the first stanza? Cadence, you've displayed your diligence looking up references, but let me put you on the spot. Why don't you get us started with your own interpretation of the first ten or so lines. Now, remember, there are no wrong answers—for the most part." The class laughed.

Cady began reading the poem for the first time:

*April is the cruelest month, breeding*
*Lilacs out of the dead land, mixing*
*Memory and desire, stirring*
*Dull roots with spring rain.*
*Winter kept us warm, covering*
*Earth in forgetful snow, feeding*
*A little life with dried tubers . . .*

Robert was quiet; Cady would have to answer this one on her own. She began slowly, "I think it's saying April is cruel because you want new things to be free from the past, but they aren't. They can't be. The dead are part of the spring."

A boy named Geoff raised his hand, waving with obnoxious exuberance. Hines motioned to him. Geoff said, "I disagree. There's no finality to death here. His verbs, 'breeding,' 'mixing,' 'stirring,' all gerunds, create a sense of constant motion, like the life cycle. The roots were only 'dull,' and they are revived by the rain. If life springs from death, then the death is false. Life is perpetual."

Hines nodded approvingly at Geoff, then turned to Cady. "What say you?"

"I guess I read that the opposite way," Cady said. "The life is false. It's just death reanimated. Life may spring from death, but it's tainted. There's no escape from the remains of the dead. See, next he says, 'Winter kept us warm, covering Earth in forgetful snow.' We want to cover up the past, white it out, erase it. But the spring reminds you it's only a temporary fix. Death was lying underneath all along, waiting to rise up again. I think these lines express that sometimes when you think you want to die you really just want things to be new again."

"And Cadence provides the Tim Burton reading of Eliot," Hines cut in. "Well argued, both of you. I like healthy debate. Let's talk about structure . . ."

Cady had contributed without making a complete ass of herself, so she counted today a victory and gave herself permission to zone out for the rest of class. She was practically asleep with her eyes open. By the time class was dismissed, she'd been daydreaming about her upcoming nap for so long, she could almost feel her downy comforter puffed around her shoulders.

She was gathering her things to leave, when Hines called to her, beckoning her with a finger as if she were a small child. "Yes?" Cady said, doing her best to look awake.

"You were unusually talkative today."

"I tried my best."

"You've studied 'The Waste Land' before, I presume."

"No, this is the first time, so it's really interesting." Cady smiled, hoping a bit of forced enthusiasm could hide her exhaustion.

"Are you a Baudelaire *scholar?*"

Cady hesitated. "No."

Professor Hines lifted his eyebrows. "So you're new to both poets, yet, from reading the words 'Unreal City,' you were able not only to recognize the allusion, but to recite lines of Baudelaire's *Les Sept Vieillards* from memory."

Cady was silent, and so was her mind. Where was Robert now? She improvised. "I'm in a French Lit class this semester, and we're reading Baudelaire. So when I was reading 'The Waste Land,' it jogged my memory, and I cross-checked it to prepare for class."

"But what you brought up today came entirely from your own head?"

"Yes."

"Why do I feel that you're lying to me?"

*Because I am,* she thought. "I'm not." Robert, Robert, Robert.

"Because if you read about that connection somewhere, it's perfectly fine to bring it up in discussion, but it's important to cite sources. Harvard has a zero-tolerance policy on plagiarism."

Cady nodded. She could feel the sweat at the back of her neck.

"Okay. Just so we're clear." Professor Hines shuffled the papers in front of him on the table for a moment before looking back up at her. "You're free to go."

"Thank you." Cady hoisted her bag to her shoulder and headed for the door.

"Oh, and one more question," Hines said, stopping her in her tracks. "What's your favorite poem in *Fleurs du Mal*? Other than '*Les Sept Vieillards.*'"

Robert. "Um." Robert, what's another title? Robert!

*Oh, sorry, I was reading. Baudelaire really is fantastic. My favorite? Gosh, it's hard to choose . . .*

"Let me think . . ." Just name one. Name one. "It's so hard to choose."

"I'm in no hurry," Professor Hines said, with the beginning of a smile on his lips.

*. . . The Sapphic ones are highly exciting, but inappropriate for you to read. They were censored in the original publication, considered pornographic. I suppose they are pornographic—*

—Dammit, Robert, I need a title!

*Got it—*

"'*La Fin de la Journée.*' 'Day's End,'" Cady said it as soon as Robert brought it to her mind.

"Ah," breathed Hines, deflating. The cat's paw lifted from the mouse's tail. "I look forward to reading your paper."

As soon as she hit the hallway, Cady yanked her sweater off over her head. Her T-shirt was tamped to her back with nervous sweat. She bent to drink from an old bronze drinking fountain, ignoring its concerning verdigris, but the cold, metallic water only let her thoughts come in clearer: Hines was on to her. He knew she was incapable of that analysis. She was a terrible liar and always had been. Still, she hadn't lied, exactly. The thoughts had "come from her head," as he said. If he'd asked from her brain, well . . .

*Oh, shoot! You should've said "To a Red-Haired Beggar Girl" for your favorite, you know, because of your hair. That would've been easy.*

Cady wiped her mouth. The halls were mostly empty now; she had little to distract her from Robert's rambling. She headed for the stairs.

How do you know so much about poetry? I thought you were a science guy.

*Can a man be defined by any one thing? I officially concentrate in chemistry, though if I weren't graduating a year early, I'd have properly switched to physics. But I indulge my broad interests—poetry, literature, language rank high among them. I seem to excel by the greatest margin in the sciences, and approbation has its charms, so I've committed myself to the more menial but more pressing business of the criteria of Bernoulli, Lexis, and Poisson, maybe make a name for myself someday.*

So, you're good at everything.

*Not true. Women. I haven't been on a date in some time. Possibly ever.*

Really?

*Don't say it like that, I've had opportunity, if not from* les jeunes filles New Yorkaises *back home. But I've come, lugubriously, to the conclusion that the two women at Wellesley and the dozen or so here that even pretend to pursue me are a sorry lot.*

A dozen?

*Well, I don't count them.*

Right, because you don't have a head for numbers.

*Ha. Ha. Don't we think we're clever?*

Cady smiled, and a guy coming up the stairs mistook it and winked in return. She blushed, reminded that she was talking to a ghost, like a madwoman. Not that she wished to stop the conversation. —You can't be that bad with women, you get along all right with me.

*Because I have no romantic interest in you.*

She snorted. —Okay, so you're not good with women.

*It's not that you aren't attractive! My heart belongs to another.*

Who?

*Whom.*

Just tell me.

*This woman, this* angel, *whose carrel in Widener is across from mine. I gaze at her when I'm supposed to be studying thermodynamics. We've never spoken, but I've written a few poems about her, though. In my fantasies, I call her Mademoiselle Spinoza, after her thesis topic.*

How do you know she's writing on Spinoza, if you've never spoken to her?

*I've looked through her books when she's not there, even read a few pages of her work. She's a brilliant writer. Her spelling could use a little help, but I find that minute weakness quite charming.*

Oh my God, Robert. You're a creeper. Stop snooping and go talk to her.

*I could never do that. Talking to her would ruin it.*

How? You don't think she could live up to your grand expectations?

*Hardly. I fear I wouldn't live up to hers.*

Cady didn't have any sharp answer to that. It wasn't the first time he surprised her that way. Robert was a genius, and he knew it, but his academic bravado didn't seem to extend beyond the classroom. For all his knowledge, sometimes he sounded so young. He reminded her of Eric that way. —Robert, why do you like talking to me? Why do you think we're friends?

*I think I perceived in your distress a certain similarity to that which I've suffered.*

Because of your baby brother?

*Not that, just the old malady. Melancholia, loneliness, a rather conflicted relationship to our own identity.*

Cady paused at the bottom of the stairs. She had thought her only problems were grief and regret over Eric, that everything was fine before he died, and yet, she couldn't say Robert was wrong. —I think you should talk to the girl. You wouldn't let her down.

*Perhaps. But isn't the promise the best part anyway? That's what's so exciting about this place—it's crackling with potential energy. Every student carries the best prospects in his pocket, fuel for every hope and dream, and we've no knowledge of how it could all go wrong. That's why this university is so glorious and so terrifying.*

Cady pushed against the big double doors of Sever and winced in the bright sunlight of a crisp Cambridge afternoon.

*It's where fate is born, sealed, and yet unknown.*

# 33

OUTSIDE, CADY STARTED down the steps of Sever Hall with Robert's words echoing in her mind. She knew too well that he was mistaken—that Harvard wasn't a safe cocoon of potential, not everyone was blissfully ignorant. The prospect of future suffering could descend sooner than he thought, as it had to Eric. But what about to her? Was she in denial about what lay in her own future? Hearing voices no longer seemed strange to her. She had accepted that there were ghosts, voices from another dimension, that they talked to her, that she talked to them. Her mental state was teetering on a precipice, and it was up to her not to fall.

Cady yelped when something grabbed her arm.

"I'm sorry!" Nikos said through his laughter. "If you saw the look on your face. You looked absolutely terrified."

Cady went to smack him, but he caught her hand and pulled her nearer to him. Sweeping his other arm round her shoulders, he tucked in close to her. "Am I so frightening?" he asked.

"No." Cady let herself lean into him. She could use some comfort, and Nikos smelled good. "You're not frightening, you're sweet. Thank you again for the Chinese food last night. I'd had the worst day, and it was just what I needed to power through an all-nighter."

"Chinese really is *the* cuisine for working late, isn't it? I learned that from American television. I don't think a detective has ever solved a case without it." Cady laughed, and Nikos brushed his palm over her hair. "But you must be knackered. Have you eaten today?"

"No, but I am *knackered*. I might just go to my room and sleep until Collegium rehearsal later tonight." And pore over those decoded numbers in Eric's notebook; this time, she didn't want to show Nikos.

"Nonsense. Apparently you don't eat if I don't feed you, and I'm not about to let you waste away, plus, I'm hungry. Dining halls are closed, so let me take you out. Hm?"

Nikos was impossible to refuse when he tilted his brows up in that puppyish way, so she gave in.

"But mind you, this is the last time I'm buying you a meal without it being a proper date."

They walked down the red brick sidewalks to Daedalus, an upscale pub-restaurant on Mount Auburn Street across from Quincy House. Inside, Daedalus was warm and inviting, with dark wood, red leather booths, and the enticing aroma of French fries. They were seated on the sunny second floor, and at four o'clock, they were the only ones there, save for a couple of guys at the bar watching ESPN on the TV. After a few minutes with the menus, Nikos asked her what she was getting, and when she told him the Portobello burger, he frowned. "A fungus sandwich?"

"Are you going to give me a hard time every time I order something vegetarian?"

"No. But I warn you, I'm going to order a steak sandwich, bloody rare. It may still answer to its name."

Cady chuckled. "Get whatever you want."

"All right, I just don't want to overwhelm you with my carnivorous virility."

"You're ridiculous."

The waitress arrived; she was a swively girl with a flirty smile and dyed red hair. Cady could always spot the fakes.

Nikos didn't appear to share Cady's skepticism. He lit up when she appeared. "Noelle! How are things?"

Of course he knows her name, Cady thought.

After some chitchat where "Noelle" pointedly pretended Cady didn't exist, Nikos ordered for them both, adding, "And two Stellas, please."

"You got it, babe." The waitress smiled and left.

"Babe?" Cady leveled her gaze at Nikos. "And I didn't ask for a beer."

"And she didn't ask for ID. Sometimes it's better not to ask. We're celebrating your paper completion."

"Ugh, it's like I already blocked it out, it's so bad. I seriously think I was sleepwalking when I wrote it. Sleep-typing."

"It's done, which is the best thing a paper can be. So, tell me, you said you had a long day yesterday, what happened?"

Cady rubbed her hands over her face; there was no makeup to mess up anyway. "Oh my God. Where do I start?"

The waitress dropped off the beers with a coy glance at Nikos, but this time he didn't pay her any attention. "Why don't we start at the foam and work our way down?"

"You were right about Lee. She was the one who hacked Eric." She left out the part about her father. "And that's not all, she was stalking him, too, well, she's stalking Prokop."

Nikos coughed on his beer. "Wait, what?"

Cady recounted what she saw on the camera and Lee's alleged sexual harassment case.

"My God," Nikos said when she was finished. "Did she say anything about me?"

"Not really." Cady felt bad she hadn't thought much of Nikos, only Eric. "I mean, she said her grades were better than yours—"

"Bollocks! She's not even fully a physics concentrator, she takes half of my courseload. And she's going to play the woman card? A victim of sexism at the hands of—wait, let me check—a *female* professor? Honestly, some people have no shame. The bitch wasn't good enough, and she knows it."

His anger surprised Cady, and his rant wasn't over. He continued,

"This is all about the Bauer. She was spying on Eric to get info on his project, prying into his private life, whatever she could, and when he quit, I became her next logical target, didn't I? I have to tell Mikaela."

"Prokop."

"Yes. Luckily our projects were submitted last spring, so Lee missed her chance at sabotage. If she copied or undermined me in some way, we won't know until after the winner is announced. I don't want to act rashly. If I take it all the way to the Ad Board right before the results and there's not sufficient evidence, I'll look like the one undermining the competition."

"Are they announcing the winner soon?"

"This weekend."

"Oh, wow." She couldn't help but think of her brother's lost hopes for the award.

"My parents are coming from London."

"Oh, right, it's Parents' Weekend." Cady took a swig of beer.

"A coincidence. They haven't come to one of these in four years. For my father to take off work, it has to be worth it. He'll come to see me win the Bauer."

"You're that confident?"

"Lee Jennings doesn't scare me." Nikos flashed her a grin. "What about you, are you looking forward to seeing your parents?"

"My dad can't, my mom's going to try to come, but I almost hope she doesn't."

"Pennsylvania's not so far."

"They're going through some stuff, and this place . . . it's painful for them."

"Of course." Nikos sighed heavily. "I'm sorry, Cadence, that was stupid of me."

Cady felt her throat tighten. She was too tired to fight off the emotions today. The best she could do was nod.

"You know you can talk to me about Eric. I see you hold it all in, but you don't have to be tough around me. I miss him, often, especially with the Bauer coming up. It's hard to be excited without him here," Nikos said, looking into his beer. "On these autumn days like this, before it got too cold, we used to go on late-afternoon runs round the river. I'd complain about whatever girl trouble I had at the moment, and he'd dutifully listen and advise. Sometimes Eric would open up on those runs, they seemed to ease his Splashberger's."

"His what?"

"Oh, just an inside joke we had. I used to kid Eric that he had Asperger's, but just a splash, 'Splashberger's.'" Nikos smiled and shook his head. "It was stupid, but it made us laugh."

"I like it." Cady smiled back. It was better than thinking of Eric as schizophrenic or depressed.

"The best part of our runs was when they were over. Straightaway, we'd go to Felipe's and get two of the largest burritos they had, loaded with guacamole and sour cream, effectively canceling out the exercise."

"Eric and his spicy food." Cady felt a pang, remembering. "When my mom made tacos, he and my dad would have contests to see who could tolerate the most Tabasco sauce. There were no winners, they'd both end up on the couch with Alka-Seltzer. I think it was just an excuse to get out of clearing the table."

"So that's an old game, eh? And here I thought we invented it!"

"You guys did that, too?"

Nikos nodded. "He beat me handily."

"I'm really glad he had you."

"We made each other better." Nikos's eyes glistened.

Cady was moving her hand toward his, when the waitress reappeared to bus their table, but by the time she had finished clearing, bending, and leaning, the moment had passed.

# 34

CADY ACTUALLY GOT herself to Wednesday's pre-exam Psychology lecture, but late, so she couldn't find Ranjoo, who apparently wasn't sitting in their old section anymore. Cady was completely screwed for the Psych exam Friday; she had accepted that. She hadn't bothered to catch up on her reading and make the most of this review lecture. All she could think about was what those numbers in the notebook meant. If she had had any leads, she wouldn't have come to class.

Professor Bernstein wore his usual outfit of black pants, black button-down, and black microphone headset wrapped around his bald dome; he looked like a member of the faculty's secret service.

"Many of you have expressed anxiety over the essay question; however, this is the one section of the exam where there's often no right or wrong answer, only stronger and weaker arguments. You will need to cite at least three secondary sources, the textbook doesn't count, but you may use a conflicting source for a counterargument as well. All relevant information should be addressed, even if it complicates your thesis."

"Can you give us an example of a typical essay question?" asked a student nearby.

"Sure, let's see." Bernstein flipped through some papers on the lectern. "Last fall's essay question dealt with deinstitutionalization.

Chapter two covered the history of psychotherapy, including the dark days of early asylums. Though vastly improved today, many mental hospitals still fall far short of the doctor's ethos: Do No Harm. Discuss the issues associated with institutionalization today, and identify areas needing the most improvement and why."

There was a collective groan.

"Now, now, is it so terrible to ask you to think critically in a science class? Let's try to answer it right now. What are some of the issues with institutionalization that we've discussed in class?"

Hands shot up. As Bernstein called on some, Cady halfheartedly jotted down their answers: "over-crowding," "over-medicating," "misdiagnosis." She felt so dreadfully behind in this class. At least, if they were discussing the topic now, the institutionalism source readings were likely among the few that would not be covered on the test, leaving her only everything else to review.

Professor Bernstein called on a young man in glasses sitting just four rows ahead of her. He stood up to ask his question and spoke in a clear, confident manner, projecting as an actor would. Cady rolled her eyes inwardly—another know-it-all.

"My name is David, and my comment is this: No one should be abused in a mental hospital, but it shouldn't be a paid vacation on the taxpayer's dime either. I think we've gotten too PC at the expense of common sense. Mental health is a public safety issue. Institutions don't only provide treatment, they also protect the rest of society from psychotic people. If keeping others safe means bending some individual rights, I think that's justified."

Professor Bernstein answered him from the stage. "That's a real issue, David, and in the case of one posing immediate danger to himself or others, what's called an involuntary commitment is possible. In my home state of California, it's known as a 5150 hold that allows an individual to be held against their will for seventy-two hours. But taking away someone's personal liberty can't be taken lightly. And we must be vigilant not to allow the stigmatization of mental illness to override constitutional rights. Another—"

"Although we already restrict the Constitution when common sense calls for it," David interrupted. "Like how we restrict the mentally ill's right to buy guns."

"In some cases, in some states, yes. But it would be a mistake to conflate mental health issues with a propensity for criminality. The statistics don't support that, and it's not in keeping with our values."

Before Professor Bernstein could call on someone else, David called out, "But what about schizophrenia?"

Cady stiffened in her seat.

"A lot of paranoid schizophrenics go on to become murderers. The Son of Sam thought he was following orders to kill people given to him by the neighbor's dog. Mark David Chapman thought he was Holden Caulfield or going to impress Jodie Foster."

Cady looked at Professor Bernstein, who calmly readjusted the microphone at his mouth. "True, but those were sensationalized examples of mental illness in our culture. It's worth noting that there was significant evidence that those particular criminals' symptoms of schizophrenia were falsified for an insanity defense."

David scoffed. "Doesn't everyone who kills another person have to be insane in some way? Some mentally ill people are a danger to the outside world. Those individuals should be committed, or 'put away' before they harm someone, whether they like it or not. They're ticking time bombs."

"They're people!" The words burst from Cady's mouth without warning. Everyone around her turned to stare, making Cady want to sink into her seat and never come out.

Unfortunately, Professor Bernstein was intrigued. "Could you stand up, repeat what you said, and say your name, please?"

Cady rose and instantly felt dizzy from the eyes on her, the room seemed to wrap around her as if she were viewing the world through a fish-eye lens. They were all waiting for her to answer, so Cady commanded her disobedient mouth to speak. "My name is Cadence. And—" She caught sight of Ranjoo sitting down to the right, whispering to a friend, probably saying, *That's my crazy roommate*. "—I said that they're people."

"They're not *normal* people," David snapped, without missing a beat. "And they're not normal medical patients. They're dangerous. If that means fewer personal liberties in order to protect others' rights to safety and life, that's a fair trade."

David's physical proximity to her, his tone, the topic's resonance—it felt to Cady like a personal attack, and she found herself unable to temper the emotion in her voice. "But what does that do to them? Being held against their will, how damaging is that? They deserve their rights, they deserve empathy. These people are victims."

The argument echoed one Cady had had in the past, a time when she had failed to be so vocal, a failure she had done everything to forget. Cady made herself stay focused on the arrogant man in front of her, her anger temporarily protecting her. She succeeded in holding off that dreadful memory, but she could sense it closing in on her. It sounded like the drumbeat of a faraway army, and she was outmanned.

"Until they victimize someone else." David turned from Cady back to Professor Bernstein onstage. "I mean, there was that story last year about a young woman who was an aide in a mental hospital and was murdered by a deranged patient with a long record of lashing out. We're not even protecting mental health workers. If the worst these patients do is kill themselves, we're lucky."

The heat in Cady's face rose to her eyeballs, she could feel them welling up with tears, but she couldn't let herself cry, not with an entire lecture hall full of people looking at her. They would see her reaction was too strong, they'd wonder what was her connection to the topic, they would all guess. And to think, if they only knew the truth.

David was looking at her again, along with the rows and rows of classmates, anticipating her response. Instead, she sank into her seat and shut down.

Bernstein stepped in and took over. "All right, so obviously there are two sides to be argued, and it's easy to get heated. In your essay questions, the important thing is to remain analytical and support whatever argument you make with texts or case studies we've discussed in class. Moving to chapter three . . ."

Cady kept her head down but didn't take any notes for the rest of the class. When the ninety minutes were finally up, the students surrounding her sprang to chatty activity. Cady relied on the others' collective motion to shepherd her out of the lecture hall.

Professor Bernstein's miked voice sounded over the crowd: "Would those students who missed last lecture's practice quiz please see me down here before you leave? Thank you, have a good day."

Cady cursed under her breath. She thought about skipping out anyway, but if she had already missed a quiz on the record, she didn't want to make things worse. She turned against the current of exiting students and plodded down the wide auditorium steps.

Professor Bernstein was talking to a male student when she came down. He patted the boy on the back and said, "All right, good luck on Friday," then turned to Cady. "You're Cadence Archer, correct?"

"Yes, and I'm sorry I missed the quiz, I was really sick that day. I'm going to make up for it on the exam and the rest of the semester."

"I actually don't care about the practice quiz. I called you down because I'm interested in how you're doing."

"Oh, I'm feeling much better, thanks."

"Not about being sick." Professor Bernstein slid his headset off with a concerned frown. "You seemed upset today in class."

"Oh, I just . . ." Cady shrugged. "I'm fine. I just strongly disagreed with his characterization of the issue."

"No kidding. That kid was a jerk."

His unexpected candor made her laugh.

"Do you have a class now?" he asked.

"Uh, no. I was just going to get lunch."

"My office hours start now. Why don't you join me for lunch in my office, we can talk about what you missed and other things."

\* \* \*

PROFESSOR BERNSTEIN'S OFFICE was on the fourteenth floor of William James Hall, the tallest building on campus and a short walk from the Science Center. His office was nice, more contemporary than some she had seen in the older buildings in the Yard. Brushed-chrome bookshelves were mounted to the wall behind his broad ash-wood desk. The desk was clean with a slim silver Apple computer on one end. A large picture window offered a spectacular panoramic view of Harvard's campus. From this height, it looked quiet and static, like a photo in a brochure. A storybook New England town, with red brick Memorial Hall looming large beside slate roofs crowned with copper cupolas, the marble pillars of Widener beyond, and Memorial Church's white spire poking through browning fall foliage like a crocus—beauty sprung from death.

"Sit down," he said, gesturing to one of two cubic armchairs. They were more comfortable than they looked; Cady sank into the gray cushion, and Professor Bernstein sat opposite her. "I know that a lecture class as large as ours can feel impersonal. But I care about my students, and I imagine this might be an especially hard time for you after your brother's passing."

Cady felt her cheeks flush. "I didn't know you knew about that."

"When a student takes his life, the entire campus feels that loss, and as a psychology professor, I take special notice. So when I saw your last name at the top of my class roster, I checked to see if there was a relation."

Cady looked down at her hands, wondering how many of her other professors had done the same.

"Today's class discussion seemed particularly tough for you."

"It brought up some stuff." The drumbeat in her temples intensified. "It's just hard to discuss something academically when you've been there personally."

"Absolutely. But I think your academic interest in the topic, despite or because of your history, is perfectly natural and healthy. Many people are drawn to the subject of psychology in order to understand themselves or their family's issues. I was."

Cady looked up.

Professor Bernstein's brow creased below his shiny pate. "My mother attempted suicide twice. Once when I was nine, and again when I was twelve. After the second attempt, she spent a year in an inpatient program and finally got some good help. So the power of psychotherapy made an impression on me. Initially I wanted to be a clinical psychologist, I thought I wanted to help people. Although you don't have to be Sigmund Freud to figure out that the only person I wanted to help was my mother." Professor Bernstein smiled. "On some level I wasn't entirely in touch with, it bothered me that I wasn't the one to save her. The idea that she had to go away from me to get better. The little-kid logic that everything has to do with you. But as I learned more, got some therapy of my own, gained more personal insight, I learned to let go of the rescue fantasy and move on, do what made me happy, which was teach. But it took time."

"I feel like I didn't get enough time," Cady began, unsure of how much to share, but talking about Eric always made her feel better, like a pressure valve releasing. "Before college, he was happy, quirky, super-smart—he was the best. And then . . . everything fell apart. I hardly had a chance to process his schizophrenia diagnosis before he was gone."

Professor Bernstein shook his head. "Suicide is unfortunately common among college students, it's not a problem exclusive to Harvard. Some studies show as much as twenty percent of undergrads consider it at some point during their college careers. It's supposed to be a time when you're about to embark on your adult life, but for many young people, that springboard looks more like a precipice."

Cady looked out the window. Eric had jumped from his window in Leverett Tower, which wasn't as high as this, but high enough. Was he scared looking down, or did he look out at the river? But Eric had jumped at night, maybe he couldn't see anything at all. Maybe he closed his eyes.

"Cadence, are you all right?"

"Sorry," she said, blinking away the sky's brightness. "I can't stop thinking about how he got to that place, how did he get that desperate? What was it that pushed him over the edge?"

"Well, schizophrenia adds another whole layer of difficulty. And we will cover that illness more broadly later in the semester, and if it's hard on you, or if you ever have questions you're not comfortable asking in section, I hope you'll ask me here."

Why wait, Cady thought? "I have this notebook of his, and I'm trying to make sense of it, but I can't yet."

"You may never be able to make sense of it. It's best not to—"

"But it's like you were saying today in class—just because someone is mentally ill doesn't mean you should discount *everything* they say, or every perception they have about themselves." Her mouth was going dry, but that only made her talk faster.

Professor Bernstein's brow furrowed as he nodded slowly. "I did say that."

"My brother was working with a physics professor, Professor Prokop. Do you know her?"

"Not well, but I know who she is."

"She had my brother as her assistant until late in the game, I mean, he was very sick. Why would a professor want a mentally ill student to be her lab assistant? That doesn't make sense, right? There's not, like, some Harvard protocol that would make her keep him on, is there?"

"Not that I'm aware of, but I'm not sure where you're going with this, or if I'm the one to help you." He sat back in his chair, eyeing her. "How do you feel now that you're at Harvard? Hard to focus?"

"Sorry, I know I was rambling a bit just then." She forced a laugh; she knew she had pushed it too far. "Just today set me off, really. Normally it's great." "Great" was too much, she should've said "fine."

"Do you ever feel depressed or anxious?"

She smiled and shrugged, but he just gazed at her calmly in return. It made her nervous. "You're worried I have it in me, the suicide gene? Diathesis-stressor theory, right?"

"Not at all. Genetics is one small piece of a very large puzzle. I'm just asking how you're holding up."

"I'm okay, thanks." She started to gather her things.

"If you change your mind"—he stopped her before she rose from the chair—"here's the info of a psychiatrist in Boston, Dr. Sharon Miller. I went to med school with her, she's terrific." He wrote her name and number down on an orange Post-it and passed it to her. "Grief is serious business."

Cady took it and thanked him.

As she was leaving, he added, "Do your best on the exam Friday. I can't cut you any breaks, I don't even grade them, my grad students do. But I can offer you this advice: Keep it in perspective. It's only a test—meaningless, in the grand scheme of things."

Precisely.

# 35

CADY THREW THE Post-it into a trash bin on her way out of William James Hall. She didn't need someone else meddling in her mind right now, rehashing her most painful emotions and memories. Perhaps there would be a time for that, but it wasn't now, not when she felt she was on the cusp of breaking through with Eric's last year. She needed to stay focused. Lee was certain Eric and Prokop had been having an affair, but Nikos dismissed it out of hand, and he knew Eric much better. But if it wasn't romantic, what *could* account for Prokop's favoritism as his mental illness worsened? Why give someone with paranoid schizophrenia access to privileged information? She strode up Quincy Street circling over the question.

She was passing Lamont Library on her way home, when a pigeon pecking on the ground caught her attention. She recognized the white feathers on one wing; it was the one from Sunday.

"How you doing, little buddy? Staying away from windows?" Cady took several steps toward him, but he toddled quickly away from her. She followed him. She wanted to pursue him enough that he took flight, to reassure herself that he still could after his accident. But he only seemed to hustle faster, veering left and flutter-hopping down the outdoor stairs to the same area she and Alex had placed him the other day. "C'mon, buddy, fly." He stopped at the shrubbery in front of Wigglesworth Hall, almost seeming to wait for Cady to catch up. When she did, the bird finally took flight toward the back of Lamont, passing over an iron gate and down a path that Cady had never seen before.

Dense foliage along the pathway prevented Cady from seeing where it led, but she followed it around the bend, the fallen yellow leaves making a hushing sound as she walked deeper, and the hubbub of campus and the square quieted. Soon it opened onto an intimate enclosed garden with a sundial in the center. The red brick of the surrounding walls could hardly be seen beneath the ivy that poured over the sides and pooled at the feet of a long, curving stone bench nestled into the shrubbery. What was once a grand wrought-iron gateway to Mass Ave had been walled off so that only the gate's embellished crown of spears remained visible from where Cady stood. The sharply peaked archway above the gate was so cloaked in ivy that its every edge was softened, and its black lantern seemed to hang from the vines like fruit. Only on the lower front wall were the curtains of ivy parted, so the engraving could be read: IN MEMORY OF THOMAS DUDLEY GOVERNOR OF THE COLONY OF THE MASSACHUSETTS BAY, followed by a lengthy inscription.

The peace and privacy of this space felt good. Cady took a seat on the bench, inhaled deeply, and let her breath out.

*This is good, no one will see us here.* Bilhah's voice sounded close, like she was whispering at Cady's neck. *It's time, I need you.*

Okay, I'm here. What's your plan?

*Tonight's the night I take Eli to the church. We'll walk all night.*

What will you say to Holyoke when he notices Eli is gone?

*Nobody in the big house hardly noticed he was born. I heard they placed the ad in the paper already: "Negro child, too young to work, free for the taking." Master can think someone answered it, likely won't give it another thought.*

How old is Eli?

*Four years old. Not that they know that. No one bothered to write down my baby's birthday, or my name, certainly not his father's name. The only thing they write for us is our price. Because they think we nobody. But a nobody can be anybody. And now my baby gon' be somebody new.*

Aren't you worried he'll ask after you?

*Eli won't talk.*

Because you told him not to? He's so young, can he understand the seriousness?

*No, he don't talk. He understands well enough, he hears all right, but he never said a word in his life. I been able to protect him somewhat so far. But him being mute will get him beat when he's older, they whip you for not answering fast enough same as they whip you for talking out of turn. People call him dumb. I say he's too clever. If you seen what he seen, you wouldn't talk neither.*

Cady didn't want to even think about it.

*Him being mute mean he don't have to keep this secret.*

A disabled black child born into slavery in 1765. Cady didn't think worse odds were possible, and yet Bilhah had found a way to turn it to her advantage. This mother's love wasn't only fierce, it was genius. But the cost to her . . .

*What other choice do I have? No Negro in this land ever been born under a lucky star. Curses all we got. But I learned from poison you can make medicine. From curses I'll make blessings. My curse is that my child is not mine to keep. Eli was of my own body, but he does not belong to me. I don't own my body neither. By natural law I do, but by the white man's laws of paper and ink, I own nothing. You can steal something with gunpowder. You can hold something down by chains. But you own it with paper.*

*I serve Master Holyoke and his guests nightly in the salon, scholars, merchants, generals, important men. Lately all they do is talk of freedom. They complain they are "slaves" to the Crown. These learned men don't know the meaning of the word. They do not blush to speak of this before me, I'm invisible to them, till they need more coffee or more rum. But with passion that moves them from their seats, they argue over so many papers, they labor over what is written, how to write it anew. They want to write a new nation into being. They will write this country a new story, as its new fathers.*

The Founding Fathers.

*The right to be one's own master, the right to rule oneself. They will write their life, liberty—*

. . . and the pursuit of happiness.

*But I'm like my son. I don't talk, I listen. I am not simple like they think I am, and I learned well. They want to write their way to freedom. I want to do the same for my son.*

*Yesterday I was the ink blot on my son's life, today I write his freedom with it.*

*With your help.*

What do you mean? What can I do?

*I need you to write the note I'll pin to my son's shirt. I stole paper and ink from the master's study. I couldn't get my hand on one of his quill pens, but I've got this white feather I trimmed the tip of with a paring knife.*

But I can't use your paper and ink.

*Please, you said you would help—*

And I will, the only question is how. I can't see you, your world, or anything in it. Can you see me?

*Yes, of course.*

Here—Cady pulled the blue notebook out of her bag and flipped to the blank pages at the back. —What if I write it with my own paper and pen, and you copy what I put down?

*I told you, I don't know my letters—*

But can you copy it like a drawing? Trace over it? I'll write it really dark, just put your paper over mine and redraw the lines. We'll keep it short. It's the only way I can think to do it.

*I'll try.*

All right. What do you want it to say?

*Say, "God have mercy on this orphan, guide him to a Christian home."*

Now watch me, I'm going to write it for you here, see? —Cady wrote slowly, in block letters:

GOD HAVE MERCY ON THIS ORPHAN
GUIDE HIM TO A CHRISTIAN HOME

*It's too small. My hand is shaking. I'm afraid I'll make a mistake.*

Okay, okay, don't worry, let me try again. I'll try to do it better for you. —Cady wrote it again below the first message, only much bigger and with more space between the letters. She redrew the lines over and over to make the letters dark and thick. At one point, she pressed so hard that her pen pushed through the paper. Cady cursed under her breath.

Hold on, wait, I'll do it fresh on another page.

Cady started over on the next page, trying hard to make this one perfect, dark, and clear.

## GOD HAVE MERCY ON THIS ORPHAN
## GUIDE HIM TO A CHRISTIAN HOME

Cady pushed the notebook away from her to the edge of her knees. —Can you see it through your paper to trace?

*I'm trying, I got to go slow.*

In the sanctity of this secret garden, on this bench shaped like a pew, Cady bowed her head and prayed. She prayed that Bilhah's plan would work, that neither she nor Eli would ever be caught or punished. She prayed that Eli would be able to live a life of opportunity and joy, that his mother's sacrifice would be worth it. She prayed Bilhah might be able to see Eli again, at least to be reassured he was all right, or to watch over him. She prayed Bilhah might find a way to escape herself.

Cady opened her eyes. Clouds passed quickly over the sun, chasing shadows over the sundial.

*There*, Bilhah said. *I'm done now.*

The note?

*Everything. I think this will do it.*

Cady broke into a smile of relief. Relief and wonder—that space-time, like the piece of parchment Bilhah now had in her hands, could fold past over present, more than two centuries apart. She couldn't comprehend exactly how it was happening, but as Professor Prokop said, the universe will always have its secrets.

Cady wished she could check it for her—You're sure it looks the same as the one I wrote for you?

*I've never been more careful. It's his letter of freedom.*

*I only wish it didn't have to be free from me.*

# 36

WHEN NIKOS HAD texted her to meet for dinner, Cady leaped at the chance. At the end of a relentlessly heavy day, she craved his levity like oxygen. He said to meet him at Lowell's squash court, located beneath Entryway A. Like many of the older river houses, Lowell had an underground tunnel network connecting rooms for various purposes, and Cady descended the damp, cool steps, trying to remember the building super's directions. She passed the first few doors and knew she'd reached the right one when she heard the squeaking of sneakers and the hollow smack of a ball.

She pushed open the door and saw the backs of Nikos and a friend whacking the ball on the court in front of her, separated by a wall of Plexiglas. The sounds of play were amplified in the echo chamber of a room, and the *whap* and *pop* of the ball was so loud, Cady flinched each time it hit. The court itself was little more than a windowless white box. The lines painted on the floor and walls offered some points of visual perspective, but the room gave a surreal, claustrophobic impression.

It was funny to see Nikos this way; Cady hadn't thought of him as an athlete. Maybe it was the accent, but he registered as an intellectual, somewhat effete. She could never have imagined him sweating before. But now, as he lunged forward to hit a low ball and his shirt rode up, she noticed the taught muscles of his V-shaped back.

"Cadence!" He turned around when he caught sight of her, and the ball bounced easily to his partner, who nailed it with his racquet. "That one didn't count," Nikos called over his shoulder as he jogged toward her. He opened the door of the court, and a puff of warm, musky air escaped, a gym-sock smell that made Cady scrunch her nose. "Sorry, we're just about finishing up here," he said. His thick hair was pulled up off his brow with an elastic headband, and his face looked flushed and healthy with a sheen of perspiration. "He's lagging, and I only have to score two points in order to beat this prat beyond recovery. Do you mind waiting?" The intonation of his question tilted down in that particular British way Cady loved.

"Sure, no problem. Good luck."

"Thanks, love. Luck won't be necessary."

Nikos sealed himself back inside the steamy court and Cady returned to the bench to watch. Both men were drenched in sweat, like they had been at it a long time. His opponent was an attractive Indian guy she didn't recognize; he was well-built and taller than Nikos, but he looked exhausted, standing drop-shouldered, wiping his face with the bottom of his shirt. Nikos, on the other hand, looked feverish with excitement.

His friend started with a powerful serve, but Nikos was agile and twice as fast. Nikos positioned himself toward the center of the court, and with quick, darting movements, managed to send his opponent running back and forth across the court. Cady didn't know much about squash, but she could tell Nikos was the better tactician of the two. Each player struck the ball only twice before Nikos sent the ball out of his partner's reach and scored. They set up again, and this time the play was more even with each volleying the ball back and forth, crossing each other on the small court.

Cady watched through squinted eyes as the players narrowly avoided collision. Nikos feinted with an intentionally short shot, but the other player anticipated and returned it with surprising force, sending the ball far to the right of where Nikos stood. Cady was sure he would miss, but he dove for it, stretching his compact body as far as possible, and caught the ball with the edge of his racquet before crash landing. But when the ball landed next, his partner was nowhere near it.

"Yes!" Nikos shouted, while the loser cussed and sent his racquet clattering to the floor. He trailed behind as Nikos burst through the door. "Did you see that?" he asked Cady with the unbridled enthusiasm of a child.

She couldn't help but laugh. "Yes, I saw it. Good job! That looked so intense."

"I'm sorry to keep you waiting, but we were tied, I couldn't leave it unfinished." Nikos wiped his face with his shirt.

When his defeated partner approached, Cady introduced herself and shook his clammy hand.

"Goodness, how rude of me." Nikos took over. "Rahul, this is Cadence, Cadence, Rahul. Cadence is a charming freshman whom I've tricked into spending time with me. And Rahul, when he isn't trying fruitlessly to beat me at squash, is a senior government concentrator in Adams House."

"Sociology," Rahul corrected.

"Whatever, one of the easy ones."

Rahul rolled his eyes. "You're like an aggro nerd, man. Anyway, good game."

"Thanks, it was." Nikos shook his hand. "Maybe next time for you, too."

"Nice meeting you," Cady said. Rahul reciprocated with only a nod.

Nikos hiked his gym bag over his shoulder and guided Cady out of the court, leaning close to her ear with a grin. "He fucking hates me right now."

Nikos was practically skipping down the dank basement hallway as Cady followed behind. "I've never seen you so giddy," she said.

"I won! That's like pure adrenaline to me. I get amped." He jumped up to smack his palm against a pipe running along the ceiling, then spun around to face her. "And that was a great game, you know, really close, that's how I like it, I like the win to *mean* something."

"Did you ever play competitively?"

"I play everything competitively," Nikos said with a smirk. "But yes, I played on my school's team before university, but now it's only a hobby. I have more important pursuits that demand my attention."

"Like your Bauer project?"

"Among other things." Nikos looked at her, and a rare sweetness came over his expression. "Would you mind if we stopped at my room? It's G-41, it's not far. I need a quick shower before we go, I'm revolting."

"Sure." Cady paused. "Do you want me to wait for you in the dining hall?"

"No, not a'tall. Come to my room, my roommate is abroad this semester, so it's not cramped like the freshman dorms, and I'll only be a minute."

NIKOS'S ROOM DIDN'T look like the average dorm room. It had a fireplace on one wall and a large window overlooking Lowell's courtyard. But more than the architectural perks, what made it stand out was the way it was decorated. There was no TV atop a microwave-mini-fridge combo or lumpy, stained futon. Instead, two tall book-shelves flanked a cherry-wood desk, and nearby, an elegant armchair looked like it would be comfy if the seat weren't stacked high with more books. In place of the standard-issue metal-framed single bed, he had a queen-sized one, neatly made with clean white linens. It looked like the home of a civilized human being instead of a college-age male.

"Back in a flash." Nikos pulled his shirt off over his head as he walked into the bathroom, offering Cady a glimpse of his toned, if furry, chest and stomach. "Make yourself comfortable," he called before shutting the door behind him.

Cady felt a little excited and a little embarrassed to be in his bedroom. The only place to sit was his bed, and she perched. She felt like she did sitting on the doctor's examining table, self-conscious, not wanting to make too much of a wrinkle.

Over the sound of the shower running, she heard Nikos begin to sing like a comical version of an operatic tenor, clearly meant for her amusement. She smiled and relaxed. Nikos was always trying to entertain her, to make her feel at ease, and he was good at it. She wondered if she could ever tell him about hearing the voices, the ghosts. No, she feared it would remind him of Eric and drive him away. No one wants to experience tragedy twice. Cady caught herself—was she a tragedy already?

She didn't want to think about that and looked out the window. The sun was setting sooner these days and had just slipped behind the roof of Lowell's opposite wing, painting the sky a seashell pink and the clouds a dusky lilac. Cady reached to turn on the lamp beside his bed. As soon as the light was on, she noticed the soft gleam of a pair of freshwater pearl earrings lying atop his bedside table.

Nikos stopped singing and Cady heard the water squeak off. Moments later, he emerged with combed-back hair, shiny pink shoulders and only a towel around his waist, smelling of boy-clean scents like wintergreen and spice. Clearly comfortable with his body, he grinned at her. "That's better."

Cady blushed. "Great. Now, put some clothes on."

"I already have a sweater." Nikos gestured at his furry torso. He crossed the room and pulled clothes from his dresser. "Relax, Archer, I'm not coming on to you, I show off like this to everyone."

"I guess so," Cady said, rapping her fingernails beside the earrings. "Or I didn't know you had your ears pierced."

"Oh." Nikos blanched. "Sorry about that." He swept the earrings off the table and into the drawer below. She had never seen him at a loss for words before.

"No, it's fine." Cady had hoped to come off playfully, but she had missed the mark and regretted mentioning it. She didn't want to appear jealous when she wasn't—was she?

"I should put these on," he said, patting the clothes in his arms.

"Do you want me to wait outside?"

"No no, I'll dress in the bathroom. One more moment, and then we'll finally get something to eat."

He disappeared again, leaving Cady to feel like she had dampened their lighthearted rapport. But when he emerged again, fully dressed, his jaunty ease had returned. "There we are."

"Ready?" she asked.

"Yes, but before we go, I want to show you something." He crossed the room to one of his bookshelves, and pulled a thin little volume from the shelf. He handed her what looked like a children's book. "Eric gave this to me."

"Really?" It was a vintage Little Golden Book of *The Sword in the Stone*. "This was his favorite Disney movie when we were kids. He used to watch it over and over. I haven't thought of it in years."

He sat down on the bed next to her. "It was one of my favorites as well. The story of a skinny nerd destined for the throne holds a certain appeal for swotty lads. We'd once lamented the lack of VHS players to indulge in the nostalgia. He gave it to me as a gag gift, but I cherish it now. He inscribed it."

She opened the inside cover, and just seeing Eric's familiar scrawl made a knot in her chest. Below the "This Book Belongs To" he had written:

*Archimedes,*

*Found this at a sidewalk sale and thought of my favorite owl.*
*Thanks for having my back on this quest, you know I have yours.*
*We'll keep the pikes off our tail.*

*Yours,*
*Wart*

Cady smiled, and her whole body relaxed. "He called you 'Archimedes'?"

"It fits. I'm Greek, short . . ."

"And the eyebrows!"

He popped one for effect. "Guilty as charged."

She laughed in delight. It was so wonderful to have a happy memory about Eric, even one that didn't belong to her. She felt a rush of gratitude for the man sitting beside her. "This is awesome, thank you." She handed it back to him. "Eric really cared about you."

"We were very good friends." He bowed his head, and Cady saw his jaw clench with emotion.

Cady put her hand on his shoulder, which seemed to revive him.

"I'm sick of dining hall food, aren't you?" he said. "I have something else I want to show you."

# 37

OUTSIDE, THE NIGHT was bitter cold but beautiful. The busy activity of Harvard Square seemed smiled upon by a crescent moon in the clear indigo sky. After they had left Lowell House, she and Nikos had gotten a quick slice of Sicilian pizza at Noch's and then stopped at Burdick's to get their extra-rich hot chocolate for the walk through the square. Nikos took her hand and held on to it inside his pocket to keep warm.

"Where are we going?" Cady asked.

"It's a surprise."

They walked up Garden Street, past the old colonial cemetery, strolling together in stride. He kept her laughing, and before she knew it, they had gone beyond the Quad dorms and turned left into a compound of buildings Cady had never seen before. It wasn't until they stopped that she read the sign on the manicured green: HARVARD-SMITHSONIAN CENTER FOR ASTROPHYSICS.

"Have you ever been to an observatory?" Nikos asked.

Her gaze traveled from his face up to the domed building behind him and she laughed in surprise. "No, but isn't it closed by now?"

"I've a friend who's an astronomy concentrator, so I called in a favor." Nikos began to nose around the shrubbery. "Look for a ski hat."

Cady poked around with the giddy anxiety of breaking the rules.

She spotted an Icelandic hat beneath a bush. "Is this it?" She lifted the hat by its red pom-pom, and when she did, a swipe card fell out of it.

Nikos snatched the card from the mulch. "We're in." He led her away from the front door and around the side. "We can enter this little annex over here, it connects to the observatory."

Cady followed him to the annex, a small building that looked like a brick box, no windows at all, so when they stepped inside, it was pitch black. Nikos used his iPhone as a flashlight to locate the light switch. When he flipped it, the light that came on was warm and dim, unlike the typical fluorescents throughout most of the science buildings, and revealed a single room packed with rows of olive-green metal shelves and a narrow passage in between. Each shelf was fully stocked with slim volumes bound in plain white cloth covers in various states of age and yellowness—a library, mummified.

"What is this place?" Cady whispered. The only sounds were the buzzing of an old lightbulb and the fan of a humidifier. She approached one of the bookshelves and peered at the strange handwritten titles made up of cryptic letters and numbers, or, on the most tattered covers, Roman numerals.

"I believe they're archival astronomy photos or slides or something. Jim, my mate who left us the swipe card, told me about it once, I was only half-listening."

*They're photographic plates of the night sky.*

Whit—Cady thought, surprised at the way she felt her heart lift.

Nikos continued, "Apparently Harvard has a half million of them from the predigital days."

*The collection stretches back to the 1880s, it's the only complete collection of both hemispheres.*

"Now they don't know what to do with them all. Jim's working with some History of Science professor to try to digitize the catalog, but each plate must be individually cleaned and scanned by hand and the process is slow, so with five hundred thousand, it would take years or something ridiculous."

*They map the night sky entire.*

"How do you know all this?" Cady asked them both.

"Jim prattles on about it, once you get him going he doesn't stop."

*I've taken several astronomy classes, so I've worked with the plates before. An airshipman is only a glorified sailor, so I ought to know how to read the stars.*

"I think it's a Sisyphean task, if there ever was one. And with the incredible telescopes and technology we have now, I don't know why we bother preserving these. But I shouldn't be surprised."

*Can you imagine?*

Nikos went on, "Harvard loves to be the sole proprietor of all things arcane and obsolete."

*Every star in the sky.*

"Every star in the sky," Cady repeated. "That's incredible."

Nikos glanced back at her. "I suppose so." He walked over to one of the shelves, pulled one of the envelopes, and began to open it.

"Are you supposed to touch them?"

"You don't think it's in good hands?" Nikos drew the glass plate from its sleeve. The plate was translucent and vaguely gray in the center, like a dirty windowpane. When he held it up to the light above, she could see it was freckled with dots no larger than a grain of sand. "Do you want to know the best part?" he asked.

"What?"

"There's no backup." Nikos loosed his grip on it for a moment, letting it drop a few inches before catching it.

"Jesus, Nikos!"

He cackled.

"Put it back right now."

"Ooh, I like this Mean Mummy voice on you. God knows how they actually read the things."

*They're photo negatives.*

"Let me see," Cady said, intrigued.

*I can show you how to read them. See that machine over there? That's the lightbox, the switch is on the side.*

Cady followed Whit's directions while Nikos watched. With his guidance, she peeled a heavy leather drape off a machine to reveal the slanted surface of the lightbox. She clipped the plate into place and hit the switch. The light flickered on, illuminating the miniature constellations and all manner of scribbled notes and numbers from astronomers long past. She traced the edge of the glass with her finger; here was a century-old record of the heavens, laid over the present.

Nikos leaned over her shoulder. "It's got writing on it."

*The annotations are my favorite part. Notes about the coordinate locations, mostly.*

"How could they possibly see what they were calculating?" Nikos asked. "They're practically microscopic."

*You'll need the magnifying loupe. Professor Johnston usually leaves one on the shelf below. Is it there?*

"Here," Cady said, locating the small cylindrical magnifying glass. "The magnifying loupe."

"Look at you!" Nikos looked at her with awe. "Magnifying 'loupe' and whatnot. Have you been here before? How do you know so much about astronomy?"

"Space camp," she lied.

Nikos smirked. "You're so full of it."

But Cady could tell he was unaccustomed to having her in the lead. Looking around this room she had never imagined existed, she was transfused with an uncanny sense of familiarity. She could feel that Whit knew his way around.

"C'mon, who wants to look at old scribblings and dots when we can see the real thing?" Nikos dismissed a century of scholarship with a wave of his hand. "Let's go to the main observatory, I want to show you the telescope." He led her through a passage to the main building and over to the elevator bay. The *ding* of the arriving elevator pinged loudly off the walls of the empty space, making Cady nervous someone would find them. Nikos seemed unconcerned, stepping aside to let her enter the elevator before him. Inside, he pushed the last button on the wall.

"It's the thirteenth floor," Cady said.

"Yes, top floor, of course."

"No, I mean, don't buildings normally skip the thirteenth floor? You know, for luck."

Nikos smiled up at the rising numbers. "We're inside a Harvard University science building. Superstition ceases to exist." The doors opened, and they found themselves surrounded by the typical classrooms and offices. Nikos turned and handed her her coat. "M'lady."

"Do I need this?"

"It will be cold outside on the roof."

Cady had been so preoccupied, it hadn't occurred to her that the observatory was literally outside on the roof of the building. She followed him up a final flight of stairs, lit with only a string of red lights along the ground; Nikos explained that red lighting is the only color that doesn't interfere with night vision. The cold air rushed in when Nikos pushed through the heavy door to the roof. It was windy so high up, but the view was beautiful. It was a clear night, she could see the dorms of the nearby Quad as a checkerboard of glowing yellow windows, and the lights of Harvard Square twinkled beyond them. They walked down a narrow metal gangway to the observatory, whose silver, domed body squatted on the concrete roof like an alien spaceship. It took another swipe with Jim's ID and an added passcode Nikos had written on scrap paper, but finally they were inside.

The observatory was a huge dome with cobalt blue walls papered with astronomical images and a white roof crisscrossed with latitudinal and longitudinal lines, but of course, the enormous telescope descending from the very center of the roof dominated the space. Its enormous diameter at the top tapered down so narrow at the bottom eyepiece that the machine gave the impression of a drill bearing down more than pointing up; Cady was reluctant to stand beneath it.

Out of the plates archive, Nikos had regained his usual commanding affect, striding to the telescope and settling into the chair that ran on a circular track.

*The Great Refractor.* Whit's voice returned. Cady found herself glad they hadn't left him in the annex. *Fifteen-inch-diameter lens, it's the most powerful telescope in the United States, its only twin is in the Poulkovo Observatory in Russia. Twenty feet of carved mahogany. Can you imagine a more glorious end for a tree?*

But the telescope in front of Cady did not match Whit's description. The machine before her was constructed of gleaming white metal, modern and cold. "When was this telescope put in?"

*In the late 1840s, I think. It's a masterpiece.*

"I'm not sure. It can't be that old. Everything here is state of the art," Nikos answered.

Cady and Whit were in the same place but looking at different things, like time folded over. She supposed Whit couldn't see Nikos, or anything else in the room as it was now, only her. He was an echo projected into her world, and she was projected into his.

"I've used this once before in a freshman seminar. Let's see if I remember." Nikos eyed some switches on a control panel near the telescope.

*First we've got to get the door open so we can actually see some sky. Over here on the wall. You can see why I like it in here. The wooden plank floor, the wheel—it feels like being aboard a ship.*

The floor was no longer wood, but Cady's eyes were drawn to a lever of sorts mounted on the wall. "Nikos, is there a door or window we have to open up to look out of?"

"Of course. How stupid of me. Yes, I think it's this handle here." Nikos released some element and punched a keypad beside it.

*I warn you, it's going to get chilly. Here, take my jacket.*

"I'm fine."

"What was that?" Nikos called.

Thankfully, a loud grinding sound answered for her as the ceiling split open. The once-hidden door retracted to reveal a widening slice of dense, dark sky. Even to the naked eye, the stars looked bright and crisp. But the telescope was not lined up with the aperture in the ceiling.

"This is my favorite part." Nikos crossed the room to hit a different button, and the ground beneath Cady growled as the entire floor rotated. She had to catch herself to keep from losing her footing.

"You could've warned me!"

"What fun would that be?" Nikos showed her how the telescope worked, first setting it up himself and then guiding her how to use it. "There. Can you see anything?"

Cady sat down in the rolling track, sliding back and forth, before steadying herself on the hull of the enormous telescope. She squeezed one eye shut and peered into it. She had never seen so many stars, or so vividly. Some were diamonds, bright and clear, others were bleary eyes of red or blue.

*They say fate is written in the stars, but the irony is that stars don't project the future, they reflect the past. If you think about it, every time you look at a star, you're looking back in time. The North Star is four hundred thirty light-years away, so when you see it shining, the light hitting your eyes is already four hundred thirty years old.*

So it's an illusion, Cady thought. The real star could be gone by the time you see it.

*No, it's all real, the star's shape, its brightness, its changes, all the stages of its life—there's nothing false about it, it's simply translated across time.*

Nikos spoke at her shoulder. "Can you see the Milky Way? Here, let me adjust it for you."

Cady scooted aside while he fussed with the telescope.

*You and I have both lost someone. I like to think they're like the stars. Their light hasn't gone out. Candlelight goes out. But something as bright as a star, or a soul, that light moves on.*

"There," he said, beckoning her back to the telescope's seat. "Now, don't move it."

This time, Cady could see the galaxy in smoky swirls of amethyst and rust, and all against the blackest sky. "I can't believe it can reach so far. When you really think of it, it's a miracle that our eyes alone can see any stars at all."

*When you love someone, time isn't such a big obstacle.*

"It's a powerful instrument," Nikos said. "All right, my turn."

Cady stepped aside. While Nikos settled with the telescope, she savored a few moments alone with Whit.

Do you believe in fate? —she thought to him.

*No.*

But what about following in your father's footsteps? You have such a sense of destiny.

*Legacy is different from fate. I chose to inherit his legacy, and I'm choosing to carry it onward. Fate implies you have no control. I admit, choice can be a burden, it would be a load off to think the future's already set. But I don't believe anything is written in the stars. I want to write it myself.*

Cady heard the hope, the possibility in his voice, and it spoke to her heart. And yet. —I want to believe you, but I'm afraid you're wrong.

*Then how does my story end?*

I don't know yet. But it does.

Nikos looked up from the telescope. "What is it? You've got a funny look on your face."

"Oh." Cady shook her head. "I was just thinking."

"About?"

"Do you believe in fate?"

Nikos walked over to her. "Absolutely."

*All of our stories end, one way or another. The stars are a reflection of the past, what you leave behind.*

"You look like you don't believe me," he said, smiling.

She shrugged. "I guess I didn't expect you to be so sentimental."

"I'm a closet romantic."

*I want to be a comet.*

Cady blushed. "Maybe I underestimated you."

"And I you. You've taken me very much by surprise, Cadence, your wit, your maturity, your beauty. Your brother was such an ugly mug"—Nikos laughed—"I'm sorry, I've a bad habit of joking when I'm nervous." He rested his hand on hers as if it steadied him, and she realized he seemed more anxious than she. "The truth is, I had always imagined you from Eric's perspective, as a little girl, 'Cady,' baby sis. And then that day in September, I looked across my piano and the woman I saw took my breath away. To be honest, I felt guilty for how attracted I was to you. I thought, if Eric were here, he would punch me in the face for thinking this way. But then, more recently, I wondered . . . if in some way, he's led me to you."

*I'm not afraid of the darkness. You shouldn't be either.*

They had drawn closer to each other without realizing it; Cady tilted her chin up and her face was inches from his. Nikos spoke the next words with nearly breath alone.

"So, in answer to your question, yes, I do believe in fate."

*You can see more in total darkness than you ever could in light.*

Cady closed her eyes.

His lips closed over her own, and she felt herself melt into his mouth, the warmth of his body, the clean smell of his neck, the pressure of his fingers on her back. The stars behind her eyes burst like champagne bubbles in a glass. It was wonderful.

And then she abruptly pulled back.

Nikos blinked in confusion. "Was that okay?"

"Yes, no, I just . . ." she stammered, unable to meet his eye. "I'm too worried we're going to get caught. Can we go?"

"Sure, I'll get our coats."

She watched him walk away. Her once-fluttering heart now raced with the real reason she had pulled away:

Cady hadn't known which one she'd been kissing.

# 38

CADY AWOKE THE next day with a gasp. The shades in her bedroom were drawn to block the morning sun, but she felt as if a bright light were shining into her brain. Last night at the observatory, Whit had pointed out the coordinate annotations on the plates, and somehow in her sleep, it clicked. She pulled her laptop out of her bag and opened it on her lap in bed. She googled "coordinates for Cambridge MA." The answer was electrifying; the coordinates for Cambridge, Massachusetts, were 42.3736° north, 71.1106° west. She found the page of Eric's notebook where she had decoded the numbers, correcting their notation to reflect her new understanding:

1. 42.371609° N—71.116840° W
2. 42.369764° N—71.125497° W
3. 42.373345° N—71.118889° W
   42.375038° N—71.119531° W

"Yes!" she cried out loud. She heard Ranjoo groan above her, but Cady was too excited to feel bad for waking her. She had cracked Eric's code, she finally understood that she was looking at geographic coordinates in the local area. Now she needed to find exactly where they were, and why they mattered to her brother.

Ranjoo's feet suddenly dropped into view, her toenails painted mint green. The bed creaked as she climbed down from her upper bunk to the floor.

"Morning." Ranjoo scratched at her silky, black ponytail. "Are you up early studying for Psych?"

"Uh, no, something else."

"Oh, you got another test? That sucks." She stretched her arms over her head and yawned. "I feel pretty good about most of it, but as you saw from those lecture notes I sent you, the statistics part trips me up. How about we get breakfast and then study for Psych together, maybe you can explain it to me?"

"I wish I could, but I have to finish this." Cady just wanted to be alone to focus.

"Oh-kay." Ranjoo sounded annoyed.

"Thanks for the notes, though," Cady added, as Ranjoo retrieved her shower caddy and headed for the door. She flashed a thumbs-up sign over her head as she walked out of the room.

Cady sighed. Not ideal roommate relations, but she didn't have time to obsess. She wanted to reread Eric's notebook armed with this new knowledge. Much of the notebook's contents seemed clearly related to some kind of Physics research notes, Cady had previously assumed they were notes for his Bauer project, but they just as likely could have been for Prokop's restricted research. The fact that Eric had encrypted the locations seemed to strengthen her hypothesis that they were related to the secret nature of Prokop's work. She also remembered Eric's refusal to discuss any of their work over email—again, Cady had previously chalked that up to yet another example of his paranoia, but now she wondered if it was lab policy.

A small note in the margin stood out to her that hadn't before. A page dated from the fall of last year that had these bullet points jotted in the margin in small print:

o   Don't be followed!
o   Out of sight

- o Publicly accessible
- o Secure but removable by hand
- o Never recheck once dropped!

If she was skeptical that these coordinates were merely part of another of Eric's paranoid fantasies, the bulleted points seemed to argue they were directions given to Eric, as if he was acting on behalf of someone else, likely Prokop, and coordinating with a third party. Cady knew Prokop was hiding *something* about their relationship, and Cady no longer felt so certain of Lee Jennings's hypothesis that they were hiding an affair. Her frontrunner guess about the coordinates was that there was some kind of meeting or handoff occurring at these spots. Although that led Cady to the disappointing conclusion that she probably wouldn't find anything remaining at these locations because they had already been removed by someone else's hand, still, she wanted to track them down. At least then she could gather more information by retracing Eric's steps, and maybe some pattern would emerge that could indicate what he was leaving, and for whom.

Cady spent the next hour giving herself a crash course in how to actually use geographical coordinates. Most of the websites she was learning from were for "geocaching," a hobby for those who enjoy scavenger hunts via coordinate clues. The amount of information on the topic was dizzying, but she'd learned there was an app that could turn your iPhone into a GPS coordinate locator. She plugged the first coordinates into her phone, 42.371940, −71.118128. It was only a quarter mile away, on Mount Auburn Street. Cady got dressed and set out.

The directions on the app led her to Mount Auburn Street, right where it splits off with Bow Street. She looked down at the app and zoomed in on the map to get more specific. She walked slowly down the sidewalk, watching her blue dot move closer and closer to the red destination dot. When the two were overlaid with one another, she looked up and smiled. She was standing outside Insomnia Cookies. Cady remembered how Eric used to rave about this cookie shop in

Harvard Square that was open at all hours of the night. He had said it was his "soulmate" shop, an idea so perfectly suited to him and his night owl habits, he was angry he didn't think of it himself. She had told him he'd have to take her there when she toured campus, but in the end, she never did tour before applying. He was so sick by her senior year, she had been afraid to ask.

If he was simply meeting someone at a cookie shop, geographical coordinates seemed like an overly specific way to make plans. Moreover, the shop was tiny. Cady peered inside and guessed it was about five hundred square feet max, not an ideal space for a clandestine discussion. So maybe there was no discussion; Eric had marked each of the coordinates with dates but no times, so maybe there was no meeting at all. Plus, Eric was awkward around new people, especially so when he was sick; Prokop would be foolish to send him on a sensitive face-to-face. But she might have sent him to make a delivery, or a drop. Cady scanned the storefront for a good hiding spot. The glass window had only a small ledge, too shallow to tuck anything underneath, but closer to the ground there was some sort of metal vent with slats like a venetian blind. She knelt down beside it and ran her fingers behind each of the horizontal slats, grimacing as her hand grew covered in the sooty filth that coated the metal.

On the third slat from the bottom, she felt something sticky. Hoping it wasn't chewing gum, she picked at it with her fingernails until she peeled it off and pulled it into the daylight. It was a silvery piece of duct tape, just the sort of thing you would use to affix something, which would already have been picked up. She was reminded of the check mark beside the first set of coordinates—confirmation, perhaps? She'd have to check all the locations for clues. A scrap of tape was far from proof, but it was enough to keep Cady going.

# 39

CADY NEARLY CHOKED on her mouthful of warm chocolate-chip cookie when she saw the email that came in on her phone. It was from david.hines@fas.harvard.edu, Professor Hines, with the subject line "Important." A wave of anxiety crashed over her. Cady had been so preoccupied with her worlds of the past, the ghosts' and her brother's, that she was completely blowing off her present. She was skipping classes, putting off assignments until the last minute, and she'd resigned herself to tanking tomorrow's Psych exam. Ironically, she'd thought her poetry seminar was the only class she wasn't actively screwing up right now. Her finger hovered over the message in her inbox as she flirted with the idea of closing her email without opening it and avoiding the message altogether. She took another massive bite of cookie for courage. "Ah, fugg it." She tapped to open it.

The message was short:

> Your paper was excellent. I'd like to meet with you to discuss it, sooner rather than later. My office hours today would be ideal, 12–2pm, Barker 135.

She actually laughed. She wrote him back, thanking him and saying she'd be there at noon sharp. It was quarter after eleven. She put

Eric's notebook back in her bag. Location number two would have to wait just a little longer.

Cady went straight to the Barker Center and arrived with time to kill before her meeting with Professor Hines, so she bought a coffee and sat in the Barker café's sunny rotunda. She was grateful for the time, as she was eager to preview the second set of coordinates. With Eric's notebook open on the table, she keyed the numbers into the app on her phone; a pin dropped on the map a little farther off campus than the first. Cady zoomed in; it was on or near the opposite bank of the Charles River. Her knee bounced under the table as she checked the clock again. She was anxious to get this Hines meeting over with and back to her main mission, figuring out what these locations meant.

At ten to twelve, she found the door to his office ajar. With her back pressed against the hallway wall, she checked the clock on her phone one last time: 11:54 a.m. Surely he wouldn't mind her being a little early, she thought. But she waited until 11:56 to knock.

"Come in," Hines called out to Cady.

She entered to find a beautiful office, artfully cluttered. The walls were painted the color of Nantucket reds, and an indigo oriental rug covered the hardwood floor. The stately mahogany desk that faced her was piled with stacks of papers and books and a boxy desktop computer, and behind the desk, a deep-silled window opened onto a view of the courtyard. Floor-to-ceiling bookshelves packed with a rainbow of volumes, some faded, cloth-bound tomes and other crisp, shiny new books, including chunks of identical ones bearing his own name on the spines. The only unappealing thing in the room was Professor Hines, leaning back in his chair with his dirty bare feet up on his desk.

"Hi," Cady said.

"Close the door." Professor Hines gestured. "Sit. You can move those papers."

"Thanks." Cady carefully lifted a stack of mail and pamphlets from the wooden chair, and, not knowing what else to do with them, sat down with them on her lap. Hines made no offer to take them from her, and instead remained in his chair with his hands clasped behind his head, staring at her.

"Do you know why you're here?"

Cady's mouth went dry; it wasn't the warm welcome she had hoped for. Her tongue worked to unstick her lips from her teeth. "I'm here to discuss my paper."

"I want to read you something." Professor Hines swung his dirty feet from the desk and reached for a book from the shelf, opening to a dog-eared page. "This is Harvard College's Student Handbook, you were given one at the beginning of the school year, yes?"

"I think so."

Hines leaned forward. "Here on page ninety-seven, in the chapter entitled, 'Academic Dishonesty,' it states that 'Students who, for whatever reason, submit work either not their own or without clear attribution to its sources will be subject to disciplinary action, up to and including requirement to withdraw from the College.'" Hines looked up from the page. "Do you understand what that means?"

"Yes."

"We don't tolerate plagiarism here."

"I know."

"And I don't suffer fools."

Cady searched his eyes for meaning, but his cold gaze betrayed nothing. She shifted in her seat. "I'm sorry, I don't understand."

Hines sat back with a sigh. "I read your paper. It was excellent."

"Thank you." Cady kept her voice soft and obedient.

"Who wrote it?"

"My paper?"

"Yes, you didn't write it. So who did?"

Cady shook her head in confusion, her thoughts too jumbled to answer. Not that Hines gave her much time to.

"The short paper you wrote last summer to get into this class, I reread it. It's competent, good enough to earn you a spot in my class, which says something. But it is nowhere near the paper you turned in this Tuesday. That paper was entirely different in style, tone, and research. It doesn't read like any freshman's paper in my eleven years of teaching. How do you explain that, Ms. Archer?"

"I don't know, I—"

"I do. You plagiarized it."

Cady gasped. "No—"

"And while some professors might just give you a zero on the paper, or fail you for the course, I'm not such a softie. I have a mind to take this all the way to the Admissions Board. Plagiarism shows a lack of character. Disrespect. Entitlement." Hines leaned over the desk and pointed at her. "Because if you don't deserve to be here, someone else does. Over forty thousand high school seniors apply for sixteen hundred spots in your class. There are easily a thousand students just as good as you who weren't so lucky. You took someone's spot, someone more worthy than you."

*I know*, Cady thought. *I took Eric's.*

"I can see the guilt on your face right now. So fess up. Tell me where you copied this from, and I might cut you a break."

"I didn't copy it, I swear."

"Look at me."

Cady obeyed. His eyes were hard.

"Last chance." Professor Hines spoke the next words slowly. "Where did this come from?"

Cady's hands were trembling. "Me. I wrote it."

"All right. Chance blown. I'm going to submit this to the Ad Board disciplinary committee for an inquiry, they have technology to identify even well-disguised plagiarism, they are very thorough. In the meantime, come to class prepared. Try to convince me you were capable of writing this paper on your own. Know that I think you are not."

Cady bit her lip and nodded.

"I'm done here. You're free to go to the ladies' room and cry."

\* \* \*

THE BARKER CENTER'S heavy glass doors hissed and groaned like hecklers as Cady pushed through them. She strode through the red brick courtyard past Hines's office window, feeling at once self-conscious that he may be watching her and hopeful that he was. Her face was red with anger as much as embarrassment, but she wanted him to know he wasn't worth one tear. Hines simply hated her, he had hated her from the first day, and the feeling was mutual. She had never been spoken to that way by a teacher, much less been accused of something as offensive as plagiarism. She might have been off her game lately, but she wasn't a cheat.

Dense clouds hung low and heavy, painting the sky the mottled gray of a tombstone. As she crossed campus toward Weld, the chill in the air cooled her anger and made room for something else—doubt. As much as she hated Hines for his condescension, the whiff of sexism in his jabs, the way he clearly enjoyed making her squirm, she had the sinking sensation that he could be right. She didn't remember the bulk of her own paper. She had been so exhausted that night, she had told herself she'd blocked it out, but had she? She knew for certain she hadn't copied the paper from anywhere. But she couldn't say she expressly remembered writing it.

As soon as she got home to her dorm room, Cady went to her laptop computer. The second the screen awoke, she searched in her Documents folder for Hines Paper 1 and clicked Open. She read the first page, which was familiar; she remembered struggling with the introductory paragraph before Collegium and spilling Chinese food on her *Norton Anthology* when looking for the quote at the bottom. But halfway through the second page, her memory grew murky. The writing tightened, the tone became more formal, and the scope of the analysis broadened. It referenced other poems in seamless support of its newly nuanced thesis statement, poems Cady had a passing familiarity with but not an expertise. The author of this paper was confident, well-read, and a little bit of a show-off.

*Robert.*

Cady's heart rate quickened. Hines was right, she hadn't written it. But she also hadn't copied it from anywhere. If she were called before the Ad Board, how could she explain this? What was she supposed to say, 'The genius that talks to me in my head wrote it'? That her study buddy is a ghost nerd from the 1920s with a penchant for French poetry? Her defense was its own indictment, only of something much worse—madness. Not that they would believe it anyway. They'd believe she was a cheat before they'd entertain the idea that she communed with dead students from another dimension.

And about that communing—how much was too much? How far was too far? Letting a ghost inhabit your mind long enough to write a paper? Was she still the one "letting" it happen at all? How far out of her control could Cady let this go before her mind was out of her control forever?

There was only one thing left she could control. She loaded the second-location coordinates into her phone and changed into running gear.

# 40

OUTSIDE, THE CLOUDS had grown darker still, as if the sun had lost its fight behind them, ashes smothering fire. Cady zipped her jacket all the way to her neck and set out toward Harvard Square. She dodged around the ambling day trippers and dashed across Mass Ave at the first break in traffic, too impatient for caution. The run had mostly been a pretense to tell her roommates while Cady tracked down the second location, but the physical exertion was helping to burn off her mounting anxiety. She ran hard, her thoughts clicking ahead with every step.

The paper thing with Robert had shaken her, made her feel naive to have let the voices into her life. Was she doing the right thing? Was she getting closer to some insight about her brother, or was she in too deep? But no, Robert was harmless, a gentle person who had only been trying to help her. All the ghosts had helped her in some way. And when she helped Bilhah to write the note, she felt more focused and purposeful than she had since before Eric died, maybe ever. She didn't understand how or why the ghosts were reaching her, but if she had crossed paths with Bilhah for only that purpose, it had been worth listening.

But still she was afraid.

The crowds thinned as she got farther down JFK Street and closer to the river, and Cady picked up speed, making her breath ragged. Fear had been her first reaction to hearing the voices. Then she'd thought only of what they had to offer her. But now she had come to care deeply about them as people. Which, ironically, brought her back to fear. She was afraid for Bilhah and Eli. Afraid they would get caught; Bilhah could be tortured, executed, and God forbid what might happen to her little boy. Cady hoped the note had come out well enough that her plan for Eli would work, but she knew Bilhah had no real safety as long as she remained a slave. Maybe Cady could help her a second time. Maybe she could help her write her own letter of freedom, forge papers as a freed woman, something so she could escape her own suffering.

She was afraid for Whit, so loyal to his family legacy and his country. He was so desperate to connect with a father he never knew that he was willing to follow him to the grave. What would happen to him if he joined the Navy at the dawn of World War II? Her mind flashed through images of the explosions and smoldering ships at Pearl Harbor, the blood-soaked beaches of Normandy, the spray of earth and bodies, men slumped in the snow outside Stalingrad; she heard shells exploding and machine-gun fire and cries of agony.

Cady remembered that night last winter when the hail had sounded like gunfire striking the car as she and her father drove behind the ambulance that held her brother, bound to a stretcher. It was Eric's loyalty that had gotten him there in the first place, his urge, however twisted, to protect Cady from terrors that had seemed real to him. For the first time, he'd had nightmares to tell her, but she hadn't listened. She had been as cold and hard as packed snow. But her mind wouldn't take her fully back there, it was still too painful. Cady's feet struck the ground harder, grinding that pain into the dirt.

The light across busy Memorial Drive was already blinking, telling her to stop, but she crossed anyway, heedless of the SUV honking at her, its headlights mere feet from her hip as she darted past. Maybe the ghosts had found her to teach her about loyalty, about sacrifice. Maybe they were a test of her willingness to put someone else before herself.

A chance to redeem herself from the last time she failed to do so and someone she loved paid the price. She pounded the concrete along the riverside, filling her lungs with the hot car exhaust and the cold air, each traitorous breath stinging more than the last, as she deserved.

The choppy bottle-green waters of the Charles River sounded angry, slapping against the banks, hocking foam at the tall grass, spitting up red Solo cups and other trash. A mallard had to flap its inky wings to ride the cresting wakes. Since there was no sun, there was no shimmer on the water, only shifting shadows on the undulating surface. The water that drew closer to the banks grew rusty and brown with the churning soil beneath. Cady heard thunder rumble in the distance, and she knew she should head back, but not yet. She needed more time to purge her anxieties, to spit up the fear and guilt and dread as violently as the river. She welcomed the weather's commiseration. A flock of geese soared overhead; their mournful voices called for escape, and their arrow urged her onward.

She turned right, taking the steps of the Weeks Footbridge two by two, the burn in her thighs barely registering. She opened her jacket down to her breast and powered up the incline and over the water. The cold wind throttled her. Cady ran hard along the far side of the river, taking a dirt path closer to the water where roots and rocks threatened to turn her ankle, but she didn't slow down. She longed to be too tired to think, and she had brain to burn. Thunder cracked again, louder this time, splitting the greedy clouds and spilling their pockets. The rain splashed on the lapping surface of the Charles, and falling drops hit Cady's hair and brow and cheeks. But she ran straight past Anderson Memorial Bridge—everything a fucking memorial. The rain would have to do better than that.

And it did. Torrents poured into the river's churning stomach, sheets of rain hit Cady sideways, and the jealous wind stole water from the river's surface and sprayed it on her feet. She checked her phone again, watching her blue dot approach its destination about a hundred yards ahead of her on the riverbank: the boathouse.

# 41

CADY FOUND THE red brick boathouse deserted, and she huddled beneath the roof's narrow shelter, wringing out her ponytail like a towel. The front of her leggings was soaked through and her jacket wasn't as waterproof as she'd thought. She pulled out her phone, wiping the wet screen with her undershirt before pulling up the coordinates app. She knew she was in the right general location, but the specific spot seemed around the corner to the river-facing side of the building, it looked almost in the river on the map. In different weather, it would be easy to investigate, but with this downpour, she could barely see five yards in front of her. The most she could do was wait for it to let up.

It showed no sign of doing so. The sound of raindrops on the roof had grown from a patter to a roar. She pressed closer to the building, flattening her body like a cat on a ledge. But as she placed her ear to the wall, she heard something else amid the rainfall: she heard music. And not just any music: jazz. She knocked lightly on the front door and whispered into it:

Whit?

*Cady.* The music suddenly sounded louder, as if a door to the interior had been opened, although the one in front of her remained shut. *Come in, quick, you're drenched.*

Even soaked, Cady's body warmed at the sound of his voice. The doorknob turned easily in her hand. She slipped inside and found herself in a cool, dark anteroom that looked part office, part mudroom. Maybe it was the old music, but her attention was drawn to the original, more elegant features of the interior, now covered with the daily stuff of modern college life. Walls with beautiful dark wood paneling served as an overdressed backdrop for a smudgy whiteboard scrawled with scheduling notes and a few frat house jokes. The metal front desk and filing cabinets were pushed against elegant beaded board. A rubber mat for scuffing wet feet lay atop what looked like an original hardwood floor, ridged and weathered with age, with grooves between each plank like front teeth that are gapped and all the lovelier for it.

What's the music?

*I've got the radio keeping me company. It's Duke Ellington, "Mood Indigo," seemed to suit the day. You like it?*

Cady nodded.

*Let me get you a towel. We've got plenty upstairs.*

I'll come with you. —Cady thought to him. With Whit especially, she always found herself wanting to preserve the illusion that they were in the same place and time. However he experienced her in his world, she wanted to play along. She didn't know whether she did it for his benefit or her own.

Cady mounted the creaking stairs. On the second floor, the walls also had wood paneling, which you could hardly see for all the framed photos covering them.

*It's this green door where we keep the clean uniforms and linens. Here's hoping someone brought in the clothesline before it rained.*

She looked for where he might mean and saw only one door, but it was painted black. Poking her head in, she found not a linen closet, but a cramped office with a small table, desktop computer, and shelves of binders, some leather-bound but most cheap plastic. But she could see the bones of its past iteration, the shelves that used to hold stacks of crisp folded linens instead of overstuffed binders, the window that opened out to a taut clothesline instead of musty shoes, she even no-

ticed an edge of green on the doorjamb where the black paint coat
had chipped. She peeked inside the dryer and found some clean, if
crumpled, towels. Boys, she thought. Eric never remembered to fold
his clean laundry either.

*Here you go.*

She draped one around her shoulders and thanked him as if he'd
given it to her.

*What were you doing out in this storm?*

I went for a run and got caught in the rain. What are you doing
here?

*Weight training. Trying to make the most of my time left on Varsity
Eight.*

Cady's gaze wandered to the team photos on the wall, one as old
as 1894, in which the men wore long shorts, lace-up leather shoes,
and turtleneck sweaters sporting a block-letter H in the center. They
looked older than their age, on account of their handlebar mustaches
and the gleam on their polished, parted hair. She scanned the dates at
the bottom of each team picture, hoping to get a glimpse of Whit. She
didn't know what he looked like, other than how she had imagined
him, but she had an irrational belief that she would recognize him.

Where's your picture?

*Our '33 crew portrait hasn't been taken yet. They'll take it in the
spring.*

The wall he was looking at might not include 1933, but hers
would. Her heart quickened as she searched for it. She was deprived of
so many senses in her experiences with Whit, the prospect of seeing
him took on the thrill of an embrace.

*You know, I was just thinking of you, and then you turn up. How do
you do that?*

I could ask you the same thing.

Finally, she found it. The photo showed one man seated with the
other seven standing tall, as straight and strong as the oars they held
beside them. Despite their sentinel pose, there was a relaxed quality
to the men in the photo; they possessed the comfortable pride of those

accustomed to winning. Their uniforms were simpler than the turn-of-the-century ones, but still looked far from modern swimwear. They wore a white tank top with a black border, or maybe crimson, the picture had no color, and the same block H on the chest, and the shorts looked like boxer briefs. She could tell the photo was taken outside on a beautiful day; even in black-and-white, she saw the sun's touch in the shade of their tan shoulders, and the way the wind tousled their hair into cowlicks or tangled it in their brows. She studied each handsome face, but to her dismay, none stood out to her.

*Do you want to see the boats?*

Cady felt a sense of being guided downstairs, visceral and compelling as instinct. She walked past the front desk and through a short hallway to two double doors. A draft of cold air came in from underneath them and tickled her ankles, giving her goose bumps. She slid one of the heavy doors aside, and this time there was no question she was in the right room.

The wood floor's aged surface softened the storm light, but against the state-of-the-art boats, the light streaked across each smooth side, gleaming in sharp geometry, daggers upon daggers. The boats were stacked vertically on racks one on top of another, like arrows in a quiver, poised to cut through water or air or whichever medium they met. They appeared impossibly long and narrow, unlike any other vessel Cady had seen before, and she found it hard to believe these razor blades could carry one man, much less eight. But despite their imposing size and shape, they appeared almost weightless hung as they were, bottom-up, all the way to the ceiling. Some were milky white and others were canary yellow, but their color was irrelevant, everything about their design conveyed their purpose—these were built for speed and aggression.

Cady walked down the corridor created by the tall boat racks on either side. She trailed her fingers along the ridge of one long boat's underside. Indirect light from the gray sky illuminated the darkened room from a large, arched, barn-style door left open on the opposite wall. A half-moon of stray rainwater shined on the floor, as if the boat room itself were perspiring.

Her phone beeped in her jacket pocket. She pulled it out, and the GPS app was alerting her that she was nearing her coordinate target. She zoomed in again on the image, where it looked like the red destination dot was just outside. She looked out on the dock, rendered white with the splashing of the heavy rain that pummeled it. She took several steps forward toward the open door, until ricocheting raindrops sprayed her ankles. From this vantage point, Cady could guess what the virtual dot coincided with: a tall, wooden post on the right-hand side of the dock, which appeared accessible via the riverbank if the torrential downpour wasn't making the water so high. It reminded her of the dock at Lake Wallenpaupack, their dock. Uncle Pete's favorite prank was to join you swimming, only to pull your dry clothes and towel into the lake when you weren't looking, but he couldn't do it from the back ones. So Eric had always hung his things on the back, right dock-post, and Cady took the left. Apparently, he hadn't changed.

*I have news.*

Cady turned around, forgetting that she couldn't search Whit's face for answers. —Good or bad?

*That depends on how you look at it.*

She listened.

*I got into the Lighter-than-Air Division of the Navy, they want me to work on the latest prototype of dirigible aircraft carrier, the USS* Akron.

The muscles in her chest tightened. —Whit, that's great, I'm so happy for you! That's your dream job, isn't it?

*Pretty much. I'd probably be doing grunt work, but it's a chance to be part of something big, a new frontier in aviation. Something that could change the course of history.*

Will this ship, the . . .

*Akron.*

Will it be seeing combat?

*No, she's still a prototype, so we'll be refining the technology, test flights, that sort of thing.*

She exhaled. —So you'll be safe. You won't be enlisting as a regular soldier, you won't be in the line of fire.

Relief flowed into her system, reviving her like water to a wilted flower. The terrible fates she had feared for him dissipated like bad dreams upon waking. He wouldn't play the role of the doomed enlisted man, after all; he would be one of the lucky ones. He would be far away and high above the spray of bullets. He would dodge them all.

*But there's no war right now, so it's an unexpected chance to serve.*

War is coming.

*Gotta be prepared, right? Hence the push to get these dirigibles ready to go, guarding the Pacific. They need men. I had expressed interest in aeronautical engineering on some forms after high school, I planned to defer until after graduation, but they're fast-tracking me, say I don't need the degree to start. If I say yes, they want me to pack up and report to Lakehurst air base in a matter of days.*

Why don't you sound excited about it? Isn't this exactly what you wanted?

*I don't know, it's happening so fast. I'd have to leave, and it's too abrupt of an ending to . . .* He trailed off.

Your education?

*No,* he said with a laugh, *not to my education. To this.*

Us?

*Is that crazy?*

Yes. —Although she had thought the same thing. If he left campus, she guessed their space-time wouldn't overlap anymore, and she wouldn't hear from him again. The thought made her surprisingly sad.

*You've been claiming you're crazy since the night I met you, it hasn't stopped us yet.*

Cady smiled, but she knew she had to make him take this job. It could save his life.

*I know it's too soon to pledge any grand emotion. If we were in high school, it'd be too soon to ask you to wear my pin. But meeting you, spend-*

*ing time with you, everything has felt . . . different. I have this gut feeling
that we could really have something here, there's . . . potential. We have this
beautiful potential, and I don't want to walk away before it begins.*

Potential is always beautiful. It's easier to imagine the happy endings and harder to imagine the bad ones. It's a mind trick to protect
ourselves when the truth hurts. You should stick to your plan, stick to
what you know is real. And the reality is, we're not on the same path.

*Then where's the room for a leap of faith? Just because you can't ex-
plain something doesn't make it untrue. I believe in intuition. The other
night in the observatory, I felt something between us—*

I did too, that was a great night. But that's all it was.

*Why don't you sound like you believe that? Your voice is all quivery.*

Whit, we can't have a future together. That we're together now
makes no sense.

*And yet we keep crossing paths.*

I don't want you to change your plans for me. I can't carry that
burden.

*It's not yours to bear. Maybe if I changed my mind, make a different
choice. The Navy will always be there.*

But it'll be more dangerous for you later—

*We don't know what's ahead of us, we can only guess. But you know
that horizon line my father laid out for me? You moved it. You let me see
beyond it for the first time in my life. To imagine a future I couldn't dream
of before. And all I want to do is keep looking.*

Cady felt her eyes well up. With this new opportunity, Whit's future was safer, his fate lashed to something lighter than air. So why did
she feel herself hesitating to send him on his way? She would miss
him. He understood Cady with an ease few in her normal life did, and
his presence entertained, comforted, even excited her. It didn't matter
that she couldn't see him, he saw her the way she wanted to be: capable, lovable, and good. She hadn't seen herself like that since before
Eric died. Whit deserved better than to feel she didn't care. He deserved the truth. But if she really cared about him, there was only one
thing to say:

I don't feel the same way about you.

He was silent. They both were.

*I'm sorry.*

Please don't apologize.

*No, I need to. I don't know what came over me to say all that, I put you in a terrible spot. You're right, I got it all wound up in my head, got carried away, jumped the gun, other clichés for being an idiot.*

You're not—

*My timing has always been terrible. You should see me dance; it's almost as embarrassing as this.*

You have nothing to be embarrassed about.

*But I want to be clear, I meant what I said. I'm sorry I told you like that and gummed up the works, but I'm glad it happened, glad and grateful to you. I'm glad we ran into each other today so I could say goodbye.*

This isn't goodbye-goodbye. —It was Cady's turn to balk at the abruptness. —When are you leaving for real?

*Monday. You can knock on my door anytime before then, if you're so inclined, Lowell G-41. But listen, Cady, you've been wonderful. You don't owe me anything.*

"Yo, can I help you?" a different voice broke in, and Cady turned to see a tall, well-built young man standing in the back of the room. He wore black spandex shorts that went to his knee and a tight Under Armour long-sleeved tee that showed every bit of muscle definition in signature crimson.

"No, I, I'm looking, taking a quick look around," Cady stammered.

"How did you get in here?" he demanded.

"It was open."

He frowned. "I doubt that. Newell's not open to the public."

"Oh, I'm not the public, I'm a Harvard student."

"Newell's not open to anyone but the men's crew and staff, no girls allowed, student or not. You want to tour a boathouse, the women's boathouse has public visiting hours. Men's is off-limits."

"Really?" A double standard more suited to Whit's time than to the present day. "Okay, I'm leaving." But Cady lingered by the door of the boat room, hesitant to leave, trying to refocus her mind's ear on Whit. She hadn't wanted to rush their goodbye, and she had a flash of anger at the rower for interrupting them. Was Whit still there?

"I mean it, you have to go," the rower called out after her. "Hey, was that one of our towels?"

Outside, Cady shut the front door behind her and leaned against it. She looked up at the pouring sky. The hurt in Whit's voice echoed in her mind and wrung her heart with regret, but she knew she had done the right thing. He would be safer and happier working on an airship that would never see combat. Maybe he could serve a few years, satisfy whatever duty to the military he felt from his family, and then go work in the music business like he wanted to. She loved talking to him, but it wasn't as if they could be together in any real, physical way. Her reasons for wanting him to stay were completely selfish. She had been selfish with Eric at the critical moment, and it had sent him to his doom. She had learned her lesson.

Cady held the towel over her head like an umbrella and sneaked around the boathouse to check that dock post before she went home. Nothing was there.

# 42

CADY HAD WANTED to go find the third drop site yesterday, but when she'd gotten home from the boathouse, her roommates had made a big deal of her being soaked from the rain. Andrea had plied her with a stack of lilac towels, and Ranjoo, normally the resident fun czar, had insisted Cady stay in with her and study for Psych. Cady had obliged that night to placate them, but she was impatient. Bernstein himself had told her that a single test was trivial, and she had time on the Hines issue, which she kept to herself; Schoolwork wasn't her priority right now. For the first time since Eric died, Cady felt focused, clear, and effective. She had helped Bilhah, she'd done the right thing by Whit, even if it pained her, and most important, she was getting closer to discovering some truth about her brother. Now that she'd found that feeling again, she wasn't going to give it up so easily. She slipped out early that morning before her roommates had a chance to slow her down with questions.

Yesterday's storms had given way to a frigid blue morning, as if the skies had been washed clean. On the virtual map, the pin had dropped right on top of the Harvard Square T station. Already, this third location seemed like an outlier, smack in the middle of Harvard Square; it seemed like an odd place to do anything secret. But perhaps there was anonymity in the recycling crowds; no one would look twice at someone loitering by a bustling subway station, it would be easy to hide in plain sight. Indeed, there were a number of invisible denizens of this particular part of the Square: the homeless.

One of the first things Cady had noticed when she arrived at Harvard was how many homeless people she saw just outside Johnston Gate. There were the regulars: the old woman outside the university bookstore with a single enormous dreadlock that fell almost to her knees, like a silver python swallowing her head whole; the cheery "Spare Change" guy to whom some people said hi but few gave cash; the Asian man who played a horrible homemade string instrument might not be homeless, but no one knew where he slept at night. Cady had taken inventory of others: a veteran in a wheelchair outside the Starbucks; the guy who thought he was funny with a sign that read NEED MONEY FOR DRUGS; an older gentleman who never asked for anything but simply sat on the ledge of the T station reading well-worn paperbacks with an empty Dunkin' Donuts cup beside him. Everyone on campus knew these people by sight, but they all looked right past them on the street. They were the fallen leaves of society, skittering haphazardly across hallowed cobblestone streets like human detritus not yet blown away.

Cady had heard that there were so many of them because back in the day, some politician cut funding and abruptly shut down the Massachusetts mental institutions, abandoning patients to find their own way without treatment, and most ended up on the streets. She'd also heard that despite the constant tourist presence, Harvard Yard contains only one bench, the unofficial reason for which is to deter the homeless from making themselves comfortable on campus. They can pass through, but they can't lie down. And still it seemed Harvard was a magnet for the homeless, hopeless, futureless members of society. Cady once thought they might enjoy the irony, but irony is a pleasure of privilege.

She wove through the throng around the T station and wondered: Would that have been Eric's fate? When Cady heard people talk about suicide—people who hadn't experienced it in their families—many called it a selfish act. She had overheard family friends say the worst part of Eric's death was his squandered potential, how he'd thrown away a promising future—Cady strongly disagreed, there were much worse parts than that—but realistically, would his future have been so bright? Did Eric sense that his course had changed, could he feel his future promise leak out like a punctured tire? Or was his choice impulsive, a reaction to pain in the present, an escape from a world that had been too cruel to him already—his illness, the stress of school and whatever Prokop was asking of him, academic rivals like Lee, his family—his sister? Cady used to wonder why potential life was held more sacred than that which existed, but now she knew. It is far easier and more pleasant to imagine happy endings, however farfetched, in all their vivid, rainbow colors than it is to face each day's reality and let time and fortune do their worst. She still told herself if her family had had more time, they could have helped him manage his illness better, live better, but of course she didn't know for sure. Maybe that's just a nice lie families tell themselves, the same lie the families of these homeless people told themselves once, too, that everything will be okay. Cady didn't even know whether she herself was going to be okay. If we could all know our futures, how many of us would choose to see it through?

She looked down at her coordinate locator app and followed its directions to the left side of the station, away from the entrance. But as soon as she looked up from her phone, she smiled in recognition. The "pit," a sunken area beside the T station, was filled with chess hustlers playing at café tables. Eric loved chess, and she could imagine him testing himself against the old pros.

The dot over the app seemed to hover over the table closest to the sidewalk. The player seated there was a middle-aged black man wearing a puffy down parka and a Red Sox cap. The young man playing him wore a bottle-green wax-coated jacket more suited to skeet shooting than street chess. A few of his friends watched the match with their arms crossed.

Cady watched the game while she waited her turn.

*Salut, mon amie.*

Hi, Robert.

*Going somewhere by train?*

Nowhere, I'm looking for something by the station.

*My friends and I enjoy taking the train to nowhere. We go to North Station, board the first train that arrives, then ride it for as long as it takes to run out of stories to embellish, and we hop off at the next stop, whatever it may be. Once we didn't get off until we were twenty miles out from Worcester at three in the morning, and it had snowed. It took hours to journey back, including an interlude of being chased by a pack of stray dogs. Have you ever run in knee-deep snow? It's invigorating, to say the least.*

This is what you do for fun?

*It's subversive. Trains are the most orderly, regimented form of transportation available. I don't see how anyone finds romance in train travel when it is so miserably predetermined. Adventure is only possible if you don't spoil the ending. The fellows and I still talk about that night with the dogs.*

If one of those dogs had bitten you, you wouldn't be so happy with your adventure.

*True, our feelings about the result of any action color our perception of past decision making. Memory is a volatile element, highly reactive, like fluorine, it cannot be trusted to yield an objective recollection, in fact, there's no such thing. So to your point, that's a case of poor scientific method, not poor judgment.*

Okay, here's a hypothetical: If I were from the future, and we were somehow communing across time, would you want to know your future?

*No.*

Really? I thought you wanted to know everything.

*Precisely why I'd beg you to please let me enjoy my ignorance for once. Knowing everything is exhausting.*

Cady chuckled. —But, for example, can you see these chess players?

*Yes.*

Maybe they were gifted kids with promising futures, but then they made one bad choice, or one bad thing happened to them, or one stroke of bad luck that denied them opportunities, and now all their potential is spent embarrassing college kids. Wouldn't they enjoy the benefit of hindsight?

*Or maybe they used their intellectual gifts to defy the odds and avoid a worse fate. There are too many variables to know. Hubris can be a mercy. I labor under my awful fact of excellence as if I am bound for extraordinary things. But even if, in the end, I've got to satisfy myself with testing tooth-paste in a lab, I don't want to know till it has happened.*

But if you knew toothpaste was on the horizon, maybe you could change course.

*Ah, again, your logic is flawed. If you could truly see my future, then the variables in fate's equation for me have been solved, and thus you've collapsed all the alternate realities that could have led to different outcomes.*

Like Schrödinger's cat.

*Whose what?*

We learned it in AP Physics, I thought you would know it. —Although maybe it was *after* his time, Cady considered. —It's a thought experiment to challenge the concept of superposition, the idea that quantum particles simultaneously exist in all positions until the moment they're observed or measured, when all possibilities but one collapse. Schrödinger said to imagine putting a cat in a box with a vial of poison that's hooked up to a bit of radioactive material and a Geiger counter. There's a fifty percent chance the radioactive material decays and registers on the Geiger counter, which would trigger the release of the poison, killing the cat. If you accept superposition in quantum mechanics, then the radioactive material has decayed and not decayed, and the cat is simultaneously alive and dead. Until you open the box. The act of observation eliminates the alternate realities. Once you look, there's no going back.

*Hm, I've never heard of it, but I understand the analogy, however absurd. Cats don't function like atomic particles. If they did, I would like them better.*

Cady smiled for a moment.

But what Robert said earlier resonated. Eric's death would forever cloud her remembrance of the past. Maybe she would never be able to know what happened to her brother, all the ways she had or hadn't let him down. But that was why understanding the meaning behind these drop locations mattered so much to her—they weren't reliant on her memory. Now she was retracing Eric's actions, trying to glean whatever objective evidence she could. There had to be better scientific method in that.

Suddenly the boys standing around the chessboard erupted in groans; the hustler had won again, and the student playing him seemed like he'd had enough. Until one of his friends pointed to the hustler. "Third to last play, you nudged that knight's position to make your move."

The hustler gravely shook his head. "No no no, I never cheat, never. I'm a man of *honor*, you understand? You friend made a mistake. Here, I show you." He then proceeded to replace the pieces and walk them backward through the last five moves from memory, while also showing the better options that his opponent failed to take at each turn. When he had finished the lesson, a few other bystanders clapped. The defeated student apologized for his friend and shook the hustler's hand, and it appeared all was forgiven.

*See? I'm not so sure this is a waste of potential. I found that delightful.*

The boys cleared off and the hustler reset the table, waiting for his next customer, but Cady was almost too intimidated to step forward. She stalled rechecking the GPS app. The coordinate location hovered directly over his chess table. Maybe the table wasn't always there. Or maybe Eric stuck something under it. —Do you think I can just ask?

*Warm him up a bit, pay for a game. I'll help you.*

"Hi, I—"

The hustler held up his hand. "Five dollars for five minutes," he said in a Haitian accent.

Cady got the cash from her wallet, and then he motioned for her to sit.

"I am Jean-Pierre. You win, you get your money back. Deal?"

Cady introduced herself and shook his hand, feeling guilty that she was essentially cheating with a genius in her ear.

"White moves first, den you hit de button."

*Start with something he won't expect, an unconventional opener. Move your king's bishop pawn out first.*

Cady did as she was told.

Jean-Pierre seemed pleased. "Not an amateur like de last one." He chuckled before making his move.

*He's a strong player. All right, take your knight . . .*

The rest of the moves went quickly, with Cady acting out Robert's instructions as if on instinct. Cady got worried only at one point when Jean-Pierre took her queen, but Robert reassured her the sacrifice was expected and decimated the black's defense, queen included, over the next few turns, making Jean-Pierre curse under his breath. With fewer black pieces remaining, it was Jean-Pierre's turn, and Robert began outlining what Cady would have to do to win the game in the next three moves. Cady was listening intently, trying to commit the plan to memory, when the black rook shot out of nowhere to knock over their king.

"Checkmate." Jean-Pierre smiled broadly, revealing some missing teeth on the sides.

*Wait, what?*

Cady actually laughed out loud.

"Good game, very good." He nodded in approval as he began setting up for the next game.

*Ah, well.* Robert sniffed. *No one can anticipate every move all of the time.*

"Oh, but before I go, can I ask you a few questions?"

"Five dollars for five minutes."

Cady pulled more cash out of her bag. He took it and started the timer.

"Do you recognize this man?" Cady brought up an image of her brother on her phone and showed it to him.

He squinted down at it. Then his face brightened. "*Mais oui,* dat is my friend. I don't know his name, but we used to play often; he never beat me, but he was good. He gave me dis fine jacket!"

Cady's heart lifted. "He did?"

"One day I wasn't here because it was too cold, I hate de cold, and he was mad, he miss me. So next time, he gave me dis, de coat off his back! I tried to refuse, but he insist. It is very warm. North Face! Good man."

"His name is Eric. He's my brother."

"Ah, de hair. I see it."

"Did he ever leave anything around here for someone?"

Jean-Pierre shot her some side-eye before reaching over to the timer once more. Cady thought he was going to say they were out of time or ask for more money, but instead he lifted the timer up and turned it over. "One time, I do a favor for my friend." He pointed to a small hollow space on its underside, beside the battery. "Here, he taped a flash drive. Someone came to get it."

Cady felt electrified. This validated the entire endeavor. She wasn't following Eric's paranoid fantasy or her own, she was on to something real. "What was on it, do you know? Did he say? Who came to get it?"

"Whoa, whoa, I know nothing. Your brother was discreet, no names, no information. He said to give it to de man who ask me to 'check de battery.' But one more rule: Your brother say I must make de man play one game at dis table before I give it to him, very important." Jean-Pierre leaned over the table conspiratorially. "Because he wanted him to lose first!" And he broke into a belly laugh.

Cady thanked him and said goodbye. Jean-Pierre tried to give her back the five dollars, and she had to refuse twice before he relented.

*I must be getting home, this chill will be the death of me. My roommate accuses me of being hypochondriacal, but I think I merely have a heightened awareness of my physiological status. I can feel the subtle swelling as millions of streptococci catarrhensae colonize the territory around my tonsils.*

Millions of what?

*What a layperson would call "strep throat."*

News flash, we *are* laypeople. You're not a doctor.

*Not yet. But I will be receiving a doctorate soon. Today I'm to hear back from the graduate research position I applied for in Cambridge— England that is. I'm going to work at the Cavendish Laboratory under Professor Rutherford, the Ernest Rutherford.*

Is he a big deal?

She heard him sigh. *He's only a world-famous physicist who discovered the true structure of the atom. He's a pioneer. It's been my dream to work with him.*

Well, congrats! I'm happy for you.

*Thank you, but I suppose I shouldn't accept congratulations yet. I won't know for certain until the mail comes later this afternoon. I do hope I don't have to wait until tomorrow.*

But you feel the odds are good?

*Very. I'm sure Professor Bridgman—he's my adviser, we're very close—wrote a very persuasive letter of recommendation. Rutherford has historically chosen the top man from Harvard. As it stands, I'm the number one student in the chemistry department, every semester I've taken five classes and audited five more, I'm graduating with top honors in three years instead of four, and my independent research concerning the pressure effect on metallic conduction is on track to be published later this year.*

Holy shit. Well, then, yeah, I'd say it's in the bag.

*Give my regrets to the toothpaste factory. Till then, I've got to get home in case the mail has arrived. Adieu!*

Cady took a seat on the cold concrete ledge of the pit and reviewed everything she had learned and tried to put herself inside Eric's head. Giving Jean-Pierre his coat wasn't out of character for her brother; Eric always had a sympathetic soul. And, if she was honest, being imprudent about his dress became a hallmark of his psychotic episodes. A small, darker worry huddled in the corner of her mind—was he giving away his belongings before he planned to die? But she pushed it away. There were practical reasons for giving Jean-Pierre the coat. Eric needed to leave something with him for the mystery person to pick up, and he would not take the choice of steward lightly; even at his most paranoid, Eric found Jean-Pierre to be trustworthy, and Cady could see why. Eric couldn't let cold weather imperil his plan for the pickup.

But Eric hadn't required an assistant for any of the other drops, so why this one? What else did Jean-Pierre say? He had to play a game first. So it was important to Eric that the pickup guy sat at that table. Cady surveyed the surrounding area to try to imagine what would have appealed to him about that location. It was right next to the busy sidewalk, facing the storefront of Cambridge Savings Bank. Eric came to hate banks, because banks had surveillance video. Even when he was doing well on his meds, a security camera could trigger his paranoia. Cady remembered when Eric was home, her mother would sometimes make him run errands with them, and if the errands involved a bank, ATM, or gas station, they were going to have a problem. He didn't even like to walk by them. Her mom could ignore it, but Cady felt so embarrassed when Eric would pull his jacket over his head to hide his face; she thought people would think he was a fugitive.

And yet Eric had chosen that specific table. So Eric had wanted to position that final location in front of a camera for at least the length of a speed-chess game.

He had wanted whatever had happened there to be seen.

# 43

CADY COULDN'T THINK with all those people around her by the T stop, so she walked to Felipe's, a Mexican restaurant beloved by the student body, especially when drunk. Its busiest hours seemed to be between nine at night and two in the morning; at regular lunch-time, she practically had the place to herself. She sat by the window facing Brattle Street and unwrapped the foil around her burrito; the steam fogged a patch of the cold glass like a puff of breath. Why would Eric want that person or that pickup recorded on camera and not the previous two? What had changed? She took a bite, careful not to drop anything on top of the blue notebook open beside her, and reviewed the coordinates page for other details that might be clues. That date stood out to her, November 20, so close to Thanksgiving. A wave of anxiety came over her, and with it a very specific memory from when he was home that Thanksgiving break.

They weren't going to the usual family gathering at Uncle Pete and Aunt Laura's house that year, because Eric had become so impossible about food preparation. Cady didn't mind a low-key holiday, because she needed to study for her second round of the SATs. So that Tuesday, she was sprawled out on the couch timing herself with a practice test, when she heard Eric upstairs yelling repeatedly for their mother—who wasn't home. By the fifth time she heard him scream

"Mom," she lost her patience. She threw her practice book down on the couch and stomped upstairs.

"Eric, shut up!" she called out before reaching the top. Eric didn't answer, but his door was open, so she knew he'd heard her. "Mom's not even here, so can you *stop scream* . . ." Cady's voice trailed off as she walked in and found Eric crouching in front of his clothes bureau with every one of the drawers pulled open. It looked like he had burglarized his own room. "What are you doing?"

"Mom's not home?" Eric looked over his shoulder from where he was currently ransacking the bottom drawer. He blinked quickly. "Then I have to call her."

"No, don't. She's meeting with the developers for that new housing complex. It's a really big deal for her." In the year since Eric's first breakdown, their mother had taken on researching schizophrenia and monitoring his treatment as a full-time job, she had majorly cut back on her work as a realtor. Cady had heard her parents arguing about it; her father thought she was losing herself playing doctor, her mother thought he wasn't engaged enough. Eric had no idea what a big opportunity this was for their mother, or how reluctant she had been to accept it because of him. "What is the problem? Can I help?"

"My clothes are in different places in the drawers."

Cady smirked. "Maybe if you did your own laundry . . ."

"Somebody has gone through my stuff, someone has *been* here!" Eric's face flushed bright pink.

"Okay, calm down. It was probably just Dad putting stuff away in the wrong spots."

Eric was pulling pairs of pants from his bottom drawer, shoving his hands in the pockets, and then throwing them on the floor. "Dad never does the laundry."

"He did this time, so Mom could prepare for her meeting. That's all."

"No. I can't risk it. All of this needs to be searched." He motioned to the heaps of clean clothes on the floor.

"Searched for what?"

"Bugs, listening devices, tracking devices, that sort of thing."

Since his official diagnosis, the whole family had taken a crash course in how to manage his schizophrenic delusions, but they were imperfect students. Her mother had been coaching her on how to handle his delusions using the LEAP method—the acronym stood for listen, empathize, agree, and partner—but Cady hadn't deployed it on her own yet. She was supposed to hide her judgment and treat his delusion as if it was a valid concern, yet stop short of validating it. But it wasn't easy to agree without judgment, especially for a sister.

"You think someone has been listening to you," she said with practiced calm. She wished her mother was here to see her 'reflective listening.' "I understand how that would be stressful."

"Stressful?" He shot her a withering look, like she was the ridiculous one. She was about to get annoyed with him, but then Eric rubbed his hand over his mouth, and she saw his hand was shaking. "I shouldn't have come home for Thanksgiving. If I'm being tracked, they know where you live now."

"It's okay, I'm not worried."

"You're not worried because you have no idea."

"So tell me, I want to help you, I'm on your side."

"I already checked that pile, but double-check it for me. Look in all the pockets, even the little tiny one inside the main pocket. And look for any buttons or grommets that don't match the others. I'm not sure who we're dealing with, FBI or Russians, but either could have technology we're not familiar with, so look for anything atypical."

Cady reluctantly picked up a pair of khakis, unsure how to sufficiently search for imaginary devices.

Luckily, it didn't seem like Eric was watching too closely. He had begun to pace, as if the agitation in his mind had spread down to his feet. "I thought someone was following me, I have for a while. And I thought, maybe it's the guy. But I'm not supposed to see him, which is a problem, because how can I know if he's following me if I don't know what he looks like? So the last time, I waited for him."

"Waited for who?"

"I don't *know* who, that's why I had to wait to see him." He shook his head in irritation. "Anyway, when he arrived, he was talking on the phone—in Russian." He opened his eyes wide with meaning, meaning utterly lost on Cady. "So I had to do something. And if my suspicions are correct, this could be retaliation."

Cady must have sighed too heavily, because he abruptly stopped pacing.

He leveled his gaze at her with a look of equal parts suspicion and hurt. "You don't believe me."

Her mind froze; she didn't know how to "partner" with him without reinforcing the delusion. "I don't know. But I'm here to help you solve your problem."

"Why are you talking to me like some sort of robot? You think I can't tell how disingenuous that sounds?"

"Eric, I'm trying my best."

"You're patronizing me."

"I think consistently taking your medication might clear your head so—"

"Oh my *God!*" Eric shouted, yanking his hair straight up where it stuck, like electroshock. "Always with the medication. I thought Dad was Nurse Ratched, but *et tu?* God! Is nobody going to listen to me anymore? Oh, right, because I'm the only sick person in this family. I've got news for you, you all could use some medication. You can start with some Midol."

"Fuck you." The LEAP method had leaped out the window. "Everyone in this family is bending over backward for you. You've been home less than a week and Mom was ready to cancel her meeting, Dad's doing your laundry, I've dropped what I was doing to come and help you. And yet you say we're all against you. You don't appreciate the sacrifices—"

"You think I don't make sacrifices? I make sacrifices for everyone and they screw me over in return! That medication that makes you and Dad feel so safe and comfortable with me—it dulls my senses at the exact moment that I need to be sharp. Half the time, I'm sedated for no reason *but* this family. I have to get better *for you*. I mean, are you kidding?" His words rushed out in a feverish pitch. "Here and there—I'm too goddamn obedient, *that's* my problem. No more. I'm not going to let you or her or Dad ruin me and my reputation. I'm looking out for myself now. I'm going to be the next giant in the physics world!" He stood there, chest heaving. "I'm calling Mom."

"Eric." Cady spoke slowly and firmly. "Don't call Mom."

"Why, because you're jealous?" he snapped.

Even in the midst of a delusion, his barb was incisive, and Cady was too wounded to speak. But Eric didn't wait to see his punch land, he was too busy tapping on his iPhone.

Cady tried to snatch it out of his hand, but he shoved her backward, hard. She was too shocked to react; he had never gotten physical with her before—and he wasn't finished. He pushed her again, got in her face, screamed at her "Get out of my room! Leave me alone!" He roughed her out the door of his bedroom, hitting her shoulder against the doorjamb and sending her stumbling into the hall. Then he slammed the door so hard the walls shook.

"Ouch! Eric, that hurt!" she yelled to the closed door, sounding like a little sister. But she retreated quickly downstairs in case he opened it again.

Eric must have called their mother, because within twenty minutes, Cady heard the car pull into the driveway. Cady was back in the living room, failing to focus on her practice test, instead mentally enumerating her causes for outrage at Eric when her mother came in and rushed upstairs without noticing Cady on the couch. Cady heard her cooing to Eric through his locked bedroom door until he finally opened it and let her in. It was another hour before her mother came down, slowly, with heavy steps. Even with her nice outfit and saleswoman makeup, her mother looked haggard.

Her first words to Cady were "What did you say to him?"

\* \* \*

NOW SHE LOOKED out onto bustling Brattle Street, at a mother who was torn in two directions, trying to console her toddler wailing in the stroller while her older child tugged at her coat for attention, and Cady's bitter feelings of that day, her frustration and jealousy of Eric, her resentment of her mother's tunnel vision on him, seemed so immature. Why hadn't she been able to see that her mother was doing her best under the most difficult circumstances? None of them knew how to cope with Eric's illness, not even Eric. She *had* said the wrong thing. She had handled his delusion badly. She had fumbled the methods her mother had taught her. And with everything she knew now— that Eric had been involved in some sort of scheme with Prokop, that Lee had been following them, exacerbating his paranoia if not legitimately fueling it, that all of her mother's worry was founded, that they could lose him forever—Cady's actions seemed only more petty and unfair. She wished she had had more patience, let him talk it out, tried harder to be a partner to him, a sister.

Instead of waiting until after he was dead.

# 44

CADY HAD WANTED to find the final drop site as soon as she finished lunch, but she hadn't realized that she'd accidentally left the GPS geocaching app open on her smartphone and drained her battery. She'd had no choice but to make a pit stop at her dorm room. Luckily, her roommates weren't home, so she wouldn't have to come up with some phony excuse for her comings and goings. While her phone charged, Cady previewed the fourth and final coordinate location on Google Maps via her laptop. She was surprised to see the dot appear on the grounds of First Parish Church, right across from Harvard Yard. "Since when do you go to church, Eric?"

Eric called himself an atheist; he believed in science, but in his way, he worshipped it. He bristled at how organized religion purported to have an answer for everything. He was humble about the limitations of our current understanding of the world around us, he embraced the unknown, and believed revelation could be found through experimentation and theoretical math. She remembered him arguing that there was no difference between believing in God versus believing we're all living in a simulation, except that one had stopped looking for proof. Professor Prokop would've been like a high priestess to him. But he didn't take anything on blind faith. Eric was a skeptic. So what had she been asking him to do? Cady rechecked her phone plugged in beside her bed: a whopping ten percent. She groaned and lay back. She was so tired.

Cady awoke to a knock on her bedroom door. Cady's eyes opened to a darkened room; the light outside nearly extinguished. Groggy and disoriented, she reached for her phone—fully charged and just after seven—she had slept through the entire afternoon.

Another knock. "Hey, Cady, can you come out? We want to talk," Ranjoo's voice said from the other side of the door.

Why didn't she just come in, Cady wondered as she rubbed the sleep from her eyes, it was her bedroom, too? And who was *we*? Her puzzlement only grew when she opened the door to the common room and saw both her roommates seated on the futon, heads together as Andrea whispered something to Ranjoo. They stopped talking when she stepped into the space.

"Hi," Cady said, instantly registering tension in the room. The two women who had been oil and water since day one now looked at Cady with matching furrowed brows. "I was napping. What's up?"

"How are you feeling?" Andrea asked.

Ranjoo's voice was more clipped. "Are you sick?"

"No, I'm fine, just tired, I guess." Cady took a seat on the nylon foldout chair they used as an armchair. She gave a nervous snort. "Why are you guys being weird?"

"Did you miss the Psych exam today?" Ranjoo asked.

Cady swore. Was *today* Friday? She'd thought she had only skipped Medieval Studies, but that was on Thursdays, so . . .

"I waited for you at the door so we could sit together, from before the lecture hall opened till Bernstein literally started passing out the blue books. I was like, unless she came late—"

"No, I missed it, okay? I forgot."

"How? You were all over that class in the beginning, your notes were better than the textbook. Then you just blow off a midterm?"

"I don't know." The ceiling light in the common room was so bright, she felt like she was in an interrogation room. "Yesterday was really busy."

"Yesterday, when you went out in the storm with no umbrella, no raincoat." Andrea widened her eyes behind her glasses. "You came home completely drenched."

"I went for a run. I got caught in the rain. It happens."

"Then there's this." Ranjoo pulled out Eric's blue notebook and set it on her lap.

Cady felt her entire body flush with heat. "So what, you're just going through my stuff now?"

Ranjoo ignored her and began flipping through the pages.

"Hey, that's not cool. Please give it to me."

Andrea leaned forward. "We wouldn't be doing this if we weren't worried about you."

"Since when are you two even *friends?*" Cady snapped. "Ranjoo, I'm serious, that's private and personal to me, it belonged to my brother who died, okay?"

"From when he was crazy?" Ranjoo's tone was blunt.

Cady was taken aback. She turned to glare at Andrea. "Nice. Thanks for keeping my confidence."

Andrea looked down at her lap, her face reddening.

Ranjoo pointed a finger at Cady. "She cares about you, which is nice of her, considering you *did* flake on her birthday, same as you've flaked on plans with me. You've been acting shitty to both of us. But I'm trying not to get pissed at you, because you weren't always like this. Something is going on with you, the least you can do is tell us what."

"Because we want to help," Andrea added, in her Good Cop voice.

"Right. So talk to us. Why are you carrying this notebook of crazy writings around?"

"It's not 'crazy writing.'" Defending Eric steadied Cady better than defending herself.

"Uhh." Ranjoo shook her head incredulously. "I'm looking at it. I mean, Jesus, is this *blood?*"

Cady blanched, her blood, from the taxicab day with Whit. "No, I fell and scraped my palm, it was nothing. And my brother wasn't 'crazy,' he was schizophrenic, and still he was smarter than any of us. He actually encrypted his notes, that's why they look like that. He used to leave me missions with messages in code, so I recognized what he was doing and cracked the code, and discovered it's a list of coordinate locations. So, I'm following them to find out why—"

"Do you hear yourself?" Ranjoo interrupted.

She scoffed and crossed her arms over her chest. "You know what? You don't get it, you didn't know him. I don't have to explain my brother to you."

"I'm not worried about his part of this, I'm worried about *yours*."

Cady squinted in confusion.

"Your writing at the back of the notebook," Andrea explained. "It looks like you used my purple pen, which is totally okay, you can borrow it."

She shrugged it off, but her heart raced. "I don't even remember. It's probably just some notes to myself."

With a nod, Ranjoo passed the notebook to Andrea, who in turn showed the page to Cady.

Cady snatched it from her hands and looked down. Written over and over again, first in print small and neat, then large and over-lined again and again, so the lettering was heavy and dark, all her practice attempts to get it right:

GOD HAVE MERCY ON THIS ORPHAN,
GUIDE HIM TO A CHRISTIAN HOME
GOD HAVE MERCY ON THIS ORPHAN
GUIDE HIM TO A CHRISTIAN HOME.
GOD HAVE MERCY ON THIS ORPHAN
GUIDE HIM TO A CHRISTIAN HOME

"This . . ." Cady's mouth went dry. When she had been writing it for Bilhah, she was only thinking of making her letters somehow visible to a person across a dimension. But now, it looked worse than she remembered, and seeing it through her roommates' eyes, it looked maniacal. "This wasn't mine, I mean, it wasn't for me. I was helping someone, I was writing it, to show her how to write it. She had to trace it, that's why it's so dark. She's illiterate."

Ranjoo raised her eyebrows. "An illiterate Harvard student?"

"She's not a student."

"Then what is she?"

Cady knew her answers weren't getting any better from here. "You've already jumped to your own conclusions, so what's the point of explaining it? You won't believe me."

"Try us," Andrea said. "We want to listen."

Cady took a deep breath. "She's a ghost."

Both the women were rendered speechless. Ranjoo's kohl-lined eyes went wide, Andrea's jaw dropped and the blue vein at her temple seemed to twitch.

"Her name is Bilhah. She comes to me from 1765, she's a slave in President Holyoke's house, she has a kid she needs to get out of there, and she needed me to write that note to do it. So I did."

It again grew quiet enough that Cady noticed the whirring of their mini-fridge.

Andrea broke the silence. "From the plaque on Wadsworth House."

"Yes!" Cady clapped her hands. "Right, you remember! See? You know I'm not making this up."

"Did I miss something?" Ranjoo looked back and forth between them.

"We saw this plaque to the slaves at Harvard . . ." Andrea said, slowly. "And then you saw a ghost of one of them?"

"No, well, first, I can't see her, I only hear her voice, and second, Bilhah had *already* talked to me—and believe me, I get how that sounds, I thought I was crazy—but *then* we saw the plaque. Remember how I freaked out when we saw it? That was why. Because it was proof that the voices were real."

"*Voices* plural." Andrea caught her slip. "So there's more than one?"

"You think you're helping a ghost escape slavery? Girl. This is some white savior fantasy."

Andrea cringed, then retrained her gaze on Cady. "Do they ever tell you to hurt yourself?"

"No! Never. They're helping me. We're helping each other." Cady raked her fingers through her hair. "Look, I'm not stupid, I know how this sounds. But there's actually real science, quantum physics, that can explain it. There are dimensions we can't perceive, where time is warped or folded over itself. These people were alive in this same place where we are now, just from different times. I wouldn't believe it either, but they tell me things I couldn't possibly know otherwise."

"Cady, you're taking a Harvard history course, our room is covered in those library books, it's obviously giving you ideas. Can't you see, you're telling yourself stories?" Ranjoo pleaded.

"There is no class, I lied. I got those books to fill in the context of what I was already hearing." Cady slumped in her chair, defeated. "This is pointless to talk about anymore, you don't believe me, it's fine. I'm fine."

Andrea looked to Ranjoo instead of Cady when she said, "I think we should go to the emergency room."

"What? No! Why?" A bolt of fear and anger staked Cady in the heart; she had never been on the other side of this. "Because I'm talking about things you don't understand?"

"Because you're under a lot of stress." Andrea stood up.

"Because you're talking about *ghosts*!" Ranjoo cried.

Andrea took a step toward her. "Let's just go and get checked out. I'll go with you, Ranjoo will stay. It'll be quick."

"No, I'm not going anywhere! I don't need an intervention. Who cares if you believe me that they're ghosts or if they are just a coping mechanism? I'm fine, in fact, I feel better than I've felt in months."

Ranjoo thew up her hands. "You're self-destructing and you don't even see it! You're skipping classes, you missed a midterm exam, you're pushing away your friends, I heard you hooked up with Teddy at the Phoenix like a half-hour after meeting him."

"Oh my God!" Cady let out a mirthless laugh. "That proves you really have *no idea* what you're talking about. I'm leaving." She shoved the notebook in her bag and grabbed her phone and coat.

"Where are you going? Don't go." Andrea anxiously bounced on her toes. "Cady, you need help—"

She slammed the door in their concerned faces.

She didn't need help.

She needed them to stay the hell out of her way.

# 45

CADY RUSHED DOWN Weld's front steps and headed toward the Square. It was dark outside, cold and windy, but Cady was hot—she was furious. How long had her roommates been gossiping about her, conspiring against her? They should have been up front with her sooner, before they jumped to conclusions. Her anger gained momentum as she barreled downhill on Holyoke Street. They had no right to go through her personal belongings, the one thing she had left of her dead brother—could there be a greater violation? And that Teddy comment? And now, in their ignorance, they were trying to interfere in her life, trying to stop her when she was *so close* to a breakthrough, to figuring out what it all meant, to understanding what she was going through—what *Eric* had been going through.

But her writing for Bilhah flashed in Cady's memory and filled her with shame. She hadn't remembered it looking like that, so messy, so frantic, so insane. She was embarrassed her roommates had seen it; it had felt like standing naked in front of them. The proof that the voices were more than just madness made so much sense in her head, and yet she'd struggled to communicate it. They were clearly unconvinced. And could she blame them?

Was their doubt enough to undermine her lived experience? No, as implausible as it seemed, she knew she was telling the truth. She was almost absolutely certain. *Just because you can't explain something doesn't make it untrue.*

There was only one person who could comfort her right now.

CADY KNOCKED ON the door of Lowell House G-41.

Nikos opened the door wearing a crisp Oxford shirt untucked and cuffed at the sleeves with gray Harvard sweatpants. He smiled when he saw her. "Well, hello! I wasn't expecting you, did you text?"

*You came.*

She threw her arms around him and held him tight.

Nikos tentatively returned her hug. "Is everything all right?"

"I needed to see you. I hated how we left things the last time."

*At the boathouse? You had every right, I sprang all that on you.*

"At the observatory? Any awkwardness was entirely my fault, I misread the moment."

"No, you didn't. I want to tell you, you were right, there was something between us. I felt it, too. I feel it now, I feel it every time we're together. I just couldn't admit it. I was too afraid."

"Afraid of what?" *Afraid of what?* Nikos and Whit asked in unison.

"Afraid of doing the wrong thing, causing the wrong outcome. But I'm tired of worrying about everyone's judgment and second-guessing myself all the time. I can't do everything right, I can't think of everything. I want to lose control, just let go, for once. Would that be so bad?"

Nikos shook his head in bewilderment. "I . . . think that's healthy?"

*Not if it means I can kiss you this minute.*

So Cady kissed him. Nikos was surprised at first, but he quickly reciprocated and pulled her inside. They stumbled around in a full-on passionate embrace. When they had to break to catch their breath, Cady reached back to the wall and turned off the light switch. The room became pitch black save for his glowing computer screen in the corner.

"That won't do. I can hardly see you now."

*Stay right there.* She heard the sound of Whit striking a match.

"Do you have a candle?" Cady asked Nikos.

He muttered something and crossed the room. She heard the ratcheting click of a lighter and suddenly the room was lit in flickering amber candlelight.

*There. And I didn't think you could look any more beautiful than by moonlight.*

"I told you, I'm a romantic." He drew her to him.

*Now for music, my cousin just sent me this record, brand-new, pre-release.*

Cady placed a hand on Nikos's chest. "Let's put on some music."

"Not a bad idea. What are you in the mood for?"

*Stormy Weather, by Ethel Waters.*

Cady repeated it verbatim.

Nikos chuckled. "Are you winding me up? I think my nan lost her virginity to that song."

*I haven't been able to think of anything but you when I hear it.*

"Play it for me."

"As you wish." He leaned over his desk and typed onto his laptop. "Ha! Spotify actually has it."

She heard soft strings and a clarinet opened the song, then one dreamy stroke of a harp before the plaintive vocal began.

*Dance with me,* Whit whispered close to her right ear.

Cady closed her eyes, smiled, and lifted her arms.

"Oh, right, dancing." Nikos took her hand in his and slipped his arm around her waist, pulling her close once more. "Mm, I take back what I said, this is an excellent idea."

They swayed to the music, and Cady leaned her cheek on Nikos's chest, feeling his warmth through the cool cotton of his shirt. He rubbed her back as they moved, and she felt the tension melt from her shoulders with each sloping note of the melody.

"You're not such a bad dancer," Cady said.

*Slow dancing is different.*

"Whatever made you think I'd be a bad dancer?"

*To turn down a slow dance with you, I'd have to be dead.*

"Did something happen today that upset you? Roommate drama?"

His accent was distracting her. "I don't want to talk about it."

They held each other dancing, and Cady listened to the song's lyrics: *"Can't go on, all I have in life is gone, stormy weather . . ."*

"This song is sad," Cady said softly.

*I know.*

"Don't blame me, you picked it."

"I didn't mean to make you feel sad," she whispered, her voice caught with emotion.

*It's not your fault. I took the position on the Akron because you were right, I do want to do it. I want you, too, but, we make choices, we hope they're the right ones. It's the best we can do in this life.*

Nikos caressed her cheek, tilting her chin up to face him. "Cadence, you couldn't make me unhappy if you tried."

*Just because it's my choice to go doesn't mean I'm not heartbroken to leave you. Promise to remember that, all right?*

She closed her eyes and kissed him softly. She ran her fingers through his thick black hair, pulling it gently at the nape of his neck. He shivered in response. He kissed her more deeply then, and she felt his biceps tighten around her shoulders, his fingers twisting the back of her shirt, his chest pressing her own. She felt her body yield to him, and he held her steady with his mouth.

His hands crept up the back of her shirt, unfastened her bra, and took them both off in one swoop. Nikos's warm brown eyes took her in. "You are so beautiful," he whispered.

Cady pulled his shirt up over his face. He yanked it the rest of the way and threw it aside. She closed her eyes and embraced him again, pressing her chest against his. The feel of his bare chest against hers, beating heart to beating heart, thrilled her.

Still tangled in a kiss, Nikos moved her to the bed and lowered her onto it. He trailed his mouth down her body, unbuttoning and slipping off her jeans when he reached them. She heard the clink of a belt buckle even as her fingers slipped into the elastic waistband of his sweats. Nikos withdrew his hands and mouth from her to get what they needed from the nightside table. In a moment, he was back, his hands sliding up her thighs, his mouth higher.

She closed her eyes, and when she looked down again, the man kissing a path up her tummy had blond hair and blue eyes that tilted down even as they looked up. She arched her back into his touch, and it felt good, so good. She raked her fingers through hair the color of wheat, her fingernails skimming his scalp, then pulled him up to her mouth. The warmth from his lips spread downward, off her tongue, down her throat, into the very center of her. She felt drugged, lost in a haze of pleasure.

His weight on top of her felt heavy, perfect. Her breathlessness heightened every sensation, lacing each with adrenaline. She wrapped her arms and legs around him and burrowed her face in his neck. She felt herself taken up in Whit's well-muscled arms, held the way she had wanted to be. He whispered her name in her ear, and she felt his hot breath, smelled its sweetness. She grazed her lips against his round shoulder, freckled by the Georgia sun, tasting of sweat and honeysuckle.

He moved over her stroke by stroke, in perfect rower's rhythm, powerful but gentle. The pleasure moved through them like waves until the heat in her was so hot it became light, the fireworks behind her eyelids so bright they became white. He was starlight shooting across time to touch her, and she was a supernova.

# 46

THE NEXT MORNING, Cady awoke with a sharp intake of breath at finding Nikos snuggled close to her. He was sharing her pillow—or she was sharing his—close enough that she could see the pores on his nose. He looked handsome and peaceful, thick hair mussed, eyelashes knit, and lips slightly parted, but Cady felt none of the intimacy one should gazing upon a lover. Instead, she felt uncomfortable and disoriented.

She got up and went to the bathroom, stepping around the condom wrapper and scooping up her crumpled clothes along the way. The bathroom tile was ice beneath her feet. She looked at herself in the mirror. Her hair was tamped down at the temples, her makeup smudged, and her eyes bloodshot; she barely recognized herself. Last night had felt like a beautiful dream, but this morning's reality was confusing, to say the least. She washed her face with cold water.

After dressing in the bathroom, Cady stepped softly back to the bed where Nikos lay sleeping. She whispered his name, suddenly shy to touch him. His breathing stayed heavy and regular. She said his name a little louder and managed to tap his shoulder.

He gave a moan and a mighty stretch, showing his body to its advantage, but Cady felt too shy to look, as if they hadn't spent most of last night entwined. "Good morning, darling." Nikos opened only one eye and squinted at her. "What are you doing all the way over there?" He pawed at her to pull her back on the bed, but she kept her footing.

"I should go."

Nikos passed his hand down the side of her body, hooking a finger in the waistband of her jeans. "It's Saturday, where could you possibly have to be that requires pants?"

"I have stuff I need to do." Cady's mind was already on finding that fourth location.

He pouted. "I was hoping we could sleep in. My parents arrive this afternoon from London, and I'm exhausted already just thinking about it. I've made a reservation at Henrietta's Table for dinner, which is the nicest restaurant in the Square, but I can only imagine the ways it will fall short of Mummy's standards."

"The Bauer Award is being given this weekend," Cady remembered, slumping into a seat at the foot of the bed. If Eric were still alive, her parents would be in town for that, too. She flashed to a fantasy of the four of them smiling around a fancy dinner table, celebrating, happy—the alternate universe where things were the way they were supposed to be.

"Yes, the presentation ceremony is Sunday evening, after a banquet reception for all the finalists and their advisers and families at the Faculty Club. I'd invite you to join us for dinner tonight, but flying commercial always puts them in a foul mood."

"No worries. You guys have a lot to celebrate. It should just be family." Cady nodded and patted his leg over the covers. She kissed him quickly on the cheek. "I gotta go."

CADY LEFT LOWELL via a side gate and emerged onto Plympton Street. She checked her phone: she had five missed text messages. Two from Andrea and one from Ranjoo concerned about where she was and looking for reassurance that she was okay. The last thing she needed was any more well-intentioned meddling from them; she wrote them both back in a group text: "I'm fine, spent the night at a friend's. Pls give me my space."

The next was from her mother, saying she was on the road, giving Cady about four hours to check the fourth and final coordinate location before her mom arrived, plenty of time. Although Cady didn't know how she was going to navigate Parents' Weekend and her new problematic roommate situation. She needed to keep her roommates from mentioning any of their concerns to her mother. Luckily, since her mother hadn't moved her in, they had never met. So as long as Cady could run interference and keep her roommates and her mother apart, they wouldn't know who to tattle to. Cady texted her mom a heart emoji.

The most recent text was from Alex: "Archives got back to me, found some docs for your slave project! What room r u? Happy to bring it over!"

No, no, no, Cady thought. She could just imagine how Ranjoo would receive the delivery of archival evidence of her ghosts. She replied: "I'm not in my room. Let's meet at Annenberg." Cady picked up her pace. She was starving, and she was excited to see what Alex had found.

The ellipses appeared, indicating he was replying.

Great! See you in 15

CADY ARRIVED AT Annenberg, the imposing freshman dining hall inside Memorial Hall. It was unnatural for a cafeteria to be so beautiful: The enormous banquet hall boasted a vaulted ceiling supported by mighty wooden trusses with stained-glass windows glittering between them, better suited to a cathedral than a mess hall. Fourteen chandeliers with lamps like medieval goblets lit the walnut-paneled space, and past Harvard presidents and distinguished graduates peered down from gold-framed portraits and cool white marble busts mounted along the walls, joined by life-sized full-body statues of John Winthrop and John Adams at the end. The intimidation factor of these esteemed figures was second only to the scores of boisterous, chattering, hungry strangers who sat below them. There was a reason Cady took any excuse to avoid eating here.

She got some scrambled eggs and a banana from the kitchen and took a seat at a relatively empty table. She was about to text Alex again when she heard her name called.

Cady looked up to see Alex happily striding toward her with his tray. He was wearing plaid pajama pants, tennis shoes, and his puffy coat. She waved him over.

"Well, now I feel like a shlub. You're all dressed for the day!" He set his tray down across from her. "And here I was worried it was too early to text you on a Saturday."

"No, you're fine." In fact the majority of the students around Cady were wearing casual, cozy clothes, and a few had freshly showered wet heads. Cady was suddenly self-conscious wearing yesterday's outfit. "I get up early."

"Me too. One perk of coming here early—no line for the Veritas waffles." Alex showed off his plate with a golden brown waffle embossed with the university crest, a shield with three open books spelling VE-RI-TAS. "I thought customized waffles were obnoxious at first, but now I feel like it's in on the joke, you know?" He squeezed syrup over the center of it.

"The truth, sugarcoated," Cady said.

He laughed. "That's good! And fitting for your project." He took a bite before pulling a manila folder out of his backpack. "So the archives librarian helped me find a few records about the slaves under Holyoke. I took photos of them and blew up copies for you. Don't get too excited, there wasn't much."

"Alex, thank you so much for doing this." Cady took the folder from him, pushing aside her breakfast to shake out its contents.

"No problem. I was happy to help," he said as she leaned over the papers.

She didn't know what she'd expected to see, but it wasn't this. The images were of hard-to-read handwritten lists, inventories, on browned, water-spotted paper. She could make out one page labeled "In the Cellar" with listed items like "Rolling Stone & Garden Tools" and "6 Old Chairs in ye. Summer House" and then "Servants Beds & Beding £1.12. Juba £40 Bilhah £12." Alex had written over the copy in blue pen: "Servant" = slave Listed with property. Eli wasn't listed. Either because he was already gone, or because he was worthless in their eyes, Cady couldn't be sure.

"Okay, now I can see you're rocking some serious bed head, so that makes me feel better about showing up in my PJs."

"Huh?" Cady reflexively touched her head and felt a huge tangle at the back of her hair.

"Oh . . ." Alex's smile faded, then reappeared, newly humbled. "You weren't home this morning, the weekday clothes on Saturday morning, rock star hair. Sorry, I'm a little slow on the uptake." He rubbed his hands over his face. "Ahh, I'm such an idiot."

"No, I'm embarrassed." Cady could feel her cheeks go hot.

"What? No, don't be. It's college, right? We're friends, we should high-five." He didn't put his hand up. "I think I see my roommates over at that table, I should join them, let you check out this stuff."

"Oh, you don't have to go." Cady felt bad, Alex was clearly disappointed that his favor wasn't paying off the way he'd hoped, but she was anxious to read the papers.

"No worries. I knew when you walked into the first day of seminar late, you were too cool for me. You still are."

Cady shook her head. "You dodged a bullet."

"See? Even that, a very cool thing to say. Anyway, good luck with the research. Professors love when you have primary docs as references, the death record was cool." He rose from the table.

"A death record—" Cady went cold. "Wait, who died?"

"Uh, it was a weird name."

"Bilhah?" She was frantically tearing into the pages he'd given her, looking for something legal and official-looking like a death record would be, but there was nothing of the sort. Was Bilhah caught? Was she executed? Was Eli punished with her?

"Yeah, Bilhah. There were only a few mentions of her, just that she birthed a son in 1761, and died in 1765, it doesn't say how old she was." He leaned over the table and pointed to one of the pages. "It's in with the kitchen inventory, see the list of food items? They made a note of her dying from accidentally eating poison mushrooms, I guess. The archives librarian said that was probably so that no one else cooked with or ate whatever she did."

Beside what looked like a shopping list of vegetables, Cady found the careless scribble: "Bilhah Negro woman supped mushroom soup & died."

A nearly soundless whimper escaped her lips. Of course, Bilhah hadn't accidentally ingested anything, the woman who could make medicine out of plants was hardly an uneducated home cook. She had killed herself.

"Love that 'supped'—good stuff. The extra credit writes itself. Anyway, I'll see you in class." Alex picked up his tray and left Cady alone to spiral.

So Bilhah killed herself the same year she dropped off Eli. The pain of saying goodbye to her son must have been too much. Or maybe with her child growing up only a few towns away, Bilhah didn't trust herself to stay away, not to risk it all for one peek to make sure he was okay. Or maybe she had been saying her suicide had been part of the plan all along and Cady was too dense to hear it. Bilhah said she was a black mark on her son's future, she wanted it expunged, she wanted him reborn a white orphan; she was never going to let a loose end remain that could endanger her son's new life, even if she was that loose end. The intensity of a mother's love was matched only by the intensity of a mother's grief.

Cady should have known.

She supposed it was good that there was no mention of Eli anywhere in the archives; it would've been big news if a former slave child belonging to the president of Harvard was caught trying to pass himself off as a white boy. Cady hoped that meant he got away with it. Bilhah's sacrifice wasn't for nothing.

But her death was.

A teardrop fell onto the paper, and Cady wiped her eyes. Suddenly the din of students talking and silverware clinking seemed to have grown in volume and become unbearable. She pushed up from the table, leaving her plate and tray behind. Cady weaved through her classmates with an increasing sense of claustrophobia, feeling as if everyone was crowding her, looking at her, judging her.

She was disgusted with herself. She had been so singularly focused on what could happen if Bilhah's plan didn't work that she had completely missed what would happen if it did. How could she have been so naive as to think she had "helped" Bilhah, so thoughtless as to have underestimated the anguish of losing a son? She had only been another white person who didn't get it—and with two hundred fifty years to know better.

Cady still would have helped her write the note that allowed Eli to escape slavery. But if Cady had thought just two steps ahead, she could have anticipated the risk of Bilhah's suicide. She could have thought of something else to write, helped her devise another plan, another way out. She could have done something, said something. She could have tried.

Cady pushed through the big double doors into the light outside. She needed to get to the last location. She needed to end this.

# 47

CADY MARCHED ACROSS the green, letting the bitter wind dry the wetness on her cheeks. The towering elm trees of the Old Yard, previously so lush with foliage and adorned with welcome banners when she'd moved in, now stood bare. All the brightly colored chairs and café tables that had sat below them in the gentler months had been taken inside. The grass was stiff and pale with frost. Cady pulled her coat tighter and hurried toward Johnston Gate on one of the long, diagonal paths of the quadrangle. The paths that crisscrossed the yards of Harvard were perhaps the only haphazard part of the entire campus. There was no divine plan or even symmetry to the irregular lattice of intersecting lines. There were only paths taken at different angles, by different people, from different times, gone over and over again and again in different combinations of all three, until they were finally, forever set in stone.

The shushing crunch of Cady's footsteps through the fallen leaves were the only sound until she heard a noisy sneeze behind her. "Bless you," she said, before turning to look over her shoulder. Only when she did, no one was there to answer.

*Pardon me. I told you, I was falling ill.*

Robert.

*You're walking awfully fast. Where are we going?*

First Parish Church.

*Bless me indeed! Church, where I should've been going along, apparently. Might I join you? Maybe I can convert.*

I'm not going inside.

*I was only joking. It's too late for me anyway. I was raised a secular humanist, so naturally I have a great sehnsucht for the supernatural. Sehnsucht is German for yearning. In truth, I could use the distraction today.*

*You already seem plenty distracted. Is everything all right?*

No. I got very bad news today. I made a mistake, I missed something that should have been obvious, and the worst happened. I'm not up for talking about it.

*That's all right, I'm in a similar fog myself. Again, the Germans have a word for the feeling: lebensmüde. Life-tired.*

Cady sighed heavily. Life-tired. She was exactly that. Or maybe death-tired. Probably both. —Where are you getting all this German?

*The German Romantic poets—I reach for them whenever I'm feeling self-pitying.*

That Eliot paper you helped me with was so good they didn't believe I wrote it. You should get your doctorate in poetry instead of physics.

*I may have to after today.*

Why, what happened?

*At the risk of stringing you a lengthy Miserere, I got my letter from Cavendish. I was rejected.*

How is that possible? Your credentials are insane.

*I couldn't understand it either. So I asked to see a copy of Bridgeman's recommendation letter. I thought the praise of an admired professor who knew me best would lift my spirits.*

And didn't it?

*Allow me to read you the final paragraph. "As appears from his name, he is a Jew, but entirely without the usual qualifications of his race. He is a tall, well-set-up young man, with a rather engaging diffidence of manner . . ." it continues with further description of my, and I quote, "pro-*

*digious power of assimilation," and my "genteel nature." I dearly hope the pun was intended.*

They rejected you because you're Jewish?

*Apparently nothing else matters as much. Not my advanced standing, not my perfect marks or published work. All that, but Bridgman knew they must be assured the Heeb tailor's son is sufficiently tall. Don't worry, I'll keep my hair short, I can pass. And yet I can't. It's not enough. Rutherford clearly didn't believe I'd "assimilate" in his lab.* Robert was trying to sound bitter, but he sounded hurt.

That's so wrong, I'm sorry. I'm sure other opportunities will open up. Not every lab can be so bigoted.

*I might make the atoms spin in the other direction, my horns could reverse the polarity. We're on the cutting edge of quantum physics and yet still riding in the turnip truck of anti-Semitism. Lowell will have to begrudgingly sign my diploma as it is.*

Lowell . . . House?

*Robert Lowell, the president of this university. He instated the quota for Jewish students, so our numbers don't get out of hand. I made the cut, but alas, an exceptional Jew is still a Jew.*

Cady had no idea there was such a policy.

*I suppose I should've expected it. I've always been an underdogger. It's not Bridgman's fault.* Robert's voice softened. *He endeavored to help me, I recognize that. It's the reality of my situation, and he had to address it. As he said, my last name gives me away.*

What is your last name?

*Oppenheimer.*

The name exploded in her mind, blinding, obliterating, inescapable. For a split second, the shock of it eliminated any further thought. Then, the boom. Synapses firing in her brain flashed on every image of the atomic bomb she had ever seen. The burst of light, bright as a thousand suns, the monstrous mushroom cloud rising with the alien grace of a jellyfish, the eerie silence before the crack of sound splits the sky and skulls of all who hear. Then the furious earth roaring after it, ash chasing fire upward until hell reaches heaven. And the victims.

Bodies, peeled back by layers, broken by shock waves, poisoned by radiation. Houses bent and burned as though they were made of paper. Cities reduced to rubble in the blink of an eye. Innocent people, with souls and dreams and pasts and futures, vaporized, annihilated, as if they had never existed at all.

Robert Oppenheimer.

The father of the atomic bomb. Each clue detonated its own tiny blast in her memory: the precocious genius, physics, thermodynamics, Niels Bohr, summers in remote New Mexico. But of course she hadn't recognized him. He wasn't *the* Robert Oppenheimer, not yet. He was only a twenty-one-year-old boy with the heart of a poet, ambitious and insecure, too shy to talk to the girl in the next carrel, too gentle to fight back at summer camp, doing his best to live up to the *awful fact of excellence.* "*If, in the end, I've got to satisfy myself with testing toothpaste, I don't want to know till it has happened.*" If only such a banal ending were possible. Her Robert didn't know what he was capable of. Her Robert didn't know he was marked to open Pandora's box. He didn't know he was carrying the potential to destroy cities, to imperil generations to come. He was only a student, arming himself in a quiet classroom to invent the end of the world. And he had no idea.

Cady leaned against the rough trunk of a tree to steady herself, as she asked one more time what she already knew was true:

You're Robert Oppenheimer?

Only no one was there to answer.

# 48

ROBERT WAS GONE.

It was like Schrödinger's cat; the alternate realities where the ghosts could exist in two places at once, or two times in one place, had collapsed now that she had seen the ending. Their known fates could not be unknown, the past could not be undone. She ached at the realization that she would never hear from him or Bilhah again.

All along, she had asked herself, why these voices, why these ghosts? There could be hundreds of spirits trapped within the gates of Harvard Yard, but something about these three marked them for her. A budding scientist, a young mother trying to save her son, an optimistic young soldier—what was the common thread between them? What did the infamous Robert Oppenheimer and the erased Bilhah share in common?

They were doomed.

All their gifts, all their potential—Robert's genius, Bilhah's love and courage—warped, twisted, and turned to ruin. They were ghosts, after all, and happy endings don't haunt anyone.

And there was one unaccounted for. Whit, who had broken through the boundaries of time to love her. Whit, who had dodged the bullet—or had he? Why would he be the exception? Whit had changed his course. He wouldn't be on the front lines of World War II.

She had saved him from that fate. But her belief in that grew brittle and cracked with doubt until it crumbled beneath her feet and plunged her into a fear so cold, it could only be true.

She fumbled to yank her phone out of her pocket, and she quickly typed "Akron dirigible" into the search engine with shaking hands. She could read the first line of the search results, like a Wikipedia article beginning, "The USS *Akron* (ZRS-4) was a helium-filled rigid airship of the United States Navy that was lost in a weather-related accident . . ."

But Wikipedia wasn't always reliable. Cady clicked the next link, a military history website, and skimmed the page:

"The mighty *Akron* soared over Washington, D.C., presiding over Franklin Delano Roosevelt's inauguration, bolstering his famous dictum, 'We have nothing to fear but fear itself.' Less than a month later, the *Akron* would be no more."

Her eyes raced over the words:

On April 3, 1933, the USS *Akron* left Lakehurst base for a routine training mission. The seventy-six men on board had no idea they were flying into one of the most violent storm-fronts to sweep the Atlantic in a decade . . .

. . . Lightning splintered the skies, radios filled with static. . . . They lowered their altitude to avoid being struck, but found themselves flying blind, with clouds above and fog below. . . . a tailwind had increased the *Akron's* speed without their knowledge, rendering their dead reckoning erroneous. What happened next has been pieced together by the survivors . . .

—Survivors, so there was hope.

Just after midnight, the winds grew extremely turbulent and the *Akron* began to nosedive. Lt. Commander Wiley released the emergency ballast, discharging nearly a ton of water to get the *Akron*'s nose up, but she began to rise rapidly, rocketing through the clouds. The crew regained control at 1600 feet, but the storm grew more violent, sucking the *Akron* into a downward current of air and pulling the ship into her final descent. Falling tail first . . .

—Cady felt her stomach drop with it.

At 800 feet, the *Akron* shook with what those on board thought was a buffeting gust of wind. What they didn't know was that the airship's tail had crashed into the ocean. Her eight engines strained, but the submerged tail acted as an anchor. Her engines stalled and her nose came crashing down. In minutes, the sea swallowed the *Akron* whole.

Seventy-three men perished that night, only three survived.

Cady's heart thundered in her chest as she clung to one last hope. She searched for "Akron crash survivors" and drew the results: "Lt. Commander Herbert V. Wiley, Richard E. Deal, boatswain's mate, second class, and Moody E. Erwin, aviation metalsmith, second class."

No James Whitaker Goodwin, Jr.

Her body froze but her heart raced. Only her eyes moved over the text, trying to rearrange the glowing words into a different ending.

Cady squeezed her eyes shut as her mind was filled with sounds of the crash. The engines gunning before they stalled out, the ghastly quiet for one awful moment before the ship's hull impacted the water. She heard the squeal and groan of the *Akron*'s steel bones breaking, rivets popping, the frame twisting, spilling her hot fuel like blood as the ship was gutted by the sea.

She closed her eyes and saw Whit in the ocean, his long, strong rower's arms cutting the waves like oars, striving to stay above water, his throat burning with salt water and gasoline. He would be looking for his fellow men, trying to help, pushing the good debris to others first, saving himself for last. How long did it take him to realize no one was coming? To understand that all his youth and muscle and courage were no match against the ocean's ageless, tireless, peerless strength. To learn that the ocean swallows krill and heroes alike.

And Cady had told him to go. Just as she had blithely listened to Robert talk atomic structure. Just as she had written Bilhah's suicide note. When Whit had discussed the airships, Cady had been thinking of the perils of war, danger from an outside enemy. She had never considered a tragedy during peacetime, nor imagined a foe as simple as a storm. How could inclement weather fell a 750-foot dirigible? That wasn't the way a soldier's story was supposed to end—in a freak accident. And yet the foolishness of anyone to rely on the constancy of the winds, the hubris of men that expect to prevail over Fortune in her heavens, was suddenly, fatally, obvious.

Cady's error in judgment was far worse than Whit's, as she had the privilege of a future perspective. She'd listened quietly as Whit described the airship's ability to protect the Pacific against an attack, when she had learned about Pearl Harbor in the sixth grade. No airships prevented the day that will live in infamy. Dirigible, what dirigible? She had barely known the meaning of the word until Whit told her. She had tried to protect him, but from the wrong danger; she had meant to save him, but from a different fate.

Another error in dead reckoning.

Of course the *Akron* was a disaster, the lighter-than-air program failed, and the dirigible aircraft carrier went extinct—just in time for the attack by the Japanese.

Just in time for Robert Oppenheimer's latest discovery.

Since her brother's suicide, Cady had entertained the impossible fantasy that if she could go back in time, she could change history. Well, she'd just gotten three more chances and had blown them all.

*Maybe that's what they have in common,* Cady thought, *the misfortune of meeting me.* She had met three people at a turning point in their lives—not the moment that would deliver their happy ending, but the one that would lead to their destruction. Her curse was having a front-row seat to their ruin, yet remaining helpless to stop them.

Helpless at best, triggerman at worst. Why would God, or the universe, or her own twisted mind, put her through this? Again. Why dangle the possibility of redemption in front of her only to snatch it away?

She raked her fingers through her hair, and when her hands dropped to her neck, she felt it—the scar, that two-inch ridge on her neck, just under her left ear—and she recalled the totality of the memory that she could never fully forget. Her heart began to race the way it had in the terror of that night. She knew exactly why this was happening to her. Why the universe had chosen her to meet these three ghosts.

Punishment.

# 49

THE MEMORY WAS always pressing in her mind, like water against a dam. Whenever Cady touched the scar, a tiny leak bubbled in the wall that she had built. But she was weaker now, and the leak split into a surge, sweeping her right back to that night last year.

She'd thought she was still dreaming when the sound of a blade shearing through something soft first registered. She didn't wake up until the cool metal touched her neck.

"Eric?" Cady jerked up and yelped at a sharp sting on her neck.

"Shhh." Her brother leaned over her in the dark and pulled her head back down onto the pillow by her hair.

"Ow! What are you doing? Stop!" She kicked at him from under the covers.

Eric groaned in frustration and hissed through gritted teeth, "Stay *still*."

"What are you *doing*?" Her hands flew to her head to get him off, and she found herself clutching at fistfuls of her own loose hair, her fingertips wet with dark blood. "Oh my God! Did you cut me?"

"Your hair. I have to cut your hair. You have to let me do this." Eric's voice sounded panicked, but his actions were forceful and deliberate. He climbed on top of her to hold her down on her bed, pressing her shoulder down with his elbow and grasping another chunk of her hair. She could see in his other hand he held a kitchen knife.

"Stop, Eric, what are you doing?" Cady writhed and flailed underneath him.

"They're going to know you by your hair."

"Eric, Eric, Eric—" She said his name over and over again as they struggled, trying to bring him back to himself. This wasn't her brother; this was a maniac. The big brother who used to comfort her after a nightmare had become one himself. His string-bean arms that had cradled and carried her now pinned her down with terrifying strength. Instead of his familiar goofy smile, he bared his teeth like an animal. Even as it was happening, Cady couldn't believe she was fighting off the same person she loved and trusted most in the world.

And despite the roughness of his grasp and the fierceness of his conviction, the look in Eric's eyes was not fury but abject fear. Terror took over his expression and blurred the subtle differences in their features, so that Cady had the uncanny sense of seeing her own face in horror. Even the panicked, high pitch of his voice unsettled her with its foreignness for him and similarity to hers, and she couldn't be sure which one of them was screaming as they struggled.

Cady could hear their parents banging on her bedroom door, but they couldn't get in, he must have locked it. It took all her might to try to keep his hands where she could see them, but mostly she caught only flashes of the cold blade as he lunged to saw off her hair.

"Stop, I have to do this! They're going to know you! I won't let them find you—"

Cady finally got hold of his wrist, but in an attempt to pry his fingers from the knife's handle, she wrapped her hand around the blade instead. She shrieked in pain. *"Mom!"*

The next thing Cady remembered was sitting in the passenger seat of their SUV with her father driving on the icy road, hunched over the steering wheel. His furrowed brow was illuminated by the bright red taillights of the ambulance that transported Eric and her mother just ahead of them. They didn't talk, although the car was barraged with constant noise as hail pummeled the roof and windshield, the wipers squeaking with metronomic regularity. Cady looked down at her bandaged hand in her lap; back at the house, the EMTs had wrapped her palm and covered the shallow cut on her neck. Dried blood caked the webbing between her fingers, and in the center of her palm, a plum spot had appeared on the snowy white gauze where the blood was seeping through.

With her good hand, Cady flipped the visor down and checked herself in its mirror; the image was grotesque. Her face was dirtied with bloody smudges and a swath of hair had been hacked off three inches from her scalp on the side of her head, leaving only a scraggly layer behind her ear. The Snow Ball was next Friday. It was the type of stupid school dance that her friend Liz liked to roll her eyes at, but that was because Liz always got asked to go. This time was the first dance for which Cady also had a date, and not a guy friend, a guy that counted—Jake Verrano. She had always thought Jake was gorgeous, but so did a lot of girls, and Cady was shocked when he'd asked her. Now she looked like a mental patient. Actually she looked worse— nobody had cut Eric's hair.

They pulled up to the emergency department, and Cady watched as a flurry of people ran to the ambulance and swept Eric and her mother inside. Her father dropped her off at the entrance and parked the car. It was three o'clock in the morning and the emergency room was mostly empty, but she still had to wait. Her father went to check on Eric. Cady was supposed to fill out the paperwork on her lap, but she couldn't hold the pen properly in her injured hand. Her writing with her left hand looked like a child's.

Her father wasn't back by the time the receptionist called Cady's name, so she met with the triage nurse by herself. The nurse took her vital signs and made inventory of her injuries.

"Will you be filing a police report?" the nurse asked.

"What for?"

"The assault."

"Oh, no, my brother did this."

"So, a domestic assault."

"He's schizophrenic."

"I'm not judging, honey. But it's procedure in these types of cases that I take pictures of your injuries, just in case you decide to press charges."

The very suggestion made Cady feel ashamed. But the hospital setting instilled obedience, so she sat quietly as the nurse took photos of the "lacerations" on her hand and neck and the "contusions" on her shoulder and arms where Eric had held her down. She turned her face away from the camera every time.

She was led to her hospital room, only it wasn't really a room, just a bed with curtains on either side. It was a while before another nurse or her dad checked on her again. Cady remembered the doctor who finally arrived was young and very good-looking, like a doctor on a TV show. She felt ugly and embarrassed while he talked to her. They had left the house in such a hurry, she hadn't changed out of her PJs of flannel pants and a threadbare, now bloodstained, T-shirt, and she couldn't stop thinking about how bizarre she must look with half the hair on her head chopped off. And her own brother had done it. She couldn't stop trembling.

Mercifully, the handsome doctor took care of her quickly. He told her she was lucky. Lucky that the neck wound wasn't deeper. Lucky that the knife didn't sever any nerves in her hand. She got nine stitches in the palm of her right hand and was prescribed antibiotics, since kitchen knives are prone to bacteria. Cady didn't feel lucky at all.

"Where's Mom?" she asked her father when the doctor left.

"She's coming."

But her mother didn't come. Cady didn't see her until they were already discharged and she and her father went to find Eric in Room 137. The door was shut. Her father gently knocked and told Cady to wait outside while he went in. She sat in a chair against the wall in the hallway, alone, a random girl in a bloodstained T-shirt and PJ pants with her hospital-socked feet shoved into flip-flops. She kept her father's giant puffy coat on even though it was too hot for it inside, because her shirt was too see-through without it, and every time a nurse or a doctor walked by, she sank lower into it. Finally her parents came out. Cady's mother looked at her with an exhausted smile. Cady's entire body relaxed and she smiled back.

"He's okay," her mother said. "They gave him a sedative, and he's resting now."

*He, him, Eric*—Cady remembered being so angry, so hurt, that those were the first words out of her mother's mouth. Cady had been attacked in her sleep, *assaulted*, and still. When her mother asked about her injuries right afterward, she shrugged her off, too furious to speak. She let her father recount what her doctor had said.

Her mother reached out to touch her face and Cady turned her cheek, which actually hurt her neck more.

"Sweetie, I just want to see the one on your neck."

"The doctor said it wasn't deep," her father said. "It should heal on its own."

"He said I was lucky it wasn't deeper," Cady added.

"That's good." Her mother took a seat next to her, so the three of them were sitting in a row, not facing one another. Her mom brushed Cady's newly short hair behind her ear. "It will grow back," she said, giving her back a rub.

"Not by next Friday," Cady muttered.

"What's next Friday?"

"The Snow Ball." Her mother knew that, they had even shopped for a dress together last week. But that was before Eric came home for holiday break, so it didn't exist.

"Oh, honestly, Cady."

A different doctor emerged from Room 137, a middle-aged woman with short salt-and-pepper hair and a serious expression. "Okay. So, we've got him stable and sleeping, we sedated him with Lexapro. He's twenty years old, correct?"

"Yes, that's right," her mother answered.

"So he's an adult. It's pretty clear from his history and what you described that he suffered a psychotic episode, but he's fine now. Normally, I would have to discharge him. However, if you feel he is a danger to himself and others, we can have him involuntarily committed for seventy-two hours to the psychiatric ward for treatment and observation, make sure he's taking his meds, et cetera. Otherwise, he'd probably do better at home."

"Yes, definitely, we want him home," her mother answered without hesitation.

"Honey," her father said softly, putting his hand on her arm. "Maybe we should just slow this decision down for a minute."

The doctor glanced over at Cady and frowned. She gestured with her clipboard. "He did this to you?"

Cady nodded.

The doctor turned to Cady's mother. "I thought you said he only cut her hair."

"He was trying to cut her hair. The nick on her neck was an accident."

"And the injury to her hand?" The doctor was already writing something down.

"Yes, that happened, but, Cady, you said you accidentally grabbed the knife yourself."

"Karen," her father said quietly.

"I'm just saying it was an accident, unintentional." Her mother went on, "It was a paranoid episode. Eric loves his sister. He would never mean to hurt her."

Her father crossed his arms. "But he did hurt her. I think we need to include Cady in this discussion, she should have a voice in the decision about if he comes home with us tonight."

Her mother grew flushed, agitated. "Eric is terrified of being institutionalized, we know that. I can barely get him to talk to a therapist. This will be a huge step backward for him."

"Our daughter should feel safe in her home."

The doctor nodded, her lips pursed. "I have to agree. Safety is the most important consideration. For everyone."

Her mother was pleading now. "I'll make sure he takes his meds. This was a fluke."

"Cady," her father said, putting a hand on her shoulder. "What do you think? How do you feel about this?"

"Are you afraid for your safety?" her mother asked, a hint of incredulity in her tone.

They were all looking at Cady. The doctor with her chin slightly raised, her face a mixture of pity and impatience. Her father stood slump-shouldered, his face gray with stubble and his eyes red with fatigue. Her mother looked ragged and desperate, her blue eyes wide, her lips cracked and dry.

Cady didn't know what to say. She was angry that her mother rode in the ambulance and didn't even check on her in the ER. She was angry that neither parent grabbed clothes for her so she didn't have to worry about her nipples showing through a threadbare T-shirt. She was angry that her hair was ruined and would take months to grow back, angry that she would have to look ugly in front of Jake Verrano on the one night she wanted to be the pretty one. She was angry that her hand hurt when she moved her fingers and her neck hurt when she turned her head. Angry that Eric got all the attention, whether he was the golden boy or the problem child, and she stayed invisible. She was angry that he went off his medication whenever he pleased, leaving everyone else to deal with the consequences. Angry that Eric didn't try hard enough to get better, that he didn't want it as much as they wanted it for him. Angry that her real brother, the big brother she adored and the easy relationship they shared, might be gone forever.

But was she afraid?

No.

"Yes," Cady answered. "I think he should stay here."

# 50

THAT QUICKSAND MEMORY wrapped around her ankles and sucked her down until her remorse was suffocating. Cady gulped at the bitingly cold air until it burned her throat, and still she felt starved of oxygen. Eric was never the same after that. The involuntary three-day stay at the hospital turned into a week. When he came home, he apologized and told her he'd never meant to hurt her. He hugged her and they cried. He was her brother again, but he was broken, in mind and spirit. Cady had broken him. From then on, he rarely complained about taking his medication, but whether he actually took it remained a mystery. He grew more isolated and depressed, the only emotion he expressed was his desperate wish to get back to Harvard, as if he couldn't stand being with the family another minute. She didn't blame him.

Cady was almost at Johnston Gate, she could see its stately red brick columns, its iron gates open to her like waiting arms, but her legs felt as weak and wobbly as her spirit. That had been *Eric's* turning point. The first step down the path toward his inevitable suicide. And Cady had set him on it, because she was angry that her hair wouldn't look pretty for a high school dance. That moment of pettiness and disloyalty would haunt her for the rest of her life. So the ghosts were a fitting punishment: to have her mind invaded, to be disbelieved, to be called crazy like the brother she'd betrayed, to be tricked into thinking she'd get a chance to make things right when she was always the one who would only make things worse.

The ground she stumbled on seemed to warp and curve up around her feet, and her stomach turned with self-disgust. Cady stopped and lifted her gaze, trying to focus on the top of the gate's frame to fight her increasing dizziness. The ornate ironwork somersaulted in a tangled filigree around the centerpiece: a cross. It was painted black.

There was nothing she could do, in this world or beyond, to redeem herself.

The cross blurred into a blot of spilled ink and smeared the sky as the gate dropped out of view. Cady's eyes rolled up to the cold, blue dome, and the gray tree branches bent inward, reaching for her with their spidery fingers, but they couldn't catch her any more than she could break her fall. She closed her eyes and let the concrete crack her behind the head.

She deserved it.

# 51

CADY HAD WOKEN up to a small huddle of concerned students and passersby. Apparently she had been out cold for a few minutes. Cady answered all the required questions correctly—her name, her location, the year, the current president, plus a political joke to prove how okay she was—but the campus police insisted she be driven in an ambulance for the barely five-minute ride to UHS, University Health Services. There, she was met with a flurry of activity on arrival: eye exam, blood pressure, blood test, CAT scan, IV inserted. It was determined she was dehydrated and had a concussion from the fall but should be fine with rest. That was nearly four hours ago. Now she was just waiting for her body to absorb the full dose of IV fluids and to be seen one more time by the attending physician before discharge. She had been texting with Nikos, but the nurse said it wasn't good for her to look at her phone, so she was relegated to staring at the ceiling from her hospital bed and trying unsuccessfully to nap. All Cady cared about was getting out of the hospital before her mother arrived.

"*Knock knock!* How's that noggin?" a gray-haired doctor in a white coat said as he entered the room, voice booming. "Dr. Sellers here. You look a lot better than you did when we first met. Color's back, blood pressure's normal." He looked appraisingly at her and the various machines around her. "Good. How's your pain?"

"Great, I feel a lot better. Can I leave?"

"Not yet. We take head injuries seriously at Harvard, it's all we have going for us." He winked. "You've got some more time before this IV bag is empty. In the meantime, I want to ask you some questions about how you were feeling leading up to your injury. Do you remember what happened just before you lost consciousness?"

*Yes*, she thought, *I let everyone die.* "Nothing, I was just walking."

"What about in the days before that? Have you been taking care of yourself?"

She shifted uneasily in bed and felt the pinch of an IV needle stuck in the inside of her left elbow, the tape pulling at her skin. "I told the nurses, I've been feeling sick, I didn't sleep much the night before . . ." She shrugged.

"Your throat and nose looked clear, temperature normal, so we can rule out the flu, but not sleeping—why's that? Academic pressure, roommate trouble?"

"My roommates are fine." Cady didn't want any medical professional reaching out to Andrea or Ranjoo. "I was out late last night."

"Alcohol can leave you pretty dehydrated."

"I wasn't drinking. I was just . . . out."

He peered at her from above his eyeglasses, his blue eyes like searchlights. "Do you want a nurse to administer a rape kit for any reason?"

"No, definitely not." What did she have to say to make him leave? "It was probably something I ate at the dining hall."

"That 'emerald beef' is a menace." Dr. Sellers was writing something down on his sheet. "Nevertheless, I'm going to send in Vanessa Hightower to say hello, she's one of our social workers. She's much younger and cooler than I am, you'll like her, everyone does. And I will check back soon." He started for the door.

The scrutiny of the hospital staff made her anxious. She fiddled with the small plastic clamp that gripped her index finger like a clothespin. "Do I still have to wear this?"

"Yes," he said without looking back.

Cady sighed and lay back, wincing when her head hit the pillow.

A short while later, a young African American woman came in and introduced herself as simply Vanessa. She had on red plastic-rimmed glasses and wore her shoulder-length hair in twists. Vanessa started with small talk before moving to more serious questions. "Did anything happen last night that might have stressed you?"

Cady said no quickly, eager to dispel this rape theory she had inadvertently implied to Dr. Sellers. Then an idea occurred to her. "Actually, there is something I didn't feel comfortable telling the doctor."

"That's okay, that's why I'm here."

"I had unprotected sex last night."

"Was it consensual?"

"Yes. But I took the morning-after pill. Then I felt really sick, I must've had a bad reaction to it."

"Emergency contraception is known to have some unpleasant side effects, abdominal pain, spotting, it varies from woman to woman. Do you remember the brand? Was it Plan B, where you take the two pills, twelve hours apart, or Plan B One-Step, where there's only one?"

"Two, and I took them both at once. I didn't know how I was supposed to do it. I just got them from a friend. It was so stupid, but I was just so nervous and embarrassed I even needed them, I wasn't thinking straight."

Vanessa nodded, and Cady felt relieved that she was buying it. Then Vanessa asked, "How did you feel right before you fainted?"

"I felt sick, dizzy. My heart was racing, I was out of breath." That part was the truth.

Vanessa pushed her glasses up her nose. "It could have been a reaction to the pill. But honestly, it sounds to me like you may have had a panic attack. Have you ever had one before?"

Cady shook her head.

"Fainting is a more severe side effect than the medication would typically produce, even if you did take several doses. However, added psychological stressors, like anxiety, can result in physical symptoms. It's what we call psychosomatic."

"You think it's all in my head?"

"No, I think it can *start* in your head. The symptoms you experience are real, but they're induced or exacerbated by mental health issues, like anxiety, depression, PTSD. We can make ourselves really sick when we don't have the right ways to cope with stress." She put a comforting hand on Cady's arm. "But that's just my hunch. And it's something we could discuss more if you want to meet at the Bureau of Study Counsel when things calm down. For now, you've been through a scare. And so have your parents."

"My parents? They're *here*, both of them?" Cady thought she might faint a second time.

"Oh, well, I was told you were unconscious for a period, it must have been then that they reached out to your emergency contact," Vanessa explained.

Cady's heart sank. Another frightening phone call from Harvard. Another panicked drive to Boston. They must have reached her mother when she was already on her way, her father would have had to leave his retreat. "You have to tell them I'm all right. They have to know, right now."

"Okay, okay, don't worry. I'm sure Dr. Sellers has assured them that you're stable and doing fine. But the details of what we tell them from here are up to you. Do you want them to come in? Because I can ask the nurses to hold off visitors."

"Yes, yes, they can come in."

"Hang in, you'll feel better soon. I can tell your parents love you very much."

Which was precisely why she needed to lie to them, she thought. Cady thanked Vanessa and she left.

Cady had only a few minutes to strategize how to deal with her parents. She looked up at the pockmarked white ceiling tiles, her eyes connecting the dots. The morning-after pill was a solid lie. It was uncomfortable enough to sound plausible, sensitive enough to put off too many questions, but not serious enough to be alarming. The conversation would be awkward, especially with her father, but not catastrophic. There was no question she would rather her parents think she was sleeping around than to think she was mentally ill.

Her mother came in first, but it was Cady who gasped at the sight of her. Not only did her mother look wild with worry, but her blond hair was now dyed as red as Cady's own. "Mom?"

"Honey! How are you feeling?" Her mother rushed to the bedside with her father following close behind. She kissed Cady's cheek so hard it hurt.

"Yes, everything is okay, I'm fine—" Seeing the fear etched on her mother's face cut Cady open. There had been a time when she longed for her mother to look at her more, to pay attention, to dote on her the way she did Eric. But now she would give anything to take this look off her face. This was the new pressure of being the only child, the last. "Mom, I'm so sorry."

"Don't apologize," her father said, petting her hair. "How are you feeling?"

"I'm good. I'm better. And Dad, you have your partners' retreat this weekend, I feel terrible, you didn't need to come. The doctors here overreacted, they shouldn't have even called you."

"Our only daughter is in the hospital, they'd better fucking call," her father snapped. "Sorry."

"They said you were in here with a psychologist?" her mother asked, her face creased with concern.

"She was only a social worker."

"Why did you want a social worker?"

"I didn't. It's just procedure." Cady repeated the lie about the morning-after pill.

When she had finished, her mother reached out and touched her arm. "Cady, you know if you wanted contraception, your dad and I support that."

"I know, I just, I made a mistake." Tears came to Cady's eyes. Her story may have been fiction, but her shame was real. "I'm so sorry I scared you."

"Oh, honey. Don't worry." Her mother shook her head and gathered Cady in a warm embrace. "I'm here, and we're going to take you home."

"What? No." Cady pushed her away. "I don't want to go home. I don't need to."

Her father stepped forward. "Cady-cake, you fainted, you have a concussion. You need to recuperate."

"No, this was all a big misunderstanding. I've been sick, that's all, and I missed my Psych exam, I have to make it up—"

"Well, we can talk about it later—"

Suddenly, Nikos appeared on the threshold, nearly breathless. "Cadence, I came as soon as I could shake my parents. . . . Oh, hello." He stopped when he spotted her parents standing on either side of the bed, staring at him. "How rude of me to barge in. I'm Nikos Niko-laides, you must be Mr. and Mrs. Archer." He shook hands with her mother, who was standing closest, then he walked around to her father and added, "I can't believe this happened. You were the picture of health last night."

Cady cringed.

"*You* were with her last night?" her father said through clenched teeth. He didn't notice Nikos's outstretched hand—by the look in his eyes, he was too busy mentally strangling him.

Nikos prattled on, oblivious. "Yes, we were dancing to jazz, of all things."

Cady sighed. "Nikos, I think—"

"Who do you think you are?" The words exploded from her fa-ther's bright red face.

"Sorry?" His eyebrows tilted in confusion.

"You take advantage of my daughter, and you don't even show her the respect to use protection?"

"Dad!"

Nikos scrunched his face like he'd just been slapped. "I beg your pardon?"

"Not helping, Andrew," her mother said.

"Oh, no? Forgive me, Karen, someone has to stand up for our daughter." Her father's tone was acid.

Nikos stood blinking, utterly bewildered, so Cady took over. "Nikos, I'm so sorry, thanks for coming, but I need time with my parents alone. Like, now."

"Of course," Nikos replied, seeming to snap back to earth, but still not understanding. "Mrs. Archer, Mr. Archer." He nodded to each of them, before turning back toward Cady. "I'll ring you later?"

Cady nodded frantically, willing him to just leave. "Go, please."

"All right, then." Nikos awkwardly backed out of the room, clicking the door shut behind him, leaving the three of them standing in a triangle, stunned silent. Tension permeated the air in the hospital room like the scent of disinfectant, and the beeping of Cady's machines was the only sound in the room, counting off each awkward second.

# 52

AFTER CADY WAS released from UHS, her mother insisted she come rest in her hotel room at the Charles instead of her dorm room, at which Cady had to stifle her delight. It was essential that she keep her parents far away from her roommates, and Cady herself wasn't keen on seeing them anyway. It wasn't until her parents pressed different buttons in the hotel elevator that Cady realized they were staying in separate rooms. Her father's floor came up first; her mother held the elevator door with her arm while he hugged Cady goodbye. Now that he had seen she was all right, he was going back to the partners' retreat, reluctantly. The doors tried to close twice before he let go of her. He did not say goodbye to her mother. It was the first time their separation felt real to Cady, even if no one was acknowledging it.

Cady remembered how much her parents had fought during Eric's illness. Even when Eric was away at school, he was the unending source of tension in their home. Her parents' differing views on his treatment crystallized the incompatibility in their personalities, and each felt the stakes were too high to compromise. Eventually, they coexisted in the house by inhabiting separate areas, like neighborhood cats with distinct territories; her father had the upstairs office, and sometimes he'd watch TV in their bedroom after dinner, while her mother would sit at the kitchen island late into the night with her reading glasses on her head, squinting at her laptop where she invariably had multiple tabs open of online support forums for schizophrenia. If her father so much as came downstairs to get a glass of water, an argument could break out. They took turns starting it. Cady's mind replayed one she had overheard from the living room:

"Amateur MD.com, again?" her father started in.

Her mother didn't so much as look up. "The Respiridone is bothering him. I'm seeing if anyone else had similar reactions and can recommend alternatives."

"Please remember they're online commenters, Internet access doesn't confer a medical degree."

"People on here share insights based on experience. Someone just shared a link to a scientific study that shows nutritional supplements like omega-3—"

"Nutritional supplements? He's battling schizophrenia, not the freshman fifteen."

"Don't belittle what you know nothing about. You have no idea the time it takes to research every medication, cross-check drug interactions, but somebody has to do it. How many of the articles that I sent have you actually read? You don't get to criticize me when you do nothing to help."

"A doctor cross-checks drug interactions, and no, I won't help you undermine his professional treatment with holistic mumbo-jumbo. Modern medicine is not the enemy, Kar', it's our son's only chance at a normal life. Good medicine can have bad side effects. If he had cancer, would you have him opt out of chemo because he didn't like losing his hair?"

"This isn't cancer. Treatment for mental illness is not so black-and-white. We have to be his advocate."

"Your 'advocacy' is enabling him to stay sick."

"How can you say that to me? I'm fighting for his life. If he's miserable on the meds, he'll stop taking them, we've seen that again and again."

"Then we show him there are consequences. If he doesn't take the meds, we threaten to stop paying for school."

"School is the only positive in his life. 'Find the wellness within the illness,' remember? It's his sole motivation."

"All the more reason to use that as leverage."

"Leverage? He's not an asset, he's our son. And he's not nine years old, we can't ground him if he disobeys. Bottom line, if he views us as the enemy, he'll cut us out of his life. He'll hate us."

"He can hate me if it keeps him healthy. That's called being a parent. I swear, sometimes I think you just don't want him to be mad at you. You don't like when he pushes you away."

"Because then I can't reach him!"

*Ding.* The elevator doors opened. Both Cady and her mother took a beat to exit.

Their hotel room was air-conditioned like a meat locker. Her mother rushed to the thermostat and pushed it up to eighty. "We can lower it once it warms up." Cady, still headachy, sat on the crisply made bed as her mother puttered around the room, turning the TV on to Cady's favorite channel and hunting down the room-service menu so they could order something to eat. Instead of the usual hotel art of landscapes or abstracts, their room featured a mock blackboard with complicated mathematical calculations. It reminded her of the earlier calculations in Eric's notebook. Cady was all but discouraged from believing the coordinates would yield any meaningful insight into Eric's psyche. The more likely scenario seemed to be that his notes would be one more wild-goose chase. But the last remaining bread crumb beckoning her onward was the fact that the final coordinate location was the only one on the list without a check mark beside it. If she was correct that the check marks meant the exchange had been completed, she held out hope that whatever Eric had left in the final spot had never been retrieved and remained there. But if she wanted to go and find it, she'd need to overcome a greater challenge: her mother.

"Did you decide what you want?"

"Uh, yeah," Cady said, glancing at the menu for the first time. One thing was for certain, her mother wasn't going to relax until she ate something. "Can I get a wedge salad and a side of fries?"

While her mother was ordering for them, Cady checked her cellphone. She was expecting to have some confused or angry texts from Nikos, but there were none—that was worse. She felt terrible for how humiliated he must have been when her father had accused him, falsely, of having unprotected sex with her. Cady fired off an email to Nikos from her phone, apologizing for involving him in her lie. She didn't explain what had really landed her in the hospital, only that she was "caught in a bind" and "had to tell them something," but that she had never meant to hurt or embarrass him. It was short and woefully inadequate, but she hoped taking responsibility could be a Band-Aid until they had a chance to talk in person, and until she had time to think of a better lie.

Her mother hung up the room phone. "They said thirty minutes, which means forty-five. Can you wait that long? We could look in the minibar—"

"I'm fine." Cady picked at the adhesive that remained on her arm from the IV. "I think I'm going to take a shower."

"Make it a bath, will you? You could still be light-headed from whatever made you sick this morning, and the steam will only make it worse. I don't want you to have two concussions in twelve hours."

Sometimes mothers were right.

Cady got into the tub as it filled and lay limp, watching the water slowly rise and swallow her toes first, then her kneecaps, until the hot water enveloped her. She thought of her mother's words: "whatever made you sick." She was sick. She was an Archer, after all, and it wasn't psychic powers that ran in her bloodline, it was self-destruction. But self-destruction is a misnomer; it leaves too much collateral damage in its wake. She turned the water off with her foot and looked around the sterile, white tile of the hotel bathroom. A small hairdryer hung on the wall in its holster like a loaded gun. She slipped her head underwater and listened to the sound of her beating heart. She thought of Whit in the ocean and imagined what it felt like to drown. She wondered if it hurt more or less than it did to lose your child. Or to burn alive. Or to be betrayed. Or any of the horrors meted out on those around her while she stood by and watched.

Yet her lungs bucked. Her body wanted to breathe, to fight, to live. She came up for air.

She lacked the nerve.

Cady washed her body and gingerly shampooed and conditioned her sore head. She dipped her head underwater again, this time to rinse, when she heard murmuring sounds in the shape of her name.

Her head broke the surface of the water. "Mom, in here," she called out, wiping the water from her eyes.

Her mother was already in the bathroom, her eyes wide with alarm. "Are you okay?"

"Yeah, I'm fine." She immediately regretted the bath for what it must have looked like.

"I called, you didn't answer."

"I didn't hear you, I'm fine."

Her mother nodded, her smile fragile. "The food's here."

"Okay, I'll be right out."

"Let me help you, I'm worried you'll slip." Her mother held open a clean towel.

Cady obliged, holding her mother's hand as she stepped out of the tub and letting her wrap her in the oversized bath sheet.

Her mother rubbed her shoulders through the towel. "This reminds me of when you were little. You loved the bath."

"I did?"

She nodded. "Eric was a handful, he would not leave the faucet knobs alone. I was so afraid he'd scald himself, I had to practically hold his arms down while I bathed him. But you would play quietly, sing yourself little songs. I could barely get you out of there when you were all pruny. You were such a good baby."

"Mom." Cady lowered her head, she couldn't look her mother in the eye. "I'm so sorry. I know how scary it must have been to get another emergency call from Harvard, that was the last thing I wanted."

"Shh, shh," her mother said, brushing Cady's hair out of her eyes the way she had since Cady was a child. "Look at me." Her blue eyes matched Cady's own. "You're all right, and that's all that matters. I'll drive here every day for good news."

Cady shook her head. "I messed up."

"Please, messing up with boys? Finally, a problem I know something about." Her mother laughed. "So what's the story with Nikos? He is handsome. Is he your boyfriend?"

"No, but I like him." Cady wrung out her hair.

"Well, that was more tepid than this bathwater. I'm old, not stupid."

"I'm not sure. He's smart and funny. And he cared about Eric, and that didn't scare him off from caring about me. But . . . I liked someone else more."

"Aw, baby." Her mother rubbed her shoulders again. "Then forget him. Who's the one you like?"

Cady shook her head, fighting a lump in her throat. "He's gone."

"Nobody's gone. You have to fight for your man." Her mother helped her into one of the hotel bathrobes. "Your father was dating a horrible woman when I first met him. I didn't let him cheat with me, but believe me, I did everything but to show him what he was missing. I had to save him from himself."

"And what about now?" Cady said softly. "Dad got an apartment?"

Her mother waved her off. "Now, it's not so simple. I don't want him to live with me anymore. I don't know how he lasted this long." She gave a tired smile. "Let's eat. We've had enough drama for one weekend, and I only just arrived."

Cady dug into the fries while her mother flipped through the TV movie options to find one that Cady would like. Her mother had never been so solicitous or tender with her, and as much as Cady had longed for it, she couldn't enjoy it knowing it came from such a painful place. As much as she wanted to let her mom be there for her, she felt like she was exploiting her mother's trauma. Being at Harvard reminded her mother of losing Eric, that was why this version of her mother—attentive, focused, doting—came out. It was for him. Not for her.

"What?" her mom asked. "You're staring at me."

"You look so different with the red hair."

"Different good?" Her mom fluffed her bangs.

"Really good. But you've been a blonde for so long, I have to get used to it. What made you change it?"

"I knew Parents' Weekend was coming up, and I want everyone to know who my baby is." She smiled. "Do you know what events they have planned?"

Cady shook her head, still unable to speak for the emotion welling up inside her.

"Maybe there's some talk of it in here." Her mother reached for the copy of *The Crimson*, the Harvard newspaper. The paper was ubiquitous throughout the hotel, set outside each door along with *USA Today* and *The New York Times*. Her mother peered down at the bottom of the front page and rummaged in her purse for her reading glasses. With them on, she looked at the paper again. "They're presenting the Bauer Award tomorrow?"

Cady watched her mother's face as if it was a spinning coin. She cleared her throat. "Don't read it if it's going to upset you."

But her mother went on reading it anyway. "Nikos is here."

"Yeah, he's probably going to win it."

"And you said he was friends with Eric?"

"Best friends, other than Matt."

"I don't really remember Eric talking about him."

"I think there were a lot of things Eric wasn't telling us about." Like the coordinates she so desperately wanted to check out. She checked the time on her phone. It would be dark soon.

Her mom folded up the paper and touched Cady's hand. "I hope you feel like you can talk to me."

"There is something." Cady hated doing what she was about to do, especially at this moment, but she didn't see another way. "I have been seeing a therapist on campus, a nice guy named Greg. Not because of anything bad, don't worry, just to deal with my grief. He's been really helpful. And with everything that happened today, and this news about you and Dad, I think I need to talk to him. I emailed him from the hospital, and he said he's free. Is that okay with you if I go do that? I'll only be gone an hour or so, and I'll come right back."

Her mother looked shocked, but she recovered quickly. "Of course, of course. I support that one hundred percent. Do you need me to drive you to his office?"

"Nope, it's only a few blocks. I think the fresh air would do me good."

To Cady's surprise and relief, she agreed. Cady got dressed, got her schoolbag, and said goodbye to her mother. Her mom hugged her one last time and watched her leave from the hotel room door. When Cady was halfway down the hallway, her mother called out her name. Cady looked back.

"I'm proud of you."

Cady had to bite her lip until the elevator doors closed.

# 53

"ERIC, YOU'RE KIDDING me." Cady had followed the map to within two hundred feet of the final coordinate location and realized he wasn't sending her to First Parish Church after all. Instead, she found herself outside the wrought-iron fence of a dilapidated cemetery she had somehow never noticed before at the corner of Mass Ave and Garden Street. Gray headstones, chipped and stained by time, jutted from the ground like loose teeth, and the interred were guarded by ancient pine trees and a skeletal canopy of barren oaks. The destination dot on her locator app blinked cheerfully from somewhere among the graves. The perimeter fence bore two signs, a pretty blue one from the Cambridge Historical Commission that read:

OLD BURYING GROUND

BURIAL PLACE OF EARLY SETTLERS

TORY LANDOWNERS AND SLAVES

SOLDIERS—PRESIDENTS OF HARVARD

AND PROMINENT MEN OF CAMBRIDGE

1635

and a dingy aluminum one with graffiti only half cleaned off:

NO LOITERING

NO TRESPASSING

BETWEEN

DUSK

&

DAWN

In other words, don't enter after dark. And it was dusk now. But they hadn't locked the gate yet, the cemetery was deserted, and none of the people hurrying past her on the sidewalk seemed to be looking up from their phones. The destination dot wasn't far; if she didn't hesitate, maybe she could be in and out quickly. She imagined Eric got a kick out of this sign, and this place. She tried to channel his enjoyment of all things peculiar instead of letting it unnerve her.

Cady gave a heavy sigh to exhale her anxiety. She had no ghosts to keep her company this time. She would have to make this final leg of the journey on her own.

She slipped through the iron gate and followed the narrow, overgrown footpath sharply to the right, farther from view of the adjacent church. Eric must have had the same idea; the dot blinked toward the far end of the cemetery, among the denser foliage near Garden Street. If she hugged the perimeter of the fence, in a passing glance, it might look as if she was on the sidewalk outside it. She kept a swift pace and didn't slow down until she was less than fifty feet from her destination.

While the GPS recalibrated to her new position, Cady observed her surroundings. The smallest headstones seemed to be the colonial ones, although she had to guess for many of them, as time had worn down the tombstones so much that the engraving was all but completely erased. She passed two tall headstones side by side marked only with the stark titles MOTHER and FATHER. But the eighteenth-century ones were engraved with elaborate designs that were in equal measure beautiful and disquieting. One tombstone that looked delicate with scalloped edges and a floral border nevertheless featured a winged skull with empty eyes and a toothy grimace. She squatted down to read the epitaph below the skull:

In memory of Mrs. Elizabeth Barrett.
Wife of Mr. Thomas Barrett who departed this life
April 17th 1785 Aged 41 years.

April, Cady thought, fucking April. Then she saw a small line added to the bottom:

Also John Barrett their son died November 7th 1784
Aged 11 months.

So her baby died first. Perhaps she died of grief. Cady said a little prayer for Bilhah.

She walked on, watching her virtual self on the GPS map close in on the destination dot, the coordinate numbers ticking closer to her target, while being careful to occasionally look at the ground and not to trip over any graves. Soon, as closely as the app could pinpoint it, it appeared that she was nearly on top of the destination. Again, she detected Eric's cleverness in the choice. If she crouched, she was safely hidden from view; on one side, an aboveground tomb blocked her from view of the church, and on the other, dense shrubbery shielded her from the foot traffic on the sidewalk. But the satellite map of the cemetery lacked detail, so it didn't help her orient herself as to which direction she should be facing, and she couldn't know how faithfully Eric had hewed to the coordinate when he hid his drop item anyway. Since Cady entered, the sun had slipped below the horizon, and the sky was almost dark. She wouldn't have much more time to find anything at all.

She knelt down and scanned the immediate area for anything interesting or unusual that might have caught Eric's eye. Straight ahead, she saw a headstone richly decorated, the arc at the top engraved with the image of a radiant willow tree sheltering an urn beneath its graceful branches. Cady read the text in the center:

> In memory of
> Mr. Samuel W.
> Son of Col. Josiah & Mrs.
> Rebecca Mower; of Saffrey
> N.H. who was drowned in
> Charles River near this
> Place, May 31, 1829
> at 23 years.

She held back the uncut grass that lay flush with the stone to read the ominous final line:

> Young Friends Prepare for Sudden Death.

She imagined her brother reading this in the last months of his life. This Samuel wasn't much older than Eric had been. Had he meant to drown himself? Is that what Eric had thought? She hated that he might have been drawn to it.

The screech of a rusty hinge made Cady jump. She peeked around the edge of the tomb to see a groundskeeper locking the gate with a clang. She wasn't protected from his sight line, so she crawled around to the far corner of the tomb and flattened herself. With her stomach against the ground, Cady waited to catch glimpses of the groundskeeper between the tombstones as he walked back to the red side door of the church.

She tried to take deep, intentional breaths, to slow her rabbit heart. "What do you want me to do, Eric?" Her breath made a tiny ghost appear and disappear in the cold air. "Freeze? Get arrested? What do you want me to see?"

The ground was hard and uneven, the grass cold; twigs poked at her, and she felt squeamish thinking of the bugs that might enjoy a cemetery. She was miserable. But Eric had always loved nature. Cady was the history buff, not him. She turned her cheek so she was facing the bushes instead of the tombstones. Then she saw it.

She slowly pushed herself up from the ground and sat back on her heels. Cady reached to touch one of the leaves on the bush. Autumn had tinged their color, but she couldn't mistake the familiar spade-shaped leaves with serrated edges. Even without its characteristic flowers, Cady knew this plant well. There was a time when three huge pots of them had greeted her daily from her own front porch, without a bloom in sight.

These were hydrangeas.

Cady ran her hands over the mulch below the bush to sweep away the top layer of wood chips. In the soil underneath, she felt something inorganic and soft, like a thin strip of fabric. She tried to pick it up, but it wouldn't budge; she could get her finger under it but couldn't pull it out. She dug her fingernails into the dirt and unearthed the top loop of a Harvard University lanyard, just like the one Cady kept her dorm room keys on. She excavated around it with a stick to loosen it from the hardened ground and pulled it out like a fishing line, gently so it wouldn't break, until she freed it from the dirt with its catch intact.

A four-inch black metal canister was attached to the lanyard's end.

She thumbed the flashlight icon on her phone and propped it against a tombstone. Under the light, she unscrewed the top of the canister, and a flash drive dropped into the palm of her hand, but that wasn't all. She stuck her finger inside and pulled out a tightly scrolled piece of paper. Her heart thundered in her chest as she unrolled and unfolded it. Cady recognized the handwriting instantly.

*I am a research assistant of Professor Mikaela Prokop, her only assistant on her work on behalf of the U.S. Department of Defense Project A-147 regarding detection of nuclear substance via electromagnetic wave particles. I have recently come to suspect the preliminary results of this research have been illegally delivered to a Russian operative instead of the D.o.D. agent for whom it was intended. I fear that I have unwittingly* participated in this act of academic espionage by facilitating dead drops per Professor Prokop's instruction. As soon as my suspicions arose, I suspended my obedience to Prof. Prokop and, at my own initiative, I supplied false data outside the T station today to serve as a decoy and buy time. Only this flash drive contains the real data results of the third trial.

At the time of writing this, I have not been able to determine for certain if a crime has taken place, so this letter has contingencies: I will give Prof. Prokop an opportunity to allay my concerns. If she succeeds, then I will release these coordinates to her to deliver, and you are the appropriate D.o.D. recipient. If that is the case, I apologize for the decoy, I believed it was a necessary step to secure our nation's intellectual property. Better safe than sorry.

If Prof. Prokop fails to provide credible proof that she has not been using me to deliver this data to a Russian agent the last two times, then you are likely a member of the F.B.I. Prof. Prokop does not have the coordinates for this location, although she may be continuing her illicit cooperation with Russia via other methods. It was her rule that I alone would choose the drop locations and text them via burner phone to the recipient, she said she was less likely to be targeted by foreign agents that way. I did not realize until recently that this was a measure to protect her plausible deniability in her ongoing contact with foreign agents, and to lay the foundation for framing me should she get caught. I've included the flash drive with the real results of the third trial as evidence of the legitimacy of my accusation. I assure you I was ignorant of this act of treason until now, my only mistake was trusting my mentor. I have been deceived and manipulated, and by the time you read this, I will have quit my position as her research assistant and cut off all contact with her. I am prepared to cooperate fully in any investigation. My email is e.archer@fas.harvard.edu, my cell is 555-539-7116, I live in Leverett House F-104. Please advise how best to proceed.

At your service,
Eric Archer

# 54

ALL NIGHT, IN the hotel bed beside her snoring mother, Cady had lain awake thinking about Eric's letter; by morning she practically had it memorized. As much as its premise seemed out of a paranoid fantasy, it struck her as highly plausible. The logic laid out in that letter was pure Eric, down to the decoy trick like the one he had devised for their childhood nemesis, Jeremy. And if true, it cast everything in a new light—Eric's close, secretive relationship with Prokop, their tumultuous parting—it wasn't indicative of a sexual affair, it was evidence of her plot to sell her research. As Nikos said, Prokop's work was government-funded and restricted for the express purpose of blocking a foreigner from exploiting access to the United States' valuable intellectual property. But what if the agent of espionage was the lead researcher herself? Cady imagined Prokop's communications within the university system were fairly closely monitored. It made sense that she would need someone with a lower profile to help her carry out any illegal sharing of information. That someone was her brother.

Unfortunately, the contents of the flash drive weren't any help in fleshing out the whole story. Cady had sneaked into the bathroom after her mother fell asleep to upload the files onto her laptop, but they were password-protected. Without Eric alive to explain the situation, all the flash drive proved was that *he* had access to privileged data, not that it was illegally shared at Prokop's orders.

The main question keeping her up that night was what it meant that the canister was still there for her to find. If Prokop had been able to prove her innocence, Eric was going to release the coordinates to the proven legitimate contact to be retrieved. Since it remained there a year later, presumably that proof never came and Eric never gave the coordinates to anyone. However, no FBI agent had picked it up either. Cady wondered if he changed his mind about Prokop's guilt or got cold feet about accusing a professor he had admired and cared for of such a serious crime. Or did he fear he himself would face repercussions for his involvement? As it was with his mental illness and paranoia, Eric already had developed a deep distrust of "the surveillance state," among which the FBI would rank enemy number one, or at least number three, behind their parents.

Or had he reported Prokop to some authority, but no one believed him? He was a diagnosed schizophrenic at the time. He was prescribed medication for it, which he had a known history of not taking. By the time he cut ties with Prokop, he had had several documented psychotic episodes and one involuntary institutionalization. Maybe Eric had anticipated his credibility challenge, and that stopped him from proceeding. Cady had viewed Prokop's continued involvement with Eric, despite his worsening mental illness, first with gratitude and more recently with confusion, but now she saw it with new clarity. Choosing a paranoid schizophrenic to carry out an actual espionage plot was genius. Eric's perceived disability was her insurance that her secret would be safe. But also, as Bilhah had taught Cady, there was an advantage to being underestimated. Eric may have suffered from mental illness, but he was nobody's fool.

"He was vulnerable. People like her are predators." That was what Lee Jennings had said. And she was the exact person Cady needed to talk to if she was going to find more evidence to corroborate Eric's claims. Cady and Lee had gotten off on the wrong foot, to put it mildly, but she bet that Lee's personal vendetta against Mikaela Prokop would be more than enough motivation for her to cooperate with Cady. Lee could be sitting on critical evidence without even realizing it. Lee had *pictures.*

The next morning, her mother was loath to let Cady out of her sight. She didn't even want to let her out of the hotel room; they ordered breakfast in. But when Cady's mom was in the shower, Cady called the university's Naval ROTC department. She pretended to be interested in joining and asked if she could sit in on a class, and the NROTC coordinator promptly gave her the time and location of the next physical training class that afternoon at one o'clock. For the next two hours Cady anxiously bopped her knee and struggled to appear normal in front of her mother. By noon, unable to stand it any longer, Cady left for "choir rehearsal."

Soldiers Field stadium looked like a concrete colosseum. The enormous structure's tiered levels served as both stairs and seating; its design and purpose were Spartan. Tucked in the shadow of one of the stadium's ground-level arches, Cady watched the NROTC midshipmen do push-ups in a row, the uniformed bodies rising and falling like keys on a player piano. She could see why the coordinator had been so accommodating—they were hard up for members. Cady counted only nine midshipmen with two officers pacing in front of them, and against the massive expanse of green and the empty stands, the group appeared even tinier. Despite the distance and the plain athletic uniform of navy shorts and a gray tee, it was easy to spot which one was Lee—she was the only woman. Although Lee's size was diminutive, she kept up with the boys, her speed and rhythm matching theirs. She appeared the picture of discipline, her body rigid, her short dark hair pulled into a low ponytail and her face down.

Soon the calisthenics gave way to stretching, and the students lined up at attention. The officers barked their final orders before dismissal, which the midshipmen marked with a salute. Cady walked over to the bench on the sidelines where the NROTC members were gathering their things. She had never seen Lee look so relaxed and affable as she was when talking to the other midshipmen.

"Hey, Jennings," Cady called, parroting the nickname she had heard the instructor use. Lee turned, her hair was tamped down with sweat at her temples, her face pink with exertion, but when she recognized Cady's face, it turned a deeper red. She started to walk in another direction, but Cady jogged in front of her path. "Wait, please," she said. "I want to talk about Prokop."

They huddled beneath an archway with the inscription: DEDICATED TO THE JOY OF MANLY CONTEST—BY THE CLASS OF 1879—JUNE 29 1904. They weren't men, but Cady felt the battle spirit was appropriate.

"What do you want?"

"I need you to give me all the photos you took of Mikaela Prokop and my brother."

"Why, so you can get me in trouble? Sue me for invasion of privacy? Remember, I don't have any money."

"No, I want to help you. You wanted to bring a sexual harassment case against Professor Prokop, but you didn't have enough evidence. I want to finish the job."

Lee crossed her arms. "Why do you care all of a sudden?"

"I found a notebook of Eric's and a letter he wrote, and it put a different spin on things." Cady was careful not to reveal too much. "You took me by surprise the other day at the Gato Rojo, but now I think you're right. Prokop hurt you and Eric. She should be held responsible. But you have too much on the line, your scholarship, the Bauer—"

"The Bauer is being awarded tonight, by tomorrow none of that matters. I'll come forward with the pictures when I feel comfortable."

"It won't get any easier. The Bauer being awarded makes it worse. If you lose, any complaint will look like sour grapes. If you win, you risk your own trophy by confessing to stalking a former rival." Cady thought of Robert's deal-breaking recommendation letter. "You know the obstacles women face in graduate science programs, you said so yourself, it's a man's world. What university is gonna take the girl who cried gender discrimination against a *female* professor? I'm not saying it's right; it's bullshit. But you're going to need those letters of recommendation from the faculty at this school."

Lee's posture softened, Cady could see her argument was working. She kept going:

"Let me do it. Give me the pictures, and I'll say they were sent to me anonymously. I have nothing to lose, and who's going to blame a grieving sister? If no one stands up to Prokop now, she'll continue to get away with it. And . . ." Cady stopped when all of a sudden Lee's face crumpled and tears began to slip down her cheeks. "Lee, are you okay?"

Lee shook her head, biting her lip. "I don't know how she got away with it, I was sure someone else must've seen her."

"What do you mean? Seen her do what?" Cady put a hand on Lee's shoulder to try to calm the crying girl. "Please, talk to me, I'm on your side."

Lee looked up to meet her gaze, and new tears did little to obscure the clear, cold certainty in her eyes. "Eric wasn't alone the night he died. Prokop was with him."

# 55

"I WAS WATCHING him, and Prokop was there in his room. I was taking photos of them right before it happened. You can see her at the window."

Cady felt a surge of vertigo, she reached to touch the cold concrete wall for balance. As Lee continued, she thought she might be sick.

"I'm not saying she played a role in his death. I missed the moment he actually jumped or she—whatever—it happened so fast. But it definitely looked like they were fighting beforehand."

Cady's heart thundered in her chest as her mind put the pieces together. Eric knew Prokop was sharing or selling her research to Russia. He had already defied her by making the decoy drop and hiding that flash drive. He had quit working for her. He was about to out her to the authorities. There was no other conclusion: "She killed him."

Lee's face was bright red. "No, I mean, I don't know. Why would she do that? She *liked* him. And I didn't see—"

"Did you tell the police?"

Lee's mouth was open, but she didn't speak.

Cady repeated the question. "You saw someone possibly be pushed out of a building, what did you do next?"

"I left."

"You *left?*" Cady's shout echoed in the concrete tunnel.

"I freaked out, okay? I was traumatized, I was probably in shock. All I wanted was to catch Prokop in a compromising position. She had been spending way less time with Eric in the weeks prior, I sensed their relationship was ending, I was desperate. My friend lived in a room in the opposite tower of Leverett with a view of Eric's room, I told her to be on the lookout. She texted me a woman was there, and I raced over. I was hoping to get a shot of them kissing or something, that was the kind of scandal I was expecting."

"So you did nothing."

"I heard the sirens a minute later, and I assumed Prokop was the one who called them. That made more sense to me than that she had actually pushed him. I read all the reporting of the incident, and I was confused that there was no mention of her. I didn't think I was the only one who knew."

"But that didn't make you do anything. You knew he wasn't alone, you have *photos,* and you've never told the police. Not the next day, not ever?"

"I wasn't sure what I had photos of, I wasn't sure what happened. You think accusing a professor of harassment is risky, how about murder? If I was wrong, forget the Bauer, forget my degree, I could be in a criminal investigation. I was in way over my head."

Cady had not known the meaning of fury before that moment. "That was my brother. You had information about his death, you didn't have the right to bide your time till it became advantageous to you."

"I freaked out, I'm so sorry. When Prokop didn't come forward, I felt terrible that I didn't call, and the more time passed, the worse I felt. But the pictures sucked, I didn't have the right lens with me, they're so blurry, you can hardly tell it's her. They prove nothing. I don't even know what they show and I took them. Soon it just felt like, it's done. He's gone. It won't bring him back. It wouldn't make any difference—"

"Of course it makes a difference!" Cady shouted, losing control.

"My brother may have been *murdered*. "Do you know what my family has gone through? The questions? The doubt? The blame? It has destroyed us. It has destroyed me!" Her chest heaved. "I need those pictures."

Lee looked frightened. "I'll give them to you. I have them saved to an external hard drive in my room. You can come to my room and get it later tonight."

"No, no 'later tonight.' You've held on to these long enough. What are you doing right now?"

"I'm supposed to meet my parents at the T station. They're here for the Bauer champagne reception at the Faculty Club. But we can go to my room—"

"No, wait, the reception might be perfect. Who's going to be there?"

"Everyone. The finalists, their families, advisers, the judging committee, and recruiters and representatives from top graduate programs and the big corporations. It's a big deal."

"Perfect. When is it?"

"The event starts at five. Afterward is the presentation ceremony, when they announce the winner."

"Here's what we're gonna do." Cady spoke with newfound authority; Lee wasn't going to be just any soldier, she would be hers. "You'll bring a flash drive with all the photos to the reception and I'll meet you there to get it. You do that, and this will never involve you again. But if you don't find me and get the drive in my hand, I'll go to the head of the Bauer committee right then and tell him what I know. In fact, I'll tell him whatever I want. And then I'll tell the police."

Lee nodded. "You got it."

But Cady was already walking away, disappearing into the shadowy tunnel. She had won the battle, but the war was far from over.

# 56

CADY CROSSED THE threshold of the Harvard Faculty Club and the air was different, filled with the sweet-stale scent of fresh-cut flowers and doors that remained shut. Her feet sank into a plush oriental rug as she took in the lobby, more like a drawing room of an elegant manor house, with leather couches and plush upholstered chairs arranged before an enormous fireplace. Wainscoted walls with damask wallpaper in a champagne hue boasted gilt-framed portraits of serious-looking white men through the ages. They looked disapproving of Cady's presence.

"Name, please?" A man wearing a crimson blazer and holding a clipboard appeared at Cady's side.

"My brother is one of the finalists," she answered. "My parents are already inside. I'm late."

"Welcome, and congratulations. The reception is in the reading room. Coat check to the left."

The reading room was a grand parlor in full-on party mode: Flower arrangements decorated every surface, groups of people, dressed more corporate than cocktail, chattered over the strains of a student string quartet, and formal waitstaff made their rounds with gleaming silver trays of hors d'oeuvres. Three robustly green ficus plants in marble pots sat framed by a large Palladian window, where just outside the trees stood bare; even the change of seasons had no power compared to the Harvard Faculty Club. Considering there were only five Bauer finalists, Cady was surprised there were so many people. Moving through the crowd, she saw many wearing name tags from major corporations, one decorated general in full Army dress uniform, and the rest were faculty from Harvard as well as other universities and graduate schools—MIT, Yale, the University of Chicago, even Stanford and Caltech. Many had a year following their name, indicating they were Harvard alumni themselves.

There was some movement in the people around her, as a line of young men wearing white tie and tails entered the room. They formed a semicircle and one announced, "Good evening, ladies and gentlemen. We are Harvard's signature all-male jazz a cappella group, the Din and Tonics . . ." As the other guests shuffled for a better view of the singers, Cady got on her tiptoes and scanned the crowd for Lee, or her real target, Prokop, but she didn't see them. Cady needed to get to the other end of the room, where the majority of the crowd was still mingling by the bar. She slipped behind the row of a cappella boys and spotted Nikos holding court with two corporate types, but unfortunately his adviser wasn't with him. He looked handsome in a trim charcoal suit with a pocket square in an appropriate shade of crimson. A beaming older couple stood nearby, they had to be his parents. Nikos clearly took after his mother; her thick, sable-colored hair matched his to a T, and she looked impossibly chic in a cream Chanel suit with a sparkling emerald brooch. His father was a shorter, silver-haired version of his son in a sharp navy suit, and he only occasionally glanced down at his smartphone. Everything about the couple looked elegant and expensively maintained, but they didn't look very huggable. She ducked in the other direction; Nikos would only complicate the confrontation with Prokop. This was something she had to do alone.

Cady almost didn't recognize Lee when she saw her standing by the buffet table, Lee looked so different in girly civilian garb, a pale blue sweater set with a black skirt and chunky black heels. She was much less threatening when she looked so uncomfortable.

Cady tapped her on the shoulder. "Do you have the flash drive?"

Lee was about to answer when a petite Asian woman stepped out from behind her.

"LeeAnn, is this one of your friends?" the woman asked expectantly.

"Cady, this is my mom, Xinwei. Mom, Cady."

Lee's mother had a warm smile, with shoulder-length hair and dated, curled bangs, and was modestly dressed in a silk floral blouse and black slacks. "So nice to meet you." She shook Cady's hand with both of hers and introduced Lee's father, Phil, a tall man with thinning light brown hair but a full handlebar mustache. He wore a bolo tie, glasses, and a serious expression that Cady recognized from Lee.

"Here." Lee discreetly pressed the flash drive into Cady's palm. "They're all there, but I have my laptop in the coatroom if you want to check it." She paused. "I am sorry."

Cady squeezed the flash drive once, savoring the cool metal in her hot hand, before slipping it into her coat pocket. She looked at Lee's face and saw someone who needed this award, who maybe had let herself down in the course of trying to get it. Cady had let herself down enough times to understand.

"I believe you," Cady said.

Lee surprised her with a hug and whispered into her ear, "Go get her."

Having the photos in her possession sent electricity coursing through her, and Cady felt a red-hot focus as she weaved through the crowd. Finally she caught sight of the flaxen mane she was looking for. Mikaela Prokop standing by the bar, wearing a long-sleeved black dress with a low scoop back. She was speaking to two smitten older gentlemen. Lithe limbs, fair hair falling on creamy skin, rose lips curling into a knowing smile, and a MacArthur Genius Award to her name. She was a bombshell with a PhD, even the old guard craved her approval. It took a woman to see through her. Prokop was purporting to laugh at something the white-haired man said, when she shot a sideways glance in Cady's direction. She excused herself from the conversation by raising a single slender finger to the gentlemen, before striding confidently toward Cady.

Prokop fixed on Cady with that predatory gaze, her eyes the color of a coming storm, betraying nothing behind her empty smile. Cady had hoped to surprise her, but now as Prokop was advancing on her, anxiety mingled with her anger and almost took her breath away.

In heels, Prokop towered over Cady. "Miss Archer, so good to see you."

"What did you do to my brother?" Her voice sounded smaller than she wanted it to.

"Ah, Eric. Of course I am thinking of him today. I always told him he was the boy who would be king, and the Bauer Award should have been his Excalibur. We should toast him." She raised her champagne flute. "To Eric."

Cady's entire body was shaking. "You killed him."

She gave the same fake laugh she had just performed for the old men. "My God! I could not have heard you right. Come, let's talk where it is more quiet." Prokop clasped her hand around Cady's upper arm with surprising force and spun her away from the crowd, keeping her close as if they were old girlfriends but never loosening her grip. She led her through a nearby door and into an empty room with an elliptical spiral staircase and checkerboard-tiled floor before Cady yanked her arm free, the physical force releasing something within her. Even as tears came to her eyes, her voice grew stronger.

"You pushed him out the window that night. You *murdered* him."

"No, no, my dear." Prokop bent at the waist and placed her hand on Cady's shoulder, speaking to her as one would console a child. "You can't possibly think that's true. I loved your brother."

Cady spat in her face.

Prokop's glass shattered on the floor as she recoiled in shock and disgust.

But now the words spurted from Cady like blood from a cut artery. "I know you were there that night—I have pictures. Pictures of you in his room, fighting with him right when it happened. You couldn't control him anymore, so you got rid of him!"

Prokop wiped the saliva from her cheek. Her rose lips curled into a sneer, but her voice remained measured and calm. "I was nowhere near your brother when he died, and I won't tolerate your baseless accusations. Security!" she called out.

"He figured out you were selling your research to Russia and using him to do it. He was going to report you for being a fucking spy! I have proof—I found the last drop!"

For a moment, Prokop's icy façade cracked. Her lips parted and her stormy eyes showed something new: fear.

Just then two blocky men in black suits jogged into the room. "Ladies, what's the problem?"

"This girl has assaulted me. Please remove her immediately."

"Miss, you're going to have to come with us." The security guard beckoned for Cady to come with him, but Cady backed away.

"No," Cady said, pointing a finger at Prokop. "You need to take her, she's a killer and a spy—"

Prokop scoffed. "She's delusional, a family history of mental illness. She *spat* on me." She raked her fingers though her hair, exposing two freshwater pearl earrings, earrings Cady remembered she had seen before—on Nikos's bedside table.

She stared, slack-jawed, at Prokop as the guard continued his approach.

"Miss, don't make this harder than it has to be." The guard's voice snapped her back to attention.

"No, listen to me, I'm telling the truth!" She backed right into the chest of the second guard, whose arms closed around her. "Let go of me, I have proof, I can show you!"

"C'mon, let's take her out this way." The first guard gestured to his partner, directing him.

The guard holding her swung her around, but just as he did, he slipped on the broken glass and spilled champagne and dropped to one knee, and Cady burst from his grasp.

"Get her!" Prokop shouted.

The security guard lunged for Cady, but she darted out of the way and bolted for a third door on the opposite side of the room, guessing it led back to the party.

Cady burst into the main parlor room only to slam into the row of Din & Tonics, breaking the line and the harmonies, falling to the ground and taking two of the singers with her. Save for a few gasps, it was deathly quiet as she struggled to untangle herself from the tuxe-doed men. From her hand and knees on the carpet, she looked up to see a roomful of eyes staring down at her.

Two sets of strong arms slipped under hers as a guard appeared on each side and easily lifted her up off the floor in one swoop, carrying her right back out of the room. As she was carried backward, she saw the receding crowd crane their necks to watch her before a frowning waiter closed the door after them. Prokop had vanished. Her body went limp with defeat.

She found herself being taken out through the staff kitchen. Staff members in chef's whites stared at her, and a waitress leaned over to whisper something to a boy washing dishes.

The younger guard on her left chuckled. "They'll be talking about that one for a while."

"Oh, for sure. You made quite a scene in there, little lady," said the older one, his gruff Boston accent coming through. "I got a daughter almost your age, full of the same piss and vinegar. Why is it you girls love drama?"

"It's not drama." Cady tried to stay focused and respectful. "That professor is a spy, she is selling U.S. government research to Russia. I have photographic proof she killed my brother to cover it up."

"Joey, didn't you say you saw that movie on Netflix?" he said, making the younger one laugh.

"You don't have to believe me. Just please let me speak to a detective, I'll show them my evidence."

"We ain't cops, hon, we're private security hired for the party. And Harvard doesn't pay enough for handling Russian spies," said the older one. They passed through the exit that led outdoors. "But if I see you coming around this building again, I'll call the police and save you the cab fare."

# 57

THE SECURITY GUARDS tossed Cady out, sending her stumbling onto the lawn, where she slipped on the frost-covered grass and fell to her hands and knees, but she was undeterred. If they wouldn't call the police, she would. She let the cold, wet ground sink into her jeans and reached into her coat pocket for her cellphone, but it was missing. It must have fallen out during the scuffle. Then a much more horrifying thought hit her: Did she still have the flash drive? Cady scrambled to her feet and frantically checked her coat and pants pockets. She laughed aloud with relief when she found it. That meant Prokop wasn't going to get away with this.

It was dark now, Cady wasn't sure what time it was. She crossed the small courtyard and sat on a bench to plot her next move. Just then, another side door of the Faculty Club opened, releasing light and Gershwin tunes. Cady's body flexed, ready to run, but the figure coming toward her wasn't one of the guards again, this man cut a much slimmer silhouette.

"Cadence!" Nikos called as he jogged over to her. "What was that? I saw those a cappella boys go flying like bowling pins and then a flash of red hair between two gorillas of security guards, was that you? Are you all right?" He threw his arms around her.

She tensed under his embrace.

"What's happened?" He looked at her with concern.

Cady searched his face, her mind swimming with new questions about the man across from her. "Prokop. I was arguing with her, she got me kicked out."

"Prokop? What on earth were you arguing about?"

"Eric."

"And? Did she say something about him that upset you?"

"She said . . ." Cady had been too distracted to make the connection at the moment, but now it was clicking into place. "She said she called him 'the boy who would be king,' and that the Bauer should've been 'his Excalibur.'"

"And this offended you in some way?"

"It's a reference to King Arthur." She leveled her gaze at him. "Eric didn't really give you that book, did he?"

"*The Sword in the Stone?* Of course he did. Maybe he spoke about it to her, too—"

"No. Archimedes is the teacher. You're not Archimedes, Prokop is."

Nikos gave a laugh, but his eyes didn't look amused. "If he gave it to her, how do I have it?"

Cady shrugged. "Maybe you took it from her house. You're sleeping with her. Her earrings were on your bedside table."

Nikos opened his mouth as if to protest, but he stopped himself, pursing his lips. "I don't know what to say."

"I don't even care. Just answer me this: Did you ever really care about Eric?"

Nikos sat back and crossed his arms, but he didn't answer.

Cady shook her head, thinking of all the pieces that didn't fit. "Eric never mentioned you to me or anyone in my family, you're nothing like him. But you were his competitor, for the Bauer Award, for Prokop's attention. I don't think you were Eric's friend. You were his rival."

He smirked. "Friend, rival, you say tomato . . ."

"So why lie about it, why paint this rosy picture to me?"

"I wanted you to like me."

"But why?"

"Revenge, I suppose."

"Revenge against Eric? What did Eric ever do to you?"

"He left me."

Cady stared at him, incredulous, but his impish affect had vanished. His jaw clenched.

"He left me when I needed him most. Love and hate are close to one another, you're likely experiencing both toward me right now. I loved having a worthy opponent in your brother, and I imagine he felt the same. Since my freshman year, beating Eric Archer was my *raison d'être*. The Bauer Award was to decide once and for all who was top dog—until your brother dropped out. Literally."

Cady recoiled. "Well, he's dead, so you won."

"Win by forfeit doesn't count!" Nikos snarled, startling her. "I wanted to *compete*. Now when I win the Bauer, it will have an asterisk beside it, because Eric wasn't there." He sprang to his feet, pacing while he spoke. "He figured out the loophole—the clever bugger— that there is nothing so sacred, so inviolate as unrealized potential. Now he's the James-fucking-Dean of the Physics Department, the Greatest Who Ever Wasn't. And it's bollocks! But now they all have to have something nice to say, even Mikaela Prokop says to you, 'Oh, *he would've won*.' Well, he wouldn't have! It was me. It was always going to be me!"

"Eric did not die to spite you. He didn't die for some stupid undergraduate award. You have no idea what he was going through, but it definitely wasn't about *you*."

"Oh, but it was. So just as he took that from me, I decided to take things from him. First I took his fantasy girl adviser, his 'Mika.' Then I took his sister. And now I'm going to take his prize."

Cady felt physically sick that she had been with this vile person. "The Bauer won't make a difference. You'll always be second place. You were nobody's first choice, not mine, not even Mikaela's."

Pain flickered across his eyes. "Eric never had Mikaela. He wanted her, but I was the first. I won her."

"You wish!" Cady stood up to get in his face. "You think you won her? She's manipulating you, using sex to distract you from seeing what she's really doing with her research, you're just too stupid to know it. Eric figured it out—sick as he was, he was too smart for her. He figured it out, and that's why he quit, he left her. And she lost it! That's why she was arguing with Eric, in his room, the night he died."

Nikos sniffed and smoothed out his jacket lapels. "Impossible. The night he died was the first night she and I spent together."

"You're lying." She put her hand in her pocket, closing her fist protectively around the flash drive. "That's what you do. You're a liar. You never cared about Eric, and you never cared about me."

"Not true. You were both very precious to me, in different ways. I do like you, Cadence, even better than your brother. You're a lovely girl, and you were a very pleasurable means to an end."

Cady shook her head, backing away from him. "I trusted you, and you deceived me."

"I didn't think you'd fall so easy. That's why I employed Ted to help my recruitment efforts that night at the Phoenix."

That knocked the wind out of her.

"Don't be cross, you were in no danger. Ted's a gifted actor, he and I had choreographed the whole thing. Except for the part when I punched him, that was improv. He was pissed, but I had to make it believable. You made a winsome damsel. And face it, you wanted to believe me."

She felt light-headed. She could barely think to speak. "You, you're . . ."

"Disgusting? Morally bankrupt? Criminally good-looking? Say whatever you want about me. You're the sister of a psychotic ex-student who is almost as psychotic herself. Whatever possible threat you might've posed to me before, you eliminated today when you emailed me an apology for falsely accusing me of having unprotected sex with you during your fake trip to UHS. I have proof you're lying and delusional, in your own hand."

She felt nauseated with the knowledge that she had played into his every trap. She began to stagger backward.

Nikos kept advancing on her. "And while we're confessing, I might as well get everything off my chest. Do you remember when you asked me if I believed in fate?"

Cady wouldn't look at him.

"You were in one of your dreamy moods, so I told you I did, that I thought the ghost of your brother had 'led me to you.' Another lie, I'm afraid. God knows that if ghosts were real, your brother would rise from the ground and punch me in the face."

Cady's right hook connected with his aristocratic nose in a crunch.

# 58

CADY STORMED ACROSS the Old Yard, furious but invigorated, despite the throbbing knuckles on her right hand. *Nikos.* All this time! As Cady's mind replayed his words, his swaggering satisfaction— satisfaction she had given him—she wanted to shake off her skin just thinking about it. It especially bothered her where Nikos was right; she had wanted to believe him. She had wanted to feel close to Eric, and Nikos's story about their friendship, the version of Eric that was healthy, social, best friends with this cool guy, played into everything she'd wanted to believe about her brother. Namely, that he wasn't so vulnerable, that she hadn't abandoned him when he needed her most. But Eric didn't have any real friends, not at the end. And now Cady realized that neither did she.

But none of that mattered now that she knew what she did about Prokop. She had come to Harvard to connect with Eric and to understand why he died, in part to redeem him and in part to redeem herself, and now she would. Prokop was the villain here. She had manipulated Eric, used him, betrayed him, and ultimately killed him. Eric had wanted to bring her to justice, but he died before he got the chance. Now Cady would finish the job. All she had to do was gather up all the parts of her case against Prokop: the photos, the drop canister with Eric's letter and flash drive, and his research notebook, and go straight to the police. But first she wanted to check Lee's photos. It would take only a minute, and her dorm room was close by.

Cady jogged up the stairs of Weld two by two. She pushed her key into her dorm room lock, fumbling with her swollen fingers. She cursed and jammed it in again, finally bursting inside.

Ranjoo looked up from her seat on the futon, lit by the glowing screen of her laptop.

"Hey, are you okay? Where have you been? We were worried."

Cady had left her own laptop in her mother's hotel room. "I need to use your computer."

"Now? What do you need it for?"

Cady sat down next to Ranjoo and took it right off her lap. "I'll be quick." She got to work minimizing the open windows and pulled the flash drive from her pocket.

"Uh, oh-kay." Ranjoo looked sideways at her. "I'm sorry if I pissed you off yesterday, I probably could've handled everything better."

Cady had plugged the drive into the USB and was trying to figure out where the files were. "Yeah, fine." She found that the contents of the drive were held in a single unnamed folder, and within that, several more folders labeled by location and date. She stopped, letting the cursor hover over the last one, marked "Leverett 3.26." March twenty-sixth last year, the day Eric died.

"But you're not making it easy to believe you're fine. Like right now, you're acting fucking weird." Ranjoo leaned over to peer at her computer screen. "What are you looking at, pictures of Leverett House?"

"Please, shut up!" Cady shouted, startling them both.

Ranjoo snorted and got up. She went into their bedroom and slammed the door. But Cady no longer cared about their fragile friendship; all that mattered were these photos. With a deep breath, she double-clicked the folder and reached a series of .jpeg files with only numbers for titles. She opened the first one.

As soon as the file opened onscreen, she had to shut her eyes to spare her heart. Although Lee was right that the image was low-quality, even the pixilated contours of her brother's face, his eyes, his chin, rocked Cady to the core. Seeing him alive, knowing these were his last moments, made the dark and shoddy image like looking at the midday sun, too bright to bear. But she urged herself to be strong. People had to identify the bodies of their loved ones, they endured such things to make sure justice was done, and this was no different.

She refocused on the picture. In it, only Eric faced the camera. He was embracing Prokop, whose back was to the camera, with his chin resting on her shoulder. Eric was a great hugger, his bear hugs used to lift Cady off her feet, and she would never feel one again. Looking at the photo, envy was all that kept her grief in check; she was jealous that his last tenderness was wasted on this evil woman. She wondered what lie Prokop had told Eric for him to let her in and greet her with forgiveness. Maybe she told him she was going to turn herself in. And in his kindness, he trusted her and let her in one last time. Cady's hand shook as she clicked on the next file.

The second image overlapped the previous one, like a playing card. This image showed Eric and Mikaela facing each other in profile. Although they weren't standing very close together, the intimacy was apparent; she was touching his forehead, perhaps brushing away his hair. But again, the vertical edge of the windowpane blocked Prokop's facial features from view. Only her arm and shoulder-length blond hair were visible.

In the next several images, Prokop was largely out of the frame; she was seated on the edge of Eric's bed, only her legs visible. In clicking through the series, however, Cady could tell Eric was angry; it was like stop-motion animation, with him traveling from side to side of the frame, pacing, gesticulating. Finally, Prokop reappeared, only again with her back to the camera. Although it did look like she was advancing on him, reaching for him, with Eric pushing her away.

There was one unopened image left, one last card to be dealt. Cady brought the cursor to the final .jpeg and found herself hesitating. She wanted to see something that would damn Prokop irrevocably, but when she considered what that might be, she didn't like it. No matter how clearly her mind spoke the words, her heart didn't like the sound, sharp, tinny, and true:

Cady wanted to see Eric pushed.

Not only because it would indict Prokop and vindicate Eric, but because it would exonerate her.

Cady opened it and her jaw dropped. What she saw was worse than she could have imagined. Eric wasn't pushed; his blurry, dark form appeared half out of the window without interference. It was the face behind him that caused her horror. The woman was also blurred in motion, not to push him, but to stop him. Cady knew because the face was one of anguish, not anger, there was no doubt of that in her mind.

The woman's identity was pixilated beyond recognition to anyone except her own daughter.

# 59

HER OWN MOTHER.

Cady crossed Mass Ave against the light and didn't flinch when a driver leaned on his horn. Expecting to see Mikaela Prokop in the photos, Cady had failed to recognize her mother at first, but the truth was evident in every picture. Her height was too short to be Prokop in the first one. And that gesture—pushing away his hair— how many times had Cady felt those very same fingertips on her forehead? And yet it was unthinkable. The only thought more appalling than her brother taking his own life was her mother watching him do it.

She passed the T station. She longed for one of Robert's trains to nowhere, but time was inescapable, and she had stepped into a moment of irreversible knowledge. In doing so, she had made permanent the most perverse alternate reality possible.

There was no chance for redemption now, for any of them. Cady wouldn't avenge her brother by nailing Prokop, the scribblings of a paranoid student wouldn't be enough to convict her, and Cady had destroyed her own credibility with her reckless behavior. Prokop didn't kill Eric, but she had used him, preyed on him in his weakest moments, and she was going to get away with it—Cady had found a way to fail her brother even in death.

Was Cady the last to know? Were both her parents keeping this secret from her, letting her drown in her guilt alone? Or had her mother kept this even from her father? There was a sick, cosmic justice that, in her father's hiring Lee, he had inadvertently paid the girl to capture the worst moment of their lives on film. She didn't recognize these people anymore, not even herself.

But the part that ripped her heart out was that for one day, Cady had allowed herself to believe that Eric hadn't wanted to leave them, that he had been someone else's victim. It didn't make not having her brother any easier, but that grief had something soft to hold on to. This was the truth stripped bare. Eric wasn't murdered. He had killed himself, and in front of their mother.

Cady passed by the street that led to her mother's hotel without stopping. She was done hunting for answers now that there were no right ones left. She broke into a run, although she could hardly feel her legs. She floated above her body and watched her mindless form race down the river like she had the other day, only now the storm raged inside her, and there was no shelter up ahead. No place or person left to put her trust in; even her own heart, her mind, her gut had led her astray.

She stopped when she reached the foot of Leverett Towers. Eric's old dorm was one of the few high-rises on campus, and with almost every window lit, it looked busy as a hive. It was full of students, talking, studying, having sex, living their lives, oblivious that someone had once lived in a room just like theirs in pure torment. That was how fickle time worked. For some, it was made of minutes strung like pearls, straight and even, moving ever onward. For others, like Cady, time was a rope with the past and present twisted together, doubled back, and looped around her neck.

As one student exited the front door of the nearer tower, Cady slipped inside after him. She headed to the elevator, but when the steel doors opened, three students burst out, boisterous and laughing. Cady backed out of their way. In a twelve-story tower with however many rooms, she would never have the elevator to herself. She took a hard left to the stairs.

The stairwell was empty, constructed entirely of unpainted concrete, lit on each floor landing by a single caged fluorescent bulb. As she climbed up the stairs, she ticked off everything she had gotten wrong:

Nikos had tricked her. Prokop had eluded her. Her mother had lied to her.

She thought of the selfless young mother who gave the last piece of her heart for her son. The brilliant young man who dreamed of advancing science but instead unleashed a scourge on mankind. The boy she loved whose safe haven turned out to be the eye of the storm.

Cady had tears for all of them, Bilhah, Robert, Whit, and Eric—it was always about Eric—for all the injustice they had suffered, the unfair hands they'd been dealt, the shortcomings of family and school and society and nation, for all their bright potential lost.

Every flight was split into two sections winding around each other without a single window. The strain, the exhaustion, the sense of futile circling—for once her body was in accordance with her mind. Her muscles trembled, her sweater clung to her back, her breathing came short and raspy, but Cady did not slow down. The ache in her legs brought the satisfaction of self-punishment. She pulled herself up by the railing, her clammy palm squeaking on the pipe. Each step brought its own bitter truth. They had a rhythm like a drumbeat.

She was disloyal.

She was deceived.

She was weak.

She was wrong.

She was bereft.

She was alone.

She was done.

Standing at the very top floor, Cady's heart pounded, yet a calm came over her. She faced a metal door with a sign reading:

ROOF ACCESS IS PROHIBITED.

CAUTION

DO NOT OPEN ALARM WILL SOUND.

Caution had its chance. Cady kicked open the door.

# 60

DEAF TO THE wailing alarm behind her, Cady walked out onto the roof as if she were sleepwalking. At the edge was a foot-high ledge before a twelve-story drop. She walked up to it as if it were a sidewalk curb. The view of the Charles River spread before her, black as an oil slick. Tears blurred her vision, smearing the lights across the river so that the buildings looked on fire. She wished they were. If the bridge sank into the black water and the stars fell from the sky like bombs, then the world would be honest. Then the world would keep its promises.

Eric had promise, and the world couldn't keep him. For all the voices that had haunted her, his was the only one she couldn't reach. He was the only one who could understand her and explain everything, and he was gone, locked away in some inaccessible past. She wanted him to tell her not to do it, or that he'd be there waiting for her when she did. She wanted to feel close to him again.

But time was two-faced. Minutes that ticked by like any other were the moments that changed a life forever, yet revealed themselves too late. And what she knew now trapped her in an unbearable present, with no way to go back or forward. Only down.

Her brother could not face his future and Cady could not escape the past, but both directions had led to the same point—here. She had longed to know why he had done it. She had thought the answer would cure her. But now that she knew the truth, she stood lonelier than ever.

She had always wondered if suicide was reckless and impulsive or reasoned and premeditated. Now she knew. It was both. Recklessness in slow motion.

Cady stepped up onto the ledge, balancing on the balls of her feet with her toes in the air. Her legs still felt like jelly from the stairs, but she commanded them to straighten and stood tall. The wind rushed by her; its cold hand felt like a caress.

Until she glanced downward, and her breath caught. Cady was back in that moment ten years ago, a little girl on the roof of Jeremy's garage, the first time she had blindly followed Eric to a precipice that was too high, only this time he wasn't there to catch her. Now she heard a voice in her head tell her, *No, get down*, but it wasn't the ghosts', and it wasn't her brother's, it was her own. She didn't want to die.

Suicide wouldn't be her escape, and it didn't have to be her destiny. Unlike Robert, Bilhah, Whit, and Eric, she still had a choice in how her story ended.

She turned to step off the ledge just in time to see Mikaela Prokop lunge to push her.

# 61

CADY TRIED TO block the push, but Prokop collided with her, and the momentum sent both women hurtling down, their arms locked in a hostile embrace. Prokop hit the roof, but Cady's lower body slipped off the building's edge, and she clawed to hold fast to her attacker, now her grappling hook. Cady screamed for help, but the blaring alarm drowned out her voice. Prokop groaned and thrashed like an alligator to wrench herself free, but Cady clutched her upper arms even tighter as her legs dangled in the air. Their faces were only inches apart, Cady looked in terror for mercy in the woman's eyes.

Prokop head-butted her with a soccer player's intensity. The shock of it loosed Cady's grip, and Prokop's arms slipped through Cady's fingers as she felt herself begin to fall. The roof's concrete edge came up fast to meet her chin—pain exploded through her jaw and she tasted the metallic tang of blood—but she held on. With her head now below the level of the roof, Cady could no longer see Prokop, but that imminent threat was replaced by the even more terrifying one, the checkerboard courtyard just a few seconds' fall and more than one hundred feet beneath her. She sputtered blood and saliva in exertion as she struggled in vain to haul herself up, her feet scrambling for purchase on the building's facade.

Her toes found a groove barely two inches deep between two concrete slabs, almost enough to let her legs hold her up but not enough to climb. Cady ground her right cheek into the rough cement to tilt her head upward. She spotted Prokop leaning over the edge, the wind blowing her hair over a face contorted in rage, then she disappeared from view. Cady knew she had to act fast before Prokop finished the job, but she couldn't pull herself up in this position, and her strength ebbed with every passing second. Soon she wouldn't have the strength to hold on at all.

Then she felt two hands close around her wrists, strong as steel, and a volt of fresh energy shot through her. She wouldn't waste it looking up again, Cady knew whose hands they were: Prokop's, trying to pry off her grip and make Cady fall to her death. But certain instincts, long buried, returned to Cady—to fight, to survive, to hope. She would hold on as tight as she could for as long as she could. And if Prokop got her fingers loose, Cady would latch on to her next, either to climb up her body or pull her down with her. She would not give up on herself. Not again.

But then the hands pulled upward. Cady felt herself rising. Then more sets of hands grabbed her biceps and she rose faster, she had to turn her face from scraping against the wall, and before she knew it, hands were hooked under her arms and lifting her up and over the ledge. She was laid out on her back on the horizontal safety of the roof, panting and alive. She finally got a look at the two police officers when they stepped back and looked down at her, while one of her rescuers refused to let her go.

"Mom?"

# 62

"I GOT YOU, baby, I got you," her mother repeated through tears as she cradled Cady's head in her lap. "You're safe now, I'm here."

Cady's entire body trembled with excess adrenaline as she looked at the faces of the two uniformed campus police officers and her own mother, struggling to make sense of them in her mental fog.

One officer lifted his hat to wipe his brow before kneeling beside her. "Ma'am, the EMTs are on their way, until then—"

"Prokop—" Cady sat bolt upright, her voice sounded high, raspy, and raw. "She pushed me, she was trying to kill me! Where is she? You have to get her!"

The officer placed a hand on her arm. "Okay, okay, we've got the suspect in custody, you're safe now."

Cady craned her neck to see past the legs of his partner standing on her other side. By the light of the open stairwell door, she saw two more officers, one speaking into his radio, the other holding Prokop by the elbow—her hands were cuffed behind her back. Cady collapsed back into her mother's arms with relief.

"That's right, take it easy, you got a pretty big welt on your head. The EMTs will be here any minute, they'll get you cleaned up, and we'll meet you at the hospital to take your full statement."

"I can tell you right now." Her body still quaked, but her gaze was steady. "Mikaela Prokop tried to kill me because I found out that she's selling her government-funded research to Russia."

The cop furrowed his brow at her, then glanced up at his partner incredulously.

"Actually, my brother was the one who discovered it," Cady added. "But he committed suicide before he could report her. I have the evidence he collected. It's in my mom's hotel room right in the Square."

"It is?" her mom asked.

The officer took a deep breath and stood up to speak to his partner: "We're gonna have to loop BPD in on this. Feds, too." His partner nodded and stepped away, chirping his radio awake as he walked. The officer started to follow him but stopped briefly to say to Cady, "We're gonna talk more about this at the hospital. A lot more."

Cady shivered again, and her mother took off her coat and draped it over her chest like a blanket. Cady gingerly sat up to look her mother in the eyes.

"How . . . how did you know?"

"My God, I had no idea you were being *attacked*, but . . ." She bit her quivering lip and paused to brush Cady's hair from her face; Cady saw that her hands shook also. "When you didn't show up for dinner, and you weren't answering your phone, I went looking for you. I must have just missed you at your room, your roommate said you were very upset about something to do with Leverett. I couldn't take the chance. I called the police that instant, and then I came straight here." Her mother looked heavenward and then squeezed her eyes shut. When her gaze returned to Cady, her eyes were awash with tears. "I couldn't let it happen again."

# 63

AT THE HOSPITAL, Cady received medical treatment to get her scrapes cleaned up, was hooked to IV fluids, and had an icepack slapped on her head before the parade of law enforcement—first local Boston police, then FBI agents—arrived to have her repeat her official statement of what happened again and again. She described her confrontation with Prokop at the faculty club, doing her best to name or describe anyone who witnessed their argument, and she gave the play-by-play of Prokop's surprise attack on the roof. She explained the history between Prokop and her brother, as best she understood it, his record-keeping on the academic espionage, the contents of his letter, where this evidence was located in the hotel room, and all the rest. She explained the decoy Eric had set up, and that if they looked at the surveillance footage from Cambridge Savings Bank on the date and time that he had listed in his notebook, they should have footage of the Russian accomplice to whom Prokop was funneling information. The questioning took so long that one of the HUPD officers who rescued her on the roof left and came back to the hospital to bring her and her mom Sicilian pizza from Noch's.

Finally the police and federal agents left, and Cady and her mother got their first moment of peace and quiet. Her mother slumped in the crummy chair she had pulled up to the side of the hospital bed, while

Cady lay beneath a triple layer of blankets—even hours later, she was still shivering with adrenaline.

Her mother rubbed her face in exhaustion. "I can't believe this happened, what that woman did to you. And I knew she was Eric's adviser, I trusted her, I even met her once, I *thanked* her. I shook the hand of the person who almost killed my daughter." She shook her head in disgust. "I didn't think I could get any more clueless."

"Not even Eric knew what she really was, not until he was too sick to ask for help, or at least too sick to be believed. That's why she picked him."

"What about you? Why didn't you tell me when you found out?"

"I thought I could take care of it better on my own." Cady picked at a loose thread on her thin blanket, and asked the next question softly, "Why didn't you tell me you were with Eric the night he died?"

Her mother looked surprised before her face crumpled into resignation. "Your father told you."

"*Dad* knows?"

Her mother's lips parted, but she didn't speak; and tears filled her eyes as she saw the hurt in her daughter's face.

"Mom, just tell me. I need to know."

Tears spilled from her eyes, as she screwed up her trembling lips to keep from crying. "I was trying to bring him *home*." She took a long, shuddering breath before she began the story. "I had been trying to get your brother to come home and take time off since Christmas. When he dropped the Bauer project, I thought he would give in, but he still wanted to finish out the year. Then he stopped taking my calls, texts, emails, everything. I had no way of keeping in touch with him. I was scared. You were away that weekend, your dad and I had a huge fight about it, and I thought, screw it, I'll go get him myself. I didn't even tell your father where I was going, I was too mad. I drove up that night."

There was no sight more unsettling to a child, even a grown one, than a parent crying. The little girl in Cady wanted to crawl into her mother's lap and hide her face in her shoulder, but she was too afraid of what her mother was about to say to touch her. So Cady listened, her heart braced for impact.

"Your brother was not happy at my drop-in visit. 'An invasion of privacy,' he said. I demanded he come home, I yelled, he yelled, I begged, we cried. He said he wasn't going to get better and that he didn't want to put us through it anymore. I tried to say the right thing, but I couldn't. Then he said goodbye to me. I thought he just wanted me to leave, so I wouldn't say it back. He said 'Say goodbye to me, say goodbye,' and I wouldn't. I told him I wasn't leaving until he came home with me, that I'd stay there all night if I had to. And then he hugged me." A smile briefly crossed her face before it went slack again. "I held him and he said, 'I love you. I'm sorry.' I was glad, because I thought he was finally agreeing to come home. I turned to get my coat, and in that second, he was at the window."

Her eyes widened with fresh horror. "It happened so fast. He pushed right through, I don't know how, if it had a screen, if he'd already loosened it, I don't know, but it happened in an instant. I couldn't reach him. He was gone." She paused while the emotion became too much, and began again. "I called the police, I was hysterical, I said that he jumped, that we needed an ambulance. I remember running down the stairs and outside and over to him." She covered her eyes as if to hide from the memory. "It was the most horrible sight, my beautiful boy, broken." When she lowered her hands, her tear-streaked face was distorted in anguish.

"So then what happened?"

"I heard the siren, I saw the lights coming, but I couldn't meet them. That would make it real, and it was already too much. Because I knew."

"Knew he was dead?"

"Knew it was my fault. And there was nothing anyone could do to undo it. And the sight, and the awful, irreversible fact of it was so horrible, I panicked, I, and I'm so ashamed of this, but I ran."

Cady fell silent as she tried to process it all. After a few moments, "So did you tell Dad, then?"

"No. I found out later that the police called the house shortly after it happened, and he answered. He still didn't know where I was sleeping, certainly didn't know I was up here. He kept calling my cell, but I didn't pick up, I couldn't. I was driving home like a maniac, in complete shock, I don't know how I stayed on the road. When I saw it was your dad calling, I had this crazy thought that he was calling to tell me Eric was all right, it was all a big mistake, I was worrying needlessly. I didn't listen to his voicemail until I pulled into the driveway at home around nine in the morning." She clutched her chest. "I could hear in his voice he was trying to stay calm, he didn't want to scare me, but he said it was very important that I come home. I thought about lying to him. I thought he would hate me forever if he knew I was there and I couldn't stop him. But when I got inside and saw him trying to break it to me gently, I hated myself more. I told him everything." Her mother paused. "And I made him promise not to tell you."

"Why?" Cady asked, anguished.

"We both agreed it would only make it worse. It had to be a secret."

"It's not a secret, it's a lie."

"I was afraid if I told you the truth, I would lose you, too. You'd just lost your brother, you needed a mother."

"But, Mom." All of her mother's decisions Cady could accept or understand, except for this one. This was a punch to the gut. "All this time. All this time I've wondered why Eric did it, what was he thinking, every unanswered question about his last minutes. And all this time, the only answer I could come up with was me. It was my fault."

"What? No, never. How could you think that?"

"How could I not?" Cady's hands shook as she finally said it out loud. "Ever since that night he cut my hair, when we were at the hospital and I said I was afraid of him so he'd have to stay. I was just mad. And you said it would break his heart, and you were right, it did. I did."

"God knows what I said that night, none of that matters."

"It did matter." Cady's throat tightened as if her guilt was choking her. "When he needed me to have his back, I turned on him. I betrayed him. He was never the same after that."

"He had been struggling long before that."

"The hospital stay was the final straw."

"Stop." Her mother got up from the chair and grabbed Cady by the hand. "Look at me. The months following that stay were some of the most stable he had that year, okay? That's the truth. I gave in to him too much, I enabled him to work around his illness instead of treat it. I found him psychiatrists outside the university healthcare system, I helped him stay in school and avoid an involuntary leave of absence. And then, when he got worse instead of better, I had none of the institutional support to get him out. That's why Eric and I were in that position that night. It was me. I did everything wrong, up to the very last minute of his life, I made every decision wrong. If you're going to blame anyone, blame me."

Cady heard her mother trace a path through her own actions that led to Eric's suicide, just as she had done herself, and neither of them was talking about Prokop and that stress, or the stress of school, or his private experience of mental illness that neither of them could ever know, and suddenly it was so obvious that there were a hundred such paths crisscrossing one another.

The line drawn by Cady's guilty conscience from that hospital stay to Eric's death had seemed so direct, and yet, as Robert said and her mother demonstrated, her memory of that night was volatile. She *was* scared that night. She was scared that her brother was so out of his mind that he could hurt her. She was scared all the time when Eric was sick, scared for him, for herself, for her family. She was scared by her helplessness, scared of how trying to make him better was tearing her family apart. She did want professionals to help so she didn't have to take it all on, and that wasn't inherently wrong, or cruel, or selfish. It had been easier to make herself the villain than accept that she had no control over her brother's actions.

Her mother went on, "I've gone over every word I said that night, thinking of how I could have arranged them differently, found the right order, the right combination that would have kept him from doing it."

"There wasn't any." For the first time, Cady felt the truth of it. "There was no one moment where you could've changed things. Time doesn't work that way. We only think it does."

"He's my kid. It was my job to keep him safe."

"He was his own person, separate from you. You couldn't control him. With the schizophrenia, he had limited control over himself. You couldn't have saved him."

Her mother nodded solemnly. "That's kind of you, but I will never believe that. When you become a mother, you'll understand."

Cady felt a deeper empathy for her mother than she had ever known. She had always thought she'd disappointed her mother by being so different from her, when it turned out that at heart they were deeply similar. They both felt enormous, unspeakable guilt for something beyond their control. They had swallowed the same drop of poison—naïveté or narcissism or codependency—that made them believe they could be responsible for another's happiness. They couldn't.

Her mother had endured the worst possible torture in seeing her child suffer and die in front of her. It had to feel like condemnation. But Cady hoped that in time her mother could see that she had no hand in Eric's illness, nor could she have guided his recovery if he wouldn't let her. And as gruesome as that night must have been, as much as she wished her mother hadn't had to witness it, on some level, Cady felt grateful that Eric had had her there. In his moment of greatest desperation, he was not alone. He knew that his mother and his whole family loved him, that in the last moment of his life, even during his most hurtful act, he was loved. They love him still.

"I'm his sister. And I understand because I felt the same way."

Her mother met her gaze, and it was as though they were seeing each other clearly for the first time.

Then the door to the room swung open and her father appeared, breathless, and pale as a ghost.

# 64

HER FATHER HAD left the retreat in Bolton Landing again to drive back to Cambridge as soon as her mother called him to say Cady hadn't turned up for dinner, just in case. One case he hadn't considered was his daughter's barely surviving attempted murder; he nearly drove off the road on I-90 when he received the second call saying they were headed to the ER. He had driven from Albany back to Cambridge in record time.

Now he stood beside Cady's hospital bed, on the far side from his estranged wife, and held Cady's hand protectively as she and her mother filled him in on the details of the last three hours.

"I can't believe this happened," he said when they were finished. "And this espionage plot Eric said he got caught up in, it's true?"

"If it had been fake, would she have tried to kill me after I told her I had proof?" Cady answered.

Her father's entire face flushed red, his jaw clenched. "I wanna kill her. I mean, in the legal sense. I take that back, in both senses. I'm sure Prokop has lawyered up by now, but she doesn't stand a chance on either charge, attempted murder *and* treason. I hope she rots in jail—*rots*."

Cady squeezed her father's hand. She knew him well enough to know that anger was his way of redirecting fear. And what happened tonight had scared the hell out of him.

"What was the proof you found?" he asked.

"It actually wasn't proof. I was mistaken when I confronted her. The photos weren't of Prokop." She looked at her mother. "They were of you. That's how I knew you were with Eric when he died."

"There are photos?" her mother asked, barely above a whisper.

Her father recoiled. "Wait, what?"

"It's okay, Mom told me about what happened the night Eric died, how she was there, and how you both lied to me about it."

He shot a cold look at his wife. "You couldn't wait to include me in that conversation?"

"Dad, listen, there's a lot to sort out," Cady interrupted before her mother could defend herself. "The girl you hired to hack Eric's web stuff, Lee Jennings—Mom, I don't know if you knew about that." From the look on her face, Cady guessed no. "Lee answered your ad because she was Eric's competitor for the Bauer, and she had an ax to grind against Prokop for choosing to advise him. Lee suspected the favoritism was sexual—she was wrong, Prokop chose him because his illness let her manipulate him and provided a good cover for her illegal activities, plus Lee is an active member of the Navy ROTC, she would literally be the last person Prokop would want around as she sold research belonging to the Department of Defense—but Lee had been stalking them and taking photos of them both in hopes of getting proof of an affair. Lee was spying on Eric the night he died."

"So she saw me, and she has photos?" Her mother looked frightened.

"You don't need to worry, Lee thinks it was Prokop in the picture, the quality is terrible, and that fits the narrative she already had in her head. Lee gave me the photos under that pretext, and that's why I told Prokop I had proof of her trying to murder Eric. When I actually looked at them, I realized Lee was wrong. Anyway, it doesn't matter now. The pictures don't incriminate Prokop, I do." She looked back at her mother and saw that her face was suddenly beet red. "Mom, what's wrong? I told you, you have nothing to worry about."

"I'm not worried about myself. I feel for you." She fought back tears from her already bloodshot eyes, her heart wrung out. "I can't believe you saw that moment, you should never have had to see that. I know I was wrong to keep it from you in the first place, but I hate to think how that made you feel, how I made you feel." She took a shaky breath. "It isn't enough, but I am so, so sorry. And I'm sorry to you, too, Andrew, for Eric, for everything."

"Karen, if anyone on this earth could've stopped Eric, it would've been you." He gave a heavy sigh. "I was just angry—angry at Eric for doing it, angry at you for going without me, and most of all angry at myself for not protecting all of us. But I couldn't talk to anyone about it. So I took it out on you, and I'd hate myself for it afterward, and round and round. You didn't deserve that, and I couldn't bear to do it to you anymore. That's why I moved out. It wasn't you. And look, you did save our baby girl. I wasn't here, and you saved her."

For the first time in a while, she saw the softness return to her father's eyes, and he looked at her mother in a way that honored their shared love, their shared history, and their shared heartbreak. Cady had thought she was one step ahead of them, analyzing their fights from the other side of a door, but now she realized she had misread so much between them. She had misread a lot.

But Cady's mother remained crestfallen. "Cady wouldn't have been on that roof if it wasn't for those photos. I've driven my husband out of the house and driven nearly both my children to suicide."

"Mom, it wasn't just the photos that got me up on that roof tonight." Cady looked between both of her parents, unsure of whether now was the right time to open up. They were all in various states of exhaustion, her dad's clothes were rumpled from the long drive, her mom looked as if she had been through a hurricane, and Cady herself was bone-tired, every muscle in her body ached, her heart most of all.

But the time for secrets was over. It was the secrets that had done this to them.

She didn't know where to start but at the beginning: "Since Eric died, I've been trying to understand why he did what he did. Once I got on campus, making sense of his suicide took over everything else. At the same time, I worried his schizophrenia was genetic and it was just a matter of time before I got it, too. I started hearing voices. I couldn't tell you, I knew what you would think, I knew what I thought. But they weren't scary or telling me to do anything bad, they were more like imaginary friends, but from the past, like ghosts." She only skimmed the surface in describing them, but it was a relief to say any of it out loud. "They had their own stories to tell, but they brought up a lot about my own, memories of Eric that I'd blocked out. I had a lot of feelings around his death that I hadn't dealt with, and the only person I could find to blame was myself. The voices helped me sort through it. Anyway, they're gone now, and I don't think they'll come back."

Even in her parents' silence, Cady could tell they were anxious at hearing this, but no more than she was at telling it. Her mouth had gone completely dry. She took a sip of water from the little plastic cup on her bedside before she continued. "When I found Eric's notebook, and the coordinates, it gave me purpose, and it gave me hope that maybe I wasn't to blame. Maybe not even Eric was responsible, maybe he hadn't wanted to die. Maybe I could blame it all on Prokop and do right by Eric by vindicating him. I hung every hope on that, it was the only thing that distracted me from my fears about myself. Then, when the pictures weren't the proof I thought they were, and the truth was even more complicated, I lost it."

She gingerly ran her hands over her bruised arms; she had goose bumps. "I wasn't on the roof of Leverett to kill myself, not really. I felt responsible for so many choices that weren't mine and situations in other people's lives, that I didn't realize I'd given up control in my own life. Consciously or not, the roof was a test—a test to see if Eric's fate was mine, or if I could trust myself to make my own choice." Cady took a deep breath. "Once I was standing on that ledge, I didn't know what I was doing, I didn't know who I was, I still might not, but I realized I'm not Eric. I'm not better or worse, I'm just myself. And I want to live to figure that out." She met her mother's gaze. "I was getting down from the ledge when Prokop pushed me."

Cady took her mother's hand and squeezed, as much to gain strength as to give it. "But after all this, I know I don't blame you, because I'm done blaming myself."

They were all silent for a few moments, the low hum of medical machines and the smell of cold pizza filling the space between them.

"So where do we go from here?" her father asked, packing much into a single question.

"The detectives said they'd like us to stay in town, in case they need us for more questioning," said her mother. "After that, I think you should come home, Cady, I think we have work to do in this family."

Cady nodded.

"Do you like that therapist you're seeing here, Greg?" her mother asked.

"Oh, I'm not really seeing a therapist, I lied about that to check out the fourth drop—but I will, I want to, I know I need help. A professor of mine gave me a name of a psychiatrist in Boston."

"I don't know about Boston," her father said. "I think you should transfer."

"I'll take this year off, but I'm coming back," Cady answered.

"Cadence, you have nothing left to prove," he said.

"It would be running away. And that's what got us into this mess in the first place. This entire family, we all run away from what's hard or what frightens us instead of facing it. Mom did it that night, Dad, you did it when you moved out, I did it plenty. But this was the first time I went toward something painful. And as difficult as it's been, I needed to do it." Cady sat up, energized by her conviction. "I didn't vindicate Eric, or myself, in the way I'd set out to. But with regard to

Prokop, I did finish what he started. That letter was his last mission for me. And I'm proud that I did it, even if he isn't here to see. It was worth it."

"It almost killed you," her mother said.

"No." Cady heard her own voice, and it sounded sure. "It saved us."

# 65

CADY AND HER parents stayed in town through the next week at the request of the authorities, who had follow-up questions. Cady used the time to recover in the hotel and pack up her room at Weld. She had a lot to explain to her roommates, and to apologize for, now that she saw their well-founded concern more clearly, but they received her with sympathy and grace. They said they were sad she was taking the year off and promised to keep in touch, and Cady hoped that they meant it. She felt genuinely choked with emotion when she hugged them goodbye, wishing she could have met them both in a better time.

Although the news of Professor Prokop's arrest for allegedly attacking an unnamed undergraduate bumped the story off the *Crimson*'s front page, Cady read that LeeAnn Jennings had won the Bauer Award, so she was definitely not coming back to claim those pictures. A later article on the Prokop saga included the footnote that she had been subsequently accused of sexual misconduct by her advisee, Nikos Nikolaides, who was additionally appealing the Bauer decision in connection with his harassment claim. The Ad Board ruled that Cady's plagiarism case was inconclusive and she should be graded without penalty. She waited for Hines's email conceding that she received an A on that paper *before* she informed him she was dropping all her classes and taking a year off. By the following Saturday night, the boxes were packed, the loose ends were tied, and the Archers were ready to go home.

That Sunday morning, her father came over to her and her mother's room to eat breakfast together before they hit the road, but it was her mother who suggested they attend Sunday services at Memorial Church. Now, walking up the steps of the church, Cady realized with a twinge that it was the first time they had all been together in a church since Eric's funeral, but she knew they could get through it. They'd been through worse.

It was also the first time Cady had been inside Memorial Church in the daytime, and it was glorious. Sunlight streamed through the floor-to-ceiling windows, filling the white room with warmth. What had seemed forbidding now felt airy and inviting, filled with light, sound, and bodies. The red carpet seemed cheery instead of lurid, like a strawberry in summer. The swath of sky seen through the window was the clear, crisp color of a blue jay's wing. The lofty, open space was filled with the bustle and chatter of its congregants, a mix of students, faculty, and members of the community.

Here, none of the students seemed to have the typical pall of Sunday dread; instead the atmosphere was social and relaxed. Cady sensed the tension subsiding from her mind and body for the first time in weeks. She and her parents took seats in the middle of a pew, not far from where she had first met Whit that night.

When the minister approached the lectern, everyone took their seats and quieted down. The clergyman was a small, round black man with even smaller, rounder eyeglasses and a halo of soft gray curls encircled his balding brown head. He had smiling eyes and a great, generous mouth; either he was born to be a preacher, or his body had grown to accommodate the calling. Cady liked him immediately. He greeted them in a baritone voice both gravelly and sonorous, with vowels drawn out by a plummy Boston Brahmin accent. His voice delivered an air of both elite intellectualism and easy comfort.

"Welcome, friends," he began. "Some of you here experienced your first Parents' Weekend last week—and you survived."

The room laughed as the Archers remained silent.

"Some of you may even be feeling a little homesick after saying goodbye to the people who raised you. They gave you food, clothing, and shelter, they are largely responsible for providing the opportunities and support in getting you here. But now they're home, and you're on your own again. So, I want to talk about what it means to be raised." The reverend lifted his arms palms up. "There are many meanings of the word. One can raise a barn, meaning to build it from the ground up. Or raise a question, meaning to offer for consideration. To raise a bet, to gamble on the unknown. To raise funds, something Harvard does very well, meaning to collect or bring together. I look around, and I am constantly reminded of those heroes and benefactors who raised this glorious church. First of course, the fallen heroes whose names are inscribed upon these walls . . ."

As he went on to point out each of the various memorial walls, Cady couldn't help but think of how Whit's name wouldn't be on any of them. How he had died serving his country just a few years after this church was dedicated, and yet, his name would be missing by a technicality that it didn't occur during wartime. But she would never forget him, James Whitaker Goodwin, Jr.

". . . the vestry of Trinity Church in Copley Square gifted this pulpit upon which I stand in memory of their rector and our distinguished alumnus, Phillips Brooks. Harvard's Phi Beta Kappa chapter gave that golden eagle lectern over there in memory of its members who died in that war. And past university president Abbot Lawrence Lowell donated the bell in our tower in memory of the World War I dead and inscribed on the lip the words 'in memory of voices that are hushed.'"

*Hushed.* There was a peace to the word, like a baby sleeping. When Cady had first heard the voices of Robert, Bilhah, and Whit, she had railed against them to be quiet; more recently she had longed to hear them. But now, for the first time, she found comfort in hoping they were hushed. At peace. Her brother most of all.

The minister had circled back to his main discussion: "To raise: to build, to offer up, to bet on, to support, to honor. To raise a child means all of the above. But perhaps the simplest definition is to lift. Many of you may recall when you were but a small child, the sensation of your father or mother lifting you onto his or her shoulders. It was a joyful gesture, one that is always sure to elicit a peal of laughter from the child and a smile from any passersby."

Cady looked over and saw her father place his hand over her mother's and give it a squeeze.

"But recall, the purpose of being raised this way was to see better. To be positioned to observe the world from a better point of view. We cannot do this all on our own . . ."

The words resonated. Cady thought of the inherent incompleteness of any single perspective, the primary and most painful example being Eric, her wonderful, troubled, brilliant, shortsighted, and beloved brother. She accepted now that his reasons for deciding to end his life could never be fully known, but it wasn't to punish them. She remembered Whit's words: *Just because it's my choice to go doesn't mean I'm not heartbroken to leave you.* But Eric hadn't given himself enough time or his loved ones enough space to carry him through the darkest times of his illness to the brighter recovery that might have been around the corner. Loving Eric wasn't always easy, but any one of them would have carried him through fire to save his life.

But it wasn't only Eric and his illness that made him think this way, it's human nature to default to our own narrow perspective. The stories we tell ourselves have such power, and yet they can be mistaken, cherry-picked, or otherwise fictitious. Cady thought of how Nikos had believed Eric's suicide was all about him and the competition. How Lee could only see Prokop in the picture. How her father, who thought he knew everything, could fail to see how he'd distanced himself from his wife and daughter. She thought of how her mother had seen only her own hand in Eric's death to the exclusion of all others, and then how Cady herself had done the same. None of them alone could ever see it clearly. They needed each other in order to see the whole picture, or as close as they could get. They needed to raise each other to see past the tragedy of Eric's death.

She thought, too, of how even the ghosts functioned to teach her this. She had thought that hearing them was her cosmic punishment for failing her brother, her curse to meet each at the turning point of their lives, to miss it, and to lose them, and repeat the agony of her missed opportunity with Eric. But the complexity of their lives showed her that that golden opportunity was never there in the first place. To think so narrowly overlooked their own agency, their limits, and her own. History is never as simple a narrative as we write in books.

She could not change the ghosts and their paths any more than she could Eric's, and she had to make peace with that. But she could let them change her. She could learn the lessons of Bilhah, that trauma does not define us, our love does, and that the story of our future is ours to write. And Whit, who carried the burden of his father's legacy but never forgot the choice was his. And Robert, that to judge ourselves in hindsight will never be fair, or proper scientific method. She could see her life better for having seen theirs.

And she could see the ways she was like her brother and the ways she was different, and cherish his memory and his lessons all the same.

"Nothing is guaranteed to you," boomed the minister. "Contrary to what you may have been told, Harvard is not a golden ticket. You will earn your keep and sing for your supper and reap what you sow. And even then, you may not get what you deserve. Nothing has changed but for this: You have been raised. So look around. Be grateful for every new perspective you encounter on this campus. Listen to the voices around you, however dissimilar to your own. Make up your own mind, forge your own path, your life is your own. That is the purpose of your new privileged position as a student at this institution of higher learning." He held a finger in the air. "And most important, do not forget upon whose shoulders you stand: family, history, and spirit. Let us pray."

Cady dropped her chin and closed her eyes but opened them again when she felt her mother's hand close over hers. She squeezed back. Now she understood that we must love people whom we cannot control, in fact, we are lucky to love and be loved by people we cannot control. If we could control the person, love wouldn't be a gift. This was the uncertainty of life, and of death. It was what made life beautiful and terrifying at once. It was the state of grace.

The three of them sat together, connected by a chain of hands, hearts, and memories. It wasn't the family Cady had grown up with; hers was, and would always be, a family of four. They would never be whole without Eric. But only these people, her family, knew the shape of what was missing. And they would fill the space as best they could, together.

# 66

*Five Years Later*

CADY RAN BAREFOOT over the cool grass with Eliot House behind her, the silk sheen of her dress flashing in the moonlight as her legs pumped beneath it. In one hand, she held the strappy heels she had worn to the Senior Soirée, and in her other she held a bath towel, and she nearly tripped for laughing. She was running alongside the friends she'd lived with in Eliot since her sophomore year; her suite mates, Imani, Olivia, and Emma, and "the boys," Jonathan, Ayush, and Max, minus Tommy, who was assisting them on secret business. They halted at the sidewalk curb to let a car pass before scampering across Memorial Drive to the banks of the Charles River.

Cady had taken the rest of her first year off after everything that had happened, and she'd started over four years ago as a new freshman in the Class of 2024. Mikaela Prokop's arrest and plea deal had garnered some publicity on and off campus, but mostly in the year Cady was home, and by the time she returned to campus, Prokop's federal prison sentence was old news. Cady's close friends knew about her past, but she wasn't labeled as The Girl Who Busted That Spy Professor as she'd feared, nor was she The Girl Whose Brother Killed Himself, certainly not to the people around her now. Asked to describe Cady, they'd tell you she was a Psych concentrator, a soprano soloist in the Veritones a cappella group, a proud resident of Eliot House, an unlikely flip-cup champion, and at the moment, a little drunk. By this time tomorrow, Cady would be a Harvard graduate.

But not before respects were paid to one final campus tradition.

Cady was having too much fun to mind the twigs and pebbles, even barefoot. She kept up with the pack as they gamboled down the banks of the river, trying to avoid drawing attention to themselves and keep quiet but failing joyfully. They couldn't stop laughing and loudly shushing each other, then laughing harder, until they reached the steps of the Weeks Footbridge.

Imani turned to face the group. "Okay guys, we're doing this, no chickening out." She stepped around the side of one of the two obelisks that bordered the base of the bridge. "Let's leave our towels here, so they'll be in reach when we need them."

"What time is it?" Olivia asked.

Ayush touched his Apple watch, which lit up in the dark. "Yikes, it's eleven fifty-three, we gotta get in formation."

Jonathan put a hand on his shoulder. "'Yush, you're gonna want to take that thing off."

"Oh, good call." He began to unbuckle it. "Tommy just texted, he's all set up on the boathouse dock."

"Cool, he'll let us know when it's midnight." Jonathan tossed his towel onto the grass, adding, "Assuming the stuff his cousin sent him actually works."

"The package said made in China, what could go wrong?" Max said, prompting a swat from Olivia.

"You're sure he's not sad he's missing this?" Emma asked.

"Believe me, I tried, but heights aren't his thing. He was happy to head up the Celebrations Committee."

Max laughed. "I thought we were calling it the Police Diversion Committee?"

"It's both." Jonathan grinned, his smile dazzling even in the dark. He met Cady's eye.

"C'mon, let's go!" Cady darted up the stone steps two by two. Although the arch of the footbridge was gentle, it was longer and higher than Cady remembered; she felt a frisson of excitement and nerves when she reached its apex. But when she turned to see her friends running up to meet her, her heart swelled.

Five years ago, Cady could never have imagined she'd be in this place, feeling this way. It had taken a lot of hard work to get here. She had gone to therapy three times a week during that gap year at home, and she maintained the progress seeing a psychiatrist once a week in Boston whom she absolutely loved, Sharon. The first year in therapy, she spent a lot of time trying to work through what she had experienced with the ghosts or auditory hallucinations. Her first psychiatrist raised the possibility that it was some variation of *folie à deux*, a shared psychotic disorder in which an otherwise healthy person comes to share the symptoms and delusions of a person with a psychotic disorder with whom he or she shares a close relationship, essentially a self-induced psychosis. Cady found that an interesting and plausible notion, although she was honest with Sharon that she didn't believe it. The issue was moot, as Cady never heard the voices again, as she knew she wouldn't.

Anyway, Sharon didn't dwell on that. She steered Cady away from trying to guess what might be "wrong" with her, in the past or the future, and kept her on the path of what was constructive, healthy, and true. With Sharon's help, Cady was learning to express her emotions instead of letting them twist inside her, and her occasional bouts of anxiety and depression grew more infrequent and manageable. And yes, she was still talking through her grief over Eric. Sharon convinced her that closure wasn't a realistic goal, only acceptance. As Cady now understood, her brother's death was an event, but his loss was an ongoing process. She was deeply grateful to Professor Bernstein for suggesting Sharon all those years ago, and for his guidance on her thesis this year; he'd become an invaluable mentor and friend.

Cady wouldn't have guessed it five years ago, but she had many friends looking out for her these days.

Ayush clapped his hands to get the group's attention. "Everyone's got a buddy, so don't swim to shore until you know their head is up and they're okay."

"Thanks, Dad!" Max teased.

Ayush snorted. "And remember, we're an odd number, so, when in doubt, leave Max."

Cady slipped the thin strap of her sheath dress off one shoulder and shot a pointed glance to the group. "We had a deal, right?"

"Yeah." Jonathan grinned, pulling his dress shirt over his head.

All seven of them stripped down to their underwear, leaving their formal dresses and suits in a glamorous heap. Then they set about climbing onto the bridge's concrete balustrade, which was shoulder high and about a foot wide. Max gave Emma and Olivia a boost and held their hands as they rose to a standing position. Imani waved him off and pushed herself up onto the balustrade effortlessly. Meanwhile, Cady had found it easy enough to climb up the chess-pawn-shaped balusters, but she was momentarily frozen in her crouching position on the top.

"You freaking out, C-dawg?" Max reached for her from the ground.

"No no no, don't touch me," she said quickly, before laughing at herself. "Sorry, I just need to take my time." It was silly to be afraid of falling, considering her intent. But she hadn't anticipated how windy it would be on top of the bridge, and she gripped the concrete balustrade so tight that white half-moons shone in her fingernails. A gust of wind blew her hair into her face, but she didn't dare lift her hand to move it aside.

She didn't want to fall, she wanted to jump.

"Here." Jonathan had stood up easily, but now he crouched down to her level. "Use me for balance."

Cady looked at him through her windswept hair. After a moment of screwing up her courage, she placed one hand on his curved back, then the other on his shoulder, and commanded her legs to straighten, slowly rising to a standing position. A glance downward at the black, lapping water still triggered a jolt of fear, but not enough to deter her. She had promised herself she'd go through with it, and she would.

"I hope it's midnight soon. I'm losing my nerve," Emma said, echoing Cady's own thoughts.

"Don't worry, I got you," Imani said from her right.

It was actually better once she was standing tall. Sandwiched between Imani and Jonathan and all the rest, facing their beloved Eliot House across the river, Cady's jelly legs felt stronger, her balance solid. The spring air swept over her bare shoulders and sent a chill down her spine. She was still a bit scared, but giddy, too—it helped that they were all in their underwear. She looked down the line at these friends who had become her family while her real one was healing itself. They had seen her through the normal college drama, the heartaches and the all-nighters, but most importantly, they hadn't flinched when she'd dared to share the heavy stuff. She couldn't believe she had almost missed the chance to meet them.

"Aw, guys," Olivia moaned. "We should have gotten someone else to take photos."

"We won't forget this," Cady said. Five years ago, she had been prepared to white-knuckle it through her undergrad years at Harvard, and yet here she stood with a lump in her throat, finding it hard to say goodbye.

Jonathan pointed. "Look!"

Fireworks shot off from the banks, small and sputtering at first, but then Tommy got them going at a good height. With a crack and a hiss, gold starbursts erupted in the inky sky and rained down over the shimmering surface of the water. Cady and her friends cheered and a few cars honked as the flashes of red and gold dazzled them.

When the last sparkly trails faded into the darkness, Max cried, "Okay, on three!"

Emma squealed. "I need more time than three!"

"Fine, ten! Ten, nine, eight . . ."

As her friends counted down in happy unison, Cady wished she could slow down time to savor this moment. She closed her eyes and heard the voices of her best friends. She breathed deeply, taking in the scent of the river and this campus in all its bitterness and beauty, say-ing goodbye to a place she never thought would feel so like home.

But home didn't mean a perfect place with only good memories, it meant a place where you grew up.

Cady raised her chin, pulled her arms slightly away from her sides for balance, and wiggled her fingers in the air, reaching for them. Then she felt Imani's warm hand close around hers and Jonathan's callused one on her left. She opened her eyes with a smile, blinking away the wetness at her lashes. Poised, knees bent, Cady joined her friends in counting down the final seconds:

"Three, two, one—"

# EPILOGUE

THE SPLASH WAS small when Cady dived into Lake Wallenpaupack. The water washed over her, warm and accepting, enveloping her with the immediacy of emotion. She swept her arms to her sides and swam underwater for a few moments, reluctant to leave its embrace. When she had to, she burst through the surface to the sunlight, filling her lungs with the air that was cool and fresh.

It was July 30, Eric's birthday. He would have been twenty-six years old.

Her family had decided to celebrate Eric's birthday with a weekend at the lake. Two years prior, her parents bought a second home there, and they had ramps installed so they could share it with Aunt Laura and Uncle Pete. Cady's parents had gone through their own counseling, individually and as a couple, and after spending a year apart, they decided to give their marriage a second shot. Buying this house was as much a reward for their hard work as it was a test, but one they had passed. It was a challenge to reclaim the location from their past life with Eric, but so far, they found the connection was a comfort in their new life without him. In fact, the house wasn't far from where they'd scattered his ashes, but it felt good to be close to him.

They had a full house this weekend, including Pete, Laura, Gram, even Grampa and Vivi. After some hard-fought apologies, things were better between Cady's mother and Vivi, although Grampa took his daughter's suggestion that he and his wife stay at a nearby lodge—for their comfort, of course. Tonight, after a dinner of Eric's favorite foods, barbecued ribs and pineapple on the grill, followed by some tearful singing over strawberry shortcake, Cady told her parents she was going to bike out to the old dock. Her father offered to drive her and keep her company, but her mother asked him to stay behind and help with cleanup. Her mother was much better at reading her these days.

Cady floated on her back, looking up at the great dome of the sky curving around her. The afternoon heat had burned off all but the thinnest haze over the water, and the sinking sun washed the sky with gold. Cady spotted the moon in a lavender corner of the sky, hovering over one of the silhouetted hilltops, waiting for its turn. She imagined the stars that would soon join her, some hundreds or thousands of light-years away, twinkling at her from across time, benevolent and eternal.

She flipped over and treaded water. Shaking the droplets from her ears, she listened to an insect chorus of crickets and grasshoppers, a bass line of hidden frogs, and the lapping of the water keeping time. Silence at the lake had a texture, and it was soft. Looking down, she could almost see clear to the silt bottom of the lake, where the underwater weeds laid their slender footholds. Nearby, a miniature school of glinting minnows feinted left, then right, in perfect unity. It struck Cady as a remarkable example of familial intuition, a bond so strong that they were connected without direct communication. Or, in Cady's case, without bodily presence. Cady thought about how Eric made up such a small part of this vast lake, and yet to her, he stretched all the way to the horizon. He was in the layered sine curves of the hills and the rapid frequency of waves upon the water's surface. His dimension was imperceptible and infinite.

She dropped back underwater and did a couple of somersaults, popping up for breath when the bubbles tickled her nose. The sensation recalled a game she and Eric used to play called The Amazing Aquabatics Show, a name he always sang out like a real announcer.

Their "aquabatics" were handstands and somersaults and sometimes dives; their audience was only each other, and sometimes their parents. Their grand finale stayed the same for years, because they never quite pulled it off. The idea was for Cady to stand straight up on Eric's shoulders, and at the end, they'd both throw their arms out—*ta-daa!* They never got it exactly right, but that was beside the point. The fun was in the trying. Over and over, Eric would hold her hands as he plunged underwater, and Cady would scramble over him to get in position for liftoff. Sometimes she'd accidentally stick her foot in his face, sometimes he'd launch her into the air on purpose, but they never lost faith that one day they would do it, rise together in perfect balance and unity. Cady remembered curling her toes around his freckled shoulders, shoulders that grew broader as the years went by, straightening her shaky legs as they both rose out of the water, squeezing his fingers until finally, at the last moment, letting go.

Cady opened her arms wide, to the lake, and to Eric.

The last rays of sunlight sparkled on the water, like stars close enough to touch.

# AUTHOR'S NOTE

The following notes on my research contain major spoilers; if you haven't finished reading the novel, I implore you to save this for the very end.

Although this novel is a work of fiction, significant research went into my imagining of the "ghosts of Harvard." I wanted to come up with characters whose stories would exemplify lost potential in different ways.

There is little a novelist can imagine that theoretical physicists have not considered seriously. It is a mind-bending field of science, with so much yet to be understood. I was particularly inspired by the work of Lisa Randall, the Frank B. Baird, Jr., Professor of Science, Department of Physics, at Harvard University. I recommend her books *Warped Passages: Unraveling the Mysteries of the Universe's Hidden Dimensions* and *Knocking on Heaven's Door* to anyone interested. Randall makes the most complex topics accessible and fascinating.

I could not think of an historical figure who better exemplifies the duality of potential and unintended consequences better than Robert Oppenheimer. Oppenheimer was a prolific letter writer, and I studied his personal correspondence during his time at Harvard in order to get a sense of his personality, passions, and voice. He was indeed a lover of poetry, especially Baudelaire, and took any chance to show off his language skills. Some of his exclamations and phrases included in the novel are taken directly from his letters to friends and family, so that his real words echo throughout the book. All of the anecdotes Robert shares with Cady are taken from Oppenheimer's life. The excerpt from Professor Bridgman's recommendation letter referring to his Judaism is authentic. Oppenheimer's charm, vulnerability, and poetic spirit made him the most unlikely young man to become the "Father of the Atomic Bomb," and I came to see him as one of American history's most tragic figures.

For those who are interested, you can find Oppenheimer's collected letters in *Robert Oppenheimer: Letters and Recollections*, edited by Alice Kimball Smith and Charles Weiner, and also in the Oppenheimer collection at the Library of Congress. Additionally, I recommend *American Prometheus: The Triumph and Tragedy of J. Robert Oppenheimer* by Kai Bird and Martin J. Sherwin.

James "Whit" Whitaker Goodwin Jr. is a fictional person, but the hope poured into rigid airships and the tragedy of the USS *Akron* disaster was real. I was spending a rainy day in the National Naval Aviation Museum in Pensacola, Florida, when I found myself fascinated by the model of a dirigible aircraft carrier that I never knew existed. It's hard to believe these enormous, rigid airships were once considered the new hope of American military aeronautics and the future of commercial air travel. The crash of the *Akron* was the greatest single loss of life in aviation at that time; seventy-three lives were lost and only three passengers survived. The tragedy was a psychological blow to a nation already in the nadir of the Depression and effectively killed the faith and funding in developing dirigible aircraft carriers to defend the Pacific. I'm not a military historian, but I wonder, had the Navy stayed with the dirigible aircraft carrier program, could they have mastered the technology and averted the attack on Pearl Harbor, forever changing the course of our entry into WWII? Or perhaps the hubris of attempting to harness the wind was always doomed to fail. In this dimension, we'll never know.

For further reading and to see truly surreal pictures of this gargantuan airship, check out *The Airships Akron & Macon: Flying Aircraft Carriers of the United States Navy*, by Richard K. Smith.

The scholarship about slavery at Harvard is extremely new. Professor Sven Beckert taught a small seminar starting in 2007, and over the next four years, he and thirty-two students unearthed forgotten records of people enslaved at Harvard. In 2011, they published a sum-mary of their groundbreaking research. And in 2016, Harvard publicly acknowledged its ties to slavery more broadly.

Four enslaved people lived in the Harvard president's residence, Wadsworth House: Titus and Venus in the household of President Benjamin Wadsworth from 1725 to 1737, and then Bilhah and Juba under President Edward Holyoke from 1737 to 1769. There is a dearth of written records about any of them, but Bilhah appears to be the only one who died while a slave in Wadsworth House, and that is why I chose her to haunt these pages.

Bilhah was enslaved in President Holyoke's household from 1755 until her death in 1765. She gave birth to a son four years before her death. There are no other known records relating to her or her child. It is not a given, and perhaps not even likely, that Bilhah got to keep her infant son with her until her death. Their lives were so devalued that better records were kept of kitchen inventory than the lives of black people during her time. So beyond those spare contours of her life and status, all the details of Bilhah's life, child, and the circumstances of her death in this novel are products of my imagination. However, my fictionalization is informed by my research of colonial life in Cambridge. For example, the executions of Mark and Phillis in Cambridge Commons in 1655 are a matter of historical record, a brutal enforcement of slavery law and public spectacle of cruelty.

I grappled with the decision on whether to use Bilhah's real name for the heavily fictionalized version of her here, and I did not make the choice lightly. In the end, I decided that her name and personhood has been buried for too long. As then-President of Harvard Drew Gilpin Faust said, upon the April 6, 2016, commemoration of the plaque at Wadsworth House, "We name the names to remember these stolen lives."

I hope further scholarship allows us to learn more about the real Bilhah and enslaved people like her. I hope more stories like hers are included in the history of our national institutions, that those stories are taught in school, and I hope future generations of Americans are better able to imagine those voices that have been silenced. Only with more perspectives and greater empathy can we urge our present moment into a more just future.

I cannot say it better than Representative John Lewis said, at the plaque commemoration:

"For nearly four centuries we have believed that the best way to cleanse this nation of the stain of slavery is to move on. We have torn down historic landmarks, blotted our names from the history books, and reworked the narrative of slavery. And we try to forget. We have gone to great lengths to wipe out every trace of slavery from America's memory, hoping that the legacy of a great moral wrong would be lost forever in a sea of forgetfulness.

"But for four hundred years, the voices of generations have been calling us to remember. We have been tossing and turning for centuries in a restless sleep. We have pleaded with them to be still. But they will not be silent. We are people suffering from amnesia. We are haunted by a past that is shut up in our bones. But we just can't stomach the truth of what it is."

To access the booklet by Sven Beckert, Katherine Stevens, and the students of the Harvard and Slavery Research Seminar and other helpful resources, visit www.HarvardandSlavery.com. For broader context on the ties between slavery and American universities, I recommend Craig Steven Wilder's book *Ebony and Ivy: Race, Slavery, and the Troubled History of America's Universities*.

# ACKNOWLEDGMENTS

A first novel is at once the most personal project and the one that needs the most helping hands at its back. In the ten years that it took me to write this book and ready it for the world, I had many hands to hold, and I have many people to thank.

Kara Cesare is the type of editor in author fairy tales. The first time we spoke was over the phone, and she understood this book so instinctively that I felt deeply seen. I've since learned that her wisdom and insight are matched only by her warmth and empathy. Her nurturing guidance gave me the confidence to rewrite fearlessly and enriched this novel immeasurably. I can't thank her enough for her role in getting everything that was in my head and heart onto the page. I'm so lucky to have her on my side.

Emma Caruso and Jesse Shuman also gave me such thoughtful reads, they are wise beyond their years, and they kept the book young and fresh. Thank you to my careful and dedicated copy editor, Emily DeHuff, who felt like a friend looking out for me from the margins.

The bench is deep at Random House, and I could not have a better team of genius professionals behind me: my publisher Andy Ward, who has believed in this book from day one and leads us all with grace and vision. Avideh Bashirrad, who makes our meetings feel like the best book club. Thank you to the most brilliant and dedicated marketing and publicity team of Barbara Fillon, Susan Corcoran, Katie Tull, and Allyson Lord. Thanks to Greg Mollica, who immersed himself in this novel, and my lengthy emails, to create the most beautiful cover of my dreams, and Virginia Norey with interior design, who perfected every detail. Everyone has shown me such enthusiasm for this book and generosity with their time and talent; I am forever grateful.

I also want to acknowledge the passing of Susan Kamil. She made such a powerful impression on me; I admired her immensely. I felt honored by her attention and eager to prove myself worthy of it, and most of all, I remember feeling so lucky to work in an industry with brilliant, strong women like Susan in charge. Her support and enthusiasm for this book changed the way I thought of my writing and myself, and there was so much more I wanted to learn from her. But writing this novel helped clarify what I believe about love and loss. I believe our hearts contain universes, ones where time folds over and wraps around us in a comforting embrace. We carry the voices of the people we've loved; we remember them always and know what they'd say, even after they can't tell us anymore. I'll always regret not having more time to work with, and, truly, to study under the great Susan Kamil. But I know I can still learn from her through the memories and lessons carried on by Andy Ward, Kara Cesare, and everyone who knew and loved Susan at Random House.

Thank you to my agents, Andrea Cirillo, Amy Tannenbaum, and Rebecca Scherer of the Jane Rotrosen Agency. These brilliant, thoughtful women were the first non-relatives who believed in this book, and their confidence breathed new energy into me when I needed it most. Each of them offered such unique gifts to this book, and their insights sparked transformative changes to the story. I'm so grateful to them for shepherding me and this novel to our happiest home at Random House. Additional thanks to my wonderful sub-rights agents, Hannah Rody-Wright and Sabrina Prestia, for introducing this novel abroad, and Chris Prestia for getting the good stuff in writing and keeping me flush with cute dog pics.

I'd like to thank Dr. Sandra Steingard, Chief Medical Director at the Howard Center, and Clinical Associate Professor of Psychiatry at the University of Vermont College of Medicine. Her decades of experience as a clinical practitioner treating patients with schizophrenia made her an invaluable resource in understanding the specific challenges faced by patients and families, always with her signature compassion. She's been like an aunt to me since I was born, having previously mentored me in feminism and Barbra Streisand, and it was a treat to learn about her *other* areas of expertise.

Thank you to two of my fellow alums for lending insight into aspects of Harvard that I was not smart or talented enough to experience firsthand. Thank you to Alvin Hough Jr. for sharing his experience as an undergraduate organist at Harvard, especially for giving me the incredible detail of midnight organ rehearsals at Mem Church. Now Alvin is a musical director for Tony Award–winning Broadway musicals; what a joy to say I knew him when. Thanks, too, to Dan Cristofaro-Gardiner, professor of mathematics and Von Neumann fellow at the Institute for Advanced Study at University of California–Santa Cruz. He kindly let this English major into his world of math geniuses and gave me a tour of Princeton's Institute of Advanced Study. Dan is the only person whose kindness can overcome the intimidation of theoretical math to someone who struggled in an undergraduate math course titled "Counting People."

Thank you to two mentors and friends at Harvard whose words have stayed with me over the years. Ryan Taliaferro, who encouraged me to pursue creative writing and avoid the pitfall of going to law school as "prestigious step two." Thank you to Bret Anthony Johnston, my former thesis adviser and creative writing director at Harvard, now the Director of the Michener Center for Writers at the University of Texas in Austin. So many of his lessons, and jokes, have stayed with me, too many to list here (although you can find them in his incredible book, *Naming the World, and Other Exercises for the Creative Writer*). He gave me the best advice a young writer can receive, "Give yourself permission to take yourself seriously." I could, because he did.

My friends are the antidote to the solitary toil writing requires. I'd like to thank all my wonderful friends who supported me during this long road. They always countered my cyclical anxiety with refreshed encouragement, patched me up after any disappointment with bitter defensiveness on my behalf, and received each incremental update as though it were cause for celebration. Special thanks to those friends I leaned on the most: my best friend Rebecca Harrington, a brilliant author in her own right and the smartest, gentlest reader and most enthusiastic brainstormer a gal could ask for; Ryder Kessler, my valiant defender and consigliere; my comrades-in-arts, Megan Amram, Janie Stolar, and Briana Hunter; in books, Siena Koncsol and Lucy Carson; Catherine Vaughan, my expert in perfect pitch and you should see her with a breakup text; my other busy and accomplished friends who moonlight as my therapists, Courtney Yip, Lauren Donahoe, Carolyn Auwaerter, Becky Singer, and Christina Zervanos, and finally my should-be sister, Katy Keating, who manages to hold me up from across an ocean.

It may seem silly to thank them here, but animals have been a part of my support system for my entire life, so I would like to acknowledge my dog, Pip, and my cat, Mimi. Thank you, Pip, for being a constant source of joy, love, and perspective, as well as the bedrock to my happiness. Thank you, Mimi, for reminding me to take breaks by blocking my view of the computer screen, insisting I move the keyboard to make room for her on my lap, and biting my hands if I typed instead of petted. And in memory of Ruby the Wonder Corgi, who frequently visited me at Harvard when I was at my most stressed and reminded me that the only way to survive a Boston winter is with aggressive optimism and a low center of gravity. May the sound of her nails scampering up the steps to my dorm room haunt the entryways of Lowell, Old Quincy, and Kirkland forever.

Thank you to my entire loving family. Laura Leonard, who has loved and supported me like family for many years, and who is my most trusted reader and sounding board. Thank you to my godmother, Franca, for radiating love and acceptance for me and my every endeavor. I'd like to remember my beloved grandmother, Mother Mary to our readers, Muggy to me, whose voice and powers are always with me. Thank you to my father for being patient all those years I was too shy to let him read this book, and then, when I finally did, for being so enthusiastic that he campaigned against edits.

I don't know how to begin to thank my mother. Everything I

know, I learned by her example. Growing up, I watched her build her career brick by brick, and yet she always made me feel like the most important person in the room. Co-authoring our nonfiction book series allowed me to learn how to be an author alongside the best. But as much as I admire her as a writer, I want to thank my mother for always staying my mom. She's my cheerleader, my fiercest defender, and my biggest fan. She's my first call when something really good or really bad happens. Her greatest lessons had nothing to do with writing. She taught me how to love in straight lines, and I always feel her love, unconditional and uncomplicated. As I wrote in this novel, *you only need one person*. Mom, you are my one.

Finally, I'd like to thank the readers who followed me from the nonfiction series I wrote with my mother and the "Chick Wit" column we still share in *The Philadelphia Inquirer*. As a memoirist, I've had the unique experience of sharing some of my most personal stories from my real life and then getting support from readers who feel like friends. I often wrote about pursuing the dream of writing this novel, and our wonderful readers encouraged me every step of the way. You asked me about the novel at every signing and on social media, so that whenever self-doubt threatened to get the best of me, I had a warm reminder that people I cared about were waiting to read it. Thank you for your support, patience, and faith in me. I hope this was worth the wait.

I especially want to thank those readers who shared their personal experiences with losing a friend or family member to suicide. Each one of your stories touched me, and I held your love and your loss close to my heart while I wrote this story. Thank you for entrusting me with your grief. I hope these pages did justice to your generosity. I cherish the connection a book can create between strangers. If you've read this far, you aren't a stranger anymore.

# ABOUT THE AUTHOR

FRANCESCA SERRITELLA IS the *New York Times* bestselling author of a nine-book series of essay collections co-written with her mother, the bestselling author Lisa Scottoline, and based on "Chick Wit," their Sunday column in *The Philadelphia Inquirer*. She graduated cum laude from Harvard University, where she won multiple awards for her fiction, including the Thomas T. Hoopes Prize. *Ghosts of Harvard* is her first novel.

francescaserritella.com

Facebook.com/FrancescaSerritellaAuthor

Twitter: @FSerritella

Instagram: @fserritella